SAVAGE®

The bronze giant, who with his five aides became world famous, whose name was as well known in the far regions of China and the jungles of Africa as in the skyscrapers of New York.

There were stories of Doc Savage's almost incredible strength; of his amazing scientific discoveries of strange weapons and dangerous exploits.

Doc had dedicated his life to aiding those faced by dangers with which they could not cope.

His name brought fear to those who sought to prey upon the unsuspecting. His name was praised by thousands he had saved.

. . . . , was
. . . cane.

Colonel Andrew Blodgett Mayfair, just five feet tall, yet over 260 pounds. His brutish exterior concealed the mind of a great scientist.

"Renny," Colonel John Renwick, his favorite sport was pounding his massive fists through heavy, paneled doors.

"Long Tom," Major Thomas J. Roberts, was the physical weakling of the crowd, but a genius at electricity.

"Johnny," William Harper Littlejohn, the scientist and greatest living expert on geology and archaeology.

**WITH THEIR LEADER, THEY WOULD
GO ANYWHERE, FIGHT ANYONE,
DARE EVERYTHING—SEEKING EXCITEMENT
AND PERILOUS ADVENTURE!**

(Coming in March 1989 is Doc Savage Omnibus #8,

Four Complete Adventures in One Volume

THE MEN VANISHED
FIVE FATHOMS DEAD
THE TERRIBLE STORK
DANGER LIES EAST

Kenneth Robeson

BANTAM BOOKS

NEW YORK • TORONTO • LONDON • SYDNEY • AUCKLAND

THE MEN VANISHED, FIVE FATHOMS DEAD,
THE TERRIBLE STORK, DANGER LIES EAST

*A Bantam Book / published by arrangement with
Conde Nast Publications, Inc.*

PRINTING HISTORY

The Men Vanished *was originally published in Doc Savage
magazine, December 1940. Copyright 1940 by Street and
Smith Publications, Inc. Copyright © renewed 1968 by The
Conde Nast Publications, Inc.*

Five Fathoms Dead *was originally published in Doc Savage
mgazine, April 1946. Copyright 1946 by Street and Smith
Publications, Inc. Copyright © renewed 1974 by The Conde
Nast Publications, Inc.*

The Terrible Stork *was originally published in Doc Savage
magazine, June 1945. Copyright 1945 by Street and Smith
Publications, Inc. Copyright © renewed 1973 by The Conde
Nast Publications, Inc.*

Danger Lies East *was originally published in Doc Savage
magazine, March/April 1947. Copyright 1947 by Street and
Smith Publications, Inc. Copyright © renewed 1975 by The
Conde Nast Publications, Inc.*

Bantam edition / November 1988

ISBN 0-553-27616-6

Published simultaneously in the United States and Canada

---

*Bantam Books are published by Bantam Books, a division of
Bantam Doubleday Dell Publishing Group, Inc. Its trademark,
consisting of the words "Bantam Books" and the portrayal of a
rooster, is Registered in U.S. Patent and Trademark Office and
in other countries. Marca Registrada. Bantam Books, 666 Fifth
Avenue, New York, New York 10103.*

PRINTED IN THE UNITED STATES OF AMERICA

O   0 9 8 7 6 5 4 3 2 1

THE MEN VANISHED

Contents

I

THE MAN WITH THE FACE

The man with the ugly face was lying. He walked up to the doorman of the Explorers League—the doorman at the service door, not the man who was accepting the engraved invitations at the main entrance—with a confident manner. He carried a press camera, a carton of photoflash bulbs, a tripod; he had a card that read PRESS stuck in his hatband.

"Photographer from the *News-Press*," he said.

He had a voice that was stilted, unnatural, somewhat strange. His words were sounded queerly, as if there was something wrong with his tongue, or as if he was not familiar with the English language.

The doorman was not suspicious. "Press section in front, to the left," he said.

Then he took another look, and his mouth became round with shock. It was a little appalling, his first look at the face of the man who had just said he was a photographer. The man's face was really two faces—that is, the left side of it was radically different from the right side. The right side was an ordinary face, rather young, almost handsome. The left side was heavy, thick-lipped, darker of cast, with an aboriginal cast to the features. The line of demarcation—the line where one half face left off, and the other began—was sharply defined, like a line drawn down through the middle of the forehead, down the nose, and on down the middle of the chin.

"Say, what done that?" The doorman was looking at the face.

The other man pointed at his camera. "Remember that powder they used to use to take flashlight pictures?" he asked. "Ever think what would happen if that stuff fell on a man's face as it burned?"

"Oh," said the doorman.

"You should have seen it," the man with the face said, "before the plastic surgeon worked on it."

"Oh," repeated the doorman. "Yeah. Well—uh—the press section's in front, and to the left, like I said."

5

The man with the ugly face strode on into the Explorers League.

His lip, the lip of his right face, curled scornfully.

"The gullible fool," he muttered to himself. "He would believe anything." He touched his face. In a secluded spot, he got out a hand mirror and looked at his face. The lip of his right face hooked up fiercely on the end; the one on his left face got a sardonic warp. In returning the mirror to his pocket, he touched the spot under his clothing where a revolver was hidden, to make sure the gun was still there.

Well satisfied with himself, he entered the auditorium. The place was normally the large main lounge of the Explorers League, but it had been converted, for the purpose of this meeting, for the presentation of the *Explorers League Ten Year Medal*, into an auditorium by the placing of folding chairs. The man with the ugly face made himself inconspicuous— not in the press section—by standing against a wall.

The auditorium was packed with a distinguished gathering. Probably there would not, for another ten years at least, be another as distinguished. Famous explorers, noted scientists, could be found in the Explorers League clubrooms any evening; but this conclave tonight was a special occasion, one so outstanding that it came but once in each ten years.

The chairman of the board of presentation was speaking. He had finished his preliminary words. He was pausing regretfully.

"We are sorry," he said, "that seven of our most valued and brilliant members cannot be here tonight. I refer to young Daniel Stage, the explorer who was lost more than a year ago in the South American jungle. And I refer also to those members of the Explorers League who went on expeditions to find Daniel Stage, and never came back, and have not been heard from. Those six are Joseph Branch, Elmo Walker Eagle, Tom Kennedy, Baron Edouard Corby, Felix Point-Mackey, and Jock van Biltmore. To those six, the history of science and exploration owes a great deal, for they were more than six wealthy men. They were men who devoted their lives to progress in science and exploration, and, when called upon to do so, went unhesitatingly into the face of unknown peril in the hope of rescuing Daniel Stage. Greater courage than that, no man has."

The speaker paused. There was somber silence. The

man with the ugly face had a look of sardonic evil. Suddenly realizing the expression that must be on his visage, he wiped it off.

"Having touched on this sad note," continued the speaker, "I will leave it. But I will pause for a few moments, and I know that each of you will pray silently that Daniel Stage and the six who have tried to find him will be able to return safely to us."

The man with the face started to sneer, caught himself. He moved back a step, to a spot where it was darker. His eyes roved over the audience.

"Tonight," said the speaker, "we are presenting the Explorers League Ten Year Medal. Each year, as you know, we make a presentation for the most outstanding achievement in the science or exploration for the year. And each ten years, we present the League's Ten Year Medal. As you know, this is the highest honor the world of science and exploration is able to pay to any man. In the past, only men of the caliber of Thomas A. Edison and Admiral Richard E. Byrd have earned distinction worthy of its bestowal."

Although his eyes still were on the audience, the gaze of the man with the ugly face had become fixed. He had singled out two stocky men. They were seated together. They saw him, stared at him. When he shook his head, they looked away quickly.

"This time, there were many worthy candidates for the award," continued the speaker, "but the board of presentation, upon its final vote, was unanimously for the award going to Clark Savage, Jr."

An apish-looking gentleman in the front row suddenly applauded loudly. His companion, a very dapperly dressed man, gave him a jab in the ribs. "Monk, you lout, this is the wrong time to applaud," snapped the dapper man. "Everybody already knows who got the award. It was on the invitation." These words rang out in the stillness, and everyone laughed; then there was applause that rose to deafening volume.

The speaker smiled, waved his arms for silence. It was some time before he got it.

"Please, please!" exhorted the speaker. "Let me tell you something of Clark Savage." He smiled and turned toward the newspapermen. "The gentlemen of the press happen to be particularly interested, because they have in the past seemed to be somewhat baffled by Mr. Savage. So much so that they refer to him as the man of mystery, or the man of bronze."

The reporters grinned.

"Gentlemen, I will refer to Clark Savage as Doc Savage, because we all know him as Doc," said the speaker. "I will also be brief. Doc Savage is probably more of a scientist than any of us, because he is a product of science. As most of you know, he was placed in the hands of scientists in childhood, and throughout youth and until early manhood, underwent rigorous training at the hands of these scientists. Most of the things the newspapers"—the speaker glanced at the press row again—"print about Doc happen to be true. They call him a mental wizard, a physical marvel. And this happens to be true. Within, of course, human limits. Doc is no fantastic, inhuman creation, as we, who are well acquainted with him, know.

"Doc Savage's career is an unusual one. It is the rather strange career of righting wrongs and bringing to justice those who are outside the law, particularly in the far corners of the earth. I imagine it is this unusual work which has contributed to the mystery which surrounds him.

"Fundamentally, though, Doc Savage is a scientist, a surgeon, an explorer. His knowledge in many fields is fabulous, his accomplishments of infinite value. I am not going to delve deeply into his work in science and exploration, any *one* of which would more than warrant his receiving this honor."

The speaker took a deep breath.

"Gentlemen," he said, "I present a truly modest man—Doc Savage."

Doc Savage appeared from an adjacent room.

The dapper man on the front row punched the apish one. "Applaud now, you mistake of nature," he said.

The admonition was not needed. Applause was tremendous, continued for minutes.

Doc Savage was a giant man of bronze, but physically so well proportioned that it was not until he stood beside the speaker, and shook hands with him, that his real size was apparent. A few small things—the sudden leaping out of bars of sinew in his neck, the flowing cables of strength in his hands—indicated fabulous physical strength. Tropical suns had given his skin a permanent bronze, his hair was a bronze hue only slightly darker.

Strength, power, vitality, all carefully reserved, was the impression he gave. His eyes in particular were striking; they were like pools of flake gold being continually stirred.

The room was full of white light popping from press camera flashbulbs. Newsreel men had turned on powerful spotlights. The engineers of two radio networks, having scuttled over to the rostrum, were making last-minute placements of their microphones. Finally quiet was restored, the confusion subsided, and Doc Savage began speaking.

The giant bronze man's voice was modulated, reserved, charged with a vibrant resonance that filled the auditorium. He spoke simply, and very briefly.

The man with the ugly face was looking at the two stocky men at whom he had shaken his head earlier. He caught their eyes. Then he made, very slowly and deliberately so that the gesture would attract no attention, a stroking motion with his hand over the left—the inhuman—side of his face. The stocky pair nodded.

The man with the face picked up his camera, his tripod, the other stuff, and left the clubrooms of the Explorers League. He had taken no pictures.

In the auditorium, departure of the man was not noticed, because Doc Savage was still speaking. He was not saying anything particularly important; acceptance speeches at award presentations are never vital. But the attention was rapt, because the bronze man's voice and manner were like a vibrant magnetic force in the room.

A tall, powerful man with a thick neck, occupying a seat on the center aisle, where he could see Doc Savage clearly, was the first to applaud on several occasions. He did so loudly, and once the bronze man's flake gold eyes rested on him for a moment.

Possibly the powerful, thick-necked man's vociferous applauding accounted for the fact that Doc Savage saw something that happened when the gathering in the Explorers League auditorium ended.

The incident created no turmoil. It attracted no notice from anyone, in fact, except Doc Savage. The bronze man saw it.

The two stocky men walked up to the thick-necked man. One of the stocky pair, keeping his right hand in his coat pocket, gouged the powerful man in the back with a hard object in the pocket.

"This is a gun, brother," he said. "If you don't want your insides to leak out, you better come with us."

The man's face was toward Doc Savage when he said that, and the light overhead was bright. Doc was watching the man's lips. And Doc Savage was an adept lip reader.

No flicker of emotion crossed the bronze man's face to show that he knew what had been said. However, he did politely excuse himself from the group where he was standing. He moved to the left, skirted the crowd swiftly.

The two stocky men and their prisoner left the auditorium, the captive walking stiffly, his face fixed. They reached the sidewalk, turned right, moved to the corner. They waited until a traffic light changed, then crossed with it into the park.

The park was a luxuriant green lung in the center of the darkened city. Farther south, and farther north, where the bordering district was less exclusive, there were people on the benches, some sleeping on the grass. But here, the park was almost empty.

Doc Savage, moving like a bronze ghost in the murk, vaulted the stone wall, vanished in the shrubbery. A moment later, the bronze man stepped from behind a bush onto the path.

The two stocky men were taken completely by surprise. One groaned involuntarily as the gun was crushed out of his fingers by a grip of terrific strength. There was a loud ripping and snapping sound as Doc Savage grabbed the other man's gun—the weapon was in an armpit holster; Doc gripped it through coat fabric—and tore it out bodily, snapping the holster straps. The man, wrenched sidewise by the force of the bronze man's strength, stumbled over a bush, fell heavily.

There was a moment of startled silence. Doc Savage said nothing. He took the two guns, one at a time—they were revolvers—and broke them. The cartridges splattered into the grass. He threw the guns, one after the other, off to the left, toward the mirrored gleam of water in the moonlight. Two chugging splashes came back, and the water rippled and danced for a moment, then became flat again.

Doc said, "Stand close together, you two."

The stocky pair got together, stood with their hands lifted shoulder-high.

The bronze man eyed them. He looked at their prisoner, the big man with the thick neck.

"None of you belong to the Explorers League," the bronze man said. "How did you get in?"

The thick-necked man suddenly pointed a hand at Doc Savage. There was a stubby black two-barreled derringer in it, and the twin snouts of steel menaced the bronze man.

"You stand still!" said the thick man. "If you as much as bat an eye, I'll blow you open, so help me!"

Doc Savage became rigid, motionless.

"Search him, Lon," ordered the thick-necked man. "And be damned careful. The guy is poison."

The stocky man, named Lon, patted his hands over Doc's clothing, reaching far out to do it, and his hands, whenever they were on the motionless bronze man, trembling.

"Clean," he said. "He's clean, Tiny."

Tiny said, "You go get the car, Bat."

Bat, frightened, said, "We're calling too many names."

"It won't make any difference," said Tiny grimly. "Go get the car."

Bat went away, breathing heavily. He headed in the direction of the street which bordered the park, and his footsteps died away.

The large man with the thick neck, Tiny, watched Doc Savage intently.

"Nice trick, didn't you think?" he asked.

"A good trick," Doc agreed.

"It took you in, didn't it?" Tiny laughed the laugh of a scared man who was feeling desperate. "By applauding, I got you to noticing me in the hall. When Bat and Lon closed in, they did it when they were sure you would notice. But the lip-reading part of it was best of all, don't you think?"

"You knew I could read lips?"

"Sure."

"What is the idea behind it?" Doc asked.

Tiny said, "Shut up!"

There followed three or four minutes of silence, then Lon muttered, "Here comes Bat with the car." Lon sounded as if he was a little ill. He kept feeling of his ribs, his shoulder, where the holster straps had bruised him when Doc snapped them. "I think I got two broken ribs," he said.

The car was a sedan, not an obtrusive one. It was black, with some chromium trim, and white-sidewall tires. They got in. Lon sat on the right of Doc Savage; Tiny straddled the jump-seat, facing the bronze man with his gun.

"Take that drive that cuts in toward the center of the park, Bat," Tiny said. "There won't be any traffic there this time of night."

The car moved. The muffler was loose, or the exhaust manifold, because the engine made a little more noise than it should have. Otherwise the car seemed to be in good condition.

Doc Savage asked, "What is behind this?"

"You said that once before," Tiny growled. "Shut up."

"You intend to kill me?"

"Oh, no, no," Tiny said. "No, of course not."

He did. There was lie all through his voice.

Doc said quietly, "You might tell me why."

Lon growled, "Because a guy was going to come to you for help, and we didn't want it that way. That's why."

"Shut up, Lon," Tiny snapped.

Doc Savage leaned back on the cushions and squirmed a little; he seemed to be relaxing. His feet were close together, and one of them rubbed the other. A moment later, the heel came off his right shoe without making enough sound to be noticed above the exhaust mutter of the engine. Doc stepped down on the heel rather hard.

Then the bronze man's body became slack, his eyes closing. He lay that way, his head rolling to the side.

"What the hell!" exclaimed Lon.

"Careful!" warned Tiny.

Lon leaned over, very cautiously, and put a hand over the bronze man's mouth and nose. He held the hand there for some moments.

"He ain't breathin'!" Lon exploded. "He's fainted."

"They keep on breathing after they've fainted," said Bat. "Maybe it was his heart?"

Tiny growled with satisfaction. "What's the difference? He's out. Pull over on the side, Bat. And hand me that thing of yours."

Bat asked, "You mean my knife?"

"Yes," Tiny said in a low voice. "Give me your knife."

And that was all they said.

II

THE MISSING MAN

Phil O'Reilly was one of the younger members of the Explorers League, and he was proud of his membership, although painfully aware that he probably had accomplished less than anyone else who belonged to the League. He hoped to remedy that. He was a wide, powerful young man, rather serious, with a good academic knowledge of general science. He happened to be quite wealthy.

He had been proud to receive an invitation to the Ten Year Medal presentation ceremonies.

For almost an hour now, he had prowled through the league clubrooms, seeking Doc Savage, and not finding him.

He accosted a steward. "Have you seen Mr. Savage? It is rather important that I talk to him."

The steward shook his head. "I believe he's gone."

"What about his two associates who were here?" Phil asked. "Monk—I mean, Lieutenant Colonel Andrew Blodgett Mayfair. And Ham Brooks—Brigadier General Theodore Marley Brooks. Do you know them?"

"Oh, yes, I know them," said the steward. "Monk was the fellow who sat on the front row and applauded, and Ham Brooks was the well-dressed man who punched him in the ribs." The steward chuckled. "You should hear those two argue some time. The things they call each other!"

"Are they still here?"

"No. They left a few minutes ago."

Phil was disappointed. "I wanted to talk to Savage about Daniel Stage," he remarked, more to himself than the steward. "I think I'll try to telephone him at his headquarters."

Phil got on the telephone, put in a call. He recognized the squeaky, childlike voice that answered—it belonged to the apish-looking Monk Mayfair, who, Phil happened to know, was one of the country's leading industrial chemists, in spite of the fact that there didn't appear to be room for more than a spoonful of brains in his head.

"Doc ain't here. I dunno where he went," Monk said with ungrammatical carelessness. "What you want with him?"

"I want to talk to him," Phil said. "I have an enormous admiration for Doc Savage."

"So have I," Monk said. "So has everybody who knows him. Who did you say you are?"

"Mr. Philip O'Reilly."

"Oh, yeah. That young squirt with a lot of money who is trying to be an explorer. I remember."

Phil, angered, said, "I *am* an explorer."

"Oh, sure. You crossed Africa in a Rolls-Royce and a trailer, complete with refrigerator and lace curtains. I heard about it."

Phil reddened with indignation. That African venture had been his initial whirl at exploring, and the newspapers had mortified him by calling it a luxury cruise, a joy jaunt, a plush-lined caravan, and other things.

He snapped, "I want to talk to Mr. Savage about Daniel Stage."

"You mean Daniel Stage, the explorer who has been lost in the South American jungles. What about him?"

"Daniel Stage was my friend."

"Yeah?"

"I am thinking about taking an expedition to hunt for him."

Monk snorted.

"Listen, sonny boy, you better stick to plush-cushion exploring," the homely chemist said. "Down where Daniel Stage went, you won't be driving a Rolls and a trailer."

"I'm perfectly competent!"

"Sure, we all think we're competent," Monk said. "It would be a tough world if we didn't. But you'll find out there's a good reason why several thousand square miles of country down there are still unexplored."

"I called you up," snapped Phil, "to ask you if Doc Savage was there. Is he?"

"No, he ain't."

"Thank you," Phil said, and hung up with an ill-tempered bang. Then he grinned wryly at the instrument. "I guess I did turn out to be kind of a panty-waist explorer the first time," he muttered. "But, you homely clown, you wait until I get another chance!"

He had a grim determination to win his spurs as an

explorer, and not have to feel uncomfortable every time he approached a group of old-timers, because he thought he detected traces of sly grins on their faces. It was this which had started him toying with the idea of organizing an expedition to hunt Daniel Stage.

He was thoughtful about the venture during the ride to his apartment in a taxicab.

In his hall, Phil O'Reilly came upon the man with the ugly face.

The encounter was brief. But it was a cat-and-dog thing while it lasted. Phil O'Reilly, being richer than a young man really should be, occupied a marble home facing the park. Tourists usually thought the place was a museum. He pushed open his door, surprised to find it unlocked.

The man with the ugly face was crouched over the mailbox. The mailbox was placed at the side of the door, with a slot that opened outside the house.

The man with the face whipped erect, whirled and ran down the hall. Apparently he had been taken by surprise.

"Hey!" Phil yelled. "Stop, you!"

He hurled his evening stick. The cane whistled over and over through the air, hit the fleeing man, and knocked him off stride. He slammed into the wall, went to his knees, skated along on all fours. But he heaved up again, went on.

"Jonas!" Phil roared.

Jonas was the butler.

Lunging in pursuit of the man, Phil hesitated momentarily to scoop up his cane. He threw it again. This time, he missed.

The man with the ugly face came to a big window in the back of the house, wrapped arms around his face, and ran through the window as if it wasn't there. Glass cascaded to the floor, leaving a big hole in the window.

Phil got his cane again, leaped out into the night. There was a small lawn, tufted with shrubbery; an entry-way led around to the street, where it was blocked by a high iron gate. The gate was easily climbed.

Taking aim, Phil hurled his stick at the man as he went over the gate. Another miss. The stick hurtled on out into the street and broke the window of a taxicab. The cab stopped; the driver stuck his head out and said some words that probably had never been heard on that street before.

The man with the face ran like an antelope, bounding up and down. He rounded the nearest corner.

Phil climbed over the gate, raced to the corner. The quarry had disappeared.

A policeman arrived on the scene. He was the patrolman on the beat; he knew Phil, and he was respectful.

"What did this intruder look like, sir?" he asked.

"His face," said Phil O'Reilly, "was the most hideous thing I ever saw on a human being. One half of it seemed to be completely different from the other half. One half was a white man's face, but the other was—well, different."

"Different how?"

"Kind of thick-lipped, and foreign, and—well—" Phil wiped his face with a handkerchief while trying to think how to describe the face. "Say, Casey, did you ever see the faces on them little images they dig up in South American ruins?"

"You mean them things they got in the museum? Them Inca things?" the officer asked. "Sure, I seen 'em."

"Well, the other half of this fellow's face was like one of those."

"Hm-m-m." Casey was confused. "He must have been a right active guy," he added, looking at Phil's height and squareness.

He knew Phil O'Reilly had been collegiate champ in several branches of athletics. Phil was also quite handsome— it was Phil's secret and horrible suspicion at times that he was pretty, and he dressed in a rough, tweedy fashion to overcome this.

"The man with the face," said Phil, "was as tough as a brass gorilla, and as active as a real one."

"I'll look around," the cop promised. "If I find him, we'll see if he can outrun a hunk of lead."

"Thanks, Casey," Phil said.

Going back to the house, Phil looked in the mailbox, and found the letter from Obidos, South America.

It was a queer-looking letter. The covering was grayish black and felt like a rubber boot. And it *was* rubber. The letter had been sealed inside a coating of crude-processed native rubber. The address was on a tag, which was attached.

Phil eyed the foreign stamps, the cancellation marks, the grime on the tag, the queerly stilted printing of the address.

Then he got a knife and chopped the crude rubber covering loose at one end.

His eyes got round as he read one of two letters that were contained inside.

It was written on some kind of animal hide that resembled buckskin. The ink was a rather strange, deep-violet color. The letter read:

Dear Phil:

This is an appeal for help. I am getting desperate. Also, it is not likely that I will be allowed to go on living much longer.

You see, Phil, I have made a fantastic discovery here in the jungle. It is the most amazing thing any explorer ever found. But now I cannot get away unaided. I have sent out other appeals for help, and those men have tried to rescue me, and failed. They are here now, all of them—Joseph Branch, Elmo Eagle, Kennedy, Baron Corby, Point-Mackey and Van Biltmore. They are here, and as helpless as myself.

Any attempt to rescue us MUST BE KEPT SECRET. You do not understand why now, but you will.

I am getting this out by Kul, a messenger who can be trusted. He will wait to guide you here, if he is able to get out with this.

Our lives depend on help, Phil. And you must keep it secret. The others let it be known they were coming to rescue me, and that is why they never came back.

Daniel Stage.

Phil O'Reilly gaped at the missive unbelievingly. He was astounded. He had been planning an expedition to rescue Daniel Stage. And here was a letter from the man!

The other note was shorter. It was scrawled on parchment in the same odd handwriting that was on the tag bearing the address.

The note informed:

Señor Phil O'Reilly:

I have forward this you. Kul are wait. You come, he guide.

You say nothing about this, please. You say, you more likely be dead. Very serious. No one understand.

You come by my trading post. Kul here. He guide.

Location of trading post you can learn in Obidos. Come secretly. I keep Kul here for you.

Niji.

Suddenly excited, Phil O'Reilly jammed the two messages in a pocket. He yelled at the butler, "Don't wait up for me, Jonas," and dashed out of the door.

He encountered Casey, the patrolman, on the sidewalk.

"Sure, and now I can't find no trace of this guy with the face," Casey said.

Phil exclaimed, "Casey, I think I know what the fellow was doing in my house."

"The devil you do! He stole something, maybe?"

"I think I surprised him before he had a chance," Phil explained. "He was bending over my mailbox. There was a letter in the box. A very unusual and valuable letter from South America."

Casey peered at Phil. "Sure, and didn't you say one half of this guy's face looked South American?"

"He didn't look like a modern South American," Phil corrected. "I said half of his face was like the face on one of those prehistoric images they dig up in ruins."

Casey scratched his head.

"A bit screwy, ain't it, sir?" he said. "You think the guy was after the letter, you say?"

"Yes."

"I'll keep looking for the guy," Casey promised.

"Thanks, Casey," Phil said. Then, as an afterthought, he declared, "I think I'll go back and get a gun."

"Have you got a permit for the carryin' of a gun, now?" Casey asked sharply.

"Yes."

"Sure, then it'll be a good idea, I'm thinkin'."

Phil dashed back into the house, ran to his gun room— the place was stocked with guns for everything from air-pistol target practice to shooting elephants—and got a dependable revolver that had a long barrel. It was his favorite weapon.

*   *   *

A taxicab took him to one of the tallest skyscrapers in the city. Alighting on the sidewalk, he peered upward. Haze concealed the top floor—the eighty-sixth floor—of the structure, so that he could not tell whether windows were lighted up there. He knew that the eighty-sixth floor housed Doc Savage's headquarters.

A private elevator carried him up. He stepped out in a rather plain hallway, approached a bronze-colored door, which was immediately opened—Phil learned later there was a capacity-type burglar-alarm device which showed when anyone came near the door—by the homely chemist, Monk Mayfair.

"Oh, you," Monk said. "What's the matter? You get mad over them remarks I made about your exploring ability, and come down here to punch me in the nose?"

Monk sounded hopeful. He sounded as if he would enjoy a fight.

"No, no," Phil said. "I've got something important to talk to you about."

A deep-throated orator's voice—this one belonged to Ham Brooks—asked from the room beyond, "Who is it, you hairy accident?"

Monk ignored the question. "Come on in," he told Phil.

Stepping back, Monk allowed Phil to enter. Noting the width of Phil's shoulders, the capable blocks that were the young man's fists, Monk grinned and rubbed his jaw. Then the homely chemist's alert eyes noted that a small electric light on the wall across the room had flashed on.

Monk's eyes narrowed. There was a metal detector device, somewhat like those used in penitentiaries to learn whether the inmates are carrying weapons, concealed in the door frame. The flashing of the light meant that their visitor had a piece of metal as large as a gun concealed on his person.

"Hey, sonny boy," Monk said. "This place is like the old-time Western saloons."

"Eh?" Phil stared at him.

"You check your guns at the door."

"Oh." Phil hesitated. Then he removed his revolver, and placed it on a large inlaid table, which, with a big safe, was the principal furniture in the reception room. "That satisfy you?"

"Partly," Monk said. "But generally, when a citizen goes around carrying a gun, there's a story connected with it."

Phil O'Reilly was looking at the other occupants of the room. There was Ham Brooks, the fashion-plate with the orator's voice. Phil knew he was an eminent lawyer.

There was a third man, a man who was a string of bones. He was longer and thinner than it seemed any man could possibly be, and still live. Phil recognized him also. He was Johnny—William Harper Littlejohn, internationally famous as an archaeologist and geologist, and noted for his big words.

"Hello, Johnny," Phil said.

"A paradisaical consociative conflux," Johnny remarked.

"I hope that's good," Phil said, smiling.

"It probably is," a feminine voice said. The woman was seated to the side, where she had not been noticed.

Phil stared at the young woman. He was dazzled. Seeing her unexpectedly was like having lightning jump out of a clear sky. She was marvelously beautiful.

"This is Patricia Savage," the dapper Ham explained. "Doc's cousin."

"I'm very glad to meet you, Miss Savage," Phil said.

He was, too. She was the most delightful thing that he could recall having happened to him. He could see the Savage family resemblance. The bronze hair, a little darker than gold, and the compelling flake-gold eyes.

Monk demanded, "O'Reilly, you say you got business?"

"Yes." Phil nodded. "Very important business."

"Any mystery connected to it?"

"Yes."

Monk jerked his thumb at Patricia Savage. "You scram, Pat."

The young woman shook her head. "Nothing doing."

"You know the orders Doc gave," Monk said ominously. "You don't get mixed up in any more of our messes. Now, don't start arguing. I know you like excitement, and I don't want any argument from you."

"I won't argue," Pat said. "I'll just stay." She turned to Phil O'Reilly and gave him a smile that would have melted a brass man. "You don't mind, do you?"

"Of course not," Phil said quickly. "In fact, I want you to stay."

There was about five minutes of heated argument, and Pat won it.

*   *   *

Phil O'Reilly took a deep breath. "Here is my story," he said.

It took him about seven or eight minutes to tell it. When Phil finished, Monk said, "It adds up to this, then: You were planning on going on an expedition to rescue Daniel Stage. And tonight, all of a sudden out of a clear sky, you get a message from him asking for help. And some guy with an ugly face tried to intercept the message, you think. That the story?"

"That's it," Phil replied.

"Ain't it a funny coincidence, you getting the message just as you had made up your mind?" Monk inquired.

"I don't think so." Phil shook his head. "You see, Daniel Stage and I were well acquainted. It is logical that he would call on me for help."

"How come he didn't call on you first? He's had several others try to rescue him."

Phil flushed. "As a matter of fact, Daniel Stage shared your opinion of my ability as an explorer. Once he told me I was a plush-chair explorer. He would call on men he thought were more competent in the beginning."

"What do you want Doc to do?" Monk asked.

"I wondered if Doc would be interested in the venture of rescuing Daniel Stage."

"You want to hire Doc?"

Phil looked indignant. "I'm not a fool. I know people do not hire Doc Savage. I hoped I might prevail on Doc leading an expedition, if I would finance it."

"You aren't just fishing for the credit of having gone on an expedition with Doc Savage?" Monk asked rather unkindly.

"No. I don't want any credit."

"I'm surprised," Monk said.

Phil O'Reilly stood up.

"You're gonna get surprised again with a bust on the nose," he told Monk, "if you don't quit making cracks about me."

Ham Brooks chuckled. "Sit down, O'Reilly," he said. "This homely baboon hasn't got any manners."

Phil subsided reluctantly. "Do you think Doc will be interested?" he asked.

"I think he might be," Ham said.

"Listen, *I'm* interested," interjected Pat Savage. "And I know Doc will be."

"You better be interested in staying out of this," Monk told her.

Pat wrinkled her nose at him. "I'm going home and get some sleep," she said. "Tomorrow, we'll find Doc and talk this over with him, and start organizing our expedition."

Ham said, "We're leaving, too. We can all go in my car, and we'll drop you and young O'Reilly."

That was all right with Phil. Already he was much interested in the attractive Pat. The idea of going on an exploring expedition with her intrigued him.

They rode down in the private elevator together. The vast lobby of the skyscraper was empty, and their heels made clickings on the parquet flooring.

They moved out onto the sidewalk in a compact group, not expecting trouble.

A man, pushing a small hot-chestnut wagon, saw them, wheeled his wagon over, stopped it in their path.

"Buy some hot chestnuts, people?" he asked.

"Naw, we don't want any," Monk said. "Hey, move that wagon outa our way."

The man said, "Sure you want some chestnuts."

He upset the wagon. Chestnuts cascaded around their feet. Along with the chestnuts, a glass bottle fell from the cart. It broke, sprayed liquid over the sidewalk, and the liquid rapidly vaporized.

The man jerked a transparent hood out of his pocket, yanked it over his head. It was equipped with an elastic which drew the hood mouth tight around his neck.

"Tear gas!" Monk yelled.

The warning was too late to do any good. The vapor surged up around them, brought stinging agony to their throats and nasal passages, blinded them.

Monk lunged forward, swung a haymaker with his fist. It missed. The chestnut vender tripped Monk; the chemist sprawled on the sidewalk. Phil O'Reilly clubbed around with both fists, yelled, "Somebody grab the guy!"

The chestnut vender waved his arms. Answering the signal, a gray car—it had been parked down the street, and was already approaching—swerved to the curb. There were two men in it, one driving, one a passenger. The driver remained at the wheel. The other got out.

Both the driver of the gray car and the fellow who alighted had pulled transparent hoods over their heads. These, while by no means gas masks, would keep out the tear gas, and a man could exist on the air inside the hood for a few minutes.

The two men, the vender and the one from the gray car, seized Pat Savage. Pat screamed. The vender struck her on the jaw.

They hurled Pat into the car, piled in after her, and the machine jumped away from the curb.

III

THE TOUGH MR. MASKET

It was then that Mr. Dink Masket made his initial appearance.

Phil O'Reilly and Ham Brooks—both of them had the same idea at once, and it was a good idea—saw Dink Masket about the same time. They had dashed out of the gas. Also, they'd had the judgment to keep their eyes shut, so that when they opened them, they could see after a fashion.

"Look!" Phil yelled.

"I see it," Ham said.

They both stared.

A very large man who was also very brown, a man Phil decided he had never seen before, had dashed across the sidewalk, and out into the street, and clamped on to the spare tire and bumper at the rear of the departing gray car. He clung there.

"He must be one of the gang they were going to leave behind!" Phil exclaimed.

"I don't think so," Ham snapped. "Come on!"

Ham's car, a limousine that looked every penny of the seven thousand-odd dollars of it had cost, was parked at the end of the block. They raced to it, piled in.

Ham made the machine leap ahead, and stop with screaming tires near Monk and Johnny, who, completely blinded, were cautiously sparring with their fists, each under the impression the other was a foe. The bony Johnny, with arms practically twice the length of Monk's, had managed to poke Monk once between the eyes.

"Quit fighting with each other!" Ham yelled. "Get in this car!" Then, as Monk and Johnny stumbled toward the sound of Ham's voice, Ham told Phil, "Steer them in the back seat."

Phil did so. He closed the glass partition between front and rear seats. "That'll keep the gas out, I hope," he said.

Ham said nothing. He dropped one eye briefly on the speedometer. It was already past fifty. He punched a button on the dash, and a police siren began howling under the hood.

"It's against the law for a private citizen to have a police siren on his car," Phil said.

"That's all right." Ham stamped the accelerator. "We've got honorary commissions."

The gray car was a pale-red tail light on the end of a rocket far ahead. But Ham's big machine was supercharged, had special low springing. It could do, on a straightaway, close to two hundred, if it had run enough. It was over ninety now.

The tail light of the gray car got closer. There was not much traffic on the streets; what there was hugged the curbings, because of the siren.

Suddenly the gray car took a corner. Ham braked at the last minute. He was doing fifty when he started into the curb, and all four tires locked and slid and smoked and howled like wolves.

In the rear seat, centrifugal force tried to throw Monk and Johnny out through the side of the car.

Monk roared, "Who's driving this thing?"

"Ham Brooks," Phil squalled back at him.

"Great grief!" Monk howled. "Let me outa here!"

The speedometer was back up to seventy.

"Go ahead and get out," Ham said.

Dark buildings, street lights went moaning past. The limousine took a high bump of a street intersection, must have gone fifty feet before its wheels got on the pavement again.

Their headlights were now splashing white glare on the gray car.

"Look!" Phil barked.

The big man, the stranger they had seen leap on the

back of the gray car, was hanging down, and, with one hand, clamping his hat over the mouth of the exhaust pipe.

"That's why we're catching up with them so fast," Ham said grimly. "You can kill a car's speed by blocking the exhaust. Sometimes you can stop the motor."

A man leaned out of the window of the gray car. A moment later, a spider-webbed design of cracks appeared in the windshield in front of Phil's nose.

"A rock flew up and cracked the windshield," he said.

"Yes, a rock made of lead," Ham said.

Phil blanched. "A bullet!"

"If you think that guy is just shaking his finger at us, you're crazy." Ham tramped down on the accelerator. "This windshield is bulletproof. I hope."

Phil sat back, white-faced. He could see the bobbing figure on the rear of the gray car. Apparently the occupants of the machine did not know the stranger was clinging there.

"He's got a knife!" Phil gasped.

"Who?"

"The guy on the back of that car." Phil pointed. "He's trying to stick it in the tires."

Ham corrected, "Trying to reach down and cut through the side wall of a tire. That's a heck of a job. He couldn't have done it on those rough streets. But we're on new pavement now."

A moment later, the man with the knife succeeded. The tire let go. The man lost his knife, clung wildly to the spare tire and bumper.

For moments, it seemed the gray car was going to dive into some one of the buildings along the street. But it straightened out, stopped.

The three men piled out of the machine instantly. Two of them dragging Pat Savage. Apparently Pat was still out from the blow on the jaw.

The man on the spare tire alighted. He was around the car, upon the trio with flashing speed. He swung a fist, and one of the three released Pat, walked backward a dozen feet or so and sat down.

The man who had been on the tire scooped up Pat, whipped around the machine, and half across the street.

Ham put all his weight on the brake pedal, stopped the limousine so that it was a barricade between Pat and her rescuer. Ham had the window down on that side a crack.

"Get in the car," he yelled. "It's armor plated!"

The rescuer wrenched open the rear door, tossed Pat inside, got in himself, and banged the door.

"Run over 'em, mates," he said.

Ham did his best. But the two occupants of the gray car had grabbed their stunned companion by the arms. A subway entrance was nearby. They ran him to that, and down the steps. Then they turned back, guns in hand. The gun muzzles emptied out fire, and noise that whooped like thunder as it echoed in the street. More spider webs appeared in the limousine glass. There were sounds like huge hammerblows against the car body.

"Monk!" Ham roared. "Give me your machine pistol!"

"I haven't got it," Monk said. "Do you think I would go to the Explorers League in a tux packing one of those things?"

"Johnny, have you got yours?"

"No, I haven't," Johnny said.

Ham grinned. "Johnny's excited. He's using small words," he told Phil O'Reilly. Then Ham drove the car up on the sidewalk and headed it for the subway entrance. It looked as if he was going to drive down the stairs themselves, and the three men with guns ducked out of sight. Ham braked in time.

Pat's rescuer flung open the limousine door. He was huge, wide, very freckled, very red-headed. He had four gold teeth in the center of his mouth, and he was showing them. He seemed as happy as a bulldog with a strange cat.

"I'm goin' after them hull worms," he said.

He did not go down that subway entrance, but ran across the street to the other one, and disappeared into that. Ham and Phil and the others strained their ears.

There was no shooting. But they *did* hear a subway train leave the station.

When the big red-thatched, freckled man came back— he had crossed from one side of the subway to the other underground—he looked disgusted.

"The swabs got away," he explained. "Jumped in the front car, and made the motorman take the train out in a hurry." He rubbed his left leg, then made kicking motions with the leg, and scowled at it. "Say, when I jumped down on them tracks to cross over, somethin' bit me."

"Bit you?"

"Yeah. Couldn't see what kind of a varmint it was."

"Maybe you touched the third rail," Phil suggested.

"Come to think of it, I was steppin' on that extra rail when the varmint bit me."

Phil gaped at him. "For the love of mud! That's supposed to kill a man."

"Kill Dink Masket?" The unusual red-headed fellow snorted. "There ain't nothin' a man can't see that is tough enough to bother Dink."

"Your name is Dink Masket?" Phil asked.

"You heard me." Dink Masket eyed Phil curiously. "Right pretty young craft, ain't you?"

Monk laughed.

Phil was insulted. But he decided to let the remark pass. "You seem to have saved this young woman," he said. "We're grateful."

Phil extended his hand. Dink Masket took it. Phil all but howled in agony. Dink Masket had a grip like a stone crusher. Dink Masket then shook hands with Ham, Johnny and Monk, all three of whom wrung their knuckles and blew on them afterward.

"Hurt you, boys?" Dink Masket asked. "I'm a little tough by nature. Sometimes I forget to be gentle."

Scowling, Monk said, "You crack my knuckles like that again, my sunset-complexioned friend, and you're gonna find out there is somebody else that is tough."

"Meaning you?" Dink Masket asked skeptically.

"Yeah, me," Monk growled.

"Ho, ho, ho!" said Dink Masket.

Monk took a step forward. "Listen, you big—"

Ham got in front of Monk and said, "You dope! He just saved Pat, didn't he?"

"Yeah," Monk admitted, subsiding. "And by remindin' me of it, you just saved *him*."

Dink Masket ambled over to the limousine, looked inside, found it was too dark to see Pat, and fumbled in his trousers pockets for a match.

"There's a dome-light switch by the door," Ham said. "Turn it on."

"Don't put no stock in them electrical contraptions," Dink Masket said. He went on fishing until he found a match, which he struck. By the illumination it shed, he inspected Pat Savage. She was still unconscious.

"Trimmest craft I've seen in some time," Dink Masket remarked of Pat's form.

Ham climbed into the car and inspected Pat anxiously. "She's just kayoed," he said, relieved.

Monk was scowling at Dink Masket. "Look here, how'd you happen to mix in this thing?" Monk asked.

"Me?" Dink showed his four gold teeth cheerfully. "I was just cruisin' past."

"You mean," Monk demanded suspiciously, "that you got mixed up in that for no reason at all?"

"Seen a squall of trouble. That's enough reason for me, mate."

"You like trouble, eh?"

"Yeah, mate, figure I must."

Monk growled, "Stop calling me mate."

Dink Masket eyed him critically. "Think I will," he said. "Guess your family was baboons a lot more recent than mine."

Ham snorted gleefully. Phil O'Reilly, who had been the victim of Monk's complete lack of manners, grinned with pleasure.

At this point, Pat Savage sat up, held her head, and opened and shut her eyes several times. She looked at their surroundings.

The limousine was still standing on the sidewalk, and a crowd had started to gather.

"I must have missed something," Pat said.

"You did," Ham assured her. "And I see no reason for us hanging around here." The lawyer climbed into the machine, waited until the others were also aboard—it was a tight fit in the back seat with Monk, Johnny, Pat and Dink Masket all wedged in—then the limousine backed off the sidewalk and left the spot.

Monk asked, "Pat, did you get a good look at those men?"

"Well, a fair look, anyway," Pat replied.

"Ever see them before?"

"No."

"Any idea why they grabbed you?" Monk persisted. "Did they say something, maybe, that would explain it?"

"Being unconscious, I wouldn't know what they said," Phil replied.

Monk scratched his head. Monk's knot of a head was covered with short red hair which had some of the appearance of rusty finishing nails. "It gets me," he said.

Phil O'Reilly leaned back on the limousine cushions, and contemplated the darkened pavement as it crawled toward them like a dark snake. "You know," he remarked cheerfully, "that was the first time I was ever shot at."

Ham threw him an approving glance. "It didn't seem to bother you much."

"Not as much as I thought it would."

Suddenly, Ham frowned. "Say, you said a guy with an ugly face tried to intercept that letter. Do you suppose—"

Phil stopped Ham by clutching his arm. "Let's get rid of this Masket," he whispered, "before we discuss anything."

Dink Masket evidently heard that, because he growled, "What's that wind you're makin' up there in the front seat?"

Producing his billfold, Phil extracted several greenbacks, the lowest denomination of which was a twenty. He turned around in the seat and extended the money toward Dink Masket.

"What's that pocket lettuce for?" Dink Masket asked.

"A reward," Phil explained.

"What for?"

"For saving Miss Savage's life."

Dink Masket blew out his cheeks indignantly. "Don't want it," he said.

"There's quite a bit of money here, and you're entitled to it for what you've done," Phil told him patiently. "With that much money, you can have yourself a time. Take it, and start painting the town red. You're a sailor, aren't you? Well, have yourself a real whoop-tearing shore-leave."

Dink Masket scowled.

"Meanin'," he demanded, "that you're tryin' to get rid of me?"

"Well, to tell the truth, we have some private business to discuss," Phil said.

"Is it about this trouble?"

"Yes, of course."

"Then," said Dink Masket triumphantly, "I'm in on it. There's no weather I like better than squally weather, at sea or ashore. Looks like I found me a squall on shore here, and durned if I don't sail right along in it."

Phil was exasperated.

He yelled, "You can't force yourself onto us."

Pat entered the conversation.

"I think Mr. Masket is right," Pat declared. "If he likes excitement, I know exactly how he feels. I like a little now and then myself. If Mr. Masket wants to help us, I see no reason why he shouldn't. I think he's earned the privilege."

"But Pat," Monk ejaculated, "we just don't want the lug along."

"I do," Pat said stubbornly.

Phil O'Reilly discovered he was caught on the horns of a dilemma. He wanted to make a hit with Pat, and here she was sponsoring Dink Masket. Phil swallowed his irritation, and reversed himself.

"If Pat thinks we need Mr. Masket, I'm in favor of his staying," Phil said.

"So am I," Ham announced.

Monk made a disgusted noise. "Why didn't you stick with me?" he growled at Phil. "We could've outvoted 'em, and got rid of this . . . this—"

"Brobdingnagian," Johnny supplied.

"What's a Brod-brodbig—whatever you call it?" Dink Masket demanded loudly.

"A large, strong fellow," Johnny explained prudently.

"That's me," Dink Masket declared. "You swabs go ahead and discuss your trouble. I want to hear it."

Ham had been thinking. "It is just possible," he said, "that this thing was an attempt to prevent us going with Phil on an expedition to hunt Daniel Stage in South America."

"If the seizure of Miss Savage had been successful," Phil suggested, "you would have had to stay here in New York and hunt her."

"That's exactly what I mean," Ham agreed.

Monk snorted. "That's a hind-foremost idea."

"How do you figure?"

"When they grabbed Pat, they had us all on the sidewalk, and they gassed us. They could have shot us all down just as easy. I would say it would've been easier than seizing Pat."

"Yes," Phil said, "but that would have been murder."

"Listen, there ain't much difference between the penalty for kidnapping and for murder."

"That *is* puzzling," Ham admitted.

Dink Masket asked, "Who is this Daniel Stage you mentioned, mates?"

Ham glanced at Phil O'Reilly. "Yes, you might tell us more about him. He was a friend of yours, wasn't he?"

"Not what you would call a close friend," Phil said. "But I *did* know him rather well." He rubbed his jaw while he was pondering. "I went to college with Daniel Stage. He was very ambitious, even then."

"Ambitious, eh?" Ham said.

"Extremely. You see, Daniel Stage came of rather poor parents, and he had an intense ambition to make a high mark in the world. He was a dreamer, rather idealistic, and impatient with a great many of life's problems. To tell the truth, he wasn't very well liked at school. He was something of a genius, I'm afraid, and eccentric after the fashion of genius."

"What would you say was his outstanding characteristic?" Ham inquired.

"An intense determination to be famous and powerful. That, and an inclination to be a reckless adventurer at heart. Just the type to be a spectacular explorer."

"He went into the back-country Amazon basin by plane, didn't he?"

"Yes."

"Where did he get the money for the plane?"

"A man named Chief John Eagle financed that," Phil explained. "You see, Daniel Stage already had a reputation as an explorer. He had been in the Smith Sound Eskimo region, and in the Rub Al Khali desert in Arabia, and some other places." Phil sighed. "As an explorer, he made me look pretty punk."

Monk leaned forward. "Any reason for John Eagle not wanting Daniel Stage to get help?"

"Oh, no," Phil said quickly. "As a matter of fact, Chief John Eagle's son is one of those who were lost hunting Daniel Stage."

"Is Elmo Walker Eagle the chief's son?"

"Yes."

"Why do they call him Chief?"

Phil smiled. "Wait until you see him. You'll understand.

The chief is an Oklahoma Indian who made millions out of oil."

"Does the chief wear feathers?"

"Not at all. He'll surprise you," Phil said. "He's a remarkable mixture of the aboriginal redskin who lived in a teepee and the modernized version."

Ham shifted the discussion to another thread. "Has Daniel Stage got any relatives around?" he asked.

"Yes, a sister," Phil replied.

Pat asked, "Good looking?"

"Er—rather," Phil admitted.

Monk enthusiastically suggested, "Maybe we'd better talk to the sister."

"We'll do that in the morning," Ham said. "It's way after midnight. We can't go rousing people out of bed at this time of night."

Johnny Littlejohn stretched his incredibly long and thin body and yawned.

"Somniferous satuvolism seems perspicacious," he remarked.

"Eh?" Phil stared at him.

"I said that time out for sleep seems wise," Johnny explained. "You might drop me at the next corner. My apartment is close."

Johnny got out at the corner, and his long frame disappeared in the darkness.

"An unusual fellow," Phil remarked.

"That's putting it mildly," Pat said. "But then, you'll find out all of Doc's associates are unusual."

Phil said, "Doc has five aids, hasn't he?"

"Yes. Monk, Ham and Johnny are three of them. Then there is Major Thomas J. Roberts, better known as Long Tom. And Colonel John Renwick, called Renny."

"Where are those two?"

"They're in South Africa on an engineering project," Pat explained. "Long Tom is an electrical engineer, and Renny Renwick is a civil engineer. They're installing a new system of mining diamonds in the Kimberly district."

Phil pondered. "I wonder what became of Doc Savage?"

Ham said, "I'll stop a minute at that drugstore yonder. Monk, you go in and try to call Doc."

A few minutes later, when Monk came out of the drugstore, he shrugged his shoulders.

"Doc hasn't showed up," he explained.

"Doesn't that worry you fellows?" Phil demanded.

Monk shrugged. "Naw, Doc often disappears. Sometimes he's gone two or three months at a time, and nobody hears from him. But he always turns up."

"Where does he go?"

"Off to a place he calls his Fortress of Solitude, to study or work on scientific experiments where he won't be bothered," Monk explained.

"Where is this Fortress of Solitude?"

"Search us," Monk said. "We don't know, except that it's in the polar regions somewhere. You see, Doc keeps a lot of valuable scientific discoveries at the place, and one time some guys found it, and we had a heck of a time. After that, he moved the Fortress. We don't know where he moved it to."

IV

THE TRICKY MR. MASKET

The attempt to shoot Phil O'Reilly was made in front of his home.

They were just alighting from the limousine. All of them had stepped out to say good night.

"Watch out!" Dink Masket bellowed suddenly.

He lunged, threw his weight against Phil, and both of them sprawled into the entryway of the house. Simultaneously, there was a sound like a sledge striking the stone side of the house. Chips of stone flew. Then the echoes of a shot banged back and forth between the buildings.

Pat dived back into the car.

"Stay down!" she shrieked at Phil. "Somebody tried to shoot you!"

Ham flung himself alongside Phil, and forced the young man to keep down.

Dink Masket and Monk crossed the street—the shot had come from the park—running in zigzag fashion, doubled low. They reached the stone fence around the park, vaulted it, charged into the bushes.

As soon as they were out of sight, Dink Masket and Monk stopped.

Dink Masket produced a revolver and fired it three times into the ground.

Monk watched, grinning. Then Monk bellowed, "There he goes! That way, Dink!"

They crashed through the brush some more.

Dink Masket fired two more shots into the ground.

"Over here, Dink!" Monk roared.

They made noise in the brush for some time. They had not seen anyone. All the shots that had been fired had been discharged by Dink Masket in Monk's presence.

They walked out of the park, and joined Phil, Ham and Pat.

Monk said, "It was that guy you described, Phil."

"You mean the man with the ugly face?" Phil was amazed. "You mean he is the one who shot at me?"

"Yep."

"Are you sure?"

"I got a good clear look at him," Monk declared.

Dink Masket said, "And I saw exactly what Monk saw."

"Which way'd he go?" Phil barked. "Let's go after him."

"He got away," Monk said. "Anyway, he's too free with that gun for anybody to go prowling around in the park after him."

Phil shuddered. "Let's get in the house," he said.

While they were entering the house, Monk got an opportunity to whisper a few words to Dink Masket. "We put that over, didn't we?" Monk breathed.

"Sh-h-h-h," said Dink Masket. "Let's not be too friendly."

In the large, comfortable O'Reilly library, they waited for the police to come. Undoubtedly, some of the neighbors would call the officers about the shooting. Phil paced the floor. He was excited, but not nervous.

"Thanks," he told Dink Masket. "I guess you saved my life, too."

"Don't mention it, mate," said Dink Masket modestly.

Phil stopped and slammed his right fist into his left palm.

"This proves one thing!" he declared. "That man with the ugly face doesn't want me going after Daniel Stage. He tried to intercept Dan's letter. Then, when that failed, he tried to shoot me."

"Let's see that letter," Dink Masket suggested.

They were examining the two missives which Phil had received in the rubber-coated envelope when the police arrived. There were two uniformed cops in a patrol car, and they were calmly efficient. Ham Brooks happened to know both officers, and they took his word for what had occurred. Ham made no mention of the letter, or of the matter of the missing explorer, Daniel Stage.

The police left, saying they would give the park a thorough search and put out a net for the man with the ugly face.

After the officers had gone, Phil eyed Ham. "Why didn't you tell them about the letter, and Daniel Stage?" he asked.

"We're working on that ourselves," Ham explained.

Pat yawned sleepily. "Well, it looks like the excitement is over for the night. How about all of us going home, and meeting in the morning?"

Phil nodded. "We're going to talk to Daniel Stage's sister in the morning—her name is Junith, incidentally. Is that our first move?"

Ham told him that it would be.

Ham drove his limousine downtown. In the seat beside him, Dink Masket was relaxed. Monk and Pat rode in the rear.

Monk chuckled for a while. "That was a nice piece of showmanship. It all came out timed right, too. When we stopped to make that telephone call to headquarters, it gave Johnny all the time he needed to get across the street from Phil O'Reilly's place with a rifle."

Dink Masket said, "I was sure glad Johnny's finger didn't slip on the trigger. He put a bullet right through where Phil had been standing."

Pat made a disgusted sound.

"A lot of good that elaborate trick did you!" she said.

Ham said, "But it did plenty of good, Pat. We feel confident now that Phil really doesn't know who that fellow with the ugly face is. We could tell that from the way he acted."

"Sure," Monk said, forgetting himself and agreeing with Ham, something he rarely did. "If Phil had been working with the man with the ugly face, and the fellow had tried to kill him, Phil would have been almost certain to give it away."

Pat sniffed. "I could have told you Phil is a straight boy."

"Oh, sure," Monk said skeptically. "He's handsome, too, ain't he?"

Pat maintained an indignant silence.

They passed two police cars cruising toward the park, evidently on their way to look for the man who had fired the shot at Phil O'Reilly.

Ham asked anxiously, "You think Johnny had time to get out of the park? It might be kind of embarrassing if they caught him wandering around in there with a rifle."

"He had plenty of time to scram," Monk said. "Big words and all."

They dropped Pat at her apartment building, which was a swanky structure on Park Avenue. Pat operated one of the most profitable beauty and reducing establishments in the city, making considerably more money from the place than she could conveniently spend.

"I'll see you in the morning," she said.

They drove next to Ham's quarters, which were in an exclusive club.

"I got to stop here and get Habeas Corpus," Monk explained. "I left him in Ham's place while we went to the Explorers League."

Habeas Corpus was Monk's pet pig, an animal with overlong legs, wing-sized ears, an inquisitive disposition, and an ability to irritate Ham unreasonably.

Ham also had a pet, a chimpanzee or dwarf baboon—there was some scientific doubt which—named Chemistry, this pet of Ham's being notable for the spit-image likeness which it bore to the homely chemist, Monk. Chemistry did not like Monk, and these sentiments were returned. Neither did Habeas Corpus like Chemistry; Ham professed no approval for Monk or Habeas Corpus, and Monk did not care for Ham or Chemistry—so that it was one large and noisy family when all four got together.

Dink Masket said, "Suppose you stay with Ham tonight, Monk. I want to borrow the car."

"I would sooner have a buck goat in my apartment," Ham declared. "But all right."

Monk looked at Dink Masket. "Where you going?"

"Got a little business, mate."

Monk grinned. "All right," he said. "Say, you do pretty well as a screwball sailor."

"Think anyone will recognize me?"

"Oh, any disguise can be seen through in time," Monk said. "But anybody would have to know you pretty well. By the way, I haven't had a chance to ask you how you really came to pile on the back of that gray car when they grabbed Pat."

"That was simple. I started to come into the building earlier, but noticed those men hanging around. Particularly the chestnut vender. That seemed peculiar, because you seldom see them selling chestnuts in that district. Of course, after they turned loose the gas and seized Pat, the only thing to do was grab on to their car."

"Well, it was fast work," Monk said.

"Be seeing you in the morning."

"Sure."

Dink Masket drove Ham's limousine toward the Hudson River, and approached a large building of brick, a warehouse that was built partially out into the river, so that it resembled nothing more than another of the shedded piers which were plentiful in that section. The place appeared disused. A barely legible sign on the front said, *Hidalgo Trading Co.*

When Dink Masket pressed a radio-control signal button on the car radio—the limousine was equipped with transmitting and receiving apparatus; the signal put out by the button was simply a dot-and-dash combination on a certain frequency—the big hangar doors opened automatically as a result. The limousine rolled inside.

Dink Masket seemed perfectly familiar with the place. He alighted, turned on the lights, closed the door. The interior of the big warehouse was deceptive. It contained a number of airplanes, one very large one for fast long-distance flights, and smaller craft, two of which were gyro planes. At the far end, there was a slip in which boats lay, the craft including a rather small submarine. All the planes were amphibians, capable of working from land or water, and there was a sloping ramp down which they could be rolled into the water, thence through large rolling doors to the Hudson River.

Striding to the river end of the hangar-warehouse, Dink Masket dropped to all fours and leaned over the edge of the slip.

Dink Masket spoke with the modulated, trained voice of Doc Savage.

"Well, well," he remarked. "The tide hasn't come in quite enough, has it?"

In the darkness below, three horror-stricken men—Tiny, Bat and Lon, the trio who had staged the trick and seized Doc Savage at the Explorers League earlier in the night— were handcuffed to three dock pilings. Only their necks were out of the water.

The tide had been coming in for some hours. When the trio had been first handcuffed there, the water had been less than waist deep. But now it was under their chins. And in a few minutes, they fully believed, it would be over their heads.

With complete amiability, Doc Savage's voice said, "You fellows have not drowned yet, have you? Well, I can always give you more time."

He reached down, felt around in the darkness, and jerked off the adhesive tape which gagged Tiny.

"You have not, by any chance, decided to tell me all about it?" he asked.

"Listen," Tiny croaked, "you ain't running no whizzer on us. We know you don't kill anybody."

Doc Savage's chuckle was grim.

"I won't be doing it," he said. "The tide might, however."

"The hell with you!" Tiny snarled.

"The tide," Doc said, "is still coming in."

Doc Savage placed the gag back over Tiny's mouth, slapped it rather hard several times to make the tape stick, then stood. He walked away, making noise with his feet. He reached the door, operated the mechanism that opened it— the rollers and motors filled the place with drumming sound as the door opened—then closed the door again. But he was still inside the warehouse-hangar when the door closed.

There was a small compartment at one side of the hangar which was completely inclosed and soundproofed. It was used for test work where a soundproof, dust-tight inclosure was necessary. It contained, among other things, a desk and telephone.

Doc entered the compartment, closed the door silently, and picked up the telephone. He got Monk Mayfair on the wire.

"They are not ready to talk yet," Doc said.

"Who do you mean?"

"The three men who tried to seize me at the Explorers League."

"Are you using truth serum on them?" Monk demanded.

"No, we have had some bad luck with that stuff, and to use it in its strongest form is always dangerous," the bronze man explained. "I am going to try to scare them badly enough to make them talk."

"Do they know you've disguised yourself, and are using the name of Dink Masket?"

"No."

Monk was thoughtful. "I been wondering if that disguise is going to help you much."

"I think it has already," the bronze man said. "These three fellows had orders to grab me tonight and kill me. They were hired by someone, I suspect. And if the person who hired them can be made to think I am dead, that will enable me to work on the thing without being suspected."

"Well, yeah, it might at that."

"I called you," Doc Savage said, "to tell you to act more worried about me. Call the police, and tell them that I am missing, and you suspect foul play. Tell the police that you got an anonymous telephone call that three men were seen forcing me into a car in the park near the Explorers League at the point of a gun. Then telephone the newspapers anonymously yourself, and give them that story. Merely say that you saw three armed men forcing me to get in a car in the park near the Explorers League at about eleven o'clock in the evening."

"I get it," Monk agreed. "You want the impression to get around that you are dead."

"Yes," Doc said. "You might, in your anonymous call to the newspapers, add that the car drove away, and that shortly afterward, you heard a shot. To dress it up a little more, you might put in that you heard me scream, 'Please don't kill me!' just before the shot. Say that you have heard my voice over the radio, and recognized it."

"Right."

"I hope you do not mind telling those lies."

"You know me," Monk said cheerfully. "Liar is my middle name. Say, had Ham and me better go to bed at all? Maybe there will be some more excitement tonight."

"No, get some sleep. I will telephone you if anything breaks."

Dropping the receiver on its prong, Doc glanced at the electric clock on the wall. He happened to know the exact minute of high tide for that day, and it was not yet that time by almost half an hour.

He settled back, and waited. The three were in no danger of drowning, actually. He had handcuffed them so that their heads were above high-tide mark for this date.

The bronze man removed one of the colored glass caps—the same type of a gadget as the so-called "invisible" eyeglasses obtained from opticians, and particularly popular with actors—with which he had disguised the flake-gold color of his eyes. The cap was irritating his eye slightly. He cleaned it carefully, and replaced it.

The rest of his disguise—the dye on his hair, his skin, and the spattering of dyed-on freckles—were giving no trouble. The gum padding in his cheeks which had the effect of widening out his face was mildly disturbing at times, but he left it in place.

V

TRAIL

Half an hour later, when Doc Savage went back to the rear of the hangar, he used the disguise of Dink Masket, including the voice. Dropping into a rowboat, he pulled himself along the slip until he reached the three men handcuffed to the piles.

He thumbed on a flashlight. The glow showed that the water was above the chins of the three. Their eyes protruded as they stared at him. All three tried to make talking noises through their noses, the result being somewhat like a swarm of bumblebees.

"So this is what he was doing to you," Dink Masket's voice remarked. "Well, I guess you had it comin' to you."

He contemplated them cold-bloodedly, listening with idle interest to the horrified buzzing they made. He glanced at the water.

"Tide is gonna fix you swabs if it comes much higher," he remarked.

One of the men looked as if he was going to faint. It was the big, thick-necked one, Tiny.

Doc plucked the gag off Tiny's face, and using the Dink Masket voice, he asked, "Any little message you'd like to send your folks?"

Tiny could only gurgle incoherently.

"Of course," Dink's voice added, "I couldn't tell your folks what happened to you. But I might pass on some other little message."

Tiny finally managed to get his voice functioning. "Turn us loose!" he bleated.

"Can't."

"Why not?"

"Doc Savage wouldn't like it. You see, I'm kind of connected with him. Tonight, I'm attending to things here in the hangar and boathouse. I knew you guys were over here, but I thought for a while I wouldn't do anything about it. Finally my curiosity got the best of me, though, and here I am."

Apparently it never entered Tiny's head that he was talking to Doc Savage.

"How did Savage happen to catch you?" Doc continued.

Tiny swore hoarsely. "It was a trick. He had some kind of gas or something in the heel of his shoe. He pulled the heel off his shoe, and we didn't notice it."

"The gas overcame you?"

"Yeah—just as we was gonna knife the bronze guy." Tiny groaned. "I guess he didn't get the gas because he held his breath, or somethin'. I remember we noticed he was holdin' his breath just before we passed out. We thought he'd had a heart attack or somethin', and had passed out. But he must 'a' been just holdin' his breath."

"That's bad. Savage won't forget that."

"You turn us loose," Tiny promised, "and I'll pay you plenty."

"How much?"

"Fifty dollars."

"Ho, ho, ho!" said Dink Masket's voice disgustedly. "You piker! I'll enjoy watchin' you drown."

Tiny kept arguing frantically, and before long, had his offer up to twenty thousand dollars, a sum it was hardly likely he could have paid.

"Nope. Can't buy me," Dink Masket's voice said finally. He seemed to ponder. "Tell you what, though. There might be one way."

Tiny got his mouth full of water, and gargled it in horror.

"I'll do anything," he croaked.

"Well, now, it kind of looked like Savage was pretty mad at you guys, and went off and left you here to drown. I think he did that, you understand, because you tried to kill him. Trying to kill him didn't get him very friendly toward you."

"Stop wasting time!" Tiny yelled. "What can you do?"

"Well, now, I might prevail on Savage not to let you drown. But I could only do that if you was to tell me the truth. If you tell me who hired you to kill him, I might have a point to argue with him. I'd be willin' to try, anyhow."

Tiny didn't like that idea. But a wave came slopping along, filled his mouth, and changed his mind.

He moaned. "We *can't* tell who hired us," he said.

Doc Savage straightened up and grunted. In the make-up as Dink Masket, he looked cold-blooded, fierce. "Well, that's too bad," he said. "I guess the tide will have to take you."

"Wait a minute!" Tiny wailed. "We'll tell you all we know."

The story came out of Tiny with babbling force. He belonged with Lon and Bat and three others, to a local crime syndicate which made a specialty of doing jobs for hire. This, Tiny insisted frantically, was their first venture into the bigger brackets of murder business.

It seemed they had been approached by a man with a strange face, a man the left side of whose face was different from the right. They did not know this man, had never learned his name. He had been vouched for, however, by a mutual acquaintance, who was a gangster. Lon, Tiny, Bat and their three colleagues had been propositioned—had been offered a tremendous, to them, sum of money to kill Doc Savage, and to seize Pat Savage and hold her. Later, it had been the understanding that they could kill Pat if they thought that would be safest.

"Why did this man with the ugly face want Doc Savage killed and Pat kidnaped?"

"Because a guy named Phil O'Reilly was coming to Doc with some kind of a proposition."

"And this man with the face didn't want Doc accepting O'Reilly's proposition?"

"That's it."

"And why was Pat to be seized?"

"To keep Doc Savage's men busy hunting her," Tiny explained. "You see, if Phil O'Reilly went to Doc's men, they might be interested in the proposition. But if this girl was kidnaped, they would have to spend their time hunting her."

Doc Savage was silent for a while. It was a reasonable story. A man hiring professional killers would hardly let them know his identity if it could be avoided.

"What is behind this whole thing?" he asked. "Why all this effort to keep Doc Savage out of South America?"

It developed that Tiny knew nothing at all about South America. Neither did the others. Nor had they ever heard of the explorer named Daniel Stage, who was lost in the Amazon back country jungle.

"This is no help," Dink Masket's voice said angrily. "You have given no indication of how Doc can get in touch with this fellow with the ugly face."

Tiny shuddered.

"Look," he said. "We was to turn up at a place and collect the rest of our pay."

"When?"

"Ten o'clock this morning."

"Where?"

Tiny described the spot frantically. "This guy with the face will be there at ten o'clock in the morning," he insisted. "He was gonna pay us. We rented Room 608 in this hotel. The guy with the face was going to meet us there."

Doc was skeptical. "Sometimes those fellows don't pay you," he reminded.

"Oh, he'll be there. The other three of our crowd, the ones who were to grab Pat Savage, were to take her to the place, and this guy with the face was going to show up and make the girl answer some questions."

That sounded more reasonable. As a whole, Tiny and the others had told all they knew, Doc concluded. However, he was still puzzled about why the three who had seized Pat had made no effort to harm Monk, Ham, Johnny or Phil O'Reilly.

He asked Tiny about that.

"Listen, we do what we get paid for," Tiny said. "If they didn't bump off them Doc Savage men, it was because they weren't getting paid for *that* job. The snatch was all they had been hired to pull."

Doc had suspected that was the reason. That, and the

fact that the kidnaping trio had not been set for a wholesale killing on the sidewalk in front of the skyscraper which housed Doc's headquarters.

The bronze man unlocked the handcuffs which held Tiny, Lon and Bat in the water. He heaved them up on the slip. They were still handcuffed, and helpless, weakened from their immersion.

Doc went to a steel cabinet which contained equipment, and came back with a hypodermic needle. He used the hypo on each of the three, although they howled protest.

The trio went to sleep shortly. The needle contained a drug that induced a state of helpless semi-consciousness that would last many hours.

Doc loaded the trio into the limousine. He drove with them to a small garage far uptown. The garage was closed for the night, but the proprietor, a rather quiet young man, lived in an apartment above the place. The young man came down, looked in the car, and, without a word, opened the door of his garage.

Inside the garage was an ambulance. Doc Savage and the garage man transferred Tiny, Lon and Bat to the ambulance.

"Will they need another shot to keep them unconscious?" the garage man asked.

"Not if you make good driving time."

"O. K. I'll start right away."

Nothing more was said. The young garage man had done this thing before—taken unconscious men to a strange institution in the remote mountainous upstate section of New York. He knew something of what it was all about. He knew that the men he hauled were criminals.

What he did not know—what no one knew except Doc Savage and his associates and the specialists immediately concerned—was that the criminals were being consigned to Doc Savage's "college" for reforming. Here they would undergo delicate brain operations which would wipe out all memory of the past—a sort of enforced amnesia. Afterward they would be taught to hate crime, would receive training at trades which would enable them to earn useful livings.

Doc's method of reforming criminals, while less painful and more effective than penitentiaries, was a little drastic for the public consumption, so he kept its existence unknown.

VI

TROUBLE LEADING TO JUNITH

At ten o'clock the next morning, it was raining.

Doc Savage studied the building where the man with the ugly face was to meet the thugs he had hired. It was a hotel, a small one, not impressive looking, not too clean, and probably not with an overly savory reputation. It was on the wrong side of Broadway.

He joined the others—Monk, Ham, Johnny, Pat and Phil O'Reilly—who were parked around the corner. Doc was still using the Dink Masket disguise. Fortunately, the dye was waterproof.

Because it would not have looked right for Dink Masket to issue orders, Monk gave them. The commands he issued were ones he had previously received from Doc.

"Me and Johnny and Phil will go to this Room 608," Monk said, "and be parked outside in the hall. We will stay under cover in the stairway, and we'll have anaesthetic gas, gas masks, and machine pistols loaded with mercy bullets.

"Johnny, you and Dink Masket park in the lobby, and keep out of sight," Monk continued. "As soon as this guy with the face shows up, you be ready to head him off should he attempt to escape."

Monk turned to Pat.

"Pat, you stay with the car," he said. "You'll be safer."

"I don't want to be safe," Pat said.

"Well, somebody's got to have the car ready for a chase," Monk snapped. "Anyway, there's another job somebody has got to do."

"What kind of a job?" Pat asked skeptically.

Monk fumbled around in a compartment, and brought out a small dark box. This container was adorned with a switch, and to it was attached a powerful clamp of the spring-and-jaws type.

"If the man with the face comes in a car," he said, "somebody has got to fasten this box on his car."

Pat peered at the box. "Isn't that one of those little

45

short-wave radio transmitters that you can locate with a direction finder?"

Monk nodded. "With this on the ugly guy's car, we can locate it, even if he should get away in the machine," he said.

Pat was more satisfied. "All right, I'll do it," she said.

They got out into the drizzling rain and separated. Monk, Phil and Johnny worked around to the rear of the hotel, their plan to enter by the back door, and get upstairs without being observed.

Pat took up a position in a drugstore across the street, with her radio-transmitter box.

Doc Savage and Ham, surveying the street carefully, decided no one was in sight. They entered the hotel lobby. The place smelled stale. A few guests occupied lobby chairs.

In the back were three telephone booths, through the glass doors of which a watch could be kept on the entrance. They took up a position there, and waited.

Ham, holding the booth door open a crack, asked, "Doc, you sure nobody shadowed us here?"

"I think not. I kept a sharp watch."

"Then, if this guy with the ugly face is tipped off, we'll figure that Phil O'Reilly must have done it."

"Don't you trust Phil?"

"I don't know," Ham said. "He seems straight. But when a thing like this starts, you're wiser if you don't trust anybody."

Doc Savage's voice dropped, became imperative. "Close your door," he said.

"Is—" Ham looked, swallowed. Their man was coming into the hotel.

He was a big, wide man. The swing of his shoulders, the lithe ease of his carriage, indicated that he had more than an average amount of agility. He wore a long tan raincoat, the collar turned up around his neck; a felt hat was yanked low over his eyes. But they could see the hideous character of his face, the inhuman aspect of it.

It was their intention to stay under cover, let the man go up to the room, and seize him along with the three men he had hired to kidnap Pat.

But the man did an unexpected thing. He stepped to one side of the door, stood there for a while, then moved over to the lobby window and looked out.

His hand leaped to his coat pocket, came out with a gun.

"He sees Pat!" Ham yelled.

Doc Savage realized that, too. Pat had rushed across the street to affix the radio-transmitter box to the man's car, and he had discovered her.

Out of the booth, Doc scooped up a light chair. He threw it. Ham's yell had attracted the ugly man's attention. He swung, faced them, started to lift his gun. Then he saw the chair coming, and dodged, at the same time trying to snap a shot. The bullet cut a long furrow in the carpet.

Doc went down, got behind a heavy divan. Ham dived for a corner, got around it. He stopped, unlimbered his machine pistol.

The machine pistols which they used, resembling oversized automatics, had been developed by Doc Savage, and could release an amazing number of bullets per minute. Although they fired various types of bullets, just now they were charged with so-called "mercy" slugs—bullets which were shells containing a potent chemical producing quick unconsciousness, without doing much damage.

Ham's pistol made a sound like a big bull fiddle. A noise that was earsplitting.

The burst missed.

The man with the ugly face got down, dived for the door, made it outside before Ham could wing him.

Ham said something violent, plunged in pursuit. The man with the ugly face ran across the sidewalk. He fired once at Pat, just as she was going into the drugstore.

Pat stumbled and was going down when she disappeared from view; either she had been hit, or she had tripped.

The man with the face dived into his car, slammed the door. The machine jumped away from the curb.

Ham leveled his machine pistol carefully, and it made another big noise. But the mercy bullets, mere shells, did not strike with enough foot-pounds of energy to break the windows of the car. The machine drove away with great speed.

"Come on!" Ham yelled. "We'll get our car and chase him!"

Pat came out of the drugstore, running with an ease that showed she had not been harmed. She joined them in the sprint toward the spot where they had left their own machine.

"Did you get that radio on his car?" Doc rapped.

"Yes," Pat said. "I was going away when he saw me. Darn it, I'm sorry I muffed that!"

"You think he saw you put the radio on?"

"No, I don't believe so. I clipped it underneath, to the chassis."

"Did you throw the switch and start the radio functioning?"

"Yes."

"Then you did all right," Doc said.

They reached their machine, piled inside, and set out in pursuit. Doc Savage, at the wheel, drove furiously for a while, using the siren, and tying up traffic.

"It's no use," he said finally.

He pulled up before a cigar store which displayed a telephone sign, and entered.

While Ham was waiting in the car, he looked at Pat anxiously. "When that guy shot at you," he said, "it looked as if he hit you."

Pat wryly exhibited a long rip in the shoulder of her expensively tailored frock.

"It was *that* close," she said. "Boy, that fellow can shoot, whoever he is."

Ham frowned. "Pat, you had better get out of this thing. We would never forgive ourselves if you got hurt."

Pat smiled and shook her head. "I like this kind of thing, believe it or not." She nodded in the direction of the cigar store. "It runs in the family. You know that Doc likes excitement."

"He never admits it," Ham said.

"Just the same, he does like it. Do you think he would follow a career like this, righting wrongs and helping other people out of trouble, if he didn't like it?"

"He was trained for it," Ham reminded her. "He was placed in the hands of scientists when he was very young and thoroughly trained for just this job."

Pat eyed Ham impishly. "What did your folks train *you* for, Ham?"

Ham looked uncomfortable. "A banker," he admitted.

"There you are. If you had liked banking, you would still be at it. You liked law, and this excitement of being one of Doc's group of assistants, so that's what you're doing."

They fell silent as Doc Savage reappeared from the cigar store. He swung into the car.

"I used the telephone and called that hotel," he said. "Monk, Johnny and Phil O'Reilly closed in on the three fellows who tried to kidnap you last night, Pat. They got them."

"What are they going to do with them?" Pat inquired.

"Question them," Doc explained. "I do not think they will know any more than the trio who tried to kill me, but there is a chance they will, so Monk and the others are going to give them a third degree."

"And afterward?"

"College," Doc said cryptically.

The bronze man switched on the sensitive radio receiver in the car, carefully adjusted the dial to the frequency of the little transmitter in the box which Pat had fastened to the chassis of the ugly man's car. Doc rotated the loop aerial, eventually picked up the signal of the transmitter. It was a steady series of staggered dots, the letter C in the continental Morse code—not the usual international wireless code—repeated over and over again.

Moving the loop control, Doc lifted the signal to its loudest point, then sank it to its lowest. He made a brief calculation.

"Going north," he decided. "Either north or south, and the car started off south, so my guess would be that he doubled back. We can make a short run and find out. If the signal drops in power, we are going the wrong way."

"How far is that little transmitter good for?" Pat asked.

"Not very far," Doc said. "That is why we can not let him get too much lead on us."

The bronze man drove carefully, but made good time. He made no effort to seek out the direct trail, but took streets where traffic was the least troublesome, so that he made, undoubtedly, a great deal better time than their quarry.

Ham said, "That guy must have been surprised when he found the trap there in the hotel. Monk called the newspapers, like you said for him to do. Every newspaper in town is carrying a story that Doc Savage has probably been murdered."

Doc nodded. "I wanted the man with the face to think that his hirelings had succeeded in killing me. If he had suspected I had escaped, he would hardly have come to the hotel."

In a miserable voice, Pat said, "Well, thanks to me, the plan blew up."

Ham laughed.

"The only way you could have helped what happened," the dapper lawyer said, "was to have been invisible."

"I guess so," Pat agreed. "Anyway, I should have been more careful. And I feel bad about it."

They caught sight of their quarry in the park. But again, luck was with the ugly man; either that, or he had faculties of extreme keenness. For he saw them; saw them in time to cut over frantically, sideswipe a car, and cause a traffic pile-up that blocked the side road into which he turned.

There were several cars jammed together. The only way to get around them was to swing out over the curbing and take to the grass. And the sod was wet, soft. Their car was heavy; its wheels knifed into the sod. The machine, bogging, slowed so fast that they were tossed against the windshield and against the front seat.

Ham snarled, "Of all the tough breaks! Three in a row!"

The machine was stuck now.

Fifty yards or so distant, there was some construction work, and a few planks piled nearby. Ham and Doc leaped out, ran toward the planks, and came back bearing a pair apiece.

By now, the car carrying the man with the ugly face had disappeared down the park driveway.

Doc took one side of the car, Ham took the other, and they jammed their planks in front of the wheels, making crude tracks.

"Gun it, Pat," Doc said. "But not too hard."

Pat tramped on the accelerator carefully. They got the car to ride the boards, and back on to the pavement. A cop arrived then, an officious patrolman of the park detail, and he had never heard of Doc Savage, and it was, in case they didn't know it, a crime to walk on the grass, much less to drive a car on it. The officer said the car tracks in the park sod were as deep as trenches in the Maginot Line. He said a great deal more. And finally they got away from him.

Doc drove.

"You work the radio finder," he directed Ham.

The trail led north, then west, then back south again. And when they sighted the ugly man's car, Doc Savage slowed down immediately, then stopped.

"We might drive past the machine," Ham suggested. "It looks empty."

"If he should happen to roll a grenade under us, it wouldn't be very funny," Doc said. "This car is armor-plated on the top and all sides, but the flooring is the same as an ordinary car."

It was Ham's limousine they were using.

"I'll have that fixed," he said.

When it became obvious that the ugly man's car was empty, Doc Savage glanced at the street name.

"Ham," he said, "did you check up on Daniel Stage's sister, Junith Stage?"

"Yes."

"Where did she live?"

"March Street. No. 1456."

"Notice what street this is?"

Ham looked. "Melrose Street," he said. "What about it?"

"Have you forgotten how the town is laid out? March Street is two blocks over. And the next block up on March will be the 1400 block."

"You mean," Pat exclaimed, "that Junith Stage lives close to where this ugly-faced man abandoned his car?"

Doc Savage nodded. "I think it might be a good idea to call on Miss Stage," he said. "And Pat—"

"Yes?" Pat said.

"You get on a telephone, call that hotel and tell Monk, Johnny and Phil O'Reilly where we are."

"Just in care something happens." Pat nodded. "I get it."

"Ham—"

"Yes?"

"You take the rear of the Stage house. And if this man with the ugly face should appear, turn loose on him with a machine pistol and mercy bullets. You remember how he was dressed."

"A greenish tweed suit," Ham said. "Black raincoat. Tan hat."

Doc nodded. "Also tan shoes, yellow-striped necktie, and the tan hat had a dark-brown band, and there was no crease in the top."

"I'll recognize him," Ham said.

"I will take the front door," Doc said.

Junith Stage was a little too tall to have a figure, yet she had one, and a very noticeable one, too. She was dark, almost

Spanish, and her beauty was the type usually associated with a tiny girl, although she was by no means tiny. As a whole, she was striking. Her voice was low, well-modulated.

She opened the door herself.

"Mr. Savage?" she said. She was puzzled for a moment. "Oh, I believe I have read of you? Doc Savage?"

The bronze man nodded.

Junith Stage remembered something, and her eyes flew wide. "But the newspapers! This morning—they said you had been killed!"

"To make a reply not exactly original," Doc said, "the report was somewhat exaggerated."

Her eyes remained wide. "What do you want?"

"A few words with you about your brother."

"Oh."

He thought she paled a little. She said nothing.

"May I come in?" he asked.

She hesitated. "Well, I—" He was sure about the paleness now. It was growing.

A pleasantly modulated voice behind her said, "By all means invite him in, Junith. We should like very much to hear about poor Daniel."

The speaker was a tall, broad-shouldered young man, as dark of hair and eyes as Junith Stage, but with features that were thin and overly handsome to the point of being aesthetic. His face was not exactly handsome. It was too thin, too intense.

Junith explained, "Mr. Marbetti. Mr. Savage, this is Mr. Marbetti."

Marbetti stepped forward, took Doc's hand. His grip was quick, hot, intense.

"I'm delighted," Marbetti said. "I have heard a great deal about you, incidentally. And the name is Rollo Marbetti."

"Rollo Marbetti," Doc said.

Marbetti smiled. "You Americans make fun of the name Rollo, I understand. But of it I am not ashamed."

Most of the time he had no accent whatever; only now and then did a twisted word, or a transposed bit of construction appear in one of his spoken sentences.

He said, "Miss Stage is my fiancée. Of that I am very proud."

"Yes," Junith Stage said quickly. "Yes, yes, Rollo and I are to be married."

"In November," Marbetti said.

"Yes, in November."

Junith Stage was still pale.

Doc Savage watched them thoughtfully. "Is there anyone else in the house?"

"Why, no," Junith said quickly.

Doc Savage's eyes narrowed. "Have you had any visitors recently?"

Marbetti answered that. "Not," he said, "within the last"—he consulted his watch—"one and three quarters hours."

Doc studied him. "Rather early to pay a call. It must have been around a quarter of nine when you came."

"Yes, exactly," Marbetti said. He smiled. "As a matter of fact, I had a good reason for an early call. Not that I see any reason why I should tell you my reasons for being here." His face darkened. "Nor, for that matter," he added, "do I see any reason for your coming in here and asking questions."

Doc said, "I want to find out some things."

Marbetti's face became even darker. "Mr. Savage, I am not in the least impressed by your reputation. Doubtless you consider that people should be, and are accustomed to taking advantage of it to force yourself in where you may have no business."

"Rollo!" Junith Stage said sharply.

Marbetti clicked his heels. "Sorry, darling," he said. "As a matter of fact, I'm not sure this fellow is Doc Savage. I saw a picture of Savage once, and he certainly did not look like this man."

"I happen to be disguised," Doc said.

"I would like to know why he came," Junith said, after hesitating.

Marbetti frowned. "Yes. So would I."

Doc asked, "Miss Stage, have you any objection to my searching the house?"

"Of course she has!" Marbetti snapped. "I call it an infernal outrage to suggest—"

"Please!" Junith said sharply. She turned to Doc. Her voice, her manner was strained. "Go ahead and search," she said.

It was then that a loud yell came from the back of the house, along with blow noises and other sounds of a fight.

VII

THE RED MAN

Doc Savage did not lunge off recklessly toward the fight. First, he laid one hand on Junith Stage's wrist, fastened the other to Marbetti's arm.

"You had better go with me," he said.

Marbetti twisted, tried to wrench his arm free. Pain, like a convulsion caused by electricity, crossed his face as the bronze man's grip tightened.

"You've . . . no . . . right!" Marbetti gasped.

Doc said, "Come on!"

There was a biting force in his tone, a quality of compelling power that caused Marbetti to subside. Doc marched them toward the rear of the house.

The fighting was not in the house; it was outdoors, in the back yard. Doc shouldered the door open, moved out on a small porch, pushing Junith Stage and Marbetti before him. He kept a watch on their faces so as to catch their expressions, and also flicked his eyes over the yard.

This house—it was far enough out of Manhattan to be in the district where the houses had yards—was surrounded with fairly extensive grounds. The house itself was not elaborate, nor was the district by any means exclusive, but it happened that the lot was very large, and covered with shrubbery, and there was an adjoining lot to the side and another to the back, both vacant, both covered with brush and high weeds.

The fight was taking place in one of the vacant lots. Doc ran toward the sound, shoving along Miss Stage and Marbetti.

Ham had lost his coat, one shirt sleeve, half his suspenders, a trouser leg, and one shoe. His foe was now endeavoring to pound him on the head with the shoe. Ham looked as if, for once in his life, he'd had enough fight.

Ham's opponent was a large redskin. There was no doubt that the man was an American Indian, because he might have been the model for the redskin depicted on buffalo nickels. He was a very large Indian, very old, very

54

active, and apparently all of his muscles were as tough as the hamstrings on a horse. He had lost his shirt, and his cabled torso heaved and writhed as he worked on Ham.

Doc reached down, got the redskin by the nape of the neck. The redskin immediately tried to clutch Doc's throat. The bronze man swung a fist expertly, and the aborigine sat down heavily. He was not knocked out, but he remained on the ground, blinking his eyes.

Ham stood up. Ham looked like a wiser man. He peered unbelievingly at the redskin.

"He looks as old as a hill," Ham said breathlessly. "But he's sure a bobcat when you get hold of him."

Junith Stage stared at the red man.

"Oh!" she gasped.

"Know him?" Doc asked.

"Why, yes!" Junith exclaimed. "Yes. He ... I have seen him following me twice. The last time I saw him was just yesterday."

Ham puffed to get his breath back.

"Hiawatha," he gasped, "was watching ... house ... when I sneaked up on him."

The redskin grunted.

"Name not Hiawatha," he said. "Name Chief John Eagle."

The red man got to his feet. He made a majestic figure, and he still retained his dignity, even while he was picking up the parts of his shirt and looking at them ruefully. He grunted, then looked at Ham.

"You have to buy me new shirt," he said.

"I will," Ham told him grimly, "if you'll pay an osteopath to put my arms and legs back in joint again."

Doc Savage watched the Indian steadily. "You are John Eagle?"

The red man nodded.

Junith Stage put her fingers to her lips. "Are you the father of Elmo Walker Eagle, one of the explorers who went to hunt my brother?"

Chief John Eagle nodded. A slight trace of sadness appeared on his otherwise inscrutable face.

"Elmo never come back," he said.

"What has that got to do with your lying out here in the brush watching Miss Stage's home?" Doc inquired.

The chief hesitated. He looked at Doc Savage, and

seemed to approve of what he saw, although Doc, in the guise of Dink Masket, fell far short of being the prepossessing figure he normally was.

"Who are you?" he asked.

"Doc Savage," Doc explained.

Chief Eagle stepped closer to Doc.

Ham exclaimed, "Watch him, Doc! He's as tricky as a fox in a hen house!"

But the chief only wanted to examine Doc more intently. "Disguise," he said. "Dye on hair and on skin, colored glass things on eyeballs." The chief extended his hand. "How do you do," he said. "Glad to meet you. Heard lot about you."

Doc shook hands with him. "I'm investigating this business of all those explorers disappearing when they went to hunt Daniel Stage," the bronze man explained. "Do you know anything that can help us?"

Chief Eagle shrugged. "Nothing really constructive," he said.

He spoke like any other American, now, having dropped the cryptic bluntness that had characterized his speech during the excitement immediately following his brawl with Ham.

"Why were you watching Miss Stage's home?" Doc inquired.

The chief glanced toward the house. "I had no very definite reason," he said. "I was here simply because I happened to be searching everywhere for the answer to this mystery, and I had gotten around to examining Miss Stage. Incidentally, I have no grounds to suspect Miss Stage of anything."

Marbetti snapped, "I should think you wouldn't!"

Chief Eagle eyed him. "Who are you?"

Rather curtly, Marbetti explained who he was, and that he was Miss Junith Stage's future husband. Ham, who had been examining Junith, looked rather disappointed when he heard this. Ham had the same failing as his sparring mate, Monk—both of them were susceptible to feminine beauty.

Doc said, "Chief Eagle, suppose you explain why you were here."

The red man nodded. "Of course. Three weeks ago, I announced my intention of organizing an expedition to go hunting for my son, Elmo, who went seeking Daniel Stage, and did not come back. Shortly after I made the announcement, my one servant, who was my valet and chauffeur and cook all in one, died. He had been poisoned. The poison, I am sure, was meant for me. The police called it suicide, and I did not argue with them. But I know someone tried to kill me."

The chief frowned, and his aboriginal face became very formidable. "Later, an attempt was made to shoot me. The shot came from a long distance, evidently from a rifle equipped with a telescopic sight. I became convinced that someone was trying to keep me from going to hunt my son."

Ham said, "That's funny."

"I see nothing humorous," Chief Eagle said bluntly.

"I don't mean humorous," Ham told him. "You see, we have decided to go hunting for Daniel Stage and the men who were lost seeking him, and somebody has been trying to kill us, too."

Chief Eagle grunted. It was very much a redskin grunt. He said nothing.

Ham asked him, "Have you seen anything of a man with an ugly face—a man with one side of his face resembling that of a South American stone image, and the other side a normal white man's face?"

"No," Chief Eagle said.

Junith Stage had made no sound, but her fingers had gone to her mouth and remained there, pressing her lips out of shape.

Doc eyed her. "Have *you* seen such a man, Miss Stage?" he asked.

For a moment, Junith seemed paralyzed. Then she shook her head. Shook it too vehemently.

"No," she said. "Oh, no, I haven't. Of course not."

Doc Savage and Ham exchanged glances.

When they were in the Stage home, Doc said, "I think I will search the place."

Marbetti, looking somewhat worried now, said, "I think that would be a good idea." He stepped forward impulsively. "Will you accept my apology for being a little abrupt earlier. I did not understand that this matter was so serious."

Doc Savage nodded agreeably.

Doc left them. The Stage house was not large, had nothing extraordinary about it. He searched very carefully, covering the place from one end to another, and finding no trace of the man with the ugly face, nothing to show that the fellow had been there.

The living room had a fireplace, an ordinary brick one with a mantel painted white. There was a fire burning in this, which was understandable because the rain had made the morning damp and slightly chilly. In the ashes were a few charred remains of what Doc Savage decided were papers.

"What are these?" Doc asked Junith Stage, indicating the ashes.

"Why, I started the fire with some old newspapers and magazines," Junith explained.

Doc Savage looked at the ashes carefully. He made no comment.

There was a knock on the door. It was Pat.

She said, "I talked to Monk, Johnny and Phil O'Reilly," she said. "They are questioning those three men who were to meet the man with the ugly face. They haven't learned anything yet, and they don't think the three know anything, but they are going to keep at the questioning."

Doc said, "I hope they will not waste too much time at that."

"They won't," Pat told him. "They will call us when they finish."

The bronze man nodded. He took a chair. Addressing Junith Stage, he said, "I wish you would tell us anything that you think might help us. Was there anything peculiar about this exploration trip your brother made to South America?"

Junith hesitated. She looked at Marbetti. "Should I tell them, Rollo?" she asked.

Marbetti's nod was abrupt. "Of course. We want to be of every assistance to Mr. Savage. It may be that this will result in the rescuing of your brother."

Junith clamped her hands together and remained very still in a chair for a few moments. Doc Savage—he might have been mistaken, he knew—thought that she shuddered.

"There was something queer about it," she said finally. "But I am afraid I cannot give you a satisfactory explanation of what it was."

"Go ahead and try," Doc suggested.

"Well, it was something that my brother—hoped to find," she said slowly, hesitating between parts of her sentences. "You see, I think that Daniel learned of some incredible discovery in the South American jungles, something that would establish him, if he managed to locate it, as one of the great explorers of all time. Once, when he did not know I was near, I heard him muttering something about, 'All Columbus discovered was America. And as for those guys who dug up those Egyptian tombs—pfft'!"

"You gathered that your brother was on the trail of something fabulous?" Doc asked.

"Yes. And fantastic."

"Any idea what?"

"No."

"No idea whatever, eh?"

"You see," Junith explained, "Daniel did not take me into his confidence. Not that he distrusted me. But, you see, I had never been in sympathy with his ambition—his ambition to be an explorer, I mean. I thought it was rather foolish, and a terribly hard way to become wealthy and famous. But Daniel seemed to think differently. We quarreled over the subject now and then, and for that reason, Dan wasn't too communicative with his information."

Doc nodded thoughtfully. "Do you know anything else?"

She considered. "Only that Daniel financed his exploration trip, indirectly, through Mr. Eagle, here." She nodded at the chief.

"What do you mean, indirectly?" the bronze man inquired.

Chief Eagle answered that. "Daniel Stage came to my son, Elmo, and asked him if he knew of a backer," the chief explained. "Elmo come to me, and I agreed to back the venture. I agreed largely because he was a friend of Elmo's, and Elmo said he was up and coming, an explorer with a future. As a matter of fact, I have never met young Daniel Stage personally."

Ham looked skeptical. "You never met young Stage, but you backed his expedition?"

"Yes."

"Strikes me as queer," Ham commented rather unpleasantly.

The chief eyed him. "I don't give a damn what strikes you as queer," he snapped. "I took my son's word for it. I trust my son."

"You think your son is still alive?" Ham asked.

Chief Eagle became stiff in his chair. His face acquired

the texture and forbidding ridges of a piece of red marble. He made no answer.

Doc Savage said, "We are not trying to antagonize you, Chief Eagle. We are merely endeavoring to find out the truth."

The chief grunted.

"Is that all you can tell us?" Doc asked Junith Stage.

She nodded.

The bronze man watched her. He was almost positive she was scared, but he wished he could be certain. He wished he was a better judge of women—or any judge at all, for that matter. He had long ago discovered that his judgment of feminine character was not to be trusted.

While he was wondering why Junith Stage was scared, the telephone bell whirred angrily. Pat picked up the receiver.

"Monk on the wire," she said.

Doc looked up. "What does he want?"

"Says they've finished with the three prisoners, and got nothing out of them," Pat said. "They turned the three over to—well, they sent the three to college."

Doc Savage nodded.

"Tell Monk, Johnny and Phil O'Reilly to come out here," he directed.

Pat relayed the information, and hung up.

Junith Stage, white-faced, asked, "Is Phil O'Reilly coming out here?"

"Yes," Pat told her.

Junith Stage took a small automatic pistol out of the front of her frock.

"You will all put your hands up," she said.

VIII

DEATH BOUND SOUTH

No one moved. The stark whiteness on the girl's face bespoke desperation. And nerves made the muzzle of her automatic jerk around in a way that was disquieting.

"Junith!" Rollo Marbetti gasped.

"Shut up!" the girl told him. "You come with me. I am going to make you drive the car."

She backed to the front door, and stood there, menacing them with the gun, while she jerked the door open. Strong breeze and a little rain came into the room, caught the girl's skirts and pounded them against her legs.

"Get out, Rollo!" she said. "Get in the car!"

"But I don't—"

"Get in the car!" Junith Stage's voice was wild.

Marbetti cast a distraught glance at Doc Savage. "I'll try to talk her out of this insane thing, Mr. Savage," he said. "I . . . I can't imagine what is wrong, but I'll try to talk her out of it."

Doc Savage nodded. Someone would have to do something. He had done what he could—he had worked the heel off his right shoe and released anaesthetic gas into the room. But the wind, coming in through the door, was sweeping the gas back, so that it was harmless. Ham and Pat were holding their breath, so that the gas had no effect upon them.

Chief Eagle drew in a deep breath, took hold of his throat, made a grunting noise, then sank to the floor. The anaesthetic gas had gotten him.

Rollo Marbetti went out of the room.

Junith stepped out after him, slammed the door.

Doc Savage, Ham and Pat leaped to windows. They saw Junith Stage leave in Doc Savage's limousine. Marbetti was driving.

Ham got the door open again, so that the wind would continue to blow the gas out of the room.

Doc flung to the telephone. "Maybe we can get the police to pick them up," he said.

"What got into that girl?" Pat asked.

"She was scared," Doc said. "She was scared all the time we were here."

"Yes, I know that," Pat told him. "But why? What was scaring her?"

The bronze man shrugged. He contacted the police, and had a call put out for the car which Junith Stage had seized and made young Marbetti drive away.

Putting down the telephone, the bronze man went to the fireplace. He examined the ashes again, giving them a closer inspection, taking a poker and raking through the coals.

"That wasn't any newspaper she burned," he said.

"Eh?" Ham came over quickly. He inspected the fragments.

"I would say it was a picture," he said. "Or pictures."

Doc nodded. He was carefully assembling some of the crumpled fragments. He kept at it, until he had enough that they could identify the subject of the photograph.

"Why, that's Junith herself!" Pat exclaimed. "Why on earth would she be burning her own picture."

Ham scowled. "Say, maybe she isn't Junith Stage at all."

"In that case," Doc said, "young Marbetti may be posing falsely also."

"Wouldn't surprise me any to find he was," Ham declared.

"I thought Marbetti was handsome," Pat said. "And he didn't look like a crook to me."

"The trouble with you, Pat," Ham assured her, "is that all handsome young men look honest to you. As gullible as you are, it's a wonder some handsome young empty head hasn't married you for all that money you make."

Pat sniffed.

Chief Eagle rolled over on the floor, and sat up. The anaesthetic gas, while its effects were quick and potent, did not render a victim unconscious for long. The after results were negligible, except for a dizziness, and a slight fuzzy confusion which would work off shortly.

The chief sat there, trying to get his mind to functioning. He must be well past sixty years of age, Doc concluded. Yet he had been active enough to take Ham to the cleaners, which was a considerable feat in itself.

Doc asked idly, "Ham, why aren't you carrying your sword-cane?"

Ham, usually, was never seen without his sword-cane, an innocent black thing that carried a long blade inside, the blade kept tipped with a chemical which produced unconsciousness.

"Monk and I got to fooling around, and broke the blade a couple of days ago," Ham explained. "I left it with a fellow to have a new blade put in. I'm going to pick it up when we leave here."

Chief Eagle decided he had his wits back sufficiently to talk.

"Did they get away?" he asked.

"They didn't do anything less," Ham told him.

Shortly, Monk, Johnny and Phil O'Reilly drove up in front of the Stage home. Ham, watching them alight from their car, was smitten by a sudden idea.

"Hey!" exploded the lawyer. "That girl—Junith Stage—she made up her mind to clear out of here when she heard young Phil O'Reilly was coming."

Doc Savage nodded. "We'll ask Phil about that," he said.

But Phil O'Reilly could shed no light on the mystery. "Yes, I know Junith," he said. "I know her quite well, in fact. I have had a number of dates with her."

"Recently?"

"Well, last week."

"Know she was engaged to marry a young man named Rollo Marbetti?"

"Great grief, no!" Phil exclaimed. "Is she?"

"So she said. Do you know Marbetti?"

"Never heard of him." Phil scratched his head and pondered. "No, I have never even heard the name."

"Well, he's got the inside track," Ham said.

They explained what had occurred—how they had trailed the man with the ugly face to this neighborhood, and how they had found Junith Stage frightened, and finally, when she heard that Phil O'Reilly was coming, she drew a gun and forced them to flee, made Marbetti drive her away in Doc's car.

"I'm dumfounded!" exclaimed Phil.

"You don't know why Miss Stage should flee because she heard you were coming out here?" Doc asked him.

"No." Phil seemed genuinely bewildered as he shook his head. "I have no idea."

Pat remarked, "Of course, we're not really sure it was Phil who scared the girl away. When it was said that Monk, Johnny and Phil were coming out—then was when she took off. It might have been Monk or Johnny who scared her."

Ham said, "If she had seen Monk's face, I could understand her being scared."

Monk eyed Ham's ripped garments and somewhat skinned and soiled person.

"You're not exactly something to soothe a baby with, yourself," the homely chemist said in a pleased voice. "What kind of a train ran over you?"

Ham became silent. It was Pat who explained about Ham's encounter with Chief John Eagle. Monk was infinitely delighted by the narrative.

"You mean this old gaffer"—Monk indicated Chief Eagle—"did all that to Ham?"

"Yes," Pat said.

Ham glared.

Monk walked over and enthusiastically shook hands with Chief Eagle.

"How," he said.

"How," said the chief.

"Me your friend," Monk said.

"How, friend," the chief said.

"How, friend," Monk replied.

Pat burst into laughter.

The telephone call came at almost exactly twelve o'clock. It was from a State police patrolman. He spoke briefly to Doc Savage over the wire.

The bronze man put down the instrument and turned to his men.

"They have found our car," he said. "Junith Stage abandoned it at the North Meadow airport, on Long Island. That is the large airport that caters to private planes, you know."

"Did Miss Stage take a plane?" Ham asked.

"Yes," Doc said. "We will go out there now and get the details."

"That's swell," Ham said.

"But you won't go along," Doc said.

"Huh?"

The bronze man drew the lawyer aside. He spoke in a voice which he was positive the others could not overhear, and also kept his face away from the others, in case Chief Eagle should be a lipreader. Doc already held considerable respect for Chief Eagle.

"Ham, I want you to take Pat with you, and check up this Chief John Eagle," Doc directed.

The lawyer was surprised. "You think he's a phony?"

"I think John Eagle is a deep river," Doc replied, "and I really know nothing whatever about him. I do know that he is extremely wealthy, and so is his son, Elmo, the young man who disappeared while hunting Daniel Stage. They got their money from Oklahoma oil. They are Osage Indians, and their family got in on the richest inheritances, and were intelligent enough to reinvest the money in oil lands, and they had luck."

Ham asked, "Just what do you want to know about the chief?"

"Anything that may be useful. Where he lives here in the city. How long he has been here. How he travels. His associates. Whether he has lost a great deal of money recently, or made a great deal. If you and Pat and Johnny all get on that, you should be able to find out considerable."

"You want us to light out on that right now?"

"Yes."

"Righto," Ham said.

Ham collected Pat, and departed. Chief Eagle and Phil O'Reilly both stared after them, then looked questioningly at Doc Savage.

"They are going to do some investigating along other lines," Doc explained. "Johnny—"

"Yes," Johnny said.

"You search the surroundings of this house," Doc directed. "Give the place a thorough search, and if you find anything, telephone the news to headquarters."

"Right," Johnny said.

Chief Eagle grunted. "My car is not far away," he said, "if you care to use it to go to the airport."

"Good," Doc said.

The chief's car turned out to be quite typical of the red man's love of color and pageantry. As Monk said later, the vehicle was a circus in itself. It was a foreign chassis with a wheelbase that must have been over two hundred inches, and the body, where it was not chrome, was covered with a basket weave of some kind of rich wicker-work.

It had five different horns. Monk tried them all out. There was one that sounded like a cow, another that imitated a dog, one ordinary horn, and two musical ones, which played different tunes.

"Oh, boy!" Monk said. "Chief, what'll you take for this boat?"

"Ugh!" said the chief.

Apparently he didn't want to sell.

The motor was as quiet as a stalking tiger under the hood, and it was hard to realize they were in motion, except for an occasional swaying lift over a particularly high bump. Monk drove. When they were clear of the city, he broke a few speed laws. Chief Eagle sat back and grinned. He seemed to like speed.

The North Meadow airport had discreetness for its keynote. There was nothing bawdy or gaudy—no hangars stuck up like modernistic nightmares, for all the hangars were disguised as English country barns. There was not even a wind sock; instead, a plume of smoke trailed from one of the chimneys and gave wind direction. Hangar rent was expensive.

An obsequious attendant answered their questions. He was obviously disturbed at the presence of a State patrolman, and horrified at the thought that a word about the airport might get in the newspapers. Publicity, it seemed, was all right for commercial ventures, but North Meadow was on a higher plane.

"The woman who answers the description of Miss Stage," he said, "drove up here about eleven thirty. She was accompanied by a young man. She asked for her plane, and also requested charts of the Atlantic coast southward, of the Caribbean, of northern South America, and of the Brazil jungle district, as much of it as has been charted."

Doc Savage made, for a brief moment, a strange small trilling sound. It was a peculiar characteristic of the bronze man, that sound, a thing which he made unconsciously in moments of mental stress. It was low, exotic, difficult of description; it was so weird that it might have been the trick of some passing breeze.

He said, "You say Miss Stage got *her* plane?"

"Yes, sir."

"How long has the plane been hangared here?"

"A little over a week, sir. A man flew it in, landing at the field here and requesting hangar space, and paying for the rent in advance. He told me personally it was Miss Junith Stage's plane, and that she was to have the craft whenever she called for it, or he was to have it, should he call. But his instructions were that no one else was to have access to the ship. I remember the occasion well because of . . . er . . . the man's unusual appearance."

Doc's flake-gold eyes—he had removed his disguise as Dink Masket—seemed to grow more intense.

"You mean the man's face?" he asked.

"Well . . . yes."

"How did it look?"

"It was a rather—well, unusual face," the attendant said.

"Was half of it different from the other half?"

"Yes. That's it exactly."

Monk grunted excitedly. "The ugly-faced man flew that plane in here and left it. Either he could get it, or Miss Stage could. That the idea?"

The attendant nodded.

Doc Savage was silent a moment. "This young man who was with Miss Stage when she took off in the plane—was it the same man who flew here with the ship?"

"Oh, no. This young man was rather handsome."

Doc Savage described Rollo Marbetti. "That the young man?"

"Yes, that was him," the attendant declared positively.

"So she took Marbetti with her," Monk muttered.

Doc asked, "And they got charts as far south as the Amazon jungle country?"

The attendant nodded. "We keep a rather complete assortment of charts here." He drew himself up. "We are proud of the service we offer."

Doc Savage went back to the car. "That settles that," he said.

"They're off for the Amazon," Monk declared. "You know something? We seem to have part of the gang on the run, anyway. That Stage girl is in on it, whatever it is."

Doc Savage shook his head slightly. He seemed doubtful. But he did not offer any explanation of his opinion.

The bronze man got behind the wheel of Chief Eagle's car. Monk, Phil O'Reilly and Chief Eagle also entered the machine, the chief riding in front. They seemed confused, said little. Doc himself did not speak until he had driven down the country road some distance and a roadhouse appeared.

Evidently the roadhouse did an afternoon luncheon business, because there were several cars and two taxis parked nearby. The place also displayed a telephone sign.

Doc stopped the car.

"I am going in here and check with Ham, Pat and Johnny," he said. "They may not have found out anything yet, but it is worth a try."

The bronze man was inside the roadhouse, crossing to the telephones, when he chanced to glance back.

Chief John Eagle was standing up in the seat. He had an enormous single-action revolver in his hand—evidently the weapon had been concealed in a door pocket of the car.

The chief forced Monk and Phil to get in the front seat.

He made Monk drive. The car left in haste, the chief riding in the back seat, keeping his gun menacingly upon Monk and Phil.

IX

STOWAWAY

Doc Savage stood there and watched them go. There was nothing he could have done—and, strangely enough, there seemed to be nothing that he cared to do. As the car disappeared down the road, the bronze man even seemed satisfied.

He lifted his voice.

"Taxi!" he called.

Two taxi drivers appeared hastily. Doc studied them, selected the more competent-looking of the two. "How fast will your cab go?"

"Ninety-five for certain," the man said quietly. "Maybe more. But I don't pay the fines."

"There won't be any fines," Doc said. "And you will get a dollar a minute."

"Yeah. What do I do?"

"You wait here for a few minutes while I make a telephone call," Doc told him. "No. Better go out and get your machine filled up with oil and gas, the tires checked and the motor warm."

The taxi driver looked at Doc appraisingly. "You Doc Savage, ain't you?"

"Yes."

"I'll be waiting," the man said.

Doc went to the telephone. Ham sounded rather disappointed over the wire.

"We haven't been working on the chief long," he said. "But he seems to be a straight Indian. We haven't dug up anything against him."

"He just kidnaped Monk and Phil O'Reilly," Doc said. "So you'd better tell me every detail you have found out."

"Well, his bank balance is about where it was a few months ago—"

"Skip his money matters for the time being."

"He lives in the Ritz-Westchester Hotel. His servant died a few days ago from what the police said was suicide—"

"He told us that."

"He controls a major oil company and two smaller ones—"

"Don't bother with his finances, I said."

"Well, the only other thing I found out," Ham said, "was that he keeps a fast plane in which he commutes from the city to Tulsa and Pawhuska, Oklahoma. Pawhuska is the capital of the Osage Indian nation—"

"Where does he hangar this plane?"

"South Shore Airport. That's out by—"

"I know where it is," Doc said quickly. "Now, listen, Ham. Continue your investigation until three o'clock this afternoon. Give it everything. Then drop it at three o'clock."

"Stop investigating at three," Ham said. "All right. Then what?"

"Go down to the warehouse-hangar on the Hudson," Doc directed. "Take off in *two* of the gyro planes. You fly one. Johnny can fly the other. But take two of the gyro planes. Leave Pat behind if you can possibly arrange it, but if you can't, let her come along. Bring plenty of jungle supplies."

"Jungle supplies?" Ham was startled.

"Head for the Amazon jungles," Doc directed.

"You mean—"

"Do you remember what that message Phil O'Reilly got said about how to find Daniel Stage?"

"Yes," Ham said. "It directed him to go to a trading post run by a guy named Niji, the location of which could be found by inquiring at Obidos, in the Amazon basin. A guide named Kul was to be waiting at Niji's place, to conduct Phil the rest of the way."

"That's right," Doc said. "You two take the gyros and head for that Niji trading post. Fly day and night, and keep together. You will lose some sleep, but by using the automatic pilots, and having Pat relieve you as pilot, you can keep in the air continuously."

"Those gyros are slow."

"I know. That is why it will be necessary for you to fly day and night."

"What will *you* be doing?"

"Never mind that," Doc said. "Now you fellows take off right after three o'clock—providing I do not call you before three to cancel the whole thing."

"If you don't call us, we take off for the Amazon," Ham said. "I understand."

The dapper lawyer sounded matter-of-fact. He was accustomed to receiving unusual orders, sudden and almost fantastic orders, from Doc Savage. But that was part of the association with the bronze man, a part of the excitement that made the whole thing so fascinating.

Doc Savage hung up. He strode out, swung in the waiting cab.

"I'll drive this thing," he said, "and we'll see if it will do ninety-five."

It would. It did—twice—a little better than ninety-seven, in fact.

South Shore airport lacked almost entirely the rigid atmosphere that characterized the North Meadow haven of snobbery. The buildings were large and looked like what they were, hangars that were as cheap as they could be built. The runway, however, was long and smooth. A slanting ramp gave access to the smooth water of an inlet, where seaplanes could arrive and depart.

Doc whipped the cab to a stop alongside the operations office. The driver, in the back, was white. Doc consulted his watch.

"Twenty-three minutes," he said. "We'll call it thirty, and make it even, providing you turn around and drive away from here right now, and say nothing about this until this afternoon, at the earliest."

The driver nodded stiffly, and Doc paid him. The hackman then got behind the wheel of his machine, and drove away. He traveled at a conservative speed of about ten miles an hour. He seemed to have had his fill of speed for some time.

The operations manager here was acquainted with Doc Savage to a slight degree. He was a man of few words. He listened to what Doc had to say.

"Eagle's plane," he said shortly. "Hangar Five. Want me to show you?"

"Please."

Chief John Eagle's plane was modern, large, fast, capable of cruising long distances without refueling. It was, moreover, an amphibian, capable of operation from land or water.

"Thank you," Doc said. He looked at the operations manager steadily. "You haven't seen me."

The man glanced about. There was no one else in the hangar. "I haven't seen you," he said. "Anything else?"

"Just one thing more," Doc said.

Doc Savage was well acquainted with the layout of the plane. Back in the body of the hull, there was a space where a man could conceal himself. Where several men could have hidden, if necessary. This cavity was back of the regular baggage compartment, and it was closed off by an opening which could be fastened from the outside, but not from the inside. It was not a very strong barricade; a man, once imprisoned in the back, could break out without much trouble.

Doc got in the cavity.

"Fasten me in here," he directed. "I do not want it to look as if I am in here."

The manager smiled slightly, but said nothing. He did as requested, then tapped on the bulkhead. "All set," he said. "Luck."

"Thanks."

Doc heard him walk away, and heard the small side door of the hangar close.

X

WEIRD JUNGLE

Doc Savage was not sure exactly how long he had been in the back of the plane. His watch had stopped, and upon investigating, he had found that nothing was wrong with the watch, that it had simply run down, and the fact worried him somewhat, because he had schooled himself not to overlook details, not even the smallest ones.

He did know that Chief John Eagle had arrived at the South Shore airport a little less than half an hour after he had taken his place of concealment. He knew Monk and Phil O'Reilly were with the chief. And he knew Monk and Phil were now lashed and gagged in the baggage compartment of the plane—he had opened a small peekhole with the blade of his knife, and had studied them. Except for a natural amount of irritation, both Monk and Phil seemed to be unharmed.

Days had passed, and the bronze man had not moved from his hiding place, had no intention of doing so as long as the plane flew south. He had slept for unusually long periods, and passage of time had become a little uncertain.

Ordinarily, during a period of confinement such as this, he would have managed to take, at least daily, the two-hour routine of exercises which he had not neglected for years, and which were largely responsible for his unusual physical development. But confined here, he had no food, and did not want to work up an appetite, so he toned down on all but the mental phases of his exercise routine. He took those.

Chief Eagle's plane was equipped with an automatic pilot of the conventional type, so that the chief could keep the ship in the air, and doze at the controls whenever he became extremely sleepy.

The plane had landed at the Miami airport for refueling, and at an airport in Haiti for the same purpose. From there, the ship had angled down to Trinidad, and taken on a load of fuel at the passenger seaplane base there. The next stop had been farther down the South American coast, and the last halt had been inland somewhere, on a river, where natives had carried fuel out in five-gallon tin drums, splashing through the shallow water while other natives with long poles beat the surface to keep the alligators away.

Doc Savage knew all this because he had punched peekholes in the thin metal skin of the plane with his knife.

While the plane had taken on gas that last time, he had watched the alligators. They were not true alligators, but caimans, although more like alligators than crocodiles. In the crocodile, the fourth tooth from the front on either side of the lower jaw fitted, when the jaw was closed, into a notch in the upper jaw, protruding so that it resembled a tusk. The same tooth, in an alligator, fitted into a pit in the upper jaw, where it was hidden when the jaw was closed. That was the principal difference between the two; that, and a difference in snout contour and slight characteristics in coloring.

The species of caimans gave him an idea of the kind of country they were getting into—well back in the Brazilian jungle, in the Amazon tributary section. These caimans were the black type, the dangerous variety sometimes reaching a length of twenty-five feet.

For a long time, there had been a wide muddy yellow river beneath. The Amazon, Doc knew. That meant the chief had swung wide, following the coast for a great deal of the distance.

The plane swung north on the Trombetas River. Doc pressed an eye to his peekhole frequently, judging their progress, noting the kind of a season the jungle was having.

This, fortunately, he thought, was not the time of the *igapo*. Twice each year, once in November and December, and once in March to June, the great flood came down and hundreds of thousands of square miles of the Amazon valley were under water. These floods were known as the *igapo*.

Chief John Eagle made a rather ragged landing on the Trombetas near the town of Obidos. Doc Savage held his breath until the descent was completed; the bronze man did not have too high an opinion of the chief's flying ability. It partook too much of the reckless abandon of a redskin riding a mustang around a covered-wagon train at which he was discharging arrows.

The plane taxied for nearly a mile. Then the chief put out a collapsible anchor, and got it to snag bottom and hold the plane. By that time, dugout canoes were paddling from shore.

The chief, it developed, wanted gasoline, oil and food—and the location of a trading post run by a man named Niji. He had trouble making himself understood, because he did not speak the Portuguese language of Brazilians, or any of the native dialects. He tried English, finally resorting in exasperation to the Osage tongue, and ended up by swearing extensively in both languages. But he finally got what he wanted.

Doc Savage was thoughtful during the loading. He had not told Chief John Eagle the contents of Phil O'Reilly's message—the orders to come to Niji's trading post to pick up a guide named Kul. He wondered how the chief knew about that.

Through the peekhole, Doc noted the food being put aboard. There was a plentiful supply of long strips of smoked *pirarucu*. That was understandable. *Pirarucu* was one of the chief items of Amazonian diet, and was noteworthy in other respects. It was one of the largest fresh-water fish in the world, and had enormous scales, frequently six inches long, the scales being used by the native women as manicuring instruments.

A *pirarucu* scale was a whole manicuring kit by itself,

the curved tip serving to press back cuticle, the upper side being rough enough to serve as a nail file, while the lower side was very good as a buffer or polisher.

Chief Eagle evidently obtained the location of Niji's trading post, because a Brazilian who spoke fair English appeared, and they spent some time consulting over charts. The Brazilian took the chief's fountain pen and drew in several rivers which weren't on the chart.

Doc could hear their speech, which took place in a dugout canoe beside the plane—Monk and Phil O'Reilly being thoroughly gagged and tied in the baggage compartment of the cabin.

"I put in parts thees reevers," the Brazilian said. "Thees what you call heem—surveyor—ees not been there yet, señor. But me, I have seen reever, so I know she ees where I draw heem."

"Thanks," said Chief Eagle.

The Brazilian eyed him curiously.

"You ees look for thees explorer, Daniel Stage?" he asked.

The chief's copper-colored face remained inscrutable. "No, not at all," he said. "What makes you think so?"

The Brazilian shrugged elaborately. "Several plane ees come thees route last year, hunt for Señor Stage," he explained.

Chief Eagle was silent for a while.

"Did a young man named Elmo Eagle stop here?" he asked.

The Brazilian nodded.

"Yes," he said. "I remember heem. Hees young man who ees look leetle like you."

Chief Eagle's face might have been made of red sandstone.

"Thanks," he said. "Did this Elmo Eagle ask for Niji, too?"

The Brazilian nodded again.

The chief climbed into the plane.

"Thanks," he said. "Has any other plane landed here within the last few days?"

"No, señor."

"The plane would have had a girl named Junith Stage aboard, and a young man named Marbetti."

"There has been no such plane."

"Good-by," the chief said.

The next morning, they landed at Niji's trading post. Part of the night had been spent on a river, the chief apparently mistrusting his night-flying ability. The distance required for the journey would have taken weeks along the jungle rivers; to penetrate the jungle itself would have taken two or three years, probably.

Niji's trading post stood in a large clearing on a bluff near the river. At the foot of the bluff ran a river, wide, sluggish, coffee-colored. On the bluff grew graceful white-stemmed *assai* palms, in their clusters of two or three. The fruit of these, a thin layer of meat over a hard stone, somewhat like a cherry, was mixed with water and became a thick dark liquid which was drunk by the natives.

Chief John Eagle landed the plane without incident on the river. When he got out of the ship, he had the big single-action six-shooter shoved in his belt, and he was carrying a stubby Model 94 lever-action .30-30 rifle.

He swung down cautiously, testing the depths of the water, and found it not much over his knees—he had anchored the plane close to shore—and started to wade to solid ground. He had taken only a few paces when he barked out in agony, and dived wildly for the beach, making a great splashing.

When the chief dashed onto solid land, two small fish were clinging to him, and he had been cut in places by others. He had also left traces of blood in the water.

Suddenly, where the blood was, the water began to boil as hundreds of the fish streaked about with frenzied ferocity. The chief knocked loose the two fish that had bitten him, and stamped on them. He stared at the water, scratched his head.

His amazed grunt was audible. Then he turned and began climbing toward the trading post, his manner alert.

Doc Savage hurriedly shoved against the fastening of the little hatch which closed off the compartment where he had been hidden. A moment later, he was bending beside Monk and Phil O'Reilly. He ungagged the two.

"Doc!" Monk exploded. "Have you been hidden back there the whole time?"

"Yes," the bronze man said.

Phil O'Reilly was speechless.

Doc worked for a time with the ropes which bound the two men.

"Now," he said finally. "The ropes look just about as they were, but by pulling here"—he showed them where to pull—"you can get free in a moment. However, stay as you are for the time being."

"Where are we?" Monk demanded. "It's a jungle river somewhere, ain't it? I can tell that by the smell."

"We're at Niji's trading post—farther back in the Amazon jungle than mapping parties have ever gone."

Monk grunted his astonishment. "Boy, that's a long ways from New York. I hope the chief has been taking us in the right direction."

"He is probably hoping the same thing," Doc said. "You stay here. I am going ashore."

He started to leave the cabin, then turned back to give a warning.

"Don't step into the river," he said. "The water is swarming with *piranha*. They nearly got the chief, who was foolish enough to wade ashore. I do not think he knew what they were."

"*Piranha*, eh?" Monk said. "Don't worry about me getting in the water, then. I saw them take a native once. He wasn't in the water more than five minutes, and all we recovered were his bones."

Phil O'Reilly had his mouth open. "What are you talking about?"

"A fish. They're shaped a little like an ordinary sole." Monk shuddered. "They go mad at the presence of blood, and they've got teeth like razors. They'll take everything off a body right down to the bones, so fast that it's incredible."

Doc Savage left the plane. He did not enter the water. Instead, he climbed on the wing—the ship was a low-wing monoplane—and by running to the tip of one wing and leaping, managed to alight on dry land.

The bronze man climbed toward Niji's trading post. He kept out of sight.

Niji was a round brown man, with the solid look of a fat man who is very strong. His brown color was deep, almost the hue of oiled teakwood. He had piercing dark eyes.

His attire consisted of a pair of red boxing trunks with silver stripes down the sides, a yellow silk shirt with flowing sleeves, and a high silk hat which had seen better days.

Niji seemed a little embarrassed by his own attire.

"You caught me," he explained sheepishly, "when I was

dressed for business. So I hope you won't get the idea from this crazy stuff that I am wearing that I'm crazy."

The chief looked at Niji's eyes, which were intent, level and intelligent, even a little masked and sinister.

"No, I wouldn't think you were crazy," the chief said.

"Thank you."

Chief John Eagle produced some papers from his pockets— papers he had taken from Phil O'Reilly—and did some lying.

"I am Phil O'Reilly," he said. "Here are some papers which prove my identity."

Niji glanced at the letters which the chief extended, letters which actually proved nothing except that the chief had them in his possession.

"You have a letter which I wrote you?"

The chief nodded. "I *did* have it," he said. "But I thought it more advisable to destroy the missive."

"Why destroy it?"

"Did you not remark in it that secrecy was essential?"

Niji nodded thoughtfully. "I did," he said.

"Well, so I destroyed the notes. As long as I remembered the gist of what was in them, what else was necessary?"

Niji shrugged. "I am sorry," he said.

"Sorry about what?"

"You remember the one you were to meet here?" Niji's eyes narrowed. "Or do you?"

"Kul," the chief said promptly. "He was to guide me to my friend, Daniel Stage."

Niji, apparently satisfied, nodded soberly.

"Kul is dead," he said.

"*What?*"

Niji shrugged again. "He stepped outdoors one dark night, and a *sucureija* found him. The *sucureija* lives partly on land and partly in water, and this one was forty-five feet long. A *sucureija*, you know, can swallow a horse or an ox whole. Their teeth slant inward, and they fasten them upon their victim, then wrap their coils around the quarry until every bone in the body is broke to fragments and the victim is nothing but a mass of bloody pulp and bones. It is not pleasant, I assure you. Then they coat it carefully with saliva, and, opening their huge jaws, begin the swallowing operations. An ox, for instance, may last a *sucureija* a month, and in case the ox should have horns, the horns are merely allowed to protrude from the creature's mouth until that part of the carcass has rotted, after which the horns are scraped off on a convenient tree."

Chief Eagle peered at him. "You mean the snakes here are *that* big?"

"The *sucureija*," said Niji, "is also called anaconda." He frowned. "Will you come with me?"

They walked a few dozen yards through the jungle. It was noticeable that the chief kept his rifle ready for quick operation.

Doc Savage followed warily, keeping out of sight. He had been close enough to hear what they were saying, and now he got close enough again. It was not difficult, because of the thickness of the jungle growth.

There was a mound of earth on the jungle floor. It was comparatively fresh, although the quick-growing tropical plants were already springing up out of it. At the head of the mound was a crude cross.

"Kul was not a Christian," Niji said thoughtfully. "But I thought I would put a cross at the head of his grave, anyway. He would have felt honored to know that a white man had placed the emblem of his religion over a poor native's grave."

The chief's face was stark. "Kul, the guide, is buried here?"

"Yes."

"Then how am I going to find Daniel Stage?"

Niji smiled thinly. "Kul did not die until some time after we found him. He had life enough to guide me in the drawing of a kind of map."

"Map?"

"I will give it to you."

Doc Savage could not get close enough to observe the map, but Chief Eagle showed a great deal of interest in it. He pored over it, using a pencil to add written designations of his own while he asked Niji questions.

"I have never been in that country," Niji said. "So I cannot tell you much. It is a great distance. Kul was on the trail four months reaching here."

"Four months?" The chief was astounded.

Niji shrugged his round shoulders. "It is a great distance."

"Then I'll need more gasoline," the chief said grimly. "Say, have you got high-test aviation gas here?"

Niji nodded. "Yes."

The chief was surprised. "How come?"

"Why, I have a plane fly in here once each month," Niji said. "I trade, a little platinum out of the natives, and the plane flies that out."

The chief eyed him. "You must get quite a bit of platinum, or a man like you wouldn't be inclined to stay in a place like this."

Niji shrugged. "That is my business," he said frankly.

Chief Eagle nodded. "That's all right. Will you sell me some gas?"

"Five dollars a gallon."

The chief said, "All right. How about food?"

"I will give you all the food you want. It will be native stuff."

"Let's get busy loading," the chief said.

Doc Savage eased away from his hiding place, and returned as rapidly and as unobtrusively as he could to the edge of the river. The current had swung the plane so that the nose pointed upstream, and, by running and leaping, he managed to grasp the edge of the wing and swing aboard. He entered the cabin.

"Don't make any move," he warned Monk and Phil O'Reilly. "I think the chief is falling into a trap."

The bronze man returned to his hiding place, closed the hatch—making a mental note that he hoped the chief would not notice the unfastened hatch—and waited.

From his peekholes—they were too small to be noticed by a casual observer—he watched the ship being loaded. Gasoline was poured into the wing-tanks. Food was piled into the cabin.

Chief Eagle paid money to Niji; then the chief climbed in the plane. The mechanical starters made their whining noise for a while, and the motors burst into life.

The plane began moving, gathered speed, rattled across the short river waves, and took the air.

Doc Savage crawled out of his hiding place. He went forward. Monk and Phil O'Reilly saw him coming, freed themselves. Doc motioned for silence.

The bronze man moved up behind Chief Eagle, grabbed the rifle and scooped the big single-action six-shooter out of the chief's belt.

Chief Eagle had the stoicism of his race. He turned, faced the bronze man. There was surprise, only a little, on the red man's face. Knots of muscle gathered in front of his ears.

Rather surprisingly, he said, "It was beginning to dawn on me that I should have brought you along."

Doc got Chief Eagle by the shoulder, hauled him away from the controls. Monk and Phil O'Reilly got in close to the chief. They could handle him.

Doc glanced downward. There was nothing but jungle below.

"Monk," Doc said sharply, "search that food. Look through it fast, and dump it overboard as you do so."

"But—"

"Hurry up!"

Monk leaped to obey.

Doc took the controls. He slanted the plane downward sharply toward the jungle. When he was a few hundred feet above the tangled mass of vegetation, he banked abruptly and headed the ship back toward Niji's trading post.

Monk dumped the food overboard rapidly. It was not long before he came back. He was pale. He had a two-gallon tin container, wrapped with wire, to which an ordinary clock and some batteries were attached.

"Time bomb," he said. "It was set to go off in an hour."

Chief Eagle grunted. "Niji crook," he said cryptically.

"Yes," Doc said. "He took you in. Furthermore, this gas he sold you is probably doped so that it will stop the motors in a short time."

The dread significance of that hit Monk before any of the others. The homely chemist let out a howl of unpleasant astonishment.

"Doc, why ain't you flyin' higher!" he yelled. "If the motors stop, that would give us a chance to pick our landing place."

"One place is about the same as another, until we reach the river," Doc told him. "And flying low, this way, Niji will not hear us returning until we get within three or four miles of the trading post!"

"You think we'll make it?" Phil asked hollowly.

The motors answered that. They stopped, one at a time.

XI

THE UNKNOWN

Phil O'Reilly became pale. But he went back in the cabin and sat down, something that took courage.

"Fasten the safety belts," Doc directed.

Monk and Chief Eagle complied. The bronze man was working furiously with the controls, the starters. But there was nothing that he could do. He gave his attention to landing the big ship. He set the controls to the slowest possible speed.

The trees were like green moss below; here and there a larger one protruded above the surrounding jungle. But for the most part the green was fairly level.

He leveled; at the last moment he kicked rudder, and fish-tailed the big plane, so that it went into a virtual stall a moment before it hit. The ship struck at the slowest speed possible.

There was a noise as if a small boy had jumped into a pile of tin cans and kicked around. That stopped. A branch came up through the floor and slapped Monk's face. The homely chemist went pale for an instant, thinking he was going to be impaled, but the stab missed him.

Doc Savage unbuckled the safety belt, turned. They seemed to be safe. Except that the earth was a good forty feet below.

The chief stuck his head out and looked at his plane. One wing was gone. Branches were sticking through the other. The fuselage was slightly out of shape.

"Sixty-three thousand dollars," he said.

Evidently that was what the plane had cost.

Doc had a small pocket compass. He gave it to Monk.

"Niji's trading post is about ten miles south and west," the bronze man explained. "But the river is only about three miles to the west. Head for the river. Make a raft, and float down to the trading post."

Monk and Phil nodded.

Chief Eagle stared at Doc. "Don't you want to know

what made me grab your two friends and head for South America, like I did?"

Doc said, "It was obvious you didn't trust us."

The faintest of grins moved the chief's lips. "I am of a suspicious people," he said. "And there is something mysterious behind this. My son *announced* that he was going to rescue Daniel Stage—and he never came back. I think *that* was why he didn't come back."

Doc Savage said, "It is rather obvious that everyone who tries to rescue Daniel Stage runs into trouble."

"Yes," the chief agreed. "So I was going to try it without letting anyone know."

"Why did you take Monk and Phil along?"

The Indian eyed him. "If you half suspected some men might know what became of your son, wouldn't you take them along?"

Doc nodded. "That's what I thought," he said. The bronze man turned to Monk and Phil. "Head for the river, then float down to the trading post," he directed. "Travel light, but take blankets to keep off the mosquitoes. And watch for *maquims*, the little red mites that burrow under your skin and cause infection and itching."

Monk nodded. "I know something about this jungle. There's another thing called a *puim*, a small louse with wings. It makes you itch terribly, and leaves a scar like a burn."

"Where you going?" Phil O'Reilly was looking at Doc.

"I hope to be there ahead of you," Doc said.

When Phil O'Reilly watched the bronze man swing away from the plane, he understood why Doc was not waiting for them. He was also astounded. He had known Doc Savage was a man of extraordinary physical ability, but he had not dreamed just how amazing an individual he was.

Doc removed his shoes, discarded them, and stripped down to trousers. He ripped the legs off his trousers above the knees. Then he got out of the plane, moved along a limb, far out into dizzy space, swayed there a moment, then pitched forward and downward. Phil yelled in horror. He thought Doc had fallen. Then, to his astonishment, he saw the bronze man grasp a thick vine, swing there a moment, move along it hand over hand, and again fly into space, this time alighting on a limb. After that, the jungle foliage hid him.

"For the love of little fishes!" Phil said wonderingly.

"Ugh!" The chief got out of the plane, peered at the ground far below, and made no effort to imitate the bronze man's example.

Niji was sitting in front of a portable radio transmitter when Doc Savage walked in on him. Niji was alone, and the radio outfit, while portable, could hardly be carried on one man's back; it was portable by airplane, or several natives could carry it. Power for the apparatus was furnished by a small generator driven by a gasoline motor, and the motor was making enough noise to cover any sound Doc might have made in approaching.

He was just finishing his communication over the instrument.

"If the bomb doesn't get this man Eagle," he was saying into the transmitter, "the doctored gasoline will. I put a chemical into the gas which I poured into the tanks."

That evidently terminated his report, because he placed the microphone on the table and switched off the apparatus. And it was then that Doc walked in.

Niji came half out of his chair, and his hand started for a gun lying on the table. He remained that way, arrested in midmovement, for a while. Then he sank back.

"You!" he said.

Obviously he recognized Doc. The bronze man studied Niji intently. He had never seen the fellow before. And he was puzzled by the expression on Niji's face.

Doc tossed the gun in a corner.

"I was on that plane," he said.

Niji blanched. "Why didn't that fool, Eagle, tell me?"

"What difference would it have made?"

"A great deal," Niji said quietly.

Doc continued to watch him. Niji looked miserable. That was puzzling.

Doc said, "You'd better explain just what you mean."

Niji's gaze was level. "You do not know me," he said. "But I have a brother. Niji is not my name, and it was not my brother's name. He was Carl Voorheis, and, four or five years ago, he was in danger of losing everything he owned, and his life and family as well. Carl is not like me; he is an honest man. Carl had a plantation in Hidalgo, a Central American republic. He— But you know what happened. You saved everything for him."

Doc remembered. "What has that to do with this?"

Niji shrugged. "I am a crook," he said. "But first, I am a man with a certain code. When a man does me or mine good, I return it. The same for wrong."

"You mean," Doc said, "that you are my friend."

Niji shook his head. "Not your friend. Crooks are never your friends. What I mean is this: If I can help you in any way, I will."

Doc was pleased. This break, unexpected, was the kind that came out of a clear sky now and then.

"You can tell me what this is all about," Doc said.

Niji hesitated. He got up and went to a window. A group of natives was husking *castanha* nuts in the clearing. The *castanha* nuts grew inside an extremely large, round cannon-ball of a shell, twenty to forty nuts inside a ball. Shipped to the American market, they were called Brazil nuts.

"You see those natives?" Niji said. "They are not my men. They will kill me if I talk."

"Then," Doc said, "you are going to refuse to talk?"

Niji shook his head. "On the contrary, I'll tell you anything you want to know. But I would like to make a deal. I would like for you to arrange some method by which I can escape."

Doc considered the point.

"That can be done," he said.

Niji left the window, went to the door, made sure no one was listening. Then he lowered his voice. "This is going to disappoint you," he said. "I don't actually know what is behind it.

"Nearly a year ago," he said, "a man came to me, and told me that exploring expeditions would begin coming to hunt a man named Daniel Stage. This man gave me several maps, all alike. I was to give each of these expeditions one of the maps, and say that a guide had brought it to me, but had died while waiting for them to come. I received a list of men, all explorers, to whom I was to write letters saying that a native had reached my trading post, a native who knew the whereabouts of Daniel Stage."

Doc Savage's metallic features were grim. "In other words, you were to decoy explorers down here, and when they got this far, you were to give them maps which would lead them on into the jungle."

"That is it."

"The maps were all alike, you say?"

"Yes."

"Then these explorers—none of them came back, incidentally—were all sent to the same spot searching for Daniel Stage?"

"Yes."

Doc pointed at the radio. "What about that?"

"That?" Niji looked at the radio. "The man who hired me supplied that. I used it to get in touch with him. It was over the radio that he told me to put a bomb in Eagle's plane and to dope the gasoline."

"What about the natives you said would kill you if they found out you were talking?"

"This man left them here." Niji frowned. "You understand, I was getting well paid for this. I am essentially a crook. Did you examine that bomb I put in the plane?"

"Monk dumped it overboard in a hurry."

"It would never have exploded," Niji said. "I am not a murderer. As for the doped gasoline, a plane could land on the top of this jungle without a great deal of danger of killing the occupants."

"You are saying you are not a murderer?"

"Yes."

Doc studied him. He believed the man. Niji was a crook, as he said, but he had a certain code that he followed.

"Did you ever think of reforming?" the bronze man asked.

"I am thinking very strongly about it."

"Would you go so far as to make a promise? I believe you are a man who keeps his word."

Niji hesitated. Finally he said, "If I get out of this, I quit. You understand, it does not take a great deal of will power on my part to do so. I have enough money to retire on."

Doc said, "There is just one more thing."

"What?"

"The name of the man who hired you."

"Marbetti."

"Rollo Marbetti? A young man, rather handsome, with a dark skin?"

"Yes. Marbetti is the man behind all this," Niji said.

It was four days before the two gyro planes arrived. They were slow, and although Ham and Johnny and Pat had made all the speed possible, their advent was delayed four days. They landed—the ships were equipped with floats—on the river.

Monk, Phil O'Reilly and Chief Eagle had reached Niji's trading post by that time. Doc had met them; they had remained encamped in the jungle, where the natives about Niji's post had not found them.

But when the gyro ships landed—the big rotors that served them instead of wings made them look like air-traveling windmills—Doc and the others stepped out on the beach.

Ham and his party taxied to land after Doc shouted a warning about the ferocious *piranha* that swarmed in the river. They sprang ashore.

"Columbus made better time crossing the Atlantic than we made in these things," Ham said disgustedly.

"There is no better ship for use in the jungle," Doc told him.

Monk was bursting with information.

"Ham, we know who is behind this thing," the homely chemist declared.

"Who?"

"Marbetti."

"I never did trust him," Ham declared. "What's he pulling? What is the idea of decoying all those explorers down here in the jungle? Why didn't any of them ever come back?"

Monk's face fell. "We don't know yet," he had to admit. "But whatever the reason, we are hot on the trail—"

A shot silenced him. It came from the direction of the trading post. A single report, evidently of a rifle. The echoes gobbled back and forth in the jungle, and a flock of birds swarmed up.

"Come on!" Doc rapped.

The bronze man led the race for the trading post. They got there in time to find natives, half-naked fellows, some of them *caboclas*, as the local breeds were called, trying to break down the door.

"Get back!" Doc told them.

Chief Eagle had his big single-action gun in his hands; Monk had the .30-30 carbine. Ham and the others held grim blue machine pistols. The natives withdrew sullenly.

"Watch them," Doc warned. "They are employed by Marbetti. They might make trouble."

The bronze man struck the door then, using his shoulder. The door was strong. It resisted. Doc said, "Locked on the inside." He said this in the native language, so the sullen half-naked men would understand.

Again he hit the door, with more force this time, and the panel flew open. Ham went in.

Niji sprawled on the floor, legs and arms twisted grotesquely. A stream of wet scarlet crawled slowly from under the body to a crack in the floor and ran down through the crack. There was a revolver by the outstretched hand.

Doc went to the door. "Get those natives in here!" he said loudly and angrily. "Find out who did this!"

He translated the order into the local vernacular, and stood there, a frowning bronze tower of a man, as natives were shoved inside. They stared at the body, not greatly concerned in the presence of death.

"None of us killed him," a man pointed out. "The door was locked, was it not?"

That was a perfectly logical argument, but Doc seemed unconvinced. He frowned for a while, and did a little brow-beating.

"We'll have to bury Niji," he said finally.

Monk and the bronze man carried Niji's form into the jungle. They placed the body in a thicket, and hastily dug a trench.

"All right," Doc said.

Niji leaped to his feet. He shook Doc's hand.

"Thanks," he said. "You will keep them thinking I am dead?"

Doc nodded.

Niji vanished in the jungle. Doc had already hidden a supply of food, and, farther down the river where the man could reach it, a dugout canoe.

Doc and Monk carefully filled in the grave they had dug, and rounded up the earth.

When they got back to the trading post, Phil O'Reilly had destroyed the radio apparatus. Chief Eagle had taken Ham, Johnny and Pat aside and informed them of the situation. "Doc Savage has one of those maps from Niji," the chief finished, "and, since Niji was a white guy, Doc is letting him go. Niji has promised to reform. What Niji does not know is that Doc is going to keep an eye on him in the future, and if Niji doesn't reform, it'll be just too bad for him. As for us, we're going on to the spot to which these missing explorers were directed."

Phil joined Doc. "I put the radio on the blink," he said.

"Collect any supplies we may need from the trading post," Doc directed. "And load everything in the gyros."

This operation took a little time. The work was made slow by the necessity for watching the hostile natives each moment. Doc, Ham and Johnny went among them, and collected several blowguns and a supply of poisoned arrows, but in spite of that, Doc shortly felt a sharp impact against his back. It was a poisoned blowgun dart that, except for the fact that he was wearing a chain-mesh shirt that had stopped the thing, would have been unpleasant. He plucked out the dart, chased the native who had blown the thing at him, caught the fellow, and gave him a trouncing in the presence of his fellows.

That put a stop to the hostility. The idea that the bronze man was invulnerable to the darts aroused a superstitious fear, and the natives skulked out of sight.

A moment before they were to take off, Monk appeared. The homely chemist was dirty and puzzled.

"Say, you remember that guide named Kul who was supposed to be waiting here?" Monk asked.

"There never was any guide named Kul."

"Oh," Monk said. "That explains why there was no body in that grave Niji showed the chief."

The bronze man indicated how they should divide their forces. Monk, Ham and Phil O'Reilly would take one gyro. Johnny, Pat, Chief Eagle and himself took the other craft, which, while no larger than the first, was a more advanced model and could carry greater weight.

They took the air without incident. The gyros—they were not true gyros with the ability to rise straight up, but neither were they the common auto-gyro plane that required considerable forward speed to keep in the air—lifted off the water after very brief runs.

Doc turned the controls over to Johnny, and spread out the chart which Niji had given him. The bronze man computed flying time, finally announced his conclusions as, "If we are lucky, we will make it by night."

It was now midmorning.

Pat said, "I never knew this jungle was so big. On the map, you think of it as just being a part of Brazil."

XII

DANGEROUS DECOY

The plateau was an astounding thing. They came upon it late that afternoon, when they were flying west, and at first it was hard to distinguish, resembling a low cloud bank on the horizon. Sun glare made the western skyline a furnace, and that did not help them to distinguish the plateau.

The plateau had a perfectly flat top, and sheer sides. There was nothing fabulous about the thing, except that it was unexpected, there in the jungle. The sides were very steep, in some places being cliffs some hundreds of feet high. In other spots, the slope was slightly less precipitous.

Chief Eagle sighed at the place, and made some mental calculations.

"The top of that thing is about two thousand feet above the surrounding jungle." He frowned at Doc. "Great blazes, isn't there any trace of that on the charts?"

"None," the bronze man said.

"It's not so amazing," Pat offered dryly. "The jungle is perpetually covered with a haze or fog, and that thing looks like a cloud bank sticking up. If we hadn't had accurate bearings, we wouldn't have noticed it."

"The map indicates that thing as our goal?" the chief demanded.

"Yes."

Doc Savage, in the leading gyro, sent the craft up toward the lip of the plateau. The size of the place, not so impressive from a distance, became somewhat breath-taking as they drew close. Its contours resembled those of the big mesas of the western United States.

There was radio for communication between the two gyros.

Doc said into the microphone, "We will circle the edge of the place. Make a quick survey before darkness."

"Right," Monk's voice said in the receivers.

"You take one direction. We'll take the other. Keep in touch with us by radio."

"Right."

The bronze man headed left. He flew almost directly above the rim, but at an altitude that would not make it too easy for a rifle shot from below. And all of them used binoculars.

The vegetation on the top of the plateau, probably because so much jungle surrounded the place that the climate was very much the same, did not differ a great deal from the lowland.

Doc distinguished *hevea* and *castilloa* trees, as well as the two drug-producing shrubs, *cinchona* and cocoa, common to higher elevations. He was surprised at the presence of *castilloa*, because he understood it was found in the upper *Negro-Branco* basin, and nowhere else.

There was also the big *massaranduba*, or cow tree, one of the largest of Amazon trees. The evening sunlight made the reddish bark of the tree seem redder—that bark, when tapped, would give a liquid similar in appearance and taste to milk, and which was even sometimes used in coffee and for other purposes which genuine milk served. However, drinking much of the milk from the cow tree would cause illness, because it coagulated into a material similar to rubber latex. The wood was very hard, so hard that nails could not be driven into it, and it had to be drilled like steel. The wood would also sink in water.

Doc said, "Monk—"

"Yes?"

"Find anything?"

"Naw, not exactly," Monk said. "There's kind of a canyon ahead, though, and it looks as if there was some paths leading down to that, and what looks like cultivated fields near it. We'll know in a minute."

Phil O'Reilly emitted a yell, grabbed Doc's arm.

"Look!" he bellowed.

Below them, to the left, there was a clearing, a meadow of some area. In this, a man had appeared. He was running, waving his arms to get their attention.

Phil glued binoculars to his eyes.

"That is Daniel Stage!" Phil shrieked.

Doc Savage turned the gyro, let it sink. He used his own glasses.

The man below appeared to be in bad shape. He was almost naked, and he was crusted with dirt. He had made himself a garment of leaves and plaited bark. He seemed hardly to have the strength to run, because he fell repeatedly. The rest of the time, he ran with an awkward leaping motion.

"That's Stage," Phil gasped. "I recognize the way he runs."

"Behind him," Doc said sharply. "Take a look!"

There was a group of men, rather light-skinned for natives, running grimly toward the fellow waving at them from the meadow.

Phil made an angry noise. "He must have yelled at us, or something, and they heard him," Phil growled.

Doc Savage fed the motor a little gas. The gyro started to lift and circle.

"Aren't you going to land?" Phil yelled.

He looked grim.

"Not immediately," Doc said.

Phil swore.

"But we've come all this way to rescue Daniel Stage!" he shrieked. "You've got a chance. You can land and pick him up before those natives get him!"

Doc said, "Not until we make sure what this is."

"But we want to rescue Stage!"

Doc's voice hardened. "We also want to find those explorers who went after him—to say nothing of Junith, Daniel Stage's sister."

Phil glared at him. Phil was not a young man who believed in sober, cautious action. When he saw a thing that seemed to need doing, he was in favor of doing it.

Suddenly Phil lunged forward. He picked a moment when Doc Savage was manipulating the controls, so he took the bronze man partly by surprise. Phil got his arm under the instrument panel, clutched the ignition wires, and wrenched them loose.

The motor stopped.

Long, bony Johnny hit Phil with his fist. Johnny did not appear to have much strength, but his blow put Phil on the floor, dazed.

"You supermagnitudinous fool!" Johnny said.

Doc worked with the controls. The gyro sank earthward.

It would land in the clearing, very close to the man staggering there.

Phil stirred on the floor.

"You can fix those wires in a minute," he muttered. "I just forced you to land."

He sounded triumphant.

Doc said, "Take a closer look at this man."

Phil got to his feet. As the gyro sank, and the man in the clearing came closer, Phil's expression changed strangely.

"Well?" Doc asked.

"It's not . . . not Daniel Stage!" Phil gasped.

"What made you think it was Stage in the first place?" Doc demanded.

"The way he ran—that loping gait," Phil muttered. "Dan always ran like that. We used to kid him a lot about it. Told him he ran like a girl."

The gyro hit with a considerable jar.

"Get him in here!" Doc rapped.

The bronze man doubled under the instrument panel, began splicing the torn ignition wires. The wires were tangled; it would take a few minutes to sort them.

Phil leaped out, yelled at the running man, "Get in here! We've got to fix the ignition wires, but we'll be able to take off."

The man Phil had thought was Daniel Stage, it developed, was not a white man at all, but a rather swarthy breed with a face that was not very pleasant. He galloped close to the plane.

Then, so unexpectedly that no one had a chance to do anything about it, he whipped two guns out of his clothing. One was an ordinary revolver; the other weapon was a big-barreled signal pistol, the type of thing called a Very gun.

He shot a hole in the gas tank. The gas ran out. He fired the Very pistol into the gasoline. With a gusty roar, flame enveloped that part of the plane.

The man then turned his revolver on them.

"Everybody sit still," he said.

The natives ran toward them, and when they arrived, the man spoke to them in a dialect which Doc Savage did not understand, although it bore some resemblance to the basic language of the tribes of the outer reaches of the Amazon region.

The natives—they were stalwart men who appeared

more white than Indian—scrambled into the gyro, seized Doc, Pat, Johnny, Chief Eagle and Phil. They had bark-plaited ropes ready to bind their prisoners.

Phil groaned. He was utterly miserable.

"Nice job you did," Johnny told him grimly.

Doc Savage shrugged.

"They might have gotten us anyway," the bronze man said. "Look." He nodded toward the other gyro, which they could distinguish in the red light of evening.

A plane, a low-wing monoplane that was fast, had climbed up from somewhere, and set upon the slow gyro plane. They could hear the enraged snarl of a machine gun from the plane, a sound that cackled across the top of the plateau in short bursts, sounding like a turkey gobbler in the distance.

The gyro landed quickly. There was nothing else to do. It did not have the speed or defensive weapons to cope with the fast plane.

XIII

THE SUN CAT

Doc Savage did not see the city until they had led him to the lip of the canyon.

He was not exactly surprised. For the last few hundred yards, they had passed through patches of cultivated ground. The fields were rather slovenly. Farming done the lazy way.

The city was like a cliff-dweller city, except that it was not under an overhanging cliff, and was not where it could be reached by rolling boulders. A ridge jutted out into the canyon, and at the end of the ridge was a round peak, where the white city stood.

"I'll be superamalgamated!" Johnny gasped.

Phil O'Reilly made a strangled noise of astonishment. Chief Eagle grunted.

"It's wonderful!" Pat exclaimed.

The captors jerked them to a halt near a path that led downward, then out along the ridge to the city. They waited there. Doc Savage studied the natives, puzzled by the shape of their features, which bore some traces of Incan ancestry, yet were predominately the features of white men.

The reason for the wait was apparent when Monk and the others were hauled into view. They were a downcast lot.

Monk looked at Doc miserably. "Doc, I had to land. That blasted plane had machine guns stuck all over it, and it could fly circles around us."

The bronze man said, "You did the intelligent thing in coming down."

"But we're prisoners."

Doc shrugged.

Monk peered at the city on the pinnacle. Then the homely chemist turned to Johnny, who, as a noted archaeologist, would know what the city meant, if anyone would.

"What kind of people live there, Johnny?" Monk demanded. "And this ain't no time to spring them big words on us!"

"The construction is entirely cubes and circles," Johnny said. "That is a characteristic of the cliff-dweller people of the Mesa Verde and other districts in Colorado, Arizona and New Mexico. It is a characteristic, too, of Incan, Mayan and Aztec architecture. The Mayans, for instance, never mastered the arch, or at least never used it. Probably they mastered it, all right, because their knowledge of astronomy and other complicated subjects was remarkable, as well as their skill at surgery. There are known instances where skulls have been found upon which fairly expert trepanning operations have been performed. I should say—"

One of the natives gave him a jab with a short spear, so they never found out what he should say. The prisoners were marched out on the ridge path.

The path was quite narrow, little over a foot wide in spots, and at intervals there were defensive arches which would make the work of an attacking force quite difficult.

The city itself was of stone and mortar. The workmanship was not as skilled as it had seemed from a distance, being not greatly superior, in fact, to the workmanship on the pueblo dwellings of the southwestern United States.

The place, however, was extensive, being at least two hundred yards in length, and probably of a greater depth. They were led up a long flight of stair-ladders—wooden arrangements which could be drawn up in case of attack.

A native grunted an order. The prisoners were searched.

They were forced, all of them, to climb down a ladder into darkness. At the bottom, perhaps fifteen feet down, they found a large circular chamber in the stone. The walls were indented with six evenly spaced pockets which were like bunks, and in the center of the room there was a large round depression, with a very small hole, no larger than a rifle barrel. To the east, in the direction of the setting sun, there was a slab of stone a foot thick, two feet wide, three feet high, projecting from the floor. And behind this in the wall was a round hole, a little larger than a man's fist, through which fresh air came.

After they were in the bottom, the ladder was pulled out.

After a few minutes, their eyes became accustomed to the darkness. The sun was not yet down, and some light penetrated through the square hole above their heads.

"This ain't so bad," Monk said.

Johnny grunted uneasily. "Personally, I think we're in a bad spot."

Monk peered at him. He did not often hear Johnny sound so concerned.

"What's eating you?" Monk asked.

"You ever been in the cliff ruins in the western United States?" Johnny asked. "Those on Mesa Verde, for instance?"

"Yeah. This place is kinda like some of them must have been when they were inhabited, only this one is bigger. What about it?"

"Remember the *kivas*?"

"The what?"

"*Kivas*. The ceremonial rooms. Circular, with six supporting pillars cut into the edge, a ventilating hole and a deflecting stone like this one, and a *see-pah-poo* in the center."

"A *what* in the center?"

"*See-pah-poo*. There are various ways of spelling it, and I'm using the easy one." Johnny spelled it out for Monk.

"Well, what about them things?"

Johnny rubbed his jaw. He looked upward. There was a reddish glow flickering over the square entrance to their strange prison, and they realized that their captors had lighted one or more fires outside.

Johnny, his tone more worried, said, "It is generally conceded that the circle was considered sacred among many of these ancient people," he explained. "Circular rooms were always their religious rooms, their temples, or rooms where they placed their grains in the hands of the gods for safekeeping. And also their sacrificial rooms."

"Sacrificial rooms?" Monk asked.

"Well—the thought just occurred to me."

"You mean—they intend to sacrifice us?"

"Now, don't get excited," Johnny said. "But at the same time, don't get too optimistic."

Phil O'Reilly flung himself down with his back against the wall. He muttered disconsolately.

"This is all my fault," he complained. "If I hadn't forced the gyro to land, we wouldn't be here."

Doc Savage said quietly, "That plane had machine guns. They could have caught us and forced us down anyhow."

Pat asked, "Has anybody seen Daniel Stage?"

No one had, apparently.

Doc asked, "Monk, who was flying the plane armed with machine guns?"

"That Rollo Marbetti. I got a good look at him."

Ham snapped, "Marbetti is the lug behind this mess."

"I wonder where Junith Stage is?" Pat pondered aloud.

No one answered.

"And my son," Chief Eagle said finally. "What became of him? And the other explorers who have come down here and vanished."

"This room is circular," Johnny said. "I don't like that."

Monk said, "While we're wondering—why not wonder what became of the guy with one half of his face different from the other half? Me, I'd like to know about him."

No one answered that.

"There must be some *reason* behind this," Pat said finally.

It was nearly two hours later when the ladder came down into the pit like a long tongue that, colored by the firelight above, looked jagged and red. A native took up a position at the top with a heavy club, and waggled the club menacingly to discourage any attempt to escape.

Another native shoved his head over the opening. It was the same man who had served as a decoy in the meadow.

"Doc Savage come alone," he said.

The bronze man climbed half up the ladder, then stopped. "What is the meaning of this?" he demanded. "Where is Daniel Stage? Where are Elmo Eagle and the others?"

The native said something in his own tongue. Doc got the general meaning of what the fellow was saying. Looking down at the others, Doc explained.

"This fellow does not speak English," he said. "He is just repeating the words he has been told to repeat."

"Doc Savage come alone," the native said impatiently.

Doc said, "Take it easy, Monk. The same for the rest of you."

The bronze man climbed the rest of the way, and men laid hold of him. They were wary, and three of them stood nearby holding small daggers made of long thorns. The sticky substance on the ends of the thorns was evidently some kind of poison.

Half a dozen long, stout cords braided of bark were tied to the bronze man's arms and legs, so that he could be spread-eagled instantly if he made any attempt at resistance. Following that, he was marched away.

Two natives went ahead carrying torches which shed smoke and some ruby-colored light that spread over the long passages of stone and mortar, and the low, worn steps which they climbed, the narrow doorways through which they passed. The air was still, and now that the sun had gone down, it was not particularly warm.

The climate at this altitude was undoubtedly pleasant, and judging from the profuse vegetation, and the fact that the surrounding jungle undoubtedly swarmed with game, life here was probably pleasant.

Doc was conducted into a room that was very long, but not wide, and—if Johnny's surmise about circles being sacred was correct—some kind of an inner temple, because the floor, walls and ceiling were ornamented with inlays of brilliant color, all circular in formation.

At the far end of the room, there were three circular, lifted platforms. They were drum-shaped. The one in the center was highest, and painted brilliant scarlet; the other two, while larger, were not as high, and one was black, the other blue.

On the black platform, perhaps a dozen natives were seated. They were elderly men, looked wise in the ways of life, and were evidently some kind of a council.

On the blue platform were half a dozen white men. Not half-breeds. These men were entirely white. They were not pleasant-looking characters.

The man with the ugly face sat on the center platform.

Doc Savage was conducted to a spot in front of the platforms, and halted, his guards keeping a firm grip on the cords which were fastened to his arms and legs.

The man with the ugly face looked at one of the elderly men on the black platform. The man arose, and spoke. His voice went on monotonously, in the manner of a man who is repeating part of a ritual.

After the elderly native finished, and sat down, the man with the face spoke in English. His handling of the speech was stilted and unnatural.

"Do you understand what was just said?" he asked.

"Not very clearly," Doc said. "This is an offshoot of the Incan language, mixed with a little Spanish, but I cannot get all of it."

"The council wishes you to understand everything," the ugly man said. "So I will repeat. You are in the presence of the Sun, the Sky and the Night." He gestured briefly at the platforms. "The colors will explain what I mean. The Sun, the Sky and the Night. Of these three things are made the things that man cannot control. In the creation of the universe, these three things were given man to teach him that he must always be modest, for there are things that he can never control."

He was silent a while, contemplating Doc Savage. There was nothing but hate in the look he gave the bronze man. Doc, in turn, was studying the fellow's face closely, this being his first opportunity to do so. Unfortunately, the torchlight furnished very poor illumination.

"The Sun, the Sky and the Night," continued the man with the face, "are beyond the control of man, hence his superiors, and therefore qualified to sit in judgment upon him. Therefore they are sitting in judgment now, the duly elected servants of these three powers, in order to pass judgment upon intruders upon our peace."

Doc said, "You are taking a long-winded way of saying what you have on your mind. Why not out with it?"

"You want it short?"

"Yes."

"All right," the man said. "On the day of the Speaking Bird, which is tomorrow, you will be tested for fitness. Only one of you need pass the test in order that all of you may live.

You have the privilege of determining which of you shall be first to take the test, and which second, and so on."

Doc watched him steadily.

"What kind of a test?" the bronze man asked.

"You will be placed with the Sun Cat," the man with the face replied. "And if you meet with approval, and are permitted to live, all of you may live."

"What is the Sun Cat?" Doc inquired curiously.

The other ignored him, turned to the elderly men and spoke in the native tongue. Doc listened closely, decided he was telling them that he had informed the prisoner of the judgment of the council, and desired to know if there was anything more he should tell the captive. The answer was that nothing more need be said.

Before Doc was led away, he eyed the white men on the blue platform.

"You fellows must have a nice racket here," he said. "I suppose you rate the sky platform because you came here by plane. As a matter of fact, I think I know what your racket is."

"A lot of good it'll do you, bozo," one of the men said.

Doc was dragged away, forced to walk down several passages, and shoved into a room which was lighted by a primitive kind of a lamp that consisted of a wick lying in a jar containing some type of oil.

There was an array of food on a low wooden platform.

He decided he was to be fed before being returned to the prison hole. Either that, or they were trying to poison him. He went over and looked at the food, smelled of it doubtfully. There was *pescada*, a fish that would taste something like cod, and *tartaruga* eggs. The *tartaruga* eggs—they were the local fresh-water turtle eggs—had the peculiar quality of the whites never hardening during cooking, so only the yolk was served very hard-boiled, resembling the dry yolk of hen's eggs.

"Psssst!"

Doc half turned, and listened.

The sound came again, from the other side of the room. It was a human sound. Doc discovered a small aperture across the room, evidently a ventilating slit, and went to it.

"Yes," he said.

"Mr. Savage," said a low feminine voice. "Come close. I want to talk to you."

It was Junith Stage.

XIV

SACRIFICE IN THE SUN

Doc Savage leaned close to the aperture and asked, "How did you get here?"

"By plane," she explained. "We left immediately after I pointed that gun at you in my house in the city, and escaped. Now listen closely. I have thought of a way—"

"Did the man with the ugly face fly down with you?" Doc asked.

She hesitated. She was silent for so long that he wondered if she could have gone away from the other end of the ventilator.

"Yes, he came with me," she said.

"Who is he?"

"I can't tell you that."

Doc Savage half opened his mouth to tell her that he believed he already knew, then he changed his mind. Instead he asked another question, beginning it with a statement.

"He is a white man," he said, "and I have been wondering how he got control over these natives."

"He doesn't control them entirely."

"You mean that he has to do what the council says?"

"On vital points," the girl answered, "he does. The council will not stand for murders, and that is why you are now alive. Although what is to happen to you is the same as murder."

Doc asked persistently, "How did he get control over these natives?"

"By coming in an airplane when he found the place," Junith Stage replied. "Like all the old Incan legendary beliefs, these people think that their deities came out of the sky, sent to them by the sun."

"They are Incans? Their language isn't pure."

"Oh, we're wasting time!" Junith snapped. "I'm trying to tell you—"

"There is Spanish mixed in their language," Doc said.

"Yes. Back during the Spanish exploration of South America, an exploring party somehow managed to get this far. How, I don't know. But they found this mesa after becoming lost and wandering for years. There was a tribe of Incans here then, and the Spanish explorers simply stayed here. They killed off most of the Incan men at the time, which accounts for the predominantly white features of these natives."

Doc said, "I supposed it was something like that."

Junith Stage's whisper was imperative. "Listen, I think that I can overpower the one guard at your door. If I can do that, you may be able—"

Interrupting, Doc asked, "What became of the other explorers who were lost?"

"They are here. But you can't help them. They are prisoners, and safe enough as long as—well, for the time being."

"What do you mean?"

She hesitated. "As long as they have money left."

"You mean that this is an extortion scheme?"

"Yes."

"The explorers were decoyed down here and seized, and held in order that money could be extorted from them?"

"Yes."

That was about what Doc Savage had thought. He did not mention the fact that he had suspected the truth.

"Where is your brother?"

"He . . . he's here." Her voice, more strained, rushed into an explanation. "That is why I acted as I did. My brother—I had to do it to save him."

Doc said, "I could tell you were not taking part in this willingly."

"Please! I think I can sneak up behind your guard from behind, and knock him out. Then you might escape."

"No," Doc said.

"But—they're going to put you in with that thing they call the Sun Cat."

"What is it?"

"A gigantic *onca*."

"Jaguar?"

"Yes."

"They are not particularly large."

"This one"—her voice was terrified—"is enormous."

"What is this test of the Sun Cat?"

"They put you in an amphitheater with the animal. There are seats around the top, and everyone watches."

The bronze man was thoughtful for a while. He made, unconsciously, the small trilling sound that was his habit in moments of intense mental stress.

"Can you reach the stuff from our planes?" he asked.

"I—yes, I believe I can." She sounded frightened.

"Will you be watching this business of a test with the Sun Cat?"

"I—hadn't intended to."

"Watch it," Doc directed. "Go to the stuff from our plane. You will find a metal case numbered eleven. In it will be a small bottle, numbered seventy-six. Get that bottle. Can you remember that? Case number eleven. Bottle seventy-six."

"Yes—I can remember."

"Tie the bottle inside a bouquet of flowers. Wrap it in a handkerchief so it will not break. Then, as I am put in the arena, toss me the flowers with the bottle inside. Can you do that?"

"I'll try."

"It will probably be the difference between life and death."

"I . . . I will do my best," she said. "I think I can."

"Good," Doc said.

She didn't think it was good. She was sobbing.

When Doc Savage was returned to the subterranean prison chamber, Monk and the rest were infinitely relieved. Ham said, "We were afraid—well, we didn't know but what they were going to bump you off."

"What happened, Doc?" Pat asked.

Pat sounded quite calm, and her quietness irritated Doc Savage. Pat enjoyed this kind of excitement, and that was a perpetual source of irritation to the bronze man. He got a kick out of it himself, he had to admit, but it was a grim kind of thrill, and he often wished he did not have a taste for adventure.

He told them what had occurred, including what Junith Stage had told him.

Chief Eagle swore in a low, guttural tone. "I have suspected they were holding my son here, and forcing him to turn over his money to them. I examined my son's bank balances and stock holdings. His money has been disappearing since he came here and vanished. They made him sign over money to them, and made him sign checks. The transactions were dated back, though, so that it would appear he had made them before he left the States."

Johnny, the long, bony geologist and archaeologist, said, "An *onca*, eh? They aren't very big."

"There are four types of jaguars," Doc reminded him. "One kind is small and yellow, and not very dangerous. Another has small spots, the third larger spots. But the fourth is the color of milk chocolate, and is ferocious."

Monk asked, "The idea is that you fight this critter, and if you lick it, we all get turned loose?"

"Something like that," Doc agreed.

It was not a pleasant prospect, and the grimness of the situation silenced them. They were tired, too. They had flown for days in the planes, and sleep had been sporadic, and strain continuous.

They took turns at trying to dig out through the ventilating tunnel. But it ran through several feet of solid rock, and they had no tools. Their belt buckles soon wore out on the stone, and after that, they made no progress whatever.

About three o'clock in the morning, Monk took up a position against the wall, Ham climbed on his shoulders, and Doc clambered atop both of them, and was able to wrap his hands over the edge of the square hole.

He drew himself up. Then he dropped back.

"That won't do," the bronze man said. "They have half a dozen *jararacas* picketed around the hole."

Phil O'Reilly asked, "What's a *jararaca*?"

"Snake," the bronze man explained cryptically. "Quite deadly. Blindness results about two minutes after one of them bites you, and death usually occurs in about five minutes."

Phil O'Reilly made a sound that had no meaning, except that it was frightened.

"I guess I'm not cut out for an explorer," he said. "I'm so scared my legs feel like sacks full of ice water."

Monk snorted. "Brother, don't let that worry you. I'm scared a lot worse."

Pat said, "We're all scared, Phil."

"You wouldn't think so, to listen to you," Phil muttered.

"Well, if I could get out of here right now," Pat said, "I would take a vow never to get mixed up in another one of these messes. Maybe."

Probably Doc Savage was the only one who really slept any at all.

*   *   *

The amphitheater had the ceremonial shape—it was round. It was somewhat like a bull ring, with seats that entirely circled it. The arena itself was deep—nearly thirty feet deep, with sides that were glass-smooth, so that the Sun Cat could not climb out.

There was one opening in the deep cup, to the west, near the base. It was circular, and surrounded by a red circle.

Above this opening were seats inclosed in boxes. They might have been seats of honor, but they were anything but that.

Monk and the others—they had shaken hands gravely with Doc Savage upon separating—were led into one of the boxes.

They stared in amazement at the occupants of the box across from them.

They were looking at several gaunt, ragged, forlorn-looking white men. Monk, who had a wide acquaintance among explorers, recognized some of them. So did Ham and Johnny.

"Hey!" Monk yelled. "Tom Kennedy! Ed Corby! How are you guys?"

A native struck Monk over the head with a long club. The homely chemist subsided, dazed; then, fighting mad, tried to rear up and assault the native. Ham and Johnny seized his arms, held him.

Chief Eagle was looking at his son, Elmo Walker Eagle. The chief's copper-colored face was utterly fixed, frozen with emotion.

The other lost explorers—Joseph Branch, Joe Biltmore, Felix Point-Mackey—were there in the adjacent box. They were confined with stout cords about their legs, and it was obvious that they had been brought here to watch the execution.

"I see the fine hand of that guy with the ugly face in this," Ham whispered. "He wants to throw a bigger scare into them."

"Lemme at 'em!" Monk snarled. "Where's that guy with the face? I'll take him, too!"

The man with the ugly face was out of reach, seated to the right, along with the white men who were his associates. He sat there, inscrutable, his evil face doubly unpleasant in the morning sunlight.

The day was glaring with sunlight. A few jungle birds, macaws and small blue *uirapuru* and *iuramimbe*, or trumpet birds, floated in the air. A few toucans, evidently pets, were about. They looked strange, their beaks almost as large as their bodies—beaks that were long for the same purpose that a giraffe's neck is long, so that the birds could reach their food, fruit that grew out on the ends of branches too fragile to support their weight. They were surprisingly light, these beaks, although they appeared ponderous.

Very high in the white-hot dome of the sky floated a *caracara-i*, a type of eagle, the cry of which, according to superstition, was an omen of death.

Pat's eyes, searching, located Junith Stage. She was seated near the ugly-faced man and his group of associates. Pat watched her closely. Pat had an inner impulse to distrust all women, and to her notion, Junith Stage had shown little reason to be trusted.

The fact that Junith was holding a bouquet of flowers was a little comforting, but not much.

Suddenly, there was a sound, a sigh, that was a kind of moan in concert. And simultaneously, every native onlooker came erect and stared down into the pit.

Monk jumped up, looked. He was in time to see a snarling, chocolate-hued streak of ferocity whip through the round opening in the wall. It was an *onca*, all right. A jaguar. But it was by far the largest of the species Monk had ever seen. Larger than a mountain lion from the Rockies. For a moment, he thought the Sun Cat was as large as a Bengal tiger, then modified his opinion somewhat. Not as large as a tiger, but fully as formidable.

"Blazes!" Monk said hoarsely.

Johnny's eyes were protruding. He had not imagined a jaguar grew this large. And this was the brownish species, the ferocious type.

Phil O'Reilly said hoarsely, "Doc hasn't a chance!"

Pat nudged him. "Keep your shirt on."

XV

BAD LOSERS

The round aperture into the arena was so low that Doc Savage had to stoop. They were holding him just back of a heavy wooden gate which closed the opening, and two natives had cut the cords loose from his arms and legs—cords of the same type which they had used to lead him about before.

When they shoved the big door open, the jaguar was in the center of the ring. Doc saw the animal, saw that it was looking toward the opening. He realized that if his captors shoved him into the ring at that moment the beast would doubtless spring upon him without delay.

He had no false ideas about his ability to cope with the jaguar in a bare-handed combat. If luck was with him, he might manage such a thing. But luck was a doubtful quantity upon which to stake his life.

The bronze man stalled. He jerked free of his captors, began making various meaningless gestures, and mumbling a singsong gibberish. The device worked. They thought he was making a preliminary supplication to some private deity, and they let him proceed.

He kept on stalling until the big cat tired of looking at the door, and stalked to the other side of the arena.

Then the bronze man entered.

His appearance brought forth a prolonged yell from the audience, as he had expected. The noise distracted the attention of the jaguar, further, and the animal snarled up at the crowd. It even made a run and a leap, and mounted to astonishing height on the wall. Its claws made a sound like steel knives ripping down a concrete wall as it slid back, and a few sparks flew.

Doc moved with flowing speed, not too fast, and not too slow, to the center of the right. He lifted his arms, turned slowly to face each side of the arena. He had a double purpose—to give the impression that he was not scared, and to locate Junith Stage.

He saw Junith's flowers before he saw Junith. She had become frightened, and thrown them too soon. The bouquet, quite large, the blossoms making it very bright, arched slowly through the sunlight and fell to the stone floor of the pit.

The jaguar sprang upon the flowers instantly. Snarling, spitting, the cat picked the bouquet up and shook it, ripped it to pieces.

Above, Junith Stage screamed. When Doc threw a glance in her direction, she was doubling over on her seat in a faint.

Doc Savage took a chance. He leaped toward the jaguar, and yelled his loudest.

Startled, the huge cat sprang back. It crouched, watching him with eyes that were utterly evil. Its tail switched slowly from one side to another.

Doc stood perfectly still. The cat was too close to the remains of the bouquet. And Doc had to reach the flowers.

The bottle which he had instructed Junith Stage to place with the flowers—she must have done so, or she would not have thrown the flowers into the arena—contained a powerful anaesthetic gas. He had hoped to use it to overcome the Sun Cat, as the natives called this enormous jaguar.

Very cautiously, the bronze man took a step toward the bouquet remnants. And the jaguar leaped for him.

The cat was a toast-colored monster of fury, paws extended, the claws showing like curved white bones. Its jaws were open.

Doc was set. His movements—they were so fast that all motion became a blur to the onlookers—were far slower than he wished they could be. But he got to one side. With his right arm, he struck at the paw of the jaguar as it lashed out for him. He managed to hit the paw without being clawed. Then the cat was past.

Doc dived ahead. His way to the flowers was clear now. He stooped, got them. The handkerchief was with them, and he felt the bottle inside it. He wrenched both bottle and handkerchief free. The handkerchief had kept the bottle from breaking.

He threw the flowers at the jaguar. That distracted the animal for a moment. But it leaped again, swiftly.

Again the bronze man went to one side at the last instant. But this time, his right hand got a grip on the jaguar's paw, fastened there with steel trap tenacity. He jerked. The impetus of the big animal's leap sent them both down. The jaguar landed heavily. Doc let it go. The cat's paws waved; it had not landed on its feet, but on its side. It twisted, rolled over to get to its feet.

Doc fell upon the animal's back, legs going around the big cat's hips and locking there, in such a position that, for the moment, it could not get its rear paws forward to claw him. He fastened his arm under the animal's throat.

The jaguar made a hideous sound. Its lashing, corded strength was incredible. It was as if the bronze man had seized a huge machine and tried to stop it with puny human strength. They went over and over, end for end, in a mad tornado of fury and motion.

Doc held his breath. He crushed the bottle on the jaguar's forehead, rubbed the saturated handkerchief over the nostrils of the beast.

It was humanly impossible to retain his grip for long. But he put forth every effort. A little time was required for the gas to take effect. Finally he got his chance, loosened his grip, sprang clear.

The jaguar, beginning to feel the effects of the gas, sprawled out, and whirled to face the bronze man. The beast showed its fangs, snarled.

Doc remained perfectly motionless. The animal was becoming dazed; its brain distracted, it might not leap. But any motion would cause it to spring. And the bronze man himself was shaken, somewhat dizzy, so that if the cat sprang now, he might not be able to avoid it.

Doc watched until the filmed blinking of the jaguar's eyes told him the animal was about to succumb.

Then the bronze man lifted his voice in a long, sustained yell that was as peculiar a sound as he could make at the moment. At the same time, he made mystic gestures with his hands.

Following the weird yell, he announced as best he could in the native language, using the Incan tongue, which the crowd could probably understand to some extent—Doc spoke some Incan vernacular, just as he had a smattering of most spoken languages—that he was exerting his power over the Sun Cat. He told the animal to lie down and go to sleep.

When the animal rolled over, overcome by the gas, it must have looked effective to the crowd.

The effect was spoiled somewhat when the man with the ugly face leaned over the pit rim and leveled a revolver at Doc Savage.

Phil O'Reilly redeemed himself for whatever mistakes he had made previously. During the excitement, he had cautiously edged toward one of their guards, with the idea of seizing the man's spear and throwing it down to Doc to use as a weapon.

Now Phil snatched the spear, whirled, hurled it at the man with the ugly face. It would have been a good job of spear-throwing for a native. Because the shaft impaled the man with the face, and he fell, without as much as screaming, into the pit.

Doc leaped, got the man's revolver, which hit the pit floor ahead of the body. With the gun, he sprang back, and menaced the other white men.

One white man had a flat automatic in his hand. Doc fired. The man shrieked, began to paw his mangled fist with his other hand.

"Don't move!" Doc warned them.

They remained motionless, watching the bronze man's gun.

"Ham, Monk, Johnny!" Doc shouted. "Get around there and disarm those fellows!"

Monk moved to obey, keeping a wary watch on their native captors. But no one made a move to interfere. Reaching the white men, Monk and the others disarmed them.

Doc said, "Ask any of those fellows if they can speak the local language."

One of the white men nodded.

"Tell these natives that we are not ordinary humans," Doc directed. "Tell them we are messengers from the outer world, and it will be very bad for them if we are interfered with. And it will be a lot worse for you if you don't say exactly that. I can understand enough of the language to tell whether you say what you've been ordered to tell them."

In a frightened voice, the man made his speech. He added a little for good measure. He announced that the man with the face—he called him some kind of a name that meant a deity from the ancestral gods of both Spaniards and Incans—had abdicated his power in favor of a new and supreme representative, who was Doc Savage.

The announcement might not have been necessary, because the overcoming of the jaguar had completely silenced the crowd.

Monk looked down into the pit, at the slack form of the man with the face.

Then the chemist glanced at Phil.

"Where'd you learn to throw a spear like that?" Monk demanded.

"Oh, I've got a trunkful of medals for javelin throwing in college," Phil explained modestly.

Monk grinned. "You remember them cracks I made about you being a plush-armchair explorer?"

Phil flushed. "Yes."

Monk extended his hand. "Well, I take 'em back. How about letting me shake hands with a real guy?"

Phil gripped the homely chemist's fist enthusiastically.

Ham said, "Phil, you don't realize what an effect you've made on Monk. This is the first time in his life he has admitted he was wrong."

From the arena, Doc called up, "Is Junith Stage conscious?"

"Not yet," Pat called back.

"Get her out of here. Wait until she is feeling all right again before you tell her what happened."

"What do you mean?" Pat asked. "Tell her about what?"

Doc Savage hesitated.

"Look," he said.

He went over to the man with the face, bent down, and worked for a moment. He stripped off a contraption of rubber and make-up which gave one half of the man's face such a grotesque appearance.

Doc straightened with the half-face mask in his hand, and the others got a look at the features of the man who had been impaled by the spear.

"Daniel Stage!" Phil O'Reilly exploded.

"No, no, his name is Rollo Marbetti," Monk declared.

Doc said, "Daniel Stage, Rollo Marbetti, and the man with the face are all the same individual."

"Is he dead?"

"Yes."

During the next hour, as a matter of safety, Doc got the rescued explorers together, and found an arms cache which had been used by Daniel Stage and the white men who were helping him.

They also located Stage's plane, concealed under trees at the edge of a clearing not far from the city.

Elmo Eagle, copper-colored like his father, and with the same stoical aquiline features, said, "It was the way Junith Stage told you, Mr. Savage."

"An extortion scheme?"

"Yes. Daniel Stage found this place while exploring, and thought he had something that would make him world famous. As a matter of fact, there is nothing really unique about the place. These people do not have even as advanced a civilization as the ancient Mayans. I think the disappoint

ment when his discovery turned out to be not so important
upset Daniel Stage's mind."

Doc said, "He deliberately disappeared, then began
getting notes out to decoy rich young explorers down here,
where he could seize them."

Young Eagle nodded.

Johnny said, "Doc—"

"Yes."

"Back there in New York, when we set that trap at the
hotel for the man with the face, then fastened the radio to his
car and trailed him. He fled to his sister's home, didn't he?
And assumed the name of Rollo Marbetti."

Doc nodded. "He was making his sister cooperate with
him. She had no choice."

"What are you going to do with the sister?" Pat asked.

"Turn her loose," Doc said. "She saved our lives when
she threw that bottle of chemical into the arena."

"At Junith's house," Johnny persisted, "did you have any
suspicion Marbetti was her brother?"

"Not until she fled," Doc said grimly. "Then I looked in
the fireplace and decided the pictures she had burned there
were really her brother's photographs. That meant she didn't
want us to find any pictures by which we could identify her
brother."

Phil O'Reilly said, "There was something else, too?"

"The fact that she fled with her brother when she heard
you were coming?" Doc suggested. "Yes, that made it very
plain that her brother was Marbetti. You see, none of us had
seen her brother except you."

Elmo Eagle had been talking to one side with the
rescued explorers.

"How we going to get out of here?" Eagle asked. "The
plane?"

"Yes. It will be necessary to make several trips, but that
will be simple. Daniel Stage had done it repeatedly."

"Will the natives interfere?" Pat asked.

"No." Eagle shook his head. "That business with the
jaguar has fixed everything."

Monk and Ham had gone off on a private mission of their
own—they were hunting Habeas Corpus and Chemistry. The
pig and the chimp had been neglected somewhat more on
this adventure than on most occasions. Both animals had
become lost when the gyro was forced down—Habeas and

Chemistry had been riding in the gyro occupied by Monk—and had been chased into the jungle by the natives.

Junith Stage revived, and, after waiting until she had fully recovered, they told her about her brother. She buried her face in her hands for a while.

"The money he extorted from those men," she said. "I can show you where it is."

"You mean it's here?" Doc asked.

She nodded. "My brother intended to stay here permanently. He had a kind of plan for setting up a little empire here in the jungle, with himself as its ruler."

She showed them where the money was stored. It was in cash, currency and silver, with some gold coins of nationalities other than American. There were quite a few bars of gold bullion. Daniel Stage had been a methodical man, for there were records of his extortions, and these would enable the money to be returned to the rightful owners.

By noon, Monk and Ham had found their pets and returned. They arrived separately, Ham about a hundred yards ahead of Monk. It was at once apparent that they were not on speaking terms.

"What's wrong?" Junith asked.

Ham exhibited his pet chimp. "Look at him!" he said sourly.

Chemistry was bedraggled, bruised, bitten in several places.

"What on earth happened to him?" Johnny demanded.

"That blasted pig of Monk's," said Ham, "found a lot of these wild hogs called peccaries—that infernal Habeas Corpus must be half peccary anyway—and somehow got to leading the pack. They had run poor Chemistry up a bush and had him half scared to death. I'll fix that hog of Monk's."

Johnny masked a grin, recalling past devilment Chemistry had perpetrated on Monk's pig.

The slight difficulty came to a climax later in the afternoon.

There was an agonized howl from another room. Monk dashed into the room, took one look, and swelled with rage.

"Whatcha mean, you shyster!" Monk yelled. "Whatcha stickin' your hand in that hog's mouth for?"

"Sticking it in, you idiot!" Ham snarled. "I'm trying to pull it out!"

FIVE FATHOMS DEAD

I

The telescope was of the type known as a spotting 'scope. They are manufactured for use on rifle ranges to locate the holes the bullets make in the targets. This one had a magnification factor of 40X. Powerful. Usually they have a power of about 20X.

For fifteen minutes, now, the man they were calling Whitey had been using the telescope. He used it patiently, intently, his lips wearing the fierce twist of a lynx waiting for a rabbit to venture within springing reach. With a telescope so powerful, any motion is a serious matter, for the objective will quickly jump out of the field of view; hence he'd made a rest for the telescope out of two bricks and a bit of fieldstone.

Presently the bushes parted nearby, a white face protruded, and said, "There's a cop coming."

"How close?"

"Pretty damn close!"

"He pay particular attention to you?"

"No. No, I don't think so."

"It's a wonder he didn't," the big man they called Whitey said bitterly. "You couldn't look more scared if you were playing in a Boris Karloff movie. Wipe that wild look off your puss. Here, have a sandwich."

Ostensibly, and for the benefit of anybody whose curiosity might be easy on the trigger, they were picnicking. This was March, late March, actually a bit early for a picnic. But today the sun was out brightly, spraying the green grass and the trees, which hadn't leafed out yet to any extent, with plenty of warm glory.

Here on the hill, the highest hill around about, it was balmy and bright, and there was just enough breeze to kick away the smell of the seashore, which was a mudflat below them. The place and the weather were all right for a picnic. The picnic baskets looked all right, and there was a raincoat in case it rained and a blanket for them to sit on.

The man they knew as Whitey handed the other man a ham sandwich, then he tossed the raincoat over the tele-

115

scope, leaned back casually and selected a sandwich for himself.

The cop, old, grizzled, apple-cheeked, looked in on them. "Nice day, huh?" he said. He whacked the bushes with his stick.

"Sure."

"Enjoying yourselves?"

"Sure."

The cop's eyes were moving continually, touching everything. Old, wise, farmed out on this placid park beat the way an old horse is put out to grass, he was alert, hoped he would see some situation that needed a policeman, just so he could defeat boredom. He was not suspicious particularly. He was just looking around.

"They don't like it if you scatter a lot of papers around," he said.

"We won't."

"Seen anything of a dog? Little girl lost one."

"What kind of a dog?"

"Black one, short legs, long hair. Scotty, I reckon."

"Haven't seen it."

"Let me know if you do."

"Sure."

"So long." The old cop hit the bushes with his nightstick again. He went away.

The man known as Whitey grinned sardonically. He popped the rest of the ham sandwich in his mouth, chewed slowly. He was very big, but the middle of him looked flabby and his shoulders slouched, and he carried his mouth loosely. His skin was just skin color, neither dark nor light, and his hair was just hair, also neither dark nor light. His eyes were the only really unusual thing about him, and they were rather shocking, for they were a pale gray—bone-colored—and he seemed to keep them closed or partly closed a good deal of the time. He wore brown sport clothes.

The other man gasped, "You think he's wise?"

The other man was named Eli Stanley. He was medium-sized and dressed in grays and would have been colorless except for a violent green necktie.

Whitey laughed. "Don't be silly." His laugh was as hard as two stones knocking together.

"Why'd he poke his nose in here?"

"Because he's a cop."

"Well, I dunno—"

"Because he's also an old cop and nothing ever happens on his beat and he wishes it would."

"But—"

"Forget it. Wipe that look off your face. Have a pickle." Whitey lifted the raincoat with which he had covered the telescope. The telescope had shifted its position slightly and, lying down to look again, he carefully changed it until it again pointed at the submarine in the anchorage westward of the cluster of brick buildings of the base. He eyed the submarine for some time.

"They're fueling," he remarked, "for the whole trip."

"How can you tell?"

He looked annoyed. "The size of the fuel lines, the length of time since a man turned on the valves. It's very simple." He frowned at the other man, added, "Eli, I hope you prove to be a better man on assaying gold and evaluating jewels than I begin to suspect."

Eli scowled. "Have I said I knew anything about a submarine? If I did, I wouldn't know anything about an ex-Nazi submarine." Eli had his jaw shoved out. But he pulled it in presently, and then he looked a little frightened for his safety. "Not that I'm squawking, you understand," he said. He was afraid of this man Whitey.

Whitey acknowledged the other's nervousness with a slight, and fierce grin. He said, "Let's go. I've learned what I wanted to know about the submarine—they're putting to sea with full fuel tanks." He began packing the telescope in the picnic basket.

Eli watched him. They are all, Eli was thinking, wary of this Whitey.

They went to one of the better hotels in town. The National Household Specialties Company had a branch office on the fifth floor, a bedroom, two sitting rooms, one of which had formerly been a bedroom, and an inner office for private business. The National Household Specialties Company was Whitey, plus eleven men. They were selling household electrical appliances—vacuum cleaners, electric mixers, refrigerators, home deep-freeze units. irons, anything electrical— door to door. They had paid their license fees. They were perfectly legal. If anyone should care to investigate the concern a bit farther, they would find that the home office in New York occupied a fairly impressive, but not too expensive, suite of offices in a midtown building, and, although the firm was expanding since the war it was not a mushroom affair. Nor was the firm a new one. It had been in existence some twenty-five years. It would have taken more digging, however, to unearth the fact that not more than a month ago the concern had changed hands.

The business of specialty selling from house to house was one which gave the salesman a logical excuse for getting around almost anywhere.

Colton, a short fat man, sold deep-freeze units, home size. He looked like a salesman; they all looked like salesmen.

Colton came in about four o'clock. He reported in the inner room. He smelled of liquor and his eyes were too bright.

He said, "This kid Flinch, this kid in the Navy—I got him a little tight. Nothing in the way of equipment has been taken off the sub. The sub put in to a South American port after the war ended, and the crew, the Nazi crew, was interned right aboard. They've been aboard most of the time since, except that they're interned ashore in barracks when the sub is in port. There was some delay because of the diplomatic red tape before the U-boat was turned over to the U.S. Navy, and the Nazi crew was still kept aboard. The idea is that the Nazi crew is to teach U.S. Navy specialists anything new they know about submarine warfare—if anything."

Colton sounded like a salesman of the door-to-door species, as well as looking the part. As a matter of fact, he had received intensive training in the art for two weeks.

Colton continued, "The sub is going to be taken around through the Canal to the West Coast. To one of the sub bases on the West Coast. There, the Nazi crew is going to teach the Navy specialists what they know, before they're shipped back to Germany."

Whitey, listening to this, could have been asleep. The lids were lowered over his strangely bone-colored eyes.

"Original equipment is all aboard?"

"Yes."

"Never been touched?"

"Untouched."

"What about torpedoes?"

"Still aboard."

"Shells for the guns?"

"On board, too."

"What about the airplanes?"

"Two airplanes," Colton corrected. "They're both on board in flyable condition."

"Okay. That's all." Whitey didn't seem to awaken.

Colton went out. He met Eli Stanley in the outer room, and they went downstairs and had a drink. " Sell any vacuum cleaners?" Colton asked ironically when they were riding down in the elevators. "Three," Eli said. "Then me and the boss went on a picnic in the park. Not a bad guy, the boss."

Colton laughed. Eli didn't mean it about the boss being a great guy, and Colton didn't mean the laugh. Over whiskies in the hotel bar, they agreed that Whitey was a so-and-so, and hell on wheels.

"But, as long as we're tying into a thing like this, I'm glad he is," Eli said.

Whitey transacted more business. He took reports from Hiller and Ward. Hiller sold, ostensibly, vacuum cleaners, as did Eli. Hiller grinned slyly and said, "Mrs. Goss is talkative. Her husband, Ensign Goss, is sailing at eight o'clock tonight, she tells me."

Whitey scowled. "You make a date?"

"Certainly not."

"Why not?"

"I make a date. I don't show up. The submarine her husband's on disappears. Okay, she's liable to think of the two in connection, give it to the cops, and there you are."

Whitey's nod was barely perceptible, but approving. "That's using your head," he said. "So the sub sails at eight tonight. Okay. Get an early dinner. Be ready to move about six-thirty."

"The crew going to move out of town?"

"Certainly the crew isn't going to move out of town. Not for a few days."

Ward was a sleepy southerner with a voice which sounded as if there was sand in his throat. He was chewing on a long, almost-black cigar which was unlighted. He said, "I don't like that damned Colorado Jones. I not only don't like him; I can't take much more of him."

"Yeah?"

"I don't take that stuff, I tell you—"

"What about the supplies?"

"They're all right."

"Aboard the *Dancing Lady?*"

"That's right. And that Colorado Jones, I can't take. So help me, I'm gonna smear him."

"Never mind Colorado Jones. I'll handle Colorado Jones. Is there plenty of fuel aboard? How about the guns? How about the gas?"

"All taken care of."

"Good. Eat an early dinner. We go aboard about six-thirty. Pass the word along. Six-thirty."

Ward nodded. He said, somewhat maliciously, "I don't notice that Colorado Jones jumping when you speak to him, either."

Whitey's eyes seemed to close completely, his voice grew lazy, and he asked, "Think I'm not able to handle the situation?"

Ward thought about it for a moment. He looked at Whitey, considered Whitey's tone, the lazy way he had spoken. Ward began to get pale.

"I never said that," he muttered, and fled.

II

The yacht *Dancing Lady* was a yacht by conversion rather than birth, having been constructed as a PT boat during the war, later sold as surplus, and converted into a fairly comfortable, and certainly speedy, private craft. In her vitals still reposed the original PT boat power-plant, a gas-devouring set of monsters which few private owners could afford to keep operating. But she was yachty-looking. She had a coat of glistening white, some mahogany and chrome had been applied here and there, and the interior was done in fairly luxurious shades of blue. At six o'clock, two men came aboard with a few cases of beer. They remained aboard. Presently others came with some food, some fishing equipment. Everyone remained aboard. Some came empty-handed, and didn't leave.

Whitey, the last to arrive, tilted a satisfied eye at the descending sun.

"Nice," he remarked. He indicated clouds which were

gathering in the sky. "Going to be dark enough to satisfy everybody."

He went into the cabin. He told Colorado Jones, "Cast off. Let's get going."

"Got some drinks to mix," Colorado Jones said briefly, and moved on.

The man they called Whitey—he signed the name of Clarence Spencer to the company payroll checks, but that, everyone felt sure, probably wasn't his name—moved sleepily, but snakily, and was suddenly standing in front of Colorado Jones.

"Beg pardon?" he said.

"Huh?"

"Beg pardon; I didn't understand you—or did I?"

Colorado Jones rolled his lips inward slightly. He was big, six feet four, and built wide where giants are built wide. His fists were enormous, and scarred as if they had hit things. After his lips had rolled in, his shoulders crawled up a little and bunched, as if getting ready to jump, and he said, "I said I had some drinks to—"

The end of his speech was a report, dull and full of force. Whitey had hit him. Colorado Jones walked backward a few feet and lay down, rather awkwardly, on the cabin floor. He said, "Why, you hit me!" His speech was perfectly clear and lucid. He got up, addressed the other with his fists, a boxer's stance. There was some movement, a little fast for the eye, and Colorado Jones lay down again, the full length of him this time. The whites of his eyes showed, and all of his teeth that would show from drawn-back lips.

Tense, silent, swift, the way people come to a fight, heads appeared in the doors, faces at the windows. Not a word was said. But they were interested; each face was as intent in expression as the face of a surgeon making first cut.

"That's twice," said Colorado Jones. His voice was a trifle thick. "Let's see if it's a habit." His words stuck together.

He started to get up. Whitey kicked him in the face. The kick was not gentle, sporting, nor did it seem necessary. Whitey lifted a foot casually and stamped down on Colorado Jones' stomach. He stamped again twice more, then watched the victim roll over and, bowing his back like an ill dog, become sick.

He said, when the other was silent, sweating and gasping, "I think the drinks can wait, don't you?"

Colorado Jones didn't say anything.

"Get us under way," Whitey said. "Then clean up your mess."

Jones didn't speak and didn't move.

Whitey kicked him where his pants were tight, hard enough to roll him half over, asked, "Something wrong with your ears?"

Colorado Jones crawled toward the deck. Hoarsely, he said, "Get the engine going. Cast off the spring-lines."

In the background, Eli nudged Colton.

"What do you think?" Eli whispered. "What do you think now?"

The *Dancing Lady* was fast. Leaving the harbor, she lifted her bow four or five feet above the water and knocked up sheets of spray that sprang outward like gull wings, sometimes thirty or forty feet long. Out beyond the breakwater and the sea buoy, when she hit the outside chop, the steersman needed a safety belt to stay in his seat.

"Slow her down," Whitey said. "Set the course about ninety degrees. Hold it for twenty minutes, then head out to sea until you lose the mainland."

"Aye, aye, sir," said Ward, who was steering.

Whitey laughed. "You're no sailor, so cut out the aye, aye stuff."

"Okay."

Colorado Jones crawled into the lounge. He crawled carefully, laboriously, on hands and knees, eyes fixed on the floor as if he wished to be very certain where he was going. Without saying anything, without looking up, he crawled aft. He was going to one of the little cabins, to a bunk. He passed from view.

Ward said, "I wonder if he's ruptured?"

Whitey asked casually, "Make any difference to you?"

"Not me," Ward said hastily. He looked frightened.

"There's a time to be sassy, if it's your nature to be sassy."

"Yes, sir."

"Also a time not to be."

"Yes, sir."

"Slow her down some more. Fifteen knots is fast enough."

"Yes, sir."

Without much humor—the way he did it was an insult—Whitey patted Ward on top of the head. "Keep saying 'yes, sir' and you'll get ahead," he said. "That's one way to do it."

He went below.

Ward's lips curled fiercely. This guy, he thought, is going to be bad. The way he is starting off, nobody is going to be able to get along with him. Ward thought of some expressive profanity, which he rolled around his tongue, but under his breath. . . . Give me a chance to fix that big guy's clock, and I will, he thought. Just gimme the chance. I hope to God I get the chance.

Whitey looked into the lounge. It was not a large room, and the occupants were sitting around, not looking too happy, most of them trying to register unconcern, as if taking a Nazi submarine away from the United States Navy was a little job they tossed off every day.

"Colton," Whitey said.

"Yeah?" Colton didn't jump, but he seemed to want to.

"Get that radar outfit set up."

"Is it dark enough?"

"Get it set up."

Rage, a dark current, deepened the color of Colton's face, made his eyes shine. But he stood up and left.

Whitey moved on. He was very big in the cabin. The size of him, the power of him, his ferocity—they had not realized quite what a nasty fellow he was until they had seen him demonstrate on Colorado Jones—left an unpleasant aura in the cabin. They all felt this, but nobody spoke of it.

Colorado Jones had crawled into his bunk. Not entirely in. One leg he hadn't managed to get quite in. But he dragged a pail to the side of the bunk, and was hanging his face over it. He was as silent as if unconscious.

Whitey closed the door.

Loudly, grimly, he said, "Think you learned anything?"

The other rolled one eye up sickly at him and said, almost as loudly, "They don't do it like that in Colorado."

"Did you think this was Colorado?"

Colorado Jones didn't answer. He did, though, lift his head. He grinned. He said—with lips only; he made no sound—and grinned as he spoke, "I think we did all right."

Whitey watched his lips, seemed to read them, and said, "The idea is to get them to hating me enough to doublecross them with the other outfit if they get a chance."

He used his lips, alone, also.

Colorado Jones nodded.

Quite loudly, he said, "Okay, this isn't Colorado."

"You willing to let it go at that?" Also loudly.

"I guess so."

"If you change your mind, let me know."

"I will."

The sun left, and drew after it a monster of blackness that took the sea and held it in its warm belly. Everything was still, limpid, damp, clammy. Far in the east a little lightning licked the clouds with red tongues, but there was no sound from it, not this far away. Presently the breeze began to blow from the land to the sea; during the day it had blown the opposite way, from sea to land, because the sun had heated the land and the air had been heated in turn and expanded and risen, but now the sea was the warmer, and the air usually moves toward warm areas.

The converted PT boat ran silently over the dark sea like a cat with its claws sheathed. It was showing lights. There would be trouble with the coast guard if it was caught running without lights. But folds of cheesecloth had been masked over the lenses of green and red side-lights and white stern-light, so that they could not be seen more than a mile away.

Whitey worked with the radio loop. He took bearings, drew lines on the chart.

"Okay," he said. "We're off the submarine base about twenty miles." He glanced at his watch. "Eight-five. The sub should be coming out presently."

He moved aft. He passed orders.

"Every man have some tear gas handy. You will know how to use it?"

They knew how. If they didn't, they wouldn't have admitted it, because they had been instructed carefully on it.

"Have your masks handy. Don't wear them unless someone has to use tear gas. Whoever uses it first, give warning. Yell out, *Freddie fell overboard!* That's the signal. Everyone got it?"

They had it.

"Okay, now the poison gas. A last resort. If some of them barricades themselves in one of the compartments, we'll use it. Not otherwise.... And get this! I use the poison gas myself. Nobody else. Understand!"

They nodded. They weren't exactly sullen, but they

weren't talkative either. Most of them, probably, had been thinking about something that was not a particularly elating thing to think about. It weighted down mouth corners and minds.

"The radar should pick up something by now," Whitey said.

He went to the bow.

III

The radar, a portable job—army surplus property sold to the public—was not the most modern type, but it was adequate for the job. The sea was not too rough to give them trouble using it but, at twenty miles, and with the boat lying as low as it did, they had difficulty picking up the submarine.

The night, now intensely black, lay around them. It was impossible to discern objects the length of the boat, the sea itself was a nothingness lost in blackness. The winking scarlet of lightning in the east was coming closer, and there was now a little thunder in short disgruntled peals.

"Nice night for it," Colton said.

"Shut up!" Whitey said.

He was fiddling with the radar, watching the screen. His mood was drawn, tense, tight. His breathing, audible, was long and harsh, but regular.

He swore violently, said, "Get to your stations! What are you crowding around for!"

The others had been gathered about. They scattered, took up their stations. This had all been planned, briefed, rehearsed. Probably few military operations had been prepared with more meticulous care, greater attention to things that might go wrong. Each man was armed with what he was supposed to be armed with. Waiting, most of them reviewed what they were to do, the tasks assigned them. There was, somehow, no feeling that their leader, Whitey, was in a temper because of fear or nervousness. Whitey's temper had at no time in the past impressed anyone as belonging to a lamb.

The plan had one bad feature. They had never been aboard the submarine. Not aboard this particular sub. But they had been on another Nazi underseas boat, one that was open for public inspection in Boston harbor; to this craft each of them had made more than one trip, the visits being in the nature of the field-trips students make. They had been studying the sub and its operation.

If there was to be any hitch, it would be in the handling of the sub, probably. Actually, only four of them—there were sixteen men packed aboard the *Dancing Lady*—had had previous submarine experience. These four were navy men—two in the English Navy and two in the U. S. Navy. One of the Americans had been dishonorably discharged, and that matter had been gone into carefully by Whitey, because it was one of the threads by which Naval Intelligence—the FBI, the police, the Treasury Department and others would be on it eventually, no doubt—might get a clue. But their schooling had been lengthy, careful, and little had been overlooked.

Whitey grunted softly.

"Okay, I've got it. It's coming this way. We'll let them parallel us."

His voice, suddenly vibrant, carried to everyone. Even to Colorado Jones, who presently came crawling out on deck.

The plan was a simple and old one. They would get ahead of the submarine, kill their engines, lie wallowing in the sea until the sub was close enough, then, being careful not to use too bright a light, and not to shoot the light toward the shore, SOS for help in the International Morse code.

In about an hour and fifty minutes, they were in position.

The submarine was carrying surface riding lights. It came toward them, the sound of its surface engines a strong accompaniment. Whitey switched off the radar, which was no longer needed, and moved back to the deckhouse, leaned inside, and addressed the man riding the radio receiver.

"They doing anything on their frequency?" he demanded.

"Just finished a position report."

"They off the air?"

"Yes."

"Keep your ears glued to their frequency. It'll be our necks if they get an alarm out."

"Right."

When the submarine was a hundred yards distant, Whitey used the light. He sent only the three letters, SOS. Three shorts, three longs, three shorts. Then he lifted his voice. "Ahoy-y-y-y, the submarine!" he yelled.

Such was the proximity of the underseas boat that they could hear the startled movement of the lookout. His, "Somebody hailing, sir!" came to them as if he were speaking in the darkness beside their boat. His voice was definitely Germanic, although he spoke English.

"Ahoy-y-y-y, the submarine!" Whitey shouted. "Can you give us some help. We need help!"

Surprise, slight excitement, swept the submarine; they could hear it making progress, first a petty officer calling out for the searchlight, someone else shouting from below to know what it was, then the sound of the cover being taken off the searchlight. At last, blinding, sudden, the searchlight beam impaled them.

"What's the trouble?" a good Yankee voice demanded.

"We need help."

"I asked you what the trouble was."

"We got a sick man, and not enough gas to get him to shore."

"Not enough fuel to reach port, you say?"

"That's right."

"We'll radio somebody to come out and get you."

"No, no, wait a minute! The guy is pretty sick. Haven't you got somebody aboard who can look at him?"

"No doctor on board."

"What's the matter with your pharmacist's mate, or somebody? You surely got somebody who knows first aid. This is important. The guy may die. In fact, we're afraid he is going to die."

"What ails him?"

"He got cut." Whitey cleared his throat, added, "We're coming alongside. We want some of you to look at this fellow." He sounded anxious to the point of terror.

The submarine fell for it, which was no surprise to anyone on the *Dancing Lady*, because the whole thing had been figured out with infinite care, the words to be shouted at the underseas boat being weighed carefully, and the nature of the various reasons they could have used as an excuse—out of fuel, sick, lost, on fire, somebody overtaking the U-boat with a naval officer—measured for convincingness. It was decided that low on fuel and a sick passenger was the surest combination which would let them get alongside the submarine, which was what they wanted.

"We're coming alongside," Whitey shouted.

The man in the sub conning tower cursed, and an officer scrambled up beside him; he also cursed, then yelled, "Take it easy! Don't ram us!"

In the *Dancing Lady's* deckhouse, the man riding the radio said, "They ain't transmitted nothing yet."

"Stay on it if they do," Whitey said. "The minute their frequency is put in use—if you think they're using it, and you can sure tell, this close—use that gadget to blanket them out."

"Okay."

The Naval officer was cursing again, yelling at some sailors to fend off the fool yachtsmen. He called them damned fools. He did some of the yelling in German which he had evidently learned from one of those courses where you have a copy book and a phonograph record. Some of it the Nazi crew understood, but the rest of it confused them.

"Keep your pants on!" Whitey yelled at him. "I can bring this boat alongside an egg without cracking it!"

He proceeded to demonstrate that he could. The sea was not very rough, and the submarine, with a hull lying very deep in the water, did not make as much leeway from wind blowing against it; the *Dancing Lady*, brought up on the leeward side, held there with motors barely turning, was in perfect position.

Men began jumping from the yacht to the submarine. Most of them had ropes in their hands as an excuse for getting on the submarine. They tied the ends of the ropes to the first thing that came handy, and then began to distribute themselves over the sub.

In a few seconds, the men were well distributed over the sub deck.

They started dropping down the hatches into the innards of the U-boat.

"Here, here, you can't do that!" the officer yelled. "This is Navy property!"

Whitey shoved a large revolver under the officer's nose and demanded, "You know what this is?"

The man said, "Good God!" hoarsely. Then he added, "Why you—" He was moving when he started to say this, so

Whitey hit him, using his left fist. The officer fell down rather heavily.

Whitey leaned over the edge of the conning tower to watch proceedings. Presently, when a square Nazi head popped up the conning tower hatch, he rapped the top of it with the revolver, grabbed the victim by the blouse front, hauled him out and spread him beside the officer. He resumed his survey of proceedings.

Things were going well.

The instructions had been—no shooting. No shooting at all. Threats, yes, and rapping of heads; then, if necessary, the tear gas. But no shooting. And, marvelously, it seemed to be coming off that way.

Eli appeared.

"We got 'em," he said.

"All of them?"

"Sure. It was a roll-over. Nobody was armed. The Nazis certainly weren't. And neither were the Navy boys, although we thought some of them might be and all of them had guns locked in their quarters or sea chests."

"Get them on deck."

"Okay."

"Without life-preservers."

Eli hesitated. "Right," he said. He sounded as if he had just shuddered.

"Wait! First, close the forward hatches. Better still, close all the hatches but the one in the conning tower."

Eli went away, after he had made some kind of a sound that denoted horror.

Whitey climbed down out of the conning tower. He sauntered forward to the point where the *Dancing Lady* lay, not nuzzling the sub now, but standing back a few yards. He called, "Colorado."

Harshly, tensely, Colorado Jones said, "Yeah?"

"Everybody off?"

"That's right."

"We made it."

"We shoulda, the way it was planned and practiced."

"You're sure nobody but you is on there?"

"I'm alone."

"Able to take her into port and tie her up?"

"I think so."

"Do that. Get going right now. Don't stick around."

"Right."

The *Dancing Lady* moved backward slowly about a hundred feet, became motionless for a few seconds, then lifted her bow slightly and turned and was lost in the darkness.

Colton had been standing near Whitey. Colton spat. He said, "You think you can trust that guy?"

"Maybe. Maybe not. But what has he got to gain by turning us in now? He's alone. The story he would have to tell is pretty cockeyed—and what would it get him? A long term in a federal jail. Maybe a rope around his neck, or the equivalent."

Colton nodded. He was convinced. "I guess you're right," he said.

The storm, for it was a storm, was coming out of the east fast. Black as the sky overhead, it was blacker in the east, and they could see, illuminated by the long crashing flashes of lightning, the nasty-looking roll-cloud that preceded the storm. A safe guess would be that it would be upon them in half an hour.

Ward, who looked and sounded like a sleepy southerner, spoke astonishingly fluent German. He used it to herd the Nazis forward. *"Wir mussen eilen!"* he shouted at them.

The Nazis went readily enough. They were confused. They didn't understand what was happening, and probably figured they had nothing to lose, for they were prisoners anyway. The U. S. Navy was keeping them in America, forcing them to disgorge what they knew about their submarine, and they had a normal amount of resentment over this over and above the fact that they were still, most of them, Nazis at heart, hence sullen about the whole thing. The Navy men were less docile.

The sub captain—he was Lieutenant Commander Charles Wake, U. S. N., a tall, hard-fisted, hard-jawed, blue-eyed man originally from Montana—was quite fierce about it. He had been thrown out of gear by the abruptness of the thing, but now he'd time to think, and he was getting ugly.

Suddenly he decided to balk.

"I'm damned if I'll go through with this!" he snarled.

Whitey scowled at him, then turned his head to ask one of the pirates, "Everybody up from below?"

"Four or five to come. All Krauts."

Whitey told the sub skipper, "Shut up!" He used a level, conversational tone. "Shut up. One more word out of you and I'll stop you permanently."

"You dirty—"

Whitey shot the skipper once. Commander Wake raised on tiptoes, threw both arms outward as if he were attempting one stroke of the breast-stroke, and went down. He struggled convulsively after he fell, and in a moment, due to the fact that he had fallen partly across the rail, floundered over and hit the slick wet hull and slid down into the sea. He drifted away. For a few minutes—several of the pirates were holding flashlights—they could see his flailing arms and legs, occasionally his face, but presently the darkness and the sea swallowed him and there was only the splashing sounds he made, these growing weaker and fewer.

There was no more resistance, no more argument.

Whitey addressed the original crew of the submarine. His voice, deep, controlled, but also harsh, was understandable to every man of the crew, all of whom were now crowded forward on the deck. He said, "You men will stay where you are. If one of you moves, he will be shot." He turned to his own men, and with almost the same tone and delivery, said, "Let's see if you know enough to get her moving on the surface."

The pirates went below.

Whitey stood in the conning tower. Colton was beside him. Colton muttered, "What if they find the Commander's body with a bullet hole in it? The body might be found."

"He was going to jump us. His men would have followed him. Somebody would have been hurt."

Colton said no more.

Shortly the submarine began moving. It did not travel fast, but everything seemed to be functioning normally, and one of the hi-jackers, calling up from below, reported, "We're not going to have any trouble with her."

Whitey said, "Get below, Mr. Colton." When Colton had descended to the control room used when the submarine was running submerged, Whitey also climbed down. He personally saw to it that the hatch was secured and fastened. His face was without expression.

"Take her under," he said.

Colton drew himself up sharply, became rigid with sick

disbelief. He said, "For God's sake!" A moment later he licked his lips, his tongue making a quick serpentine swipe like the tongue of a serpent. Much the same feeling went through some of the others; no one was untouched by emotion, for the command was charged with evil. It meant, in effect, the death of everyone who had been aboard the submarine, Nazi and U. S. sailor alike.

The shore was fully thirty miles away, with an offshore wind and an offshore set to the tide and currents, so that it was somewhat too supernatural a feat to expect anyone to swim to shore. Too, the storm was brewing, would break with whistling ferocity before long, would fill the air with driving rain and lash the sea into surface madness. The storm was an asset they had not reckoned on. It was, in effect, a gift conveyed on them by the forces of evil.

Harsh, fierce, Whitey snarled, "Take her under! What are you waiting on!"

Presently the sub dived.

They had not expected to be able to hear the men on deck scream as the green sea came up and poured over the steel hull and swallowed the sub—but they did. They heard the screams. They were not very loud. They were like kittens mewing, terrified kittens in a sack that had been dropped into a creek. The mewings did not last long, for the sub sank as the sack would have sunk.

"Keep your heads on your shoulders!" Whitey said. "This is the first dive. Don't muff it!"

The sub went down, and the meters read twenty, thirty, then forty feet. Whitey said, "Deep enough." The vessel leveled out at that depth. It planed along, driven by the electric motors, and the strangeness of the new medium held them, gripped them, held their minds motionless and helpless to be stabbed anew by thoughts of the men left behind in the sea to die.

Whitey sensed this. He showed no concern. He went over and fiddled with an intercommunicator gadget, a device by which, if he spoke into a microphone at the command position, his voice would be carried throughout the submarine. He got the thing working, blew into it to test it, and, satisfied, said sharply, "Your attention, brothers. In fifteen minutes, we will surface, and run on the surface until one hour before daylight. The day run will be made submerged.

The following night, practice maneuvers will begin, and will continue for one week as scheduled.... May I congratulate you, gentlemen? You are a fine, bloody bunch of cut-throats, and Henry Morgan and Captain Kidd would love you. Goodnight."

The loudspeakers stopped hissing, died an abrupt unreasoning death, but probably there was not an eye on board that did not continue to stare at the mechanical gadgets with hypnotized, and emotionally tortured, intensity. They were hardened men; they had also the advantage of knowing before hand what was to happen, since it had been planned, discussed, rehearsed, for days; but there had been something in the speech—deliberate, unmoved, cold—that had stunned them. Whitey's voice and words had been completely natural, hence entirely abnormal. The man should have had emotion. Elation or fear or horror. There certainly should have been horror, but there had been none, and it had been sickening, because this man was their leader, and nobody likes to follow an abnormal leader, not even an abnormal genius, nor an abnormally courageous man, for abnormality of any kind is too close to insanity to be comfortable.

There were, too, the men in the sea, the men swept off the deck when the submarine submerged, the men now far behind in the darkness and—for the storm would be here by now—the suffocating welter of water and wind that was a squall at sea. These men would be dying. They were quite possibly dying now. A sigh, the cast-off effusion of this death, seemed to sweep the neat steel walls and bulkheads and pipes and conduits, to linger and cling, to work its way into their minds and settle there, a clammy bat-like indescribable monster of a thing that could not be dislodged.

The submarine, moving forty feet below the surface, went its way as steadily as a coffin.

IV

Miss Brenda Linahan, on the staff of *Solar, The News Weekly,* was one of those young women who over-awe men. The over-awing was the final effect; she produced other effects first, because she was not difficult to gaze upon, and she always dressed well, or better, or—as Pete Idle, article editor of *Solar*, often said—just a little too sexy. Anyway, the first effects she produced were wolf-stirring. But getting to know her better was like listening and being intrigued by a wonderful symphonic radio program, then going backstage during rehearsals and suddenly discovering what an alarming, and unromantic, amount of cussing and sweating and confusion and downright genius went into the construction of the show. Brenda was something like that. She would never fit in any guy's kitchen, unless it was a small kitchen equipped with nothing much but a cocktail shaker.

Brenda had been born in Texas, and Texas was button-busting proud of her in spite of all that Texas already had, or claimed it had, to be proud about. She had been a remarkably stupid little girl, people had thought, which only meant that she hadn't given a tap about doing the things little girls do. They seemed silly to Brenda, who had just simply been born too matured. This detached attitude lasted until college, and college proved barely adult enough to get her interest. People couldn't understand how she made the record she did, nor why she shot like a skyrocket through the succession of newspaper, magazine, and photo-magazine jobs she proceeded to hold and discard. It was no mystery to her co-workers. She was just too out and out good to be held by one firm very long. She was now with *Solar*, which was tops.

"Hello, Brenda," said Article Editor Pete Idle one morning in early, very early, April. "Sit down. Have a cigarette. I'll get O. J."

The morning was bright, but cold, and Brenda had sought to tone it down and defeat it with a brown tweed outfit. She was quite fetching. But fetching or not, she inspired no amour in Pete Idle, who was always alarmed by Brenda.

O. J. was the publisher. He was Mr. Big. He was the alpha and the omega, and Brenda was surprised, because O. J. was what is known as a business office man, and never, if it could be helped, confused himself by trying to deal personally with his writing, photographic or reportorial geniuses. Brenda lit a cigarette.

"Now what?" she wondered.

O. J., a tall man with an aristocratic silver streak in his hair and a roving eye for a pretty leg, looked at Brenda with the kind of approval you lick your lips over, then, almost instantly, with fully equal disapproval. "What," he said darkly to Pete Idle, "are you trying to pull on me?"

"Me?" Pete was astonished.

"Listen, Pete," said O. J.. "This is no job to try to run your girl friends in on."

"She's not my girl friend!" Pete disclaimed.

"Why, darling, that's treason," Brenda said lightly.

Pete pointed his finger at O. J. "Look, you don't know who this girl is. I guess you only know her name, which is Brenda Linahan. I guess you had better make some inquiries about her."

O. J. grinned. "Later. Later. Is she good?"

"She's terrific."

"She looks it," said O. J., his grin on Brenda.

"Her looks are very fooling, boss."

"I like to be fooled," said O. J. "Miss Linahan, how about dinner with me tonight to discuss business and things."

"No, thanks," Brenda replied. She turned to Pete and added, "I don't know what this is, but I don't like it, I think."

"You will."

"Like it?"

"Sure."

"Make with words," Brenda invited, "and we'll see."

O. J. had one eye half-closed, probably wondering how he should react to a lady employee refusing him a date rather casually and as though she meant it. Somewhat disturbed, he said, "I think we're taking this too lightly. It isn't a small, frothy matter. Quite the contrary. It is a terrific matter."

"How can I take it seriously, when I don't know what it is?" Brenda asked. "Or do you simply mean that there is a law around here that says to take O. J. seriously?"

Pete winced.

"Cut it out," he said hastily, making soothing gestures. "Listen to me a minute, and I'll sober you up."

"Sober away."

Pete stared at Brenda impressively.

"Did you know that, in the last six months, four American ships have disappeared on the high seas, and seven have been boarded and looted by pirates?" he asked.

Brenda was drawing on a cigarette at the moment, and astonishment put smoke up her nostrils, so that she sneezed.

"Are you kidding?" she asked, brushing at ashes.

"Nary a kid."

Brenda's eyes narrowed. "There have been some newspaper items about ships lost. I didn't pay particular attention to them. After years of reading, during the war, of almost daily sinkings of ships, I suppose it becomes something you don't notice specially."

"That's why it hasn't created a rumpus."

"Disappearances, you said, didn't you?"

"Yes."

"A disappearance is different from a sinking. Or is it? Warships were usually announced as unreported and presumed lost, so one might become inured to that."

"Wreckage was found in three instances."

"Oh."

"The fourth just vanished—but it probably went down, too."

Brenda frowned at him. "You said seven have been boarded and looted by pirates?"

"Seven."

"Big ones?"

"Fairly. Two were."

"Now wait a minute," Brenda said. "Pirates take seven ships and not a word appears in the newspapers about it. That's not reasonable. What kind of bug dust are you giving me?"

"It's true."

"It can't be true."

"Oh, yes it can," Pete said. "Because the United States government, plus the other Allied governments, are keeping a blanket on it."

Brenda was skeptical. "They can't blanket something like that."

"They have."

"Well, I guess they could," Brenda admitted. "They kept some pretty big things quiet during the war, like atomic bombs and things." She examined Pete thoughtfully, then somewhat suspiciously. "What do you think you're going to talk me into?" she demanded.

"You," Pete said, "are going to find those pirates."

Brenda leaned back, placed her purse neatly on her knees, knocked ash from her cigarette onto Pete's desk, something she knew he didn't like anyone to do, then she said, "A very funny joke. Now, what have you really got on your mind?"

"I'm not kidding."

"Then God help *Solar, The News Weekly,* because its article editor has gone nuts. You really mean I'm to turn pirate catcher?"

"Pirate finder, I said."

"Finder, catcher, what's the difference?" Brenda still didn't quite believe the whole thing. Although the world had been full of fantastic, cockeyed stories the last few years, this one was a little bit fuzzy, even for 1946. She said thoughtfully, "Four ships have disappeared or sunk, and five have been hi-jacked. Who did the hi-jacking?"

"A submarine."

"You mean men on a submarine, don't you? It strikes me that—"

O. J. cleared his throat, doing this so that it said: Hold on, young lady, this is a serious matter. He said it aloud: "Hold on, young lady, this is serious."

"That's just what I started to say," Brenda assured him. "Such a serious matter should be presented more completely, and so that I can understand it."

"What don't you understand?" Pete demanded.

Brenda numbered off by holding one finger up. "First, the pirates are on a submarine?"

"Yes."

"Two, how do they know it isn't a Nazi or Jap submarine and crew which has decided not to give up the war?"

"The pirates were Americans."

"How could anybody be sure of that? Did they have passports, or something?"

"By their talk—"

"I've heard Nazis talk English that you would swear was Brooklyn American," Brenda interrupted. "Is there any more proof than that?"

"The U. S. Navy seems to think they're American renegades."

"What else does the U. S. Navy think?"

"They haven't said," Pete replied grimly. "As a matter of fact, they haven't said anything. All I know is what drifted out of the Navy Department through—well—through certain sources I have."

Brenda was intent now. She knew about Pete's sources in

the Navy—he had them in the Army, and in a lot of other unexpected places, too; it had even been rumored that Pete had a pipeline direct to a top Nazi during the war—all of which meant that Pete's information was probably correct. He thought it was, anyway. Otherwise he wouldn't have O. J. in on the thing. O. J. was known as a man who canned his employees when they made a fool out of *Solar, The News Weekly*. If Pete said there were pirates, there must be pirates. Brenda's eyes brightened. Her face lighted with interest. She shuddered.

"This is hotter than a frog in a frying-pan—if true," she said.

O. J. hit his knee a lick with his fist. "Exactly! That's what I told Pete. It's just what *Solar* needs in the way of a news exclusive." He caught himself up, and added hastily, "Not that we don't lead the field as it is."

Brenda was tempted to mention that she knew as well as anybody that *Solar, The News Weekly* was taking a beating now that the war was over and hot spot news photo coverage wasn't as important as it had been, and particularly since *Solar* had been a little slow to convert its coverage to interesting peacetime features.

"You can," she said, "count on me."

Pete grinned happily. "I knew we could depend on you. The other mags, those goats we've got for competition, will stick reporters on it when they get wind of it. Incidentally, I don't think they've got it yet. I think we've got an exclusive. *Solar*, with a girl on the story, getting in first—story, pictures of the pirates—will be a world-beater. You'll be famous, Brenda. You can write your own ticket. Hollywood, anything. We'll raise your salary."

"We'll talk about money later," O. J. said cautiously. "The point Pete is making is this, Brenda: you have to deliver. You have to show up the men."

Brenda said suspiciously, "This must be pretty tough, the way you're selling it to me."

"I wouldn't kid you—it might be," Pete admitted.

"You know damned well it will be," Brenda said. "Now, where do I start?"

"There's one other angle," Pete said. "It won't help you, maybe, but you should know about it. Two weeks ago, the Navy lost a submarine. It disappeared. It was a Nazi sub, and it was enroute from New London to the Canal and around to

the Pacific to the submarine facility at San Diego. Most of the
Nazi crew was aboard, and some Navy officers, and they were
going to have the Nazis cough up some more secrets of their
sub warfare. The whole lot—sub, Nazis, Navy boys—vanished.
Maybe the pirates got them, and maybe they didn't. Nobody
seems to know, and they're keeping it quiet."

"Why keep it quiet?" Brenda was puzzled.

"God knows. Maybe because the Navy isn't happy unless
it's keeping a secret."

O. J. said grimly, "I'm going to do an editorial on this
business of secrecy when the time is ripe. I'll burn their
pants off."

Brenda pondered.

"Where do I start?" she wished to know. "Where do I
get on the trail of my first pirate?"

"That," said Pete, "is your problem."

"Oh, now, wait a minute! That's ridiculous. Surely you've
got some ideas or an idea or—well, something."

"I have an idea," Pete confessed.

Brenda eyed him. "Your ideas generally stand my hair on
end. Let's hear this one."

"Try Doc Savage."

Brenda started with surprise, then her eyes widened,
became round and bright with pleasure, and she leaped to
her feet. She told Pete, "Pete, you're a genius. You really are.
A lovely genius, and you even have a brain. That's a wonderful idea."

O. J. was not so enthusiastic. "Doc Savage will throw
you out on that lovely shell-pink ear, Miss Linahan," he
predicted.

V

Brenda Linahan began operations by going to the Colony
for lunch, because she was under the impression that she did
her best thinking while consuming excellent food. Also there
was an eminent scientist, a Mr. Ivanitz, who lunched there
regularly. Mr. Ivanitz was twenty-eight years old and one of
the brain-trust which had worked out the atomic bomb. He
was also, Brenda happened to know, acquainted with Clark
Savage, Jr., or Doc Savage, as he was known. Mr. Ivanitz was

at the Colony, and Brenda showed him her teeth, the required amount of leg, and presently had Mr. Ivanitz dying to do her a favor.

"Oh, now, wait a minute!" Mr. Ivanitz gasped, when he found out what he had gotten himself into. "That's out of the question."

"You know him, don't you?"

"Sure, but—uh—not that well."

"I understand," said Brenda, "that this Doc Savage makes a business of punishing evil-doers and righting wrongs, and I have a job that is right in his lines."

"Stop your kidding," said Mr. Ivanitz, who had a shock of dark hair and was quite handsome.

"But I've heard that's his profession."

"But it sounds silly when you put it that way, and there isn't anything silly about the man himself, I can assure you. He's a great scientist." Mr. Ivanitz became enthusiastic. "In the field of electronic research, he has done marvelous work. Why, without his contribution to the development of the mass spectograph that was used to separate uranium isotopes, the big colutron wouldn't have been—"

"Hold it, Ivy, hold it," Brenda said. "You're getting technical, and also you're getting beside the point, which is: can you introduce me?"

"Well . . ."

Brenda seized his arm. "Come on, sonny, before you change your mind."

Doc Savage's headquarters was on the eighty-sixth floor of a midtown building but, it developed, there was a certain process you went through, involving a visit to an office on the fifth floor for a screening inspection at the hands of what seemed to be a private detective agency. "If we're lucky," Mr. Ivanitz explained, "we'll find one of Doc Savage's assistants—he has five, all quite prominent in their professions—on the fifth floor. That will enhance our chances of getting in."

They were lucky. They found a very dapper gentleman, thin-waisted, with the wide mobile mouth of an orator. He was rather hatchet-faced, but otherwise modestly handsome. His clothing, however, was a sartorial experience, for everything he wore seemed to be impeccable and exactly the right thing for the time of day, the occasion.

"Brigadier General Theodore Marley Brooks," Mr. Ivanitz said, introducing the well-dressed gentleman.

Ham Brooks, thought Brenda, who had heard of him. And he has the eye, too. Mr. Brooks' eye was on her leg. She stood so as to give him a good view.

Mr. Ivanitz explained that Miss Linahan had an important matter to discuss with Doc Savage, and could a meeting be managed?... Ham took his eye off Brenda's curves long enough to state, enthusiastically, that he thought it could. He would go up right now, personally, and see. Would Mr. Ivanitz go along, while Miss Linahan waited?

They were back sooner than Brenda expected.

Their faces were longer than she had expected.

Ham Brooks apologized, "I'm sorry..."

"We was throwed out on our ears," said Mr. Ivanitz inelegantly. "That is, figuratively speaking."

"What's the matter with your influence?" Brenda asked Ham Brooks.

"It was your squire's fault." Ham indicated Mr. Ivanitz. "Everything went fine until Ivy happened to mention *Solar, The News Weekly.*"

"You would have thought," said Mr. Ivanitz, "that I had withdrawn a snake from my mouth."

"Is something wrong with *Solar, The News Weekly?*" Brenda inquired.

Ham Brooks nodded. "Doc Savage is not on good terms with the publication."

"How come?"

"Doc doesn't like publicity. They tried to give it to him. Someone up there, a Mr. Pete Idle, attempted to force the matter, making, as I understand it, some threats about adverse publicity."

Brenda nodded. "That's Pete's approach on hard-to-gets. It has earned him a couple of pokes in the nose."

"Well, you're out of luck," Ham said regretfully. "However, I think that if you and I got together this evening for a little dinner and theater, I might figure out—"

"I'm figuring way ahead of you," Brenda said. "No sale. Thanks."

Escaping from Mr. Ivanitz was a simple matter. He had, it developed, a conference uptown which he must, absolutely must, attend. He helped Brenda into a cab and gave the driver the *Solar* building address, then stood back and waved goodbye regretfully. Three blocks up the street, Brenda told the driver, "Turn around and take me back to where you picked me up. I forgot something."

There was, in the same building which housed Doc Savage's headquarters, a rather impressive restaurant-bar. This bistro was on the street level and, Brenda had chanced to notice, probably had tables from which it was possible to observe, through plate glass windows, the lobby of the building. She found her surmise correct. There was a window, and a table nearby, unoccupied.

"A Russian and his helper," she told the waiter. The waiter, surprising her, nodded knowingly and left.

Brenda had no very definite plan—except that she wasn't giving up. She hoped that, if she concentrated on it, she would think of a way of getting to Doc Savage. Once she had him collared, selling him on this pirate story might be tough, and that needed thinking about also.

Probably, Brenda thought, he'll call the birdie wagon for me. The pirate story, she suddenly realized, sounded as crazy as anything. She kept an eye on the lobby area in front of the elevators. She believed she would know some of Doc Savage's other assistants by sight. There were, as Mr. Ivanitz had said, five of them. There was Monk Mayfair, a chemist; Renny Renwick, an engineer; Long Tom Roberts, an electrical wizard; and also Johnny Littlejohn, archaeologist and geologist. And, of course, the wolfish Ham Brooks. Brenda hoped she wouldn't have to add Ham Brooks, who certainly had an eye. And, speaking of eyes—what was wrong with the long, very capable looking man sitting at the next table. He had barely glanced at her.

It took about a minute more for Brenda to realize that the man, like herself, was watching the lobby.

The waiter came with Brenda's vodka and beer chaser. She paid the check, knowing she might wish to leave in a hurry.

Finally the man stiffened, showed sharp interest. Looking beyond him, Brenda saw that Ham Brooks had left one of the elevators, was in front of the cigar stand making—she had a good idea—a tentative pass at the blonde there. Brenda shifted her gaze back to the man who was interested.

He was as interested as a bird watching a worm.

Ham crossed the lobby, departed.

The man remained where he was.

*   *   *

He was, Brenda decided, a man of more than ordinary sort, probably. At least he was more than just a long and capable looking man. He was distinctive. It was the sort of distinction that goes with accomplishing things, or rather becomes a habit when one accomplishes things. She knew the manner. There were plenty of bright young men around *Solar, The News Weekly* who had it. This man, however, was not particularly young. He was, she surmised, at least thirty-five, but he had not started going to seed. She would have pegged him as younger than thirty-five, except for the distinguished flash of white in the hair over his temples, a little more white on one side than the other.

He had merely resumed his waiting, as far as she could tell.

There is a chance, Brenda thought, that he only knew Ham Brooks by sight. The fellow might only be aware that Ham Brooks was a Doc Savage aide, and he might have enough interest, or be sufficiently impressed, by Doc Savage to create the excitement he had displayed. For the fellow had, for a moment when Ham was in view, been quite excited. Or was it tense? Brenda believed it was tense, rather than ordinary interested excitement. The idea intrigued her.

The gray-haired man sprang suddenly to his feet, did it so that it was almost a commotion. He headed for the exit.

Brenda swung her gaze over the lobby. She expected to see Doc Savage. But the only individual in sight who was at all distinctive was a very large man who was making his way toward the street. Not Doc Savage, Brenda decided immediately. Doc was a big man. But this fellow was more flabby, more rounded of shoulder, and carried himself as if he did not have much ambition.

Impulsively, Brenda decided to follow the white-haired man who had been watching the lobby, follow him far enough, at least, to ascertain whether there was anything mysterious afoot. She'd had a cute idea, or one that she hoped was cute. If she could approach Doc Savage from the angle that a mysterious man had been very interested in one of his aides, and hanging around his headquarters, it might get her a hearing.

The tall, white-haired man carried one shoulder lower than the other when he walked. He made his way to the street, paused to examine a haberdashery display in a shop, and Brenda was quite sure that he was waiting and watching for someone.

The one waited and watched for proved to be the big, shapeless man with the slouching walk. He came to the corner, glanced idly about—enough of a glance for Brenda to catch a glimpse of his eyes and be shocked—after which he moved up the street. The drop-shouldered man trailed him. Brenda fell in behind.

Presently, thinking again of the shapeless man's strange, bone-colored eyes, she shivered.

The owner of the bone-colored eyes walked north on Fifth, turned right, crossed Madison and Lexington and had spaghetti and meat balls in a noisy and popular place on Forty-second Street. He ate in a booth, alone for the first ten minutes, after which he was joined by a guest.

The guest was a nondescript brown-haired man of slightly less than middle age whose principal characteristic was that he had no outstanding characteristics. He was just a man of about forty, and, taken out of the uniform he was wearing, it would have been difficult to pick him out of a crowd of more than a half dozen.

The low-shouldered man had coffee and ravioli and consumed it at a table. He spent most of the time pretending to read a newspaper. Brenda was sure about the pretending.

The bleach-eyed man and his visitor ate mostly in silence, the visitor less than his host—for the bigger man picked up the check. The visitor was ill at ease. When he spoke it was probably in a low voice and he leaned forward. He received an envelope. It was fat. He put it carefully in his inside coat pocket, buttoned the coat.

Money, Brenda thought. He wouldn't handle anything but money that way, and with that look on his face.

The guest arose and left, and, as he passed Brenda, she was able to read the lettering over his coat pocket: Security Armored Car Service.

The bone-eyed man left presently, paid his check and bought a package of peppermints, then sauntered outdoors.

The drop-shouldered man took up the trail. So did Brenda, and the trail led to a good hotel on Madison Avenue, where the big man seemed to have a room. He went to his room, or disappeared into the elevators, and the man with the low shoulder resumed reading, this time a magazine, in the lobby.

I wish, Brenda thought, I had someone a little less conspicuous than me to do this shadowing.

She glanced at a clock, decided it might not be too late to catch Editor Pete Idle at the office, and tried it on the telephone.

"Pete, do you know anything about the Security Armored Car Service?" she asked.

"One of the big ones. They move your valuables from here to there. Why?"

"Can you find out if they have moved, or are going to move in the near future, any merchandise that would interest a pirate?"

"What the hell!?" Pete gasped. She could visualize him beginning to spout excitement like a Roman candle.

"Can you?"

"I can try."

"Do that. And make it sizzle, will you. And ship me down a private detective or somebody who can do a following job. I think I'm a little conspicuous to get away with it forever myself."

"I'll say you're conspicuous. . . . Say, what is this, anyway? Have you turned up anything?"

"I wouldn't kid you, I'm just fishing," Brenda said soothingly. "Call me back at"—she glanced at the number on the telephone—"Vanderbilt 0-7821. If I don't answer, don't page me. It's a hotel lobby pay booth. I don't want attention called to me. And don't forget the nice, mouse-like, unobtrusive detective."

"Listen, give me the details of what you've—"

"And be laughed at?" Brenda said. "Nothing doing."

She purchased a fashion magazine at the newsstand and began reading in a chair near the phone booth.

Sixteen minutes later, the phone rang, but it was a male voice which inquired for Daisy, then tried to tell Brenda that she might do instead of Daisy Still. "Call Newhouse 9-0031, and ask for Miss Still," Brenda suggested. Newhouse 9-0031 was the number of the city morgue. A couple of minutes afterward, the phone rang again, and this time it was Pete, who sounded as if he had just lunched on lighted firecrackers.

"For God's sake, don't ball up whatever you've got!" he

blurted. "Because I think you've got something hot. How did you do it, anyway? Did Doc Savage set you on to it? Did he? I never thought you'd see the guy."

"What have you found out?"

"Listen, why don't you—"

"Come on, come on, don't waste my time."

"The Security Armored Car Service this morning transferred some seven odd million dollars in gold bullion from the Federal Reserve vaults to the steamship *Poinsettia,* which sails for Cherbourg at midnight tonight. The heavy stuff is going to the French national banking system as part of a deal to stabilize the franc."

"How much?"

"Seven odd million."

"There's nothing odd about seven million of Uncle's little men. The ship is the *Poinsettia?*"

"*Poinsettia* is right."

"And it sails when?"

"Midnight."

"That's what I thought you said. Okay, Pete. You know where my apartment is. Dash over there and find my passport in the bookcase, upper left hand corner, and get it in the hands of whoever's hands it has to be in so I can sail on the *Poinsettia.* Incidentally, buy me a ticket on the ship, and deposit some expense money with the ship's purser. Better make it quite a sum."

"Listen, you want—I mean, I want more information!" Pete was beginning to stutter.

"You've got most of it. I simply picked up a suspicious fellow at Doc Savage's building and followed him and he met a driver for Security and some money changed hands. Oh yes, I mixed that up a little—I'm following another suspicious fellow who is following the first suspicious fellow."

"Untangle that," Pete requested.

"Untangle it yourself. What did you mean, suggesting I go see Doc Savage when you knew *Solar, The News Weekly,* and particularly a guy named Pete Idle, was on his dark list?"

"I couldn't think of anything better. I knew that if I hit a spark to get you started, something would develop. What did Doc Savage tell you?"

"Nothing."

"Why not? Isn't he interested in this pirate thing? It's

big enough and right up his alley. What ails the guy? Why
didn't he—"

"He threw me out. I didn't see him."

"Is Doc Savage involved in this affair?"

"How do I know! What about the detective?"

"I hope he is!" Pete said excitedly. "My God, I've always
wanted a firsthand story of one of his cases in Solar! I've tried
half a dozen times, and every time I get kicked in the snoot."

"What about an unnoticeable detective?"

"Oh, hell, I haven't had time."

"Well, get him down here," Brenda said sharply. "And
get my passport to the ship."

"How'll I get in your apartment? What about a key?"

"Kick down the door," Brenda said, and hung up. She
was exasperated because Pete hadn't sent someone to do the
shadowing. The neglect was likely to prove serious.

Presently she knew it was serious, because Low-shoulder
got up and sauntered out of the hotel, Bone-eye ahead of
him, and there was nothing for Brenda to do but take up the
tail end of the procession.

All of them rode three taxicabs downtown four blocks
then across town to the North River piers, the journey
ending at a pier around which swarmed the motor and foot
traffic incidental to a sailing.

The honey which was drawing this bee-like activity was a
passenger liner, modest in size as passenger liners went, but
new and crisp looking. Brenda, as soon as she lost trace of
both her quarry—this happened almost at once in the confusion—
moved over to get a look at the name of the craft. *Poinsettia*.
She was not surprised.

VI

The Gulf Stream, that great current that slides warmly
across the Atlantic, has its beginning in the Gulf of Mexico,
where it is born under the continuing tropical sun that nurses
it and raises its temperature until it is many degrees warmer
than almost any other sea. Then the forces, the mysterious
astral and terrestrial forces that make tides, hurl it out
through the narrow channel between Florida and the Baha-
mas, a channel about a mile deep and only fifty miles wide,

where it moves with terrific speed for an ocean current, faster than a man would care to run for any great distance.

Almost blood-warm, charged with force, power, the current swings north and for innumerable leagues its line of demarcation with the rest of the Atlantic is as sharply drawn as a pencil mark, and its vitality is not spent until it reaches the coasts of England, Scotland, Norway. They say that without the Gulf Stream, England would be as grim in climate as Labrador. All of which was contained in a lengthy speech which Brenda Linahan made to Pete Idle. Brenda was goading Pete, a rather agreeable pastime and quite a change for Pete.

"Shaddup!" Pete said morosely. "I don't give a damn about ocean currents and the climate of England. I also know when I'm being ridden."

Brenda explained that she was just pointing out the advantages of an ocean voyage, and the reason for the enjoyable weather they were having.

"Lay off," Pete requested.

They were occupying steamer chairs on the boat deck of the *Poinsettia*, new deck chairs, and the steamer rugs which were draped over their knees were also new; the ship had been used as a troop transport during the war, and since refurbished with new post-war equipment.

"You needed a rest, anyway," Brenda said.

"I know of nothing I needed less. I don't like boats. I get seasick. I don't like my cabin. I'm in a stall in the steerage with three other guys and all three are poker sharks. They play all night." He scowled darkly, added, "I bet I'd get a private cabin if they knew who I was."

Alarmed, Brenda warned, "Don't you start showing off! If news got out that you were aboard, it'd create a commotion."

Pete snorted. "I'm not that important."

"Who said you were important? All I mean is that our competition would think you were on the trail of a big story and stir up a fuss trying to find out what it was."

Pete thought this was probable. "The laugh would be on them. There isn't any story."

"We're not sure."

"I am! Three days, we've been at sea, and nothing has happened."

"Bone-eye and Droopy-shoulder are aboard."

"Means nothing, I've decided." Pete closed his eyes. "Go away. You irritate me. Everything irritates me."

Brenda laughed. "Well, you had to be chivalrous and dash aboard."

Pete lifted both hands in a gesture of holy horror and denied this. "God, don't accuse me of chivalry! Of drunkenness, yes. Of thievery, arson, libel, plagiarism, okay. Chivalry, no!" He closed his eyes again. "Let me sleep. I think the whole pirate scare was a damned lie somebody fed me, and I'm going to skin somebody alive for it. Go away. Goodbye."

"I think you were born a stinker," Brenda assured him, and went to her cabin to put on her bathing suit, then to the pool to see whether she was good enough bait to get some gullible guy to feed her free drinks.

Actually she was mighty glad good old Pete Idle was aboard, and she appreciated the sterling feelings of concern which had led him to drop everything at the office and sail with her. It was not, she knew, that Pete just wanted to be in on a big story. Pete, she suspected, didn't really believe this stuff about pirates. But he had been afraid he could be wrong, and he had sailed with her because he didn't have the kind of conscience that would let her face danger alone. It was nice of him. Also, O. J. would raise hell, the office would gossip, and Pete's girl friend would probably crown him.

The pool was not crowded. The weather outside was too nice, for the *Poinsettia* was ploughing lazily through the marvelous aquamarine blue of the Gulf Stream on an almost motionless sea.

"Hy'ah, lovely," a voice said.

Brenda jumped violently, looked around, and gave an even bigger jump. It was the man she had come to refer to as Drop-shoulder. He was grinning at her.

"Nice pool," he said. "And you make it very ornamental."

"Uh—thanks," Brenda said, feeling that her brain had stopped functioning for a moment. Did the fellow suspect her? Or was he just trying to make a pick-up.

"I was watching your diving form," the man said. "It was nice. Would it make you mad if I introduced myself?"

"Me, mad? Should it?" Brenda was trying not to be confused.

"I'm Davey Govern, and I hope not," the man said

amiably. "My next move is to offer to buy you a drink. But should I make it now, or wait a while?"

"That," said Brenda, "is exactly why I put on this next-to-nothing bathing suit."

Govern laughed. He beckoned a waiter.

Brenda decided suddenly that she didn't like him, and more than that, she disliked him terrifically. The dislike, she concluded, was spark-plugged by fear. She tried to analyze the feeling in relation to the man's appearance.

He seemed, at close range, a younger man than she had thought. He was made of sinews and hard flesh and a skin that looked as if it should have been a pouch for bullets. His gray hair fooled me, she thought. He's only about thirty, but they've been a very busy thirty years. She could not quite put her finger on the reason for her fear, which she realized was going to grow into terror.

"Are you going to keep your name a secret?" he inquired.

"Name?" She felt jittery, as if she was unhooked for the moment.

"Something to call you by, at least."

"Oh! Brenda. Brenda Linahan." She decided to talk fast and get loosened up. "I'm a writer, if you could call a trained seal on the staff of *Solar, The News Weekly* a writer. I'm enroute to"—she tried to think where she could be enroute to—"Switzerland. I'm going to do a story about the resurgence of the tourist trade in Switzerland." She thought this sounded rather plausible in view of how scared she felt.

Mr. Govern grinned. "That must explain the feeling I had that I'd seen you somewhere." His teeth were short, as if he'd been chewing on a file. "I did have a familiar feeling about you, you know."

"Oh, did you?"

"I must have seen your picture somewhere. I imagine it has appeared in the magazine, hasn't it?"

"Oh, yes," Brenda said, and realized she had a terrified desire to convince this fellow that she was nothing whatever except a staff writer headed for Switzerland. She wanted him to believe this. She felt, without knowing why she felt it so strongly, that it was worth her life to make him believe this.

"What'll you have?" The waiter was at their side.

"A Russian and his helper," Brenda said, then could have bitten the end off her tongue, for she remembered that was what she'd been drinking in the New York bistro where she had first seen him.

"Yes, I imagine a picture would explain why I seem to recall you," said Mr. Govern.

Pete Idle was alarmed when he cornered Brenda in the lounge later. "I saw you talking to that yegg. You scared the dickens out of me!"

"I scared myself." Brenda shivered. "I'm still weak in the knees. I don't why, either. I never met anybody before who made me think so much about a trunkful of rattlesnakes."

"What did you find out about him? Anything?"

Brenda permitted herself a satisfying shudder before she replied.

"I listened to his smoke screen, at least. He says his name is Mr. Davey Govern, and he is on his way to France to—he asked me not to laugh at this—learn to cook the way the French do. I didn't laugh. In fact, I could have screamed my head off. I tell you, that fellow—"

"Think he's a pirate?"

"If he isn't, Blackbeard certainly missed a bet."

"Think he suspects you?"

"Oh God, I wish I knew!" Brenda said fervently. "There's something about him that's horrible, that turns my blood cold, that—"

"Ps-s-s-s-t!" hissed Pete. "Speak of the devil..."

Mr. Govern was approaching them. He was neat in a hard razor-like fashion in evening clothes, and he smiled at Brenda, said, "I was wondering if you'd have dinner with me, Miss Linahan."

Save me, somebody, Brenda thought.

She said, "Oh, I'm awfully sorry. I have an engagement with Mr. Idle here."

"You're both invited," the man said, his face registering no visible emotion whatever.

"Nothing doing," Pete said abruptly. "I mean—well—nothing doing."

Mr. Govern said coldly, "Don't blame you, buddy."

He went away.

Pete said nothing in an impressed way for a little while after Mr. Govern had gone, then he muttered, "That clattering sound you hear is my knees knocking together." Brenda was surprised at how hoarsely impressed he sounded.

"What's the matter?"

"He scared me, too," Pete said. "Look, you lay off that guy. You've been trailing him around shipboard to see what he does, haven't you? Well, cut that out."

"But someone should—"

"I'll do it. I'll follow him." Pete considered this offer uneasily, added, "I wish to God I'd dug up that detective and we had him aboard. But I sent him down to that hotel in New York and he's probably waiting there yet. Say, if I'm going to follow him, is there anything in particular I should know? Has he got any little habits, and does he carry a gun?"

"I visualize guns sticking on him like scales on a fish, but I haven't seen any," Brenda said. "All he does is occasionally follow the bone-eyed man around the ship. I think, in fact, that he keeps track of the bone-eyed man most of the time. You'll notice the fellow is now in the dining room."

Pete shuddered. "I wish you'd quit calling him bone-eyed!"

"Why?"

"It's too—uh—prophetic."

It was agreed that Brenda was to switch her surveillance to the big man with the strange, pale eyes, and she was mighty glad to do it. She felt sorry for Pete, in case anything went wrong, because she suspected this guy Govern would make a grease spot of Pete. During dinner, though, she gave her concern for Pete an anesthetic by recalling several occasions when he had made her as mad as a hornet around the office. Finally she worked herself up to the point where she felt Pete would deserve most of whatever he got. It is never very hard to get mad at the boss.

The big man with the bone-colored eyes—he was down on the ship register as Mr. Case, which meant nothing except that he must have a passport with that name and his picture on it—ate a leisurely meal. Then he went out and strolled the deck, rather purposefully it seemed to Brenda, for he ended up in a deck chair near the bow on the upper deck.

This part of the ship was a lonely spot, being too windy for any but the hardy passengers. The only sound of any consequence was the snarl of code and an occasional clatter of static from the radio shack which was nearby. A generator was also singing inside the radio shack. But the spot where the big man's chair was, Brenda noticed, gave a view of the sea ahead. She recalled that he had used this chair once or twice before. What was he doing? Settling down to watch the sea ahead?

Brenda decided to remain where she was, in the shadowy niche between a ventilator and a lifeboat, and watch.

Presently the big man put on a rather peculiar looking pair of goggles. She thought these were just goggles, until an operator stepped out of the radio shack letting a sweep of light from the door fall across the big man, and she discovered— before he hastily lowered the goggles—that they weren't ordinary.

Oh damn! Brenda thought.

She happened to know what kind of goggles they were because she had once done a story for Solar about them—not those particular goggles, but similar ones. They were ingenius filters which permitted the user to see black-light signals which, without the gadget, were quite invisible to the unaided eye.

I'd better get Pete, she thought.

But she didn't go for Pete, because the night suddenly got full of events.

First, the big bone-eyed man arose with speed and purpose, put the goggles in his coat pocket, walked straight to the radio room and went inside. In a moment, there was a sound which Brenda knew absolutely was someone being hit with a fist, and hit hard.

A voice said, "Here! What's the big—" The voice must belong to one of the radio operators. It ended rather ominously, in a series of struggle sounds that were not very loud.

Brenda slipped off her footgear so that she wouldn't make any noise, and moved hastily to a point from which she had a view through the door into the radio shack.

The big bone-eyed man was systematically choking one radioman and the other one lay on the floor, motionless.

The radio shack, which contained all of the transmitting equipment for the *Poinsettia*, was not a large room, but it was crowded with shining black instrument panels in which indicator lights glowed, and the usual complicated looking array of stuff that one saw in radio shacks.

The bone-eyed man withdrew his right hand from the radio operator's throat, made a fist of it, and slammed the man on the jaw. He laid the unconscious radioman on the floor.

He began systematically smashing the transmitting equipment. He seemed to know what he was doing, for he was careful to pull a number of switches before he reached into the apparatus and tore out wires, or used a paperweight to batter radiotronic tubes into fragments.

The bridge, Brenda thought! I'd better tell the Captain!

But it would be necessary to pass the radio shack and climb a companionway to reach the bridge, and she was afraid she would be observed. Go back. That seemed the only thing to do. She whirled, ran swiftly, but only for about forty feet, whereupon a figure stopped her. She gasped, "Mister, a man is in the radio shack— Oh! Oh!"

"What did you say?" asked Mr. Govern quietly.

"Oh!"

"That's as good a comment as any, probably," he said dryly. "I would, however, confine myself to that and no more, if I were you."

He permitted her to look at the pistol, the destructive end of the pistol, which he was holding.

"See the nice big bullets in there?" he asked. "They're for you, my dear, if you open that pretty kisser."

VII

Frozen, horror fighting to get out of her throat, Brenda thought: I mustn't scream. I mustn't. He'll shoot. And yet, for three, five, ten seconds, it was almost impossible to keep from shrieking. Finally she realized that Pete Idle was standing beside the droop-shouldered Govern.

"Why don't you do something, you dope!" Brenda gasped.

Pete's eyes looked like boiled eggs in the darkness. "That's a gun he's got," he said. He sounded as if he hadn't been breathing for some time.

"How did he—"

"Catch me? I was following you. I was playing bodyguard. He came up behind me." Pete sounded bitter.

He sounded so tense and upset that Brenda became afraid he would try something reckless.

"Don't try anything, Pete," she urged.

"You're telling me," Pete mumbled.

Mr. Govern said softly, "Do you mind lapsing into silence? And stepping over there in those shadows. I prefer, incidentally, that you stand a bit ahead of me. About a yard ahead."

They moved over to the designated place, a spot where they were not very noticeable, because of the darkness and the intrusion of a ventilator scoop, from the radio shack.

Pete whispered, "What's that guy doing in the radio—"

"Do you want your brains knocked out?" Mr. Govern inquired savagely.

Pete didn't. He was silent. Brenda was silent. If they breathed, they didn't notice it, and they didn't dare turn their heads, didn't feel any kind of a move was at all safe. They could see the radio shack door, and presently it swung lazily open, and the big bone-eyed man came out. He seemed in no hurry, but sauntered over to the rail and lounged there.

Hard, ominous, threatening, the gun in Mr. Govern's hand gouged Brenda's back.

"He disable the radio equipment?" Mr. Govern demanded in a very low whisper. "Nod, or shake your head. Don't speak."

Brenda nodded.

"Ah," said Mr. Govern. "I guess this is it. Just keep your mouths shut and your eyes open and I surmise you will see something interesting and exciting. If you are really an article writer for that magazine, Miss Linahan, you will possibly get some interesting material for a future article." He chuckled, and added, "If you are ever able to write it."

"May I ask a question?" Brenda whispered.

"Ummmmm. One. Yes, one only."

"Are you and that man working together?"

"No," said Mr. Govern. He sounded bitter. "Now shut up!"

Brenda knew, certainly, positively, that the stage must be set for a pirate attack, and that it was going to come at any moment, but when it did come—about two minutes later—she was so astonished that she thought she was going to pass out. She could give no justification for her astonishment. She had been forewarned. But she was astonished anyway, because it was so unbelievable, so incredible. *Crack! . . . thump! First*, a fused shell exploded in front of the *Poinsettia,* and a moment later the sound reached them from the gun that had fired. The shell arrived an instant ahead of the gun sound.

There was, at first, only confusion on the bridge. Exclamations. Men running. A searchlight stuck a stiff rod-like beam of light into the sky; then the rod dipped.

A loud voice from the dark sea hailed them. It came, obviously, from a loudspeaker capable of great power and projection.

The mechanical voice said: "Extinguish that searchlight if you don't want a torpedo in your guts!"

A voice, from one of the liner's officers, bellowed through the darkness: "What's the idea?"

Either not hearing, or ignoring the man, the loudspeaker said, "Heave to, if you don't want to be torpedoed. This is an act of piracy. You are being held up and robbed. Follow instructions and your ship and passengers will not be harmed. Get funny, or disobey orders, and you will be sunk!"

There was a normal amount of cursing. A man came flying down from the bridge, dashed to the radio shack, looked inside, yelled, "Good God, both operators have been killed! The radio apparatus is smashed!"

There was another *Crack* and *thump!* as a second fused shell was exploded over the bows, but far enough ahead that there was no danger.

"That's good shooting," said Mr. Govern critically.

Brenda demanded, "Is this a trap?"

"What kind of a trap could it be?" Govern countered. "They picked a spot where there's not likely to be any ocean traffic along. It's night, so planes won't sight them, if there should be any planes, which is unlikely."

"I thought maybe it was a trap the Navy had set," Brenda explained. "Aren't you a Navy man?"

Mr. Govern laughed softly.

"No, darling," he said. "And shut up, will you?"

They noticed that the big man with the colorless eyes had merged into the shadows near the radio shack. He did not seem alarmed by the excitement, nor possessed of any urgency to do anything immediately.

From the bridge: "Who are you? What kind of crazy business is this?"

From the sea: "Put your searchlight on us for one minute, no longer. One minute only, or we'll shoot the bridge off your ship and you with it. Then you have another minute to decide to follow orders."

Stiffly, as if it were startled and confused, the searchlight beam dipped. The submarine was closer than Brenda had expected it to be. It was by no means alongside, however. The searchlight, in considerably less than a minute, lifted off the submarine. The operator seemed to be frightened.

Presently, the ship surrendered.

There was, considering the magnitude of the thing, remarkably little confusion about the act of piracy. It was evident that the corsairs knew exactly what they intended to do, and also that they knew the construction of the *Poinsettia*. They even, as the sub drew near, asked for the liner's captain by name. Captain Gristell. He cursed them miserably.

The loudspeaker said, "Captain, our man will now assume charge of your ship."

"Send him aboard," the Captain snarled.

"He is already aboard. He will come on the bridge now. He is not to be harmed, and his orders are to be followed implicitly. The alternative is a torpedo in your vessel, and we shall also machine-gun officers and passengers when they take to the life-boats."

Pete muttered to Mr. Govern, "Isn't that your cue?"

"Not me. Who the hell do you think I am?" Govern demanded sourly.

"Who *are* you?"

"The guy who's gonna deposit some lead in you if you don't shaddup!" Mr. Govern seemed to be getting tense.

The man with the colorless eyes had gone on the bridge, they suddenly realized. They could hear Captain Gristell swearing, hear the big man silence him in short order. Amid a rapid-fire issuing of instructions across the narrowing stretch of sea between the submarine and the steamer, the merger of sub and liner was effected. In the meantime, a cargo port on a lower deck had been opened, and some kind of a landing stage lowered.

There was, while the sub was maneuvering, an interval of quiet, and they heard the bone-eyed man on the bridge instruct the Captain, "If your vault can be opened by anyone aboard, have it opened. Otherwise, we shall be forced to blow it, and the result might be some damage to your ship and passengers."

"Get the purser," the Captain mumbled. He seemed to be defeated.

"I'm going below to oversee the opening of the vault,"

the bone-eyed man said. "You will continue to follow instructions as they come from the loudspeaker on the submarine."

The big man left the bridge.

Mr. Govern nudged Brenda with his gun, then used it to gouge Pete. "Get going. We'll drop down and watch the excitement."

Pete, his reportorial instincts aroused by the drama, was quite willing. Excitement had, for the time being, put aside some of his fears. They found a companionway and descended. On the lower decks, there was all the confusion that the situation called for. Stewards and crew members, hastily put to work by the bridge, were trying to keep things from getting out of hand, but were not doing too well, most of them being as confused as the passengers. There was a general, and normal, inclination on the part of everybody not to believe that there could not be such a thing as pirates holding up the ship.

Mr. Govern had placed his gun in the pocket of his dress coat.

"Don't think I won't, or can't, shoot," he warned. "Keep going."

Brenda suggested, "Why don't you just let us go?"

"Sister, I've got plans for you and the boy friend here," Mr. Govern said. "Don't irk me. Do what I tell you. A part of my plans consists of killing you if you give me trouble."

Somehow they had not the slightest doubt but that he meant this.

The robbery of the ship went forward, seemingly, in slow motion, but this was purely an illusion; when Pete Idle glanced at his watch and saw how little time had elapsed, he whistled in astonishment. Govern nudged him in the back, said, "Never mind being amazed. Keep going, or they'll have this job done and off here before we can tie into them."

"Godamighty!" Pete croaked. "Tie into them! Are you kidding?"

"Keep moving!"

It was early enough in the evening that almost no one had gone to bed, and the excitement had drawn everyone out on deck. They had some trouble with the crowds.

Mr. Govern seemed to know where he was going, and the route to get there, because presently they opened a door, stepped out on naked steel plates—and were confronted by a man with a gun. The fellow was obviously a pirate. He advised, "You'd better stay where you are."

He watched them intently. Behind him, men were either climbing aboard the liner, or going back aboard the submarine. Brenda's eyes flew wide. Those going aboard the sub were carrying small and extremely heavy burdens.

They'd already opened the vault!

"Goodbye seven million bucks," Brenda whispered to Pete.

Mr. Govern overheard. He asked, "How'd you know about the gold, my lovely?"

Brenda decided she'd said something wrong. Very wrong, probably, because she got the idea that Govern had drawn some kind of conclusion from her innocent remark, or had solidified some conclusion which he'd already had.

Intensely, terrifyingly, she began to wonder what Mr. Govern planned to do with Pete and herself. She had imagined that she was already about as scared as she could become. This was wrong. Terror grew until it began to make the ends of her fingers numb. There was something horrifying about the methodical efficiency with which the pirates marched back and forth. Not the least frightening fact was that they didn't look like the pirates always looked in the movies. They didn't even look tough. They were just men like—well—like poor old Pete, who was looking down at his knees, probably to see if they were shaking as hard as he thought they were.

Through the open loading port, Brenda could see the wet, hard iron hide of the submarine. She could hear the moist sob of water as waves sloshed over the deck of the under-seas boat. The pirate who was watching her grinned lewdly. He was about twenty-five, had a small moustache, wore spectacles. He said, "Hy'ah, babe." Brenda shivered.

Unexpectedly, the man with the bone-colored eyes appeared. He seemed larger, more formidable. In an unpleasant tone, he said, "Snap it up! You're five minutes off schedule now!"

The pace of the burden-carriers quickened visibly.

They're afraid of him, Brenda thought. He must be the head guy.

The big man went to the landing stage, threw a glance downward, demanded, "Have they brought the old geezer aboard?"

Someone replied in the negative. The big man was indignant. "What the hell's keeping them! They should—" He paused, wheeled, shouted, "It's about time!"

Two pirates appeared, drag-carrying a slender man with perfectly white hair and a young-looking face. The prisoner had been somewhat manhandled and was leaking blood from scalp and lips. They straightened him out on the landing stage, kicked his rear, and went down to the submarine with him.

"Whoeee!" Pete said softly.

"What's the matter?" Brenda asked.

"That guy they took aboard—he's got a mint of money," Pete said. "Name's Ingraham. Oil man and Wall Street operator. I talked to him a few times. Knows a lot of people I know—or rather, he knew most of the prominent people I knew."

"Why did they take him aboard, do you suppose?" Brenda wanted to know.

The young pirate, the one keeping an eye on them, grinned sardonically at her. "Don't be naïve, baby. Didn't you ever hear of ransom? It's done in the best of pirate circles."

Brenda shivered.

The young corsair eyed her. "You're not rich, are you, tutz?"

Brenda shook her head definitely not.

He sighed. "Too bad, because I'd like to kidnap you, tutz."

Mr. Govern spoke in a conversational tone to the young pirate. He said, "I think I can make you happy, sonny."

"Huh?"

"Tutz, here, and her pot-bellied friend are my prisoners," Mr. Govern explained. "Now don't get confused. And don't start shooting. I'm going to walk them out and talk to your head guy. I've got something to say to him. You understand?"

"I'm damned if I do." The young pirate was confused. "You wanta talk to Whitey?"

Govern nodded at the big man with the bone-colored eyes. "He Whitey?"

"Yeah."

"He's the one I wanta talk to." He started to nudge Brenda and Pete forward. The pirate's gun, suddenly leveled, made a distinct click as it cocked. "No, no, stick where you are!"

Mr. Govern froze. His hand with the gun was still in his jacket pocket. In a moment, the young pirate began staring intently at the hand. He licked his lips with a quick swipe of his tongue, asked, "Got a gun in there?"

"That's right. Don't make me use it. Call Whitey over here."

"You haven't got a chance."

"I know it," Mr. Govern said.

Brenda suddenly had a great respect for Mr. Govern's nerve. She hadn't imagined a man could sound so coldly determined when he was on the point of getting himself shot.

The young pirate did not take long to get a decision made.

"Whitey!" he called. "This guy's got a gun. He wants to talk to you. He's got something on his mind."

Whitey came over, coldly, without hesitation. . . . Just like in the films, Brenda thought in horror. Only such things never happen in life.

"Well?" Whitey examined Mr. Govern bleakly.

"I got things to say."

"Say them."

"This girl and this guy were following you around in New York."

Tension tightened Whitey's eyes down until they seemed closed. "Why?"

"That's what I thought you might like to ask them."

"How do you know they were following me?"

"Saw them."

"You were doing some following yourself?"

"That's right."

Whitey used his jaw to indicate the landing stage and said, "Go aboard. But first give that gun to Timmy, here, and if you've got more than one, give them all to Timmy."

"All three of us go aboard the sub?"

"That's right."

Mr. Govern used care not to move suddenly enough to alarm anyone and removed the gun from his pocket and passed it to Timmy, the young pirate, who was grinning. Timmy pocketed the gun, told Brenda, "Glad to have you aboard, tutz," and bowed at the landing stage. "Get moving."

Brenda presently discovered, stupefied, that she was

going down wet iron steps toward a steel submarine deck over which waves broke and sent sheets of water sliding. She was walking, but she had no wish to be walking, and very little, almost none, of the physical feeling of movement. She supposed this must be what they meant when they spoke of fright and used the term petrified. It was very descriptive. Petrified. She would always know what it meant.

Behind them, above them, Whitey said, "Lock these guests up. If they start anything, shoot them in a not too messy way."

VIII

A submarine was not a completely new experience to Miss Brenda Linahan. The smallness of quarters, the cramped confines of passages, did not astonish her, but did give her an acute attack of claustrophobia. She knew the tiny cubicle in which they were locked was the quarters of the skipper because of the presence of depth and speed gauges and a directional indicator, two telephones. . . . Mr. Govern immediately began going through a desk, yanking out the drawers, examining the contents. Pete glared at him and said, "Brother, you got us in a hell of a mess! I hope you're satisfied."

Mr. Govern grunted in triumph, and held up some official looking correspondence. "This submarine," he announced, "is a Nazi war prize which was stolen from the U. S. Navy about ten days ago." He made satisfied smacking noises with his lips. "By golly, I'm glad to know that. I was only able to get rumors that a submarine had been stolen, and wasn't able to confirm them. But they were the straight goods. That's fine."

"What's fine about it?" Pete snarled.

"Why, it proves they're just beginning pirates," Mr. Govern said. His lips curled with scorn. "Amateurs. First-timers. Punks." He sounded as if he didn't think much of the pirates.

Pete scowled at him.

"They seem pretty efficient to me, amateurs or not," Pete said.

Mr. Govern continued his search.

Brenda listened to movements on deck. She believed

the sounds indicated the looting of the seven odd million dollars from the vaults of the *Poinsettia* was about finished, and that preparations were being made to escape with the loot. This proved to be correct, because presently the motors started. The motors, not the engines, she realized; that probably meant they were going to submerge at once, because the motors were used for underwater headway. She exclaimed, "They're going to submerge!"

"Naturally," said Mr. Govern contemptuously. "They don't want to give the steamer a chance to ram them."

Irked, Pete said, "Maybe they're not as dumb as you thought."

"Oh, they're not dumb," Mr. Govern admitted. "Just amateurs." He said amachoors for amateurs. He sounded as if he was relapsing into a tough manner that was more natural with him.

Brenda suddenly realized that it was going to be a horrible experience when the sub dived. She pressed against the double-decker bunk, hands clenching the cold metal stanchions. She wished mightily that she had paid more attention to sensations on the one other occasion when she had been aboard a submarine when it dove. This had been about a year ago, and, unfortunately, there had been a handsome Naval lieutenant present who was more interesting than a submarine diving. She began to tremble violently, and finally blurted, "I'm scared!"

"What of?" asked Mr. Govern.

"Of what may happen when the submarine submerges!"

"Forget it. We've already submerged," said Mr. Govern in a conversational tone. Then—cruelly, considering how casually he had spoken—he swung his right fist from behind his hip and landed it on Pete's jaw. The blow was loud. Pete instantly fell down, eyes closed. "Glass jaw," said Mr. Govern, admiring his handiwork.

Brenda, suddenly more angry than she was afraid, looked around for some weapon with which to attack Mr. Govern.

"Cut it out, baby," he advised.

"Why did you hit Pete?" Brenda flared.

"Partly for satisfaction," said Mr. Govern. "I don't like the idea of him having such a pretty girl as you. And also he was thinking of bopping me. I could see it in his eye."

Brenda subsided and put herself to wondering who, and

what, and why, Mr. Govern was. He was extraordinary. Extraordinarily horrible, she decided.

Half an hour later, the door to the tiny stateroom opened and a pair of gun muzzles looked in at them, Whitey back of the weapons. He examined Pete—Pete had just partially revived, was sitting on the floor holding his head with both hands—and did not seem surprised nor concerned. He glanced at Brenda. "Comfortable?"

"You let us go, if you know that's good for you!" she said angrily and, she realized when the words were out, foolishly.

Whitey laughed.

He gestured for Mr. Govern to step outside.

"You and I are going to talk now," he advised.

Govern shrugged. "Okay by me." He moved into the corridor, noted two armed men backing up Whitey, and grinned at them. Whitey closed and secured the cabin door and directed one of the armed men, "Better stick here on guard."

Mr. Govern was escorted to the control station, where it was possible to talk in comfort. He noted from the instruments that they were submerged and traveling southeast at about twelve knots. The fact that the instruments were German and marked in German gave him some trouble. He said, "You guys must have been busy practicing the last ten days."

Whitey looked at him unpleasantly. "How do you figure ten days?"

"I heard a rumor that the Navy had lost this sub ten days ago."

"Who are you, brother?" Whitey asked harshly.

Mr. Govern grinned, without, however, putting much humor into the grimace. "Look, I'm going to give you the whole thing in a small package. First, I'm using the name of Govern, and it isn't my name and you don't give a damn what my name is, or if you do, it won't do you any good, because that's a personal matter I intend to keep to myself. Who am I, you say? Well, I'll tell you: I'm one of a group of men who, nearly a year ago, decided that as long as the world had gone crazy, they might as well do it too."

When Whitey looked as if he was going to interrupt, Govern held up a hand, said hastily, "Listen to it, will you, even if the build-up isn't interesting."

"Go ahead."

Originally—and by originally, he meant prior to a year ago, Mr. Govern explained—the men concerned in the story he was going to tell had been involved, most of them, in the war in one way or another. He compressed his lips, said sharply, "None of us were Japs, Germans or wops. Don't get that idea. We're Americans. Well, maybe a South American or two, and a couple of black boys who are as American as you or I, or maybe I should say English. They're Bimini Negroes. They knew the Bahama Island waters better than you know the palm of your hand.

"I'll not burden you with how we got together, but we did. Actually, we were gotten together by one man. This guy—and we might as well start calling him Cavu right now, because that is what he's called—is an extraordinary sort of fellow. He is a man of extreme vision, infinite patience for planning, startling imagination, and he is not troubled at all by morals, honesty, or conscience. A perfect man for the job. A man capable of organizing a band of pirates able to function in this year of 1946. And that is what he did."

Whitey sneered, said, "What are you giving me?"

"You already know about this, don't you? Not the details I'm giving you, but of our existence?"

Whitey said nothing.

"First, let me finish," Mr. Govern requested. "We were fairly well organized by the end of the war with Japan, and when that came, we managed to grab us a Japanese submarine. A nice one. Complete with airplane, torpedoes, and fuel supply. With that sub, we took another one. Five months were devoted to organization and drill, then we established a base and began operating. Now don't tell me you haven't heard of us."

Whitey scowled. "Okay. I heard rumors."

"Gave you the idea of going into the racket yourself, didn't it?"

"Maybe."

"Okay, now you know who I am and—"

"You haven't said who you were!" Whitey interrupted harshly.

"I represent the gentleman I've called Cavu. I'm supposed to ask you, and persuade you if possible to make a deal."

"Deal? What kind of a deal?"

"One big organization," said Mr. Govern, "can function with a lot more safety than two."

"Yeah? That's just a statement, and you're not going to be able to prove it."

"Look, I can give an example: take this ship you've knocked over tonight. What do you think will happen now? They'll set a bunch of booby traps on ships that sail in the future. But the main thing is, they'll keep this quiet. They've kept our own activities quiet, figuring, I imagine, that we'll get reckless or worried because of it. Anyway, there'll be booby traps from now on, and supposing we didn't know this and tried to knock off one of the ships. Suppose we did that? Too bad for us. Or suppose it had been us tonight and you tried it later. Too bad for you. Get the point?"

"You mean," said Whitey, "that, working separately, and neither one of us knowing what the other is doing, one of us is liable to stir up a hornet's nest that the other will fall into?"

"That's it."

"You've got something."

"What about it?"

"What about what?"

"How about joining up with us?"

Whitey frowned. "That'll take some talking over with the crew."

"Fair enough. Put it up to them."

Whitey moved over to examine the gauges, check the course and tell the steersman that there was no reason why they shouldn't surface and increase speed. "Where's Colorado Jones?" he demanded. The steersman, who was Colton, said, "He went back to check an oil leak to see if it's getting any worse." Presently Colorado Jones, big, sullen, sour-faced, returned. Whitey told him to surface and cruise, same course, at about three quarters speed.

Whitey went back to Mr. Govern. "You left out the girl and the guy with her."

"Uh-huh. They're magazine people, they say. I don't know about that. Maybe they are."

"Work for a magazine, eh? Why the hell'd you bring them aboard?"

"I gave it to you straight the first time. They were following you around in New York."

"Yeah? How do I know that's so?"

Mr. Govern explained where he had first noticed Brenda, describing the bar—he had, he explained, noticed Brenda at once, but without immediately realizing she was following Whitey—and continuing the description of the trailing to the restaurant where the driver of the armored truck had been paid off, then to the hotel, finally to the *Poinsettia*. The story was correct in detail except that it gave the impression that he, Mr. Govern, had followed Brenda, instead of the reverse being true. Finishing the story, he eyed Whitey narrowly, said suddenly, "That building where I picked her up—Doc Savage has his headquarters there, doesn't he?"

Whitey jumped. So did Colton and Colorado Jones, who were listening. Whitey recovered himself, scowled, blew out his cheeks. He said, "The office we use for a front is in that building. I located it there because I figured it would be a good idea to keep an eye on Doc Savage, because, sooner or later, he would probably stick his nose into this thing."

Govern nodded. "I knew your front was in the building. I also heard that was why."

Whitey said bitterly, "How'd you get that information?"

"You'll never know."

"Somebody in my outfit tipped you off."

Mr. Govern grinned. "I'll let you worry about it. Point is, thought the girl and the guy might know too much—about you, not about me. So I brought them along. By force. They didn't wanna come. I did you a favor, see?"

"I wonder." Whitey was sullen, mulling over the suspicion, apparently, that someone in his crew had approached Whitey, or had been persuaded to talk.

"How about having a meeting of your crew to discuss my proposition?"

Whitey swung to Colton. "What do you think about it?"

"I dunno." Colton was indecisive. "It's got its points. But I dunno. Would depend on whether we had to kick back a share to"—he nodded at Mr. Govern—"this guy's crowd."

"Why don't you," said Mr. Govern, "all assemble and I'll talk it over."

Whitey became sourly purposeful. "We'll do that. Colorado, pass the word along to Ward, Eli and the rest. Have the first watch assemble in the wardroom. We'll have to do this in two shifts."

*   *   *

The conference turned out to be a hard-fisted affair with nobody trusting anyone else and taking no special pains to be polite. Mr. Govern seemed to enjoy it and before the arguing recessed had conveyed the impression that he was able to be as hard as any occasion would warrant.

He said, "This is a merger, see? That's all. We share expenses, and the only expenses will be maintaining a base for operations. We've already got a damned good base. If you guys have one, we'll vote on which one we'll use, or we might want to use both. Everybody contributes to maintaining the base."

They would keep books, Govern explained, and the expenses incidental to each act of piracy—items like buying off the armored truck guard who had tipped Whitey off that seven million dollars in bullion had been put aboard the *Poinsettia*—would be charged against the individual job, to be paid out of the proceeds of that haul. It was, Mr. Govern pointed out, a matter of business, a profitable deal bringing a profitable return to the operators.

"About this gold. It's hard to move gold these days. We may have to buy somebody to get it done, and another way is to go into the gold mining business and sell the gold as a product of the mine. That's complicated, because experts can tell pretty much where a piece of gold comes from, but it can be done, I've been assured. Any expenses of that sort would have to be paid out of the general fund to which you guys will contribute."

"What about ransom dough?" Ward asked.

Mr. Govern didn't think much of ransom, and he felt that his chief, Cavu, agreed with this in principle. "I know you've got a guy aboard you want to ransom," he said. "My vote would be to shoot him and forget it, but that's up to you guys, although I think Cavu will want a general vote by both crews on it."

Someone wished to know where the head guy got that name Cavu. "He a foreigner, or something?"

Mr. Govern laughed. "No foreigner. It sounds silly, but you know that Air Force term CAVU, meaning, 'ceiling and visibility unlimited'? Somebody hung it on the chief early in the deal, because of the uncanny way he had of figuring out what would happen. It stuck. Cavu. It isn't his name, but that doesn't matter."

Colorado Jones spit on the wardroom floor and said, "I don't think so damned much of the whole idea."

"By me, it don't look like a bad deal," Colton said. "It's

got advantages. You take a syndicate, they always got it their way." His opinion seemed to be the majority one.

Whitey said, "It's up to you guys. I'm for it, or against it, whatever you say. But I want to do some more brain-beating over it before I commit myself finally."

It was decided everybody would do some thinking.

IX

Mr. Calvin R. Ingraham, the financier, had been lying on his back in a bunk staring fixedly at the oddly shaped steel ceiling plates overhead. Suddenly he sat up, grimacing with the effort, unlaced one shoe, pulled it off, stumbled to the door, a matter of hardly three feet, and beat on the door with the heel of the shoe. Over the hammering sound this made, he screamed, "Help! Help! Let me out of here!" Presently someone on the other side of the door said angrily, "Cut that out, you old buzzard. You want me to hafta kick your pants up around your neck?" Ingraham continued hammering, and in a moment the door was wrenched open, Colorado Jones stepped inside, measured Ingraham carefully, and swung his fist. The blow drove Ingraham backward and he fell across the bunk, bending backward, shoulders, head and arms lying in the bunk. He hung there, dazed, his breathing blowing red bubbles off his lips. "I'm tryin' ta think, and you're botherin' me, dammit," Colorado Jones said, and went out and shut the door.

Calm fell again in that part of the submarine, and Colorado Jones appeared to immerse himself in thought, watched grinningly by a pirate who was about forty years old and having some difficulty with asthma, brought on, he claimed, by the bad air in the sub.

Presently Whitey approached and asked, "How's the old goose?"

"He's fine," Colorado Jones said.

Whitey growled, "Let's have a look at him," and, shoving open the door, swore in anger. Mr. Ingraham, the intended ransom victim, was now lying on the bunk, hanging his head over the edge and bleeding on the floor. "Who hit him?" Whitey demanded.

"The old goofer was makin' a racket," Colorado said angrily.

Whitey slammed the door and fastened it. "You keep your hands off him. You might kill him." He wheeled on the asthma sufferer, ordered, "Clench, you take over. Colorado hasn't got sense enough to do it." He scowled at Colorado, said, "You come along with me. I'm going to talk to the girl and her boy friend."

Colorado hitched his pants. He didn't say anything. He was insulted.

Whitey posted Colorado Jones outside the stateroom which held Brenda Linahan and Pete Idle. He told the man who had been on watch there, "Colorado'll relieve you for a while. Had any trouble from inside?"

"Nah. I think tutz has been bawling though."

"You haven't molested her?"

The guard was the young pirate who had been on the landing stage of the *Poinsettia* when Mr. Govern made his entrance.

"Nah," he said.

"If there's any molesting, you're going to get into trouble," Whitey warned.

The boy grinned. "Match you for first crack," he offered. When Whitey didn't say anything, he sauntered off.

Colorado Jones, in a very low, very bitter, very enraged voice that reached only Whitey, said, "I can't take much more of that kid. I'll smear him, the dirty little rat, so help me God! I can't take him. I really can't take him!"

Whitey glanced about swiftly, but there was no one in earshot. He said, "Take it easy, Renny. I think this thing is about in the bag."

"Figure they'll vote to join up?"

"Yes."

"I think so, too."

Whitey said, "That's what all the hell has been for, wasn't it?" He indicated the door. "I'm going in. If anyone comes, tap on the door with a coin if they show any inclination to stop and hang around."

"What are you going to tell the girl and the guy?"

"The truth, I suppose."

"I hope they can take it."

Whitey said he hoped so, too, and entered the cabin,

actually the commander's cabin when the sub was under the Nazi flag.

Brenda Linahan had been sobbing—it had been a hysterical outbreak of frenzied rage and helplessness during which she had beaten the berth with her fists and said words a lady shouldn't know—but she had things under control. Pete Idle had been looking at her in amazement, reflecting that the guy she married had better watch out about getting her mad.

"Get out of here!" Brenda screamed at Whitey.

Whitey ignored her uneasily, and finally indicated Pete's face. "What happened to your lip?"

"That guy Govern slugged me," Pete said, and added a personal opinion of Mr. Govern, using some of the words he had heard Brenda use a few moments ago.

"Cut that out!" Whitey said. "There's a lady present."

"I'm glad you told me," Pete said sourly. "Listen, she cusses like a stevedore. I just found it out."

Brenda addressed Pete angrily. "Why don't you hit him! He's probably got a gun. Take it away from him and use it to get us out of this mess!"

Pete examined Whitey for size. "No, I'll wait until something a little smaller, say a Sherman tank, comes along."

"Sit on the berth, you two," Whitey ordered.

The cabin, while not large, was fitted with the comforts to which Nazi commanders had considered themselves entitled. There was, in a corner, an ingenious folding lavatory and shaving mirror arrangement similar to those found in railway pullman roomettes. Whitey folded the basin down, ran water into it, removed a small case from his pocket, bent over the basin, and seemed to be doing something with his eyes. Still engaged in that, he remarked, "These contact lenses aren't what they're cracked up to be when you have to wear them over an extended period of time. I think the fumes in the air aboard a submarine tend to cause irritation, also."

He straightened, turned, and they saw that he had used a small rubber suction cup to remove contact lenses from his eyes.

Pete and Brenda stared at him. Pete nearly fell off the bunk.

"Oh, for God's sake! . . . You're Doc Savage!" Pete said weakly.

Brenda flopped back on the bunk, brought both hands to her face and clamped them over her lips, fingers criss-crossed and pressing hard, and presently she giggled. Pete groaned. "She's going to have another attack!" he gasped. He seized Brenda's arms at the elbows, tried to pull her hands from her lips, failed, then shook her violently and said, "Stop it! Stop it, you hear!" He sounded small and frightened, like a child.

Brenda giggled again uncontrollably through and around her fingers, then said, "It's a silly damn comedy show, that's what it is! . . . The pirates have got poor Brenda and up gallops that gallant hero in disguise. Hurrah, here comes the cavalry!"

Doc Savage, with the removal of the contact lenses—they were tinted and gave his eyes the nasty bonelike coloration—had, seemingly, shed the whole character of Whitey, the pirate leader. The roundness went out of his shoulders, his face settled into more normal lines, and he became competent, composed, quick-moving. He went to the bunk. "Let's see what we can do with her, Pete." He leaned over, slapped the girl's face once without much gentleness. The shock silenced her. He said quickly, "Comic opera or no comic opera, you are still on a submarine operated by pirates. They are, with the exception of myself and two other men who are my assistants, all genuine pirates. They fully intend to kill you. Now go ahead and have your little-girl tantrum."

Motionless, tense, Brenda kept her hands over her mouth for a few moments, but finally she took them away. Her eyes were again rational, but quite frightened.

"I guess," she said, "my hinges were a little loose. Having you turn up like that—you *are* Doc Savage, aren't you?"

"Yes."

"You handed me the shock of my life."

"Feel better?"

"I probably won't feel exactly right until I'm back in my apartment in New York and under the bed. But I think I've got hold of myself. Only, if you've got any more surprises, give me some warning."

Doc glanced at Pete. "Did Govern knock out any teeth when he hit you?"

Pete shook his head. "What is this, anyway? In case you don't know us, I'm Pete Idle, article editor of *Solar, The News Weekly,* and this is Miss—"

"I know who you are," Doc said. "Ham Brooks described

Miss Linahan quite thoroughly when she came to see me in New York."

Brenda said, "Only I didn't see you. You remember?"

"Naturally not. But you should have told Ham you were working on this pirate affair." Doc smiled slightly. "Not that you would have gotten to see me—I think you can see why. I was quite busy being Whitey. But if you had told Ham what your business was, I think we would have managed to give you a bum steer that would have kept you out of the affair. At least, you wouldn't be here, now."

Brenda was impressed. "After this, I tell everybody all my business," she declared.

Pete made some frantic gestures. "I don't get this! I don't get it at all!"

"You bungled," Doc told him, "smack into the middle of a pirate-catching scheme."

Doc Savage sketched briefly—and Brenda and Pete immediately realized he must be skipping an enormous amount of detail—the scattered developments which had gradually gathered and funneled themselves into the present tense situation. First, as would be obvious, the regularly constituted channels of authority, federal—Navy, Coast Guard, Marine—as well as civil, had been unable to make effective headway toward finding and catching the corsairs. The pirates, Doc explained, had planned too well, organized too tightly, and were too extremely cautious to be caught. The pirates had provided against every normal device of detection and apprehension. . . . Finally, Doc was called into the case, and given free rein—over the doubts and objections of several—to use his own methods, which were usually shaded with the bizarre.

"It takes a thief to catch a thief," Doc explained. "That was the theme we decided to work on. We were fortunate enough to get the cooperation of the Navy department, who enabled us to seize this submarine in a manner I believe was quite convincing."

Brenda, amazed, demanded, "You mean most of these men aboard are genuine pirates?"

"All but two."

"But how on earth did you manage to assemble a gang of genuine crooks?"

Doc said, "It wasn't too easy." He added that the gathering together of such a crew of rascals had been an essential part of the plan, however. "The whole object was to let the genuine pirates find out that another crew was going into the buccaneering business, on the theory that we would eventually get a line on them. We thought they might approach us as brother pirates. To use another old saw: 'Birds of a feather flock together.' Actually, we have just received a merger proposition from the other pirate gang, and we're thinking it over. Mr. Govern made the offer."

"Govern is one of the other pirate crew?"

"Quite a prominent member, evidently."

Brenda's reporter instinct asserted itself, and she demanded, "But how did you manage to take this sub away from the U. S. Navy so that it would look natural?"

Doc packed an outline of the operation into half a dozen sentences.

"You mean you submerged and left the Navy men in the sea to drown! Surely not—"

"That was part of the act," Doc explained. "The PT boat that had been converted into a yacht was standing by about a quarter of a mile away. It could not be seen in the darkness. Only one man was aboard—Colorado Jones, who, incidentally, is Renny Renwick—Lieutenant Colonel John Renwick—one of my associates. After we submerged, Renwick simply came back and picked up the Navy men. None of them, you may be sure, drowned."

"Wasn't that risky?"

"The sea wasn't rough. And the Navy had picked men who could swim, and who also wore, under their clothing, small emergency life belts which they could inflate."

Brenda shook her head. "I mean, later, wasn't it risky? Suppose the genuine pirates investigated to learn whether any of the Navy men were supposed to be lost were really lost. Consulted their families, for instance?"

"They did that, as a matter of fact," Doc said. "But we were unable to find and shadow the men who did the inquiring. That was a very disappointing failure. But to answer your question—the Navy crew, and the Nazis, from the submarine, were put aboard a battleship enroute to the Orient. They are being kept out of sight."

"Why, I think it was marvelous!" Brenda exclaimed.

Pete said he didn't feel it was so marvelous. "We're in a hell of a predicament, if you ask me," he said. "I would rather be locked up in the lion house at the zoo."

*   *   *

"But I don't understand why you brought Pete and me aboard," Brenda said to Doc Savage.

This made Doc uncomfortable. "There wasn't anything else to do. I was afraid leaving you behind would make Govern suspicious. He told me you had been shadowing me in New York, you remember. That was enough to make me very suspicious of you and a genuine pirate would have brought you aboard to question you, so that is what I had to do."

"I guess so," Brenda admitted.

"It was our own fault." Pete was very gloomy. "After this, I'm going to stick to my desk."

Doc explained, "In case you're wondering why I am telling you this, it's because your help will probably be needed. We're outnumbered. There's two of my men, myself and you two. That's five. There'll be at least seventy men against us, including the other pirates. That's odds of fourteen to one. Probably that is the best we can expect."

"Oh my God!" Pete groaned.

"Colorado Jones is Renny Renwick," Brenda said. "Who is your other man?"

"I'd rather not tell you."

"Why not?"

"You might unconsciously give his identity away, if you knew him. He's an ace in the hole."

Pete muttered, "He can't be in any deeper hole than we're in. What's the program? What do you think will happen next?"

Doc said he was almost positive his crew would vote to talk over a merger with the other pirates and, in order to do this, they would probably visit the base from which the other pirates were operating. "I sincerely hope I'm right," he added. "Once I know where the pirate hangout is, I can contact the Navy and arrange for a raid on the place. That'll wind the whole thing up satisfactorily."

"Please don't make it sound so simple," Pete said nervously. "As scared as I am, it can't be that simple."

"Take it easy. Just hold everything, and wait for orders," Doc said. "Incidentally, I'm going to separate you and Miss Linahan, so you can get some sleep in privacy."

Brenda retained the Nazi captain's cabin. Pete was

consigned to a smaller cubicle which was used for storage. While Pete was being locked up, Colton approached and said, "The guys want to take a vote. If we're going to talk it over with this other outfit, it will save time to head for their hideout now, and save maybe retracing our course."

"Okay," Whitey said.

The submarine was surfaced, and the machinery was stopped to permit everyone to attend except a single lookout who took a position at the radar apparatus, keeping an eye on the 'scope for ships or planes in the neighborhood.

The vote to confer with the other corsair organization about a merger was heavily affirmative, only three voting against it.

Doc Savage—he had replaced the contact lenses in his eyes and was again in the character of Whitey—stood up abruptly.

"Now wait a minute!" he said sharply. "This may be a hi-jacking gag. It may be a scheme to get us blocked up in some little harbor, or get us alongside a ship that will put a shell in us, disabling us so they can take that bullion away from us. We're not going to any base until I find out that it's safe."

Mr. Govern grinned.

"That's plain talk, and now I'll give you some of the same. If you think I'm going to tell you where our base is, you're crazy."

Colton asked, "How we going to get together, then?"

Mr. Govern said, "You've got a plane aboard, haven't you?"

"It's a Nazi plane."

"On floats?"

"Naturally."

"That's fine. I can fly one of them, I think. I wouldn't want to take it off on a rough sea, but if you can do that, I'll blindfold one of you and fly it to our base. Is it a two-place ship?"

"It's two-place."

"Okay. What do you think of the proposition?"

The suggestion seemed to be acceptable. Doc faced the assemblage and demanded, "Do you want to elect a man to make the trip? Or shall I go?"

"If you want the job, you're welcome to it," Colton said, and there was a general laugh.

X

Four days later, the submarine lay under a gray sky smoky with fog. The sea, infinitely clear, as blue as cobalt, ran in long lazy swells, but there were few small waves. The whole sea, in fact, had a greasy, limpid look.

"The plane's got radar," Doc said. "I can find the sub coming back. But can you find your island?"

"Who said it was an island?" Mr. Govern countered. "You leave it to me."

"In this fog?"

"In this fog," Mr. Govern said. "I'll find it, don't you worry."

Colorado Jones leaned over the rail. He said, "You don't come back, I take command."

"You do not! We've been into that." Doc scowled at him, trying to make it good. "Colton is the man. Colton takes over. But I'll be back."

Colorado—Renny—spat disgustedly. He didn't say anything more.

They were getting the plane over the side, which was somewhat of a ticklish job, but not entirely new to them. They had done it twice before during training, and held many dry runs, not actually putting the plane on the sea, several times. There was a catapult for launching the ship, but Doc did not have too much faith in it, and had decided to take the ship off from the water. Conditions for a surface take-off were about as nearly ideal as they ever were at sea.

"You fly the forward cockpit," he told Mr. Govern. "The Nazis were too tight to put flight instruments in both cockpits. Coming back, I'll take the front cockpit."

Mr. Govern had made a black hood which was to serve as a blindfold, and he passed this over.

"That do for a blindfold?"

"Don't see why not."

They got in the ship, and fastened the safety belts. Doc was uneasy about the plane, not trusting it, which was hardly justifiable, because the Nazis, regardless of what one thought of their political thinking, had been excellent mechanical workmen. He ran cockpit check twice, then got the engine turning. He felt completely unnatural in the cockpit, and remembered, with acute distress, that he hadn't test-flown the plane, and didn't know whether anyone else had. He fiddled with the controls, testing, examining, calculating.

"What's the holdup?" Govern demanded, turning his head.

"You want to take it off?" Doc demanded angrily. Govern said no more, and Doc felt he must be grinning. He eased the throttle open; they began to move. Presently they were in the air. So easily, so quickly, that it was surprising. The plane had good characteristics. It had vaulted off the top of a swell, and Doc eased it carefully over the next swell, began climbing.

He felt Govern take the stick. The man did some gentle S-turns, some coordination exercises, and seemed satisfied. He made a gesture of drawing his hands down over his eyes. The hood.

After that, for about two hours, it was intensely black.

He heard Govern beating the side of the fuselage, heard the man's voice, faint, torn by the wind, saying, "Take the hood off!"

Govern had changed the clock. That was the first thing Doc noticed, and it was important, and in an instant, Doc realized he had no way of knowing exactly how long they had flown, or knowing, probably, within half an hour's span. Tension would do that to a man. Destroy his judgment of time passage. Govern, a clever man, had thought of that.

They were still flying. Govern, pointing downward, yelled, "Look her over."

It wasn't an island. No island, Doc thought, astonished. Then he realized he really should have expected something like this. A ship. A rusty, small old tramp steamer. It looked like a rattletrap even from a thousand feet in the air.

No island. But there was a reef, or rather two parallel reefs with deep water between them in which the tramp lay. The reef formation was coral, and this was the Bahama region, somewhere near the edge of the Bahama Banks, which took in a lot of territory, many thousands of square miles.

Doc decided he did not recognize the place, but it would make no difference one way or the other if he did; tomorrow, even today, they could move the old steamer. The steamer was the thing. He watched it intently, examining it.

Cunning judgment they'd used on the ship. It was a

liberty ship, an old one, but there were hundreds of standardized models exactly like it which had been turned out in the early rush of war shipbuilding. Proving it was a ship of specific identity would be difficult without a close range inspection. He imagined he wouldn't be allowed to take a close look, and he wasn't.

They landed. Doc did the landing, knew that Govern must be a little dubious of his ability to handle the Nazi ship, which was quite a sensible feeling to have. They got down all right.

"Taxi over to the lee of that reef to the right," Govern yelled. "And wait for a boat."

The boat, a launch which displayed considerably more speed than was to be expected of a tender from such a decrepit steamer, streaked toward, but not directly to them. It circled, warily, its motor went silent, and the occupants, half a dozen tough-looking men, stood staring at them.

"It's a great dog that has no tail," Mr. Govern told them loudly. Evidently this was some kind of password, because the launch approached at once.

"Your friends," Doc remarked, "look like a bunch of cut-throats."

"They are." Mr. Govern sounded amiable.

Doc concluded presently that Cavu, whoever he was, was not in the launch, because a surly looking fellow with no forehead worth mentioning and twice as much jaw as he needed looked up at Govern and advised, "Big boy says for you to come aboard first. He wants to know what the hell you're doing before you bring this guy on board."

Govern turned to Doc. "Mind waiting?"

"I don't like it."

"Fat lot of good it'll do you." Govern got in the launch, and there was an argument about whether the launch would contribute its anchor, a small mushroom affair, to keep the plane from drifting. Nobody seemed in a very cooperative humor, but they finally tied the anchor line to the seaplane nose-cleat and dropped the anchor in the water, which was about two fathoms deep here. The launch left for the tramp steamer with Mr. Govern.

Doc Savage wished he had brought a pair of binoculars. It had not occurred to him to do so, because usually they were not very effective from a plane. He studied the steamer

intently, and decided he probably could not identify it again if
they took the trouble to make small changes in its rigging,
which they probably would. As a measure of caution, he got
the plane motor ready to start, and climbed out on the float
and re-tied the anchor line in a knot which would slip loose if
he ran for it, but would hold as long as the plane merely rode
at anchor. That way, he could get away if necessary. He was
glad to note that the cockpit was armored, however, so he
moved up there to wait. Half an hour dragged past.

Only Govern and the helmsman were in the launch
when it came back.

"Okay. I got him soothed down," Govern beckoned.
"Get aboard."

"How does he feel about the proposition?" Doc climbed
into the launch.

"Skittish. A lot depends on you. But the business details
as I outlined them are still okay."

"Good enough."

"You got that black sack?"

"In my pocket."

"Put it over your head."

Later, when Doc got out on a landing stage, he fell over
something and bruised his knees. "Get somebody to lead me,
or I'm going to take this rag off my eyes!" he said angrily.
Somebody laughed and said, "Tough guy, huh?" But he was
taken by the elbow and guided up a considerable number of
not too steady steel steps, then onto a deck, across the deck
and over a raised ship threshold—he skinned one of his shins
here—and the smell of a none too clean cabin assailed his
nostrils.

"Sit down," Govern said.

"Do I take this hood off?"

"You leave it on."

"That wasn't in the bargain."

"It's in the bargain now," Govern said. "You try taking
that off, and you'll get a knife or a bullet."

"This," Doc said, "is a good way to start a business
conference."

"You don't have to see anybody to talk, do you?"

"Bring on your man!" Doc said angrily.

He tried to decide, by ear only, what was going on, but
this proved difficult because of the amount of walking about,

whispering, shuffling of feet, moving of furniture. He began to feel very creepy. Not that he had felt at ease before he came aboard.

The voice, when it finally addressed him, was disguised, he decided, by the speaker holding something in his mouth.

"I'm the stud duck around here," the voice advised.

"You're Cavu?"

"That's as good a name as any. Let's hear your proposition."

"Brother," Doc said violently, "we didn't make any proposition. Your man made it."

The voice became conciliatory. "I understand that. Go ahead and outline the thing as you conceive it. I want to see whether we understand each other."

Doc said that was reasonable. He ran over the terms that had been discussed—each group of pirates to keep its own swag, expenses on each job to be charged to that job, general expenses of maintaining the base—which would be the tramp steamer—divided among everyone. He reviewed the suggested method of using a gold mine to move gold bullion, and sharing expense of that. He said, "I think a better method would be to pro-rate the mine expenses in proportion to the amount of bullion each outfit moves."

"That's about what I had in mind." The voice sounded satisfied. "What guarantees have you got in mind?"

"Guarantees of what, for God's sake?"

"That you're on the up-and-up."

Doc snorted, and endeavored to sound as disgusted as Whitey should sound. "Listen, brother, we've both got to take chances until we get acquainted. We've got seven million in bullion aboard, and a good ransom prospect, and if anybody should worry about being doublecrossed, it's us."

"Ransom is out."

"That," Doc said, "reminds me of another point. Who's going to be top dog of this thing? And don't say you are, because you'll get an argument."

"Any objections to a joint command?"

"Not if it's really joint."

"Willing to abide by a general vote on this ransom question?"

"I suppose so."

"It's a deal."

When, a moment later, Doc asked, "Anything else you

want to discuss?" it was Mr. Govern who answered. "He's gone. It's over. I'll go back with you."

"What the hell? Don't I get to take this blindfold off?"

"In the plane. In the plane."

In the launch, riding back to the plane, Doc realized gloomily that he had no idea what the steamer looked like at close range and that he stood no chance whatever of going before a court and identifying the man known as Cavu. It had been, the whole interview, melodramatic to the point of being silly, but it had been cautiously effective. They were clever.

"Take it off," Govern said. They were at the plane. Govern had a chart which he spread out when they were in the seaplane. "This is where we are." He marked a spot. "You know the position of your sub, so you can get us back."

Doc saw, astonished, that the submarine was not quite a hundred miles from the reef anchorage. "Do we bring our sub here?"

"Why not?"

"I just wanted to know." Doc eyed him narrowly. "I thought you guys had two subs. I haven't seen any sign of them."

Mr. Govern said he thought that was funny indeed. Did anybody think he, or Cavu either, was sucker enough to lay both subs in where they could be picked up without much effort? "Anyway, they're out on jobs," he added. "One of them isn't due back for about thirty days. The other one will be in next week sometime."

"You don't," Doc said, "seem to trust me."

"Sure we trust you—as much as you trust us."

Doc said dryly, "This should be one big happy family. You ready to take off?" Mr. Govern said he was set. Both engines started without hesitancy, all the dials behaved as they should. The man in the launch had untied the anchor line, showing surprise at the kind of knot he found it tied with. The launch moved away. Doc let the plane weathercock itself into the wind, then opened the throttle and took off, passing near the tramp steamer at about the level of the vessel's deck.

On the steamer, there was some profanity, and nervous fingers on half a dozen machine guns which, concealed back of portholes, had been following the plane.

Somebody said, "Damn him! He came close so he could get a look at the deck."

Another man, who evidently had done some flying, said soothingly, "You can't see any detail to speak of, going past in a plane that fast. If he had taken a picture, that would be a different matter. But Govern will see he didn't."

"I say, we had him. Why let him go?"

"Because there's more of his men on the sub. Why not clean up the crowd, all at one lick?"

They watched the plane, climbing steadily, become indistinguishable against the somber sky. After that, there was a relaxing, and lighting of cigarettes. Amidships, they were lowering a box of hand grenades into the launch.

"They're a hundred miles away," said a man who, on the bridge, was working over a chart. "Give the plane an hour to reach there. Say the sub will make twenty knots. They won't cruise that, but say they do to be safe. That gives us six hours."

"Plenty of time."

The launch headed out toward the entrance to the pocket-like anchorage surrounded by the reef formation. Here there were two fingerboard markers of the type used to mark channels in shoal water, but which obviously did not indicate a channel. They were range sights. The launch, passing out to sea, kept them aligned behind and ran for about fifteen minutes at fair speed.

Hand grenades, tossed overboard, now made four loud gulping noises astern as they exploded; there was a pause, then another gulp. The launch made a lazy turning circle, and by the time this was completed, an underseas boat was breaking water. A few moments later, another surfaced. Both craft were of Japanese manufacture, and they had been lying in water of sufficient depth, and on dark bottom which blended with their hull coloring, effectively concealed.

The launch collected the commander and an officer from each sub, then headed back for the tramp.

"We've got a pretty set-up," the launch pilot volunteered.

The submarine officers were interested. Their vessels, equipped with radar, had submerged at the approach of the plane. The radar, effective at far more than eye range, had given them time to get down safely, and they had lain on the bottom until the signal, four explosions, a pause and another blast, indicated there was no longer danger. That was all they knew about the situation.

The launch pilot grinned at them.

"Doc Savage just paid us a visit," he said, blowing their hats off.

The conference aboard the steamer was a grim matter. One of the sub captains, whom they called Blackman, demanded to know the background of the whole thing.

"You remember Willie Colton?"

Blackman said sure he remembered Willie, the thieving so-and-so. What had he done, cut his own mother's throat?

"Nah, just sold out his pals again. You see Willie got himself in with a gang that was planning to seize a Nazi submarine from the U. S. Navy and go into the same business we're in. When the scheme got far enough along that Willie knew it would probably come off, he got word, indirectly, to Govern. The next time Govern was in New York, he looked up Willie, and Willie gave him the dope. So right away, plans were laid. Govern was to contact these new pirates and offer a merger, and get them down here where we could knock them off and grab us another submarine, plus whatever in the way of gravy they had aboard the sub at the time."

"Where does Doc Savage come in?"

"Right where he was least expected. He's the leader of this pirate gang."

"Oh, hell! I don't believe it!" Blackman's eyes narrowed speculatively. "Say, if Savage has turned pirate, he would be a damned good man to tie up with!"

"He ain't so don't start licking your lips, brother. Savage and some of his men are on the sub. Govern doesn't know how many of Savage's men, and neither does Willie Colton. Willie hadn't dreamed this pirate—they call him Whitey—was Doc Savage."

Blackman was skeptical. "You meanta tell me the rest of the crew on the sub don't know Savage is their stud duck?"

"That's right. They're all genuine pirates but Savage, some of his men—Govern doesn't think it can be more than three or four aboard—and a newspaper or magazine writer, a girl, and some guy with her, and another guy they've got for ransom."

"Well, for God's sake! How did Govern get wise?"

"Govern," the other said, "used to be a college professor.

You knew that, didn't you? He taught speech, and like some speech professors, he learned to read lips. Okay, he reads lips still. So he saw, saw mind you, a big guy they call Colorado Jones address this Whitey as Doc. That might have been all right—a lot of guys call other guys by the nickname Doc. But Whitey and this Colorado Jones said something about Pete somebody now having a gun, and Pete somebody is the magazine guy with the girl. That, and using his bean, tipped Govern off."

The explanations out of the way, the plan for trapping the submarine was laid. Govern, it was explained, was to convince Doc Savage that the other two submarines belonging to the pirates were absent on forays and would not return, the first one, for at least a week.

Returning for the conference, Doc's sub was to be induced to enter the anchorage within the reefs.

"Once inside, they're cornered. One of our subs takes up a position near the mouth of the channel to block escape. The other sub will be lying in position, and all it has to do is raise its periscope for a signal, and let fly a torpedo when Savage's sub is in target position. Then it will surface and help shoot any survivors."

"What about Govern?"

"He won't be on Savage's sub then."

"How come?"

"He'll be in the launch, going ahead, showing the way into the channel. That way, he'll be in the clear."

"Think they'll fall for that?"

"Why not? It's a pipe. A pushover."

"Hell, he might just lie off the reef and keep us penned up in here until the Navy shows up."

"No, no, he can't. Because he's got a crew of genuine pirates. Govern figured out his whole plan. It must have been to turn pirate to get trace of us, then notify the Navy. That's what he'll try to do—play along until he can notify the Navy."

"Yeah, but what if—"

"Radio them before he gets here? Govern is gonna take care of that."

Blackman said, "It sounds okay to me, except the part about coming inside the anchorage with the subs. I don't like that entrance channel. It's pretty narrow, and not too deep."

"You've been in before, haven't you?"

"Sure, sure." Blackman consulted his watch. "What if they get here during daylight and see us? You'll never get them inside then."

"You'll be submerged inside the anchorage. There's plenty of water to cover you. And they'll come in at night. Govern will see to that. They won't notice you."

"Then we better get active," Blackman said.

XI

The seaplane, veering suddenly, rammed its float into the hull of the submarine. There was a crunching as the tip of the left wing was mangled by the deck stanchions. Mr. Govern, looking as sorry as he could, yelled, "Hell, that was my fault! I tripped on the rudder by accident!" He was not sorry. He thought: boy, that fixes it so they won't be taking no other looks at the anchorage from the air right away. They won't find the subs.

There was some profanity and shoving, and a pirate fell overboard and was hauled back again, before the hoist gear was made fast and the plane lifted aboard and, wings folded, was inserted in the deck hangar. Doc and Govern had gone below.

"One thing more, I forgot to tell you. Radio silence. You keep radio silence," Govern said.

"Haven't we been?" Doc scowled. "What is this, anyway?"

Govern shrugged. "That's Cavu's orders, not mine. I told him I didn't think there was a chance of you having pals you would call in after you got us located. He said it wouldn't hurt anyway."

"Pals?"

Mr. Govern grinned. "You'd be surprised how many million bucks there are on that old tramp steamer."

"Yeah? We weren't going to use the radio anyway. But that don't apply to radar."

"Not to radar," Mr. Govern said. "But I'm gonna fritz the radio, if you don't mind."

"The hell you are! I'm not going to have that set disabled!"

Mr. Govern said it wouldn't be disabled. He would merely take out some tubes. He said he was quite familiar with radio apparatus, and this seemed to be true, because he did nothing but remove the tubes, the strategic ones. Doc watched him.

They marked out the course on the chart, and turned it over to Eli Stanley, who was in charge of the current watch. After he had fiddled with a computer, Eli said, "We'll probably get there before midnight."

Doc Savage and Govern, enroute to the galley to get something to eat, stopped to look in at the millionaire who was being held for ransom, Mr. Calvin R. Ingraham. A slender, tired, bruised and frightened figure, Mr. Ingraham scowled at them from the bunk. He cursed them bitterly. Govern laughed. Doc said, "You're on thin ice, brother." They re-fastened the door.

"My advice," said Govern when they were walking on to the galley, "is to tap that guy on the head and drop him overboard."

"You speak too lightly," Doc said, "of a hundred thousand dollars."

"Think we'll get that much out of him?"

"Why not?"

They had corned beef hash and biscuits and fruit, all from cans, in the galley. Mr. Govern said he thought he would get some sleep.

Doc Savage made sure Govern was, if not asleep, at least in his bunk, after which he collected Renny Renwick, alias Colorado Jones, and they got Pete Idle. They held a conference in Brenda Linahan's cabin.

"We're in a jam," Doc said bluntly. "They know I'm Doc Savage."

The cigarette Pete Idle held between his lips split and broke as his lips tightened and terror seemed to make his eyes go out of focus for a few moments, then cross, the left eye remaining fixed, the right one moving inward slowly until Pete had a vacuous, imbecile-like expression. Foolishly, he removed the wreck of the cigarette and pulled shreds of tobacco off his lip.

Brenda's reaction, more inward, hence probably more violent, was curtained quickly by an instinctive rush of disbelief.

"I don't like the time you pick for jokes," she said.

Doc shook his head. "No joke. I wish it were."

"But how. . . ?"

"I don't know. We slipped somewhere. I'm sure Govern

didn't know it when he came aboard, but I'm also positive he knows it now."

Renny Renwick was examining his large fists bitterly. "Holy cow! I wonder—you say you're sure? What gave you the tip-off?"

"It was largely, I think, the way they're doing this," Doc explained. He described with considerable exactness the flight, the landing, the interview—he was quite detailed about the interview, repeating much of it word for word—and the return. "Notice anything phony about the interview?" he asked Renny.

Renny stirred doubtfully. "Was that all that was said?"

"Yes."

"It seems to me this guy who talked to you when you were blindfolded, Cavu or whoever he was, might have shown more interest in practical details like how many men we've got, what kind of equipment, our contacts ashore, and such. You had a lot of such detail prepared, didn't you, stuff that was phony, but would check out as being true if they investigated it?"

"That's it."

Brenda was skeptical. "It seems to me you've based a terrible conclusion on awfully little.

"Well, add a little guesswork and hunching," Doc said.

"That's what I thought! You don't really know."

"I'm going to act as if I did," Doc assured her.

Pete, who was impressed by Doc Savage, asked Brenda, "Want to put a little bet on it? I'll lay you he's right. This thing was too good, and maybe too complicated, to last."

"Damn both your hunches! I wish I were back in New York," Brenda said bitterly. "I'm scared. I don't care who knows it. I've been scared for days. When Govern pointed that gun at me on the *Poinsettia*, I thought I was as frightened as I was capable of becoming. Every day since I've thought the same thing, and I keep being wrong."

Renny wished to know what Doc thought they should do about it. "We could, as a last resort, circulate a rumor in our crew and get them to thinking this other gang of pirates is going to hi-jack them out of their loot." He frowned, added, "But that wouldn't be too good. The tramp steamer would haul out of that anchorage, and probably be hard to find, no more identification than we've got. There was no name on it, you say?"

"No name. And it was exactly like most of the other Liberty ships that were turned out early in the war. Likewise, I think you're right about it skipping out. Probably if we're not there by midnight, the steamer will be gone by daylight."

"But surely Navy planes could find it," Brenda exclaimed.

"Might. But maybe not. And if they did, could they prove anything? As cunning as these fellows are, I'll bet you that by the time a boarding party went aboard, there wouldn't be a shred of evidence."

Renny thought so too. "They would find an innocent tramp steamer engaged in trading in the islands."

"Exactly what," Pete Idle wanted to know, "have they ordered you to do?"

"Enter the anchorage."

"The lagoon"

"It's not a lagoon. Just an anchorage. It's a horse-shoe shaped coral reef formation, partly exposed at low tide in a few places. But it won't be a coral island and a lagoon for a few thousand more years."

"Then what?"

"I don't know. And I don't intend to find out," Doc said.

"But—"

"We can't wait until they spring their trap." Doc was emphatic on that point. "If we do, we'll have to fight our own crew as well as theirs. Too big odds."

"Have you got a plan?"

Doc nodded. He got a paper out of the former Nazi skipper's desk and proceeded to sketch, with remarkable accuracy considering the brief time he'd had to study it, the anchorage. "This is fairly close to scale," he said. He marked figures here and there. "These are the approximate soundings in feet, as nearly as I could guess the depth." He sketched in the tramp steamer. "The old Liberty was there, but they may move it." He added some more soundings around the inlet.

Renny, who had been watching, grunted suddenly. "Holy cow! We can block the inlet!"

Pete leaned over his shoulder to look. "How?"

"With this sub."

Pete quickly turned the color of white lead. "Oh, cripes! Is that safe?"

"We'll be glad to have you come up with a better idea," Renny told him grimly.

XII

At twenty minutes past eleven, standard time, Mr. Govern said, "They see us." He whipped a flashlight across the conning tower rail, aimed it carefully, and gave four rapid blinks of light, a pause, then another blink. From the distant steamer in the anchorage came a single answering wink. "Good." Govern thrust the flashlight in his coat pocket. "Now we go in. The launch will pick us up outside and lead us in through the channel."

Doc Savage concluded that Mr. Govern had missed his calling in not having been an actor. He had said as much to Renny earlier, and Renny agreed, except that he added this could have been the next best thing to Mr. Govern not having been born at all. Renny now stood at Doc's elbow.

"Colorado," Doc said.

"Yeah?" Renny grunted.

"Go below. Check to make sure everyone is at emergency stations. No leaving posts because of curiosity. Impress that on them."

"Okay." Renny slouched away.

Mr. Govern did not approve of Renny. "That fellow," he said, "should serve a hitch in the Navy. Teach him discipline."

"The only discipline Colorado understands is a hard fist."

"Yes. . . . I heard you had a fight with him the night you took the sub."

Doc made no comment. He put a pair of night glasses on the distant steamer, and observed the launch just leaving the landing stage. "They're coming," he remarked. He passed the glasses to Govern who, Doc noted, scanned the entire lagoon with them. A grim suspicion hit Doc. He thought: the man's not interested in the launch or steamer. He's searching the surface inside the anchorage. Why?

Doc became convinced that one or more of the pirate submarines was inside the anchorage.

The sub moved forward lazily under surface-engine power. Govern was still peering at the anchorage, but presently he handed the glasses back, and Doc, wary lest his attention was being cunningly misdirected, made a slow turn, covering the whole horizon with the lenses. He saw nothing, but the night was hazy, almost foggy, so not seeing anything did not necessarily mean there was nothing there.

He could hear the launch engine now, It was quite noisy, and he wondered suddenly why they had taken off the muffler, then he remembered that on the other occasion he had heard the launch he had been deafened slightly by riding in the plane, so the launch exhaust might be no louder now than it had been.

Eli Stanley and Colton were on the outside bridge with Doc and Govern. "Maybe we oughta get the gratings off the boat islands," Eli suggested.

"What good could you do against them floating around in a lifeboat?" Doc asked.

Renny came up from below. "Everything okay," he said.

Govern, on edge, easily irritated, snarled at him, "Why don't you phrase it the proper way! Say, 'Everything secure, sir.'"

Renny looked at him coldly. "Nuts to you."

Doc Savage stepped close to Mr. Govern and swung his right fist against Govern's jaw. Govern saw the blow coming too late, and there was a bare instant when surprise and horror contorted his whole face. He fell heavily, and Renny caught him, lowered him to the deck.

"His hat and coat," Doc said. "Take them off. They're the same ones he was wearing this afternoon."

Eli and Colton gaped, mouths widely and roundly open, not, for the moment, able to breathe, they were so taken by astonishment.

Doc gave them as evil a look as he could put on over excitement and said, "We're not going into this like sheep. But don't alarm the guys below."

Renny had Govern's coat and hat. Doc said, "Put them on."

Renny was reluctant. He knew the launch would be the safest spot when hell broke loose. "Hadn't you better—"

"No, you'll go in the launch."

The launch was close now. There were two men in it. If they were armed, the weapons were not in sight. The small boat made a circle, came in astern, and put-putted alongside. Doc gave orders. Eli and Colton, with boathooks, laid hold of the launch, and it laid heavily against the hull.

Doc jumped aboard the launch.

The pirates stared at him. "Hell, thought you were—where's Govern?" one muttered.

"Govern's indisposed. He's not coming."

The two men froze. It did them no good. Eli and Colton held the launch. Renny had a gun in his hand.

Doc also produced a gun. "Sit down. Act natural. And after you're down, take your guns out and drop them overboard. You're going to pilot us through the channel, and no funny business."

The two pirates stared at the menacing guns, at each other. Their eyes were wide, glittering in the darkness. "Better do it, Ken," one said. And Ken nodded, then cursed bitterly. He shut up when Doc ordered him to do so.

"Get aboard," Doc told Renny. When Renny was in the launch, Doc himself climbed on deck. "Cast off."

As the launch eased forward, they heard Renny order, "Take us through the inlet. And if the sub goes aground, I'm going to shoot both of you immediately."

The two pirates seemed somewhat relieved.

"So that's what's eating you," one exclaimed.

Doc wheeled on Eli and Colton. "Get out on the bow, clear out. Use sounding leads, and use them fast. One of you on port and one on starboard. We don't want to take any chances of running out of water."

The pair moved with willing alacrity. Now they probably thought they understood the reasons for the violence and surprise. Doc was merely afraid the sub was going to be led aground. That was what they must think.

Doc took over the steering control. He called down, "Speed six knots ahead." And, a moment later, he also ordered, "Blow safety. Blow all tanks." That was a natural command, because they would know that the submarine should ride as high as possible while passing through the gap in the reef into the anchorage.

It would keep them busy below, too, give them something to think about.

Lifting slowly until, cork-like, it rode high on the surface, the submarine moved forward. A short wake streamed out aft. From the launch, Renny called out changes of course as they occurred, because the approach to the inlet was not direct. Reefs, coral heads, had to be dodged.

"By the mark, five." Eli sang out soundings.

Doc swung a gaze at the tramp steamer. Nothing alarming there. His eyes searched the comparatively calm water of the anchorage. There, he felt, was where trouble would come from when it came. Let it come, he thought. He left the wheel a moment to slug Govern's jaw again, insuring the man's continued unconsciousness.

"And a half, four!" Colton called the depth of water.

Four and a half fathoms. Twenty-seven feet. The depth should not get any less—he hardly expected it to be this shallow, and he listened intently, suspiciously.

"On the mark, five!" Colton yelled.

The bar! That was it. They had passed over the bar, where the water always shoaled up somewhat. He listened to Eli and Colton shout soundings, and the water deepened slightly. They were entering the channel.

Anxiously, he swung his eyes, trying to ascertain just how far they were into the inlet channel. Suddenly he broke out in cold perspiration. This was deadly. If they didn't get in far enough, or got too far.

"How much farther before we're out of the channel?" he shouted at Renny.

He could distinguish Renny leaning over one of the pirates in the launch. Then Renny bellowed, "Over halfway through!"

He saw Renny's arm rise, fall, saw the pirate go down. He saw Renny close with the other pirate, begin fighting, and saw a gun muzzle spit pale red flame.

He saw this, actually, while he was bawling into the speaking tube, "Full speed ahead! Full speed! Quick!"

Feverishly, he put the wheel to port. Put it over as far as it would go, to emergency turn. He could feel, distinctly, the power surge from the engines. The vessel gained speed. It was already going fairly fast, better than six knots, which was almost enough by itself. He held his breath, waiting.

The bow hit the left side of the channel. It hit hard and harshly, grinding, lifting, tearing at the coral, embedding itself.

"Kill starboard engine! Full speed, port engine!" he roared into the tubes.

Then he locked the rudder hard over, left it, and dropped below down the hatch.

Amazed, frightened, angry faces confronted him. He repeated his engine order. "Kill starboard engine. Full speed on port engine. Quick! Give it everything!" To the bewildered faces, he said, "Stay below! For God's sake, stay below!" He didn't want them out on deck if he possibly could prevent it. It was something he couldn't prevent. But he might delay.

He squeezed past, went toward the bow. Reaching the cubicle where Pete Idle was confined first, he wrenched open the door, said, "This is it. Come on."

Pete was, he saw with relief, going to be all right. There was no more than a natural amount of fear and excitement on Pete's rather homely face. Pete had been supplied with a revolver and a box of cartridges, and he got these from where he had hidden them.

Doc indicated the gun. "You may not have to shoot it. Keep it out of sight. Shoot only as a last resort to save somebody's life."

Pete nodded, then shuddered and said, "Hell, don't scare me!"

"We'll get Miss Linahan."

Brenda was ready. Her color wasn't normal and she wasn't as talkative as usual. She also had a gun, which she had declared she wouldn't be able to shoot, and in addition she carried a folded sheet and the essential parts of a first-aid kit which she had made into a package. "Red Cross service," she explained. Pete grinned through his nervousness and assured her, "You're wonderful, baby."

"One more," Doc explained.

He reached the little cubicle where Mr. Calvin R. Ingraham, financier, was confined.

Pete was dubious. "Will that old gaffer be any help? Of course we ought to save his neck, but maybe he'll be safer—"

"I've been holding out on you." Doc was unfastening the door to the cubicle, which was hardly more than a locker. "This guy will be a lot of help. He's Ham Brooks—Brigadier General Theodore Marley Brooks. One of my associates."

Ham Brooks still looked like Mr. Ingraham, financier. But his manner wasn't Mr. Ingraham's cowed, how-dare-you manner.

Doc looked into the cubicle. "You hide the evidence?"

"Sure," Ham said. "If this flops, I hope they throw me back in there." He grinned at Brenda. "Haven't I seen you somewhere?"

"You should remember," she said.

Doc moved forward. "We'll go out through a gun access hatch. It'll be quicker."

The releasing of Brenda, Pete and Ham had taken time, although not as much time, probably, as it had seemed to Doc to require. He was pitting himself against astonishment, hoping confusion would hold the crew long enough for him to gain the deck. He realized now that he was going to lose. But he had expected that. Another thing he hadn't expected was four men, crowding around the gun access hatch, fighting to get it open and outside.

He said grimly, "One apiece for us. Don't shoot."

As he spoke, Ham went in ahead of him, grimly. Ham was fresh. Ham said loudly, "Here, boys, you've got to undog it at the top. Look at the top!" The subterfuge didn't quite work, because one man turned his head, recognized Ham as the prisoner for ransom, and yelled.

Ham clubbed the man, who promptly went down and slid past Ham's legs. Ham, probably thinking the man was knocked out, closed with another, but not as successfully. His intended victim got hold of Ham's gun arm with both hands, leaped up, and instantly locked both legs around Ham's middle in a scissors.

Action was vicious, silent, too fast for conscious thinking, planning, too swift for clear understanding. Doc, going forward, had his legs embraced by the man Ham had clubbed. If the clubbing had slowed up this fellow, it was not at all apparent.

Doc stumbled forward, knowing he was going to fall, but he got his hands on another man and pulled that one down. He was hit in the face. He struck back. He was down now. One man had his legs. He had one with his hands. Suddenly, somehow, Ham and the man he was wrestling with fell into the pile. Presently Pete Idle walked over the top of all of them to get at the remaining enemy, stepping, in the process, on Ham's face.

Pete was hit between the eyes with a gun barrel. There seemed no good reason why the blow should not have killed him. But it did not. All it did was start him batting his eyes uncontrollably at the rate of about twice a second, a symptom that persisted, to his alarm, for several hours. Pete grabbed the gun that had hit him. He got it, fell over backward with it. His enemy, overbalanced, upset on top of him.

Now and for the following seconds, the cramped area was

a senseless tangle of anatomy, gasps, curses, and sinew-wrenching effort. Brenda kept saying, "Hold him, so I can hit him!" to someone. She sounded, it seemed to Doc, so calm that he wondered about her sanity whenever he had time to wonder about anything.

Doc struck, twisted, gouged, bit whoever and whatever he could strike, twist, gouge or bite. In return he was struck, twisted, gouged and hit. He had, presently, the horrible feeling that they were going to fight there, like a barrelful of wildcats and snakes, forever, for all eternity.

He hardly knew when or how it was over, but it was, and Brenda was saying angrily to someone farther back in the submarine, "Go away, you!" and firing her gun.

They got the hatch open.

Doc had, fortunately, the foresight to yell, "Renny! Renny, be careful!" before they went out on deck. It was fortunate because Renny, in the launch which was now alongside the submarine, was calmly taking pot-shots at each and every head that appeared.

They scrambled out on the wet, slippery deck.

"In the launch," Doc said.

Brenda held back, gasping, "Mr. Ingraham—Ham Brooks is hit! He's down!"

Doc shoved her toward the launch, not gently, said, "Get going!" He turned back to see about Ham, but Ham came out of the hatch. "I got it," Ham said.

What he had got was a light machine gun, a Reising. They had planted it there previously. They had, as a matter of fact, planted the guns in several places on the sub for an emergency. But this seemed to be the only one they were going to be able to reach.

"Into the launch!"

Their boarding of the launch was, when they looked back on it later, comical, and it was certainly painful. Because each of them without exception lost footing on the slick sub hull and fell ignominiously into the craft. It was moving before they got untangled, and Renny was yelling angrily, "Holy cow, quit clowning! Use that machine gun! Use it!"

Doc, bruised and irked, said, "Run the launch!"

A moment later, Ham unlimbered the machine gun, and it frightened them all with its roar. He dusted off the conning tower. They could see a couple of tracers arch off strangely into the night.

Doc decided he would steer the launch. It would be very bad if they hit the reef at any point, or collided with a coral head. He took the helm from Renny, who demanded, "What kept you?"

Before he could answer, the launch hit a coral horn. The impact, not inconsiderable, upset them all, piled them against seats and thwarts. The launch heeling, grinding and rending, seemed to be on the point of capsizing, then didn't, and slid off the coral head and started moving again.

"We have a leak!" Brenda gasped, making what was probably the understatement of the night. A fire hose could not have put water in the launch faster than it was coming in.

Doc Savage, trying to visualize the lay of the reef, swung the launch so as to parallel it. There might be more coral heads, but they would have to take a chance with those. Renny, on all fours with a flashlight, was stuffing his coat in a rent. He said, "Five minutes, maybe, is all we can stay afloat."

"Enough," Doc said.

Pete Idle yelled, pointed, yelled again. Neither cry was words.

"To submarines!" Brenda exclaimed.

I was right, Doc reflected grimly. *They were inside, where I thought they were. Both subs in the anchorage. Trapped.*

"We get a break," he said grimly.

"A good one would be a change," Brenda told him. "How do you figure—"

"Watch."

On the submarine jammed across the inlet, they had manned one of the deck guns, and it now fired, the flash lighting up the night, dashing dark red light across the water about them. Far away, far out beyond one of the submarines, the shell exploded.

Ham's grunt was disgusted. "I don't see how they missed at that point-blank range."

"They'll plant the next one," Renny said.

He was right. The second shot was a clean hit on a conning tower. Renny, with the appraising guess of an expert, said, "They didn't do any real damage. Just messed up the conning tower and probably killed a few guys." He strained his eyes. "Why don't those birds turn loose torpedoes?"

Doc said, "We could hardly see the wake." He was maneuvering the launch in toward the reef, beginning to wonder if they were going to go aground before they sank. He could see breakers ahead. That, he hoped, would be a part of the reef which was hardly below the surface. They grounded.

"Out and behind the launch," he advised. "Better work away from the launch, in case somebody pops a shell into it."

Brenda said, "I hear an airplane."

"Your imagination," Pete assured her. "Can you swim?"

"Of course."

"Well, I can't, so—"

The sea seemed to jump around them, and the tops fell off the small waves. The explosion, probably not as gigantic as they thought it was, did not upset them, but its shock, through the water, made their legs tingle.

"Torpedo," Doc said. "There should be three"—he paused to let three more terrific explosions occur in succession—"more, and there they are. One sub emptied all the bow tubes."

"I tell you, I hear an airplane—more than one," Brenda exclaimed.

The submarine lying in the inlet was badly mangled, but by no means demolished. There was no more firing from it, though.

Down through the darkened sky above, dropping from beneath the cloud overcast, two planes came slanting. Approximately over the inlet, they leveled out, and both of them dropped flares. The amount of light suddenly over the anchorage was stunning. Doc could see the faces of his companions clearly. He wheeled toward the northern horizon, and in a moment saw the flash of a medium caliber gun.

Pete heard the shell approaching, gasped, "Oh, oh, I know what that is." He dived under the surface. Doc hauled him out, explained, "The concussion might—"

Two thousand yards beyond the tramp steamer, the shell burst. It was not spectacular; its shock was a faint slap against their legs, stomachs, brought by the water. A second one fell a hundred yards short of the steamer. Renny said, "The planes overhead are spotting!"

Then Brenda screamed, "Look! Look!" She was pointing into the north where, visibly outlined at intervals by the flash of its guns, stood a light cruiser.

Ham was laughing. "If I wasn't an old Army man, I'd say a kind word for the Navy," he said. "I'd say—" He didn't explain what he would have said, didn't finish, for his mouth roundly opened with horror, his eyes swelled and protruded, and in his neck, sinews whipped tight with horror.

Mr. Govern was walking out of the deep water on to the reef. It was incredible that he could have gotten there without being seen, heard, incredible that he could have gotten there at all. But he was there, and the revolver in his hand shaking just enough to make it frightening.

XIII

Another shell arched through the sky, hit the tramp steamer squarely; flame, pieces of ship, pieces of men, smoke, climbed around crazily above the deck; there was enough noise to interfere with what Mr. Govern was saying, but not enough noise to drown it out.

"Five of you," he was saying. "Five. Just right. Just enough to go around." His voice, guttural, hoarse, veined with fear, was not quite rational. He did not explain why five was such a good number. They knew he must mean there were five bullets in his gun.

He peered at Ham and said, "So they bothered with you!" He seemed surprised. A wave, curling over the reef, breaking, sloshed past Govern's shoulders, for a moment immersing his arms, the gun. But he kept his balance and the wave was gone in a moment. He said, "These cartridges are waterproof." He scowled at Ham, asked, "Who the hell are you?"

Doc Savage said swiftly, "Tell him the story, Ham! Tell him! He should know it, before he does anything!"

"Radio!" Ham said. He was hoarse. He had to fight down the impulse to yell words. His story—the story wouldn't help them. It wouldn't stop Govern. Govern would shoot them as quick after he heard the story as before. But the story would do one thing; it would get them time. Govern might listen. Time. Time was, at this moment, all there was of life. "Radio!" Ham blurted. "I kept the cruiser posted by radio. As a matter of fact, the cruiser was following the *Poinsettia*, keeping out of sight below the horizon, from the time we sailed from New York."

Flames were climbing up from the tramp steamer. They gave enough light to stain Govern's face redly. He was pushing out his lower lip at them, disbelievingly. He said, "You, Mr. Calvin R. Ingraham, didn't have a radio."

"I'm Ham Brooks."

"We searched you," Govern said. "I searched you myself."

"It was planted."

"Where?"

"In that compartment where they imprisoned me on the sub. A good job of hiding it, too. Outside antenna and everything. Used one of the regular antenna, through concealed wiring."

A wave broke around, but not quite over, Mr. Govern again. It didn't bother him. He stood like a post. His gun and hand were one rigid object. The revolver, a hammer model, was cocked.

"How," he demanded, "did you know you'd get locked up in that compartment?"

Ham said, "Doc Savage was giving the orders aboard, remember? And also, that little cubbyhole was a logical place for a prisoner like me."

Govern licked salt water off his lips. "So you went aboard as a prisoner for that. Cute."

Ham was frightened now. Afraid they would be shot at once. It was pretty certain. He said, "I kept the radio operating almost steadily. It was the most feasible way of keeping an operator at a secret radio."

"Cute," Govern said.

Doc, urgently, said, "There's another angle. You better hear it." There was no other angle.

No other angle. But there was another wave, coming in slowly, swelling the way waves do when they move into shoal water. Not as large a wave as the others, a feeble wave. Doc watched it, and knew it was life and death. A very small wave, feeble, futile.

A shell hit one of the submarines. Hit it squarely, opening it forward of the conning tower, making a hole with jagged curled edges as if a piece the shape of a sunflower had been cut out of the steel.

Govern cocked his gun. He said, "Nothing I do will get

me hanged any quicker. That's one satisfaction." He was waiting for the wave.

"One thing more!" Doc said urgently. "There's Cavu. Cavu. Let me tell you—"

"I'm Cavu," Mr. Govern said. "You can't tell me a damned thing about Cavu, because Cavu is me."

"I knew that," Doc said.

Govern stared. "For God's sake, when? The hell with it, never mind! Time is—" The wave came up around him. He went silent. The rising water covered his gun. He could have raised it, but he didn't because the gun had gotten wet when he was swimming and one more wetting would make no difference. The cartridges were, as he said, waterproof.

Doc said, "Take him, Renny!" He didn't, probably, get it all out. Because he was going forward, forward and down, diving into the wave. Now, for two or three seconds, Govern's—Cavu's—gun would be immersed. They had to do it all in that time.

Govern's gun exploded. It did his ears no good. Did the gun no good, either, because, when the bullet trying to get out of the barrel encountered the resistance of water, the back-pressure of powder split the cylinder. The rest was merely a matter of beating Mr. Govern down, of holding him under water, of hammering him, choking him, of tying his wrists with his own belt. This they did with enthusiasm.

The light cruiser was coming in fast. Its guns were silent, and its searchlights thrust out long, white, rod-like beams that probed and searched. The submarine that had been hit was down by the stern; the other was flying a white cloth of some sort.

Doc watched the steamer.

"They're going to beach it," he said. "I hope they do. The loot they've taken may be aboard." He wheeled on Govern, demanded, "What about that? Is the loot your outfit has picked up on board the steamer?"

Govern said nothing most expressively.

"Cavu is silent," Ham said. He laughed. "It's aboard. He wouldn't have that look on his face if it weren't." He nudged Govern. "What about it?"

Pete Idle grinned. "Cavu wishes he could walk the plank." Pete looked at the burning steamer, the two subs, the oncoming cruiser. He became miserable, disgusted. "No cameraman!" he complained. "All this, and no cameraman!"

Doc Savage relaxed. It was all right; things were back to normal. Pete Idle was again a magazine editor, worrying about *Solar, The News Weekly* and everything was fine.

Brenda clutched his arm, pointed happily at the cruiser. "They've seen us," she said.

THE TERRIBLE STORK

I

"What? Sixty-five?" screamed the auctioneer. He clutched his forehead, indicating that the shock was about to kill him. He said, "I'm dying! I'm murdered!"

This got just one titter, from one man, out of the eighty or so in the auction room. The others were silent; it was hot in the room, the chairs were hard, and nothing much was happening.

"Sixty-five *dollars*!" the auctioneer said. "Who'll bid seventy?"

But this didn't get a laugh either, until he yelled, "Okay, okay, my error, the bid was sixty-five *cents*. Seventy? Do I hear seventy *cents*?"

Monk Mayfair, the famous chemist, said, "That auctioneer is quite a comedian. Bob Hope had better watch out."

Ham Brooks, the equally famous lawyer, shifted miserably on the hard wood chair. "He's about as unfunny as you are," Ham said, wishing he had a pillow to sit on. He stared at his black cane.

"Ain't I unfunnier 'n that?" Monk Mayfair asked. He was a short, wide, hairy man. It was obvious why he was called Monk. "Shucks, now you got me worried," he said anxiously. "You've really got me worried."

"Worried about what?"

"When we're gonna get outa here," Monk said. "That's what's worrying me."

"I agree heartily," Ham said.

"Seventy," a voice said.

"Sold!" the auctioneer said.

"Oh, dry up!" muttered Ham. He wondered if a crack in the seat of the chair was going to catch him and pinch him. That was all he needed to make the afternoon complete.

Doc Savage asked, "Why don't you two take a nap?"

Doc Savage was a bronze-colored giant of a man who was conspicuous in the auction room in spite of the long raincoat he'd worn so as not to be conspicuous. Monk and Ham looked at Doc Savage. Ham asked, "Go to sleep? On these chairs!"

"Doc's being funny," Monk said. "He made a joke. Yes, sir, the auctioneer's humor is contagious." Monk's very large humorous mouth was all that saved his face from being frighteningly homely. He added, "No kidding, why don't we go somewhere else? What've we lost in here?"

Ham Brooks showed lively interest. "You bet! Go somewhere else. We've got the afternoon off, and we just started out for a walk, got tired, and came in here for a rest. Now what are we staying for?"

"Why don't we repair to a burley-cue show?" Monk asked.

"That's two good ideas from you in a row," Ham said. "Goodness, what kind of vitamins are you taking?"

The auctioneer held up a small shiny metal statuette of some kind of a bird, apparently a stork. "Who'll start it at fifty cents?" asked the auctioneer.

"Fifty," a voice said.

"Fifty cents is bid. Who'll give—"

"Fifty *dollars* is bid," the bidder corrected.

Doc Savage straightened on his chair. Straightening made him taller than anyone in the room, enabled him to see over people's heads. He said, "What on earth!" His eyes, which had been sleepy, became wide with interest—his eyes were more gold than brown, like pools of flake gold. He added, "Fifty dollars for that thing!"

"What is that thing?" Ham pondered.

"Some kind of a boid," Monk said. "This is gettin' dull, pal. What say we scrammo to the girlies?"

"Fifty *dollars*!" The auctioneer got his eyes back in their sockets. "Who'll give a hundred?"

"Good God!" Monk sat up suddenly. "Fifty *dollars*?" He added, "Say, what's that thing made of, platinum?"

Clear and tight as a bell, a voice came from the other side of the auction room.

"Two hundred dollars," it said.

Monk swallowed. "My, my," he said.

Doc Savage had swung his head. The bell-like voice of the second bidder belonged to a clear-skinned young man who looked brown and outdoorsy.

"Five hundred!"

This was the first bidder again.

Doc located him. He saw a wide man who had blue eyes and the cherubic smile of a cupid.

Ham asked, "Know the bidders, Doc?"

"No."

The bell-voiced young man said, "Five hundred and one dollars is bid."

"A thousand," said the fat, wide, smiling man.

"A thousand and one."

"Two thousand." The fat, wide man's smile wasn't genuine. Apparently his face just happened to be shaped that way.

"Two thousand and one."

"Three thousand."

"Three thousand and one."

Monk swallowed.

"Five thousand."

"Five thousand and one," said the bell-voiced young man grimly.

Astonishment was sweeping the auction room. Here and there customers were getting to their feet in order not to miss anything; some still dozed, not knowing what was going on.

A lull had hit the bidding. Outside, the noises of Forty-sixth Street made a quarrelsome background. The auction room itself was large, forty feet wide and about sixty feet long. It was a ground-floor storeroom which, for lack of any more permanent tenant, had been rented to the auction company, together with an upstairs floor and mezzanine for storage purposes. The auction firm itself was not a large one, but it was reliable. It made a business of disposing of estates, usually art objects and furniture collections.

"Five thousand and two dollars," a voice said.

Doc Savage and Ham Brooks both started violently, for the bid had come from between them. It was Monk Mayfair.

"You fool!" Ham was dumfounded. "You haven't got five thousand and two dollars!"

"Huh? Gosh, I haven't, have I?"

"Why'd you bid?" Ham demanded.

"The suspense got me," Monk muttered. "I guess I became hypnotized or something."

"What do you want with that thing?" Ham asked angrily.

"I don't want it." Monk became alarmed. "My God, do you reckon I'll get it?"

Ham looked at him bitterly. "I hope you do," he said. "I

would like to see what you would do with a five-thousand-and-two-dollar tin stork."

"You think it's tin?"

"How the hell do I know what it's made of!" Ham was irritated with his friend. "If you think you're going to borrow a single thin dime off me to pay—"

"Ten thousand and three dollars," bid the bell-voiced young man.

"Whoosh!" Monk subsided gratefully. "Saved by the bell," he said. Sweat had popped out on his narrow forehead. "What'd I bid on the thing for?"

Doc Savage's flake-gold eyes were alert, interested. He said, "Ham, that thing can't be worth ten thousand." His size, which was considerable, was deceptive until one was close to him. "The intrinsic value of the statuette cannot possibly be ten thousand," he added.

"How about platinum?" Ham was doubtful. "Would it be worth that kind of money if it were platinum?"

"Very doubtful."

Monk had an idea. "Maybe it's got diamonds and rubies in it." He became enthused. "I'm gonna bid again!"

Doc and Ham eyed him in alarm.

"Ten thousand on something you don't know what it is!" The usually punctilious Ham was getting mixed up.

"Ten thousand and four dollars," Monk explained. "That's what I think I'll—"

"Fifteen thousand dollars!" bid the fat man. He seemed angry. His smile was beatific.

Monk swallowed.

"Go ahead, bid," Ham sneered at him. "You didn't have five thousand, so it won't hurt you to bid fifteen."

"Fifteen thousand and one," said bell-voice.

Doc Savage was on the edge of his chair. "Monk." He nudged the homely chemist, directed, "Monk, go up and take a look at that thing. See what it is."

Monk batted his eyes. He was dazed by the bandying of so much money around an eight-inch-high statuette of a skinny bird, apparently made of tin. He seemed stupefied.

Ham said, "Dopey has dropped his marbles." He added, "While he's picking them up, I'll go look at that thing."

Doc shook his head. "Monk is a chemist. Let him look. Or both of you go look."

Ham leaped erect. "Come on, Gunga Din." He began

tramping on toes, reaching the aisle. Monk lumbered after him, and the seat occupants hastily removed their toes from danger. Monk was mumbling, "I'm a chemist. I can tell what kind of tin that thing's made of. God bless us!"

The fat, smiling, cherub man had drawn a gun and was pointing it at Monk and Ham. "Get back!" he said. The gun was about two and a half pounds of blue steel, an impressive cannon. "Sit down!" he added. He sounded determined.

Monk and Ham halted.

"Hey!" Monk yelled. "That guy's got a gun!"

Suddenly this was no longer an amusing interlude in a dull afternoon.

Monk and Ham froze. There was nothing else they could do. Doc Savage instinctively ducked for safety. So did the others who were quick thinkers.

"Here, here," said the auctioneer loudly. "Sit down! Don't interrupt the auction." He hadn't noticed the gun. "Sit down!" he yelled. Then he saw the gun and turned remarkably white.

Doc warned, "Be careful, Monk!"

Monk addressed the fat man loudly. He asked, "Brother, you wouldn't want to shoot me, would you? You don't even know who I am."

Ham said, "Sit down, you fool!"

"Sit down!" the smiling fat man said.

He didn't sound as determined this time. Monk was encouraged to be foolish.

"Brother, I'll sit down," Monk said, "as soon as you put away that gun. Not before. I won't be threatened. I won't be—"

Blam-m-m-m! Gun sound was the voice of thunder in the auction room.

Monk croaked, "Oh, God!" He went down, upsetting two chairs and also bringing Ham Brooks to the floor.

Ham thought Monk had been shot. He gasped, "Why, the dirty—" He started to grab for his own armpit holster. Monk clutched him, kept him from getting to his feet. "Stay here," Monk said. "There's nothing like having something solid under you when you quake with terror."

"They shot you!" Ham was gasping with rage. "I'll show the fat so-and-so—"

"Shot me! Where?" Alarmed, Monk felt of himself in search of wounds. "Where? Are you sure? I thought the fat man got shot. I thought the guy with the bell voice shot him."

Ham reversed himself. "Go ahead, stand up, get shot," he said. "I've got a notion to shoot you myself. What's the idea, scaring people?"

Monk said, "Who's more scared than I am?" He started to lift up and look around, changed his mind. "Take a look and find out what's going on, will you?" he suggested.

"I wonder if we can crawl to the door without getting shot at?" Ham pondered. He didn't do any looking.

Suddenly, deafening, the gun sounded in the room again. *Blam-m-m-m!* It sounded like the same gun. *Blam-blam-blam-m-m-m!* That time it seemed to be a different gun. It ran more to soprano.

"Who're they shooting at now?" Monk wanted to know.

"Doc, probably," Ham said.

"Serve him right, too," Monk said. "It was his suggesting we look at that stork thing that got everybody all worked up."

Except for the ear-splitting sounds of the guns, it had been remarkably quiet in the room. It was a paralytic sort of a stillness. Born of astonishment, it lasted only until understanding arrived. Everyone seemed to get the idea simultaneously: the idea was that bullets were flashing about. Suddenly every man was trying to get behind or under something, preferably two or three of his neighbors. The noise was an avalanche.

The auctioneer gazed in horror at the confusion before him. Abruptly he emitted a girl-like scream, whirled and dashed into the nearest refuge, which happened to be a large vault in a rear corner of the room—the premises had once been tenanted by a bank. The auctioneer hauled the door shut behind him, foolishly locking himself inside the vault.

He had taken the stork statuette with him because he had been holding it in his hand at the time.

The fat, smiling man and the young, bell-voiced man now got cautiously to their feet. They saw each other. *Blam-m-m! Blam-mm!* Each shot at the other. Neither hit his target.

Crawling on the floor, the fat, smiling man and the young, bell-voiced man now departed. The fat man reached the street ahead of the other and was out of sight down a subway kiosk by the time his enemy appeared. Fortunately the latter did not choose the subway. He ran a block and hailed a taxi.

II

Noisily, and too late, the police arrived, two green and white carloads of them. The sirens fell silent in the street as they entered the auction gallery premises. There they began collaring everyone who had lacked the foresight to make a discreet departure.

Half an hour later, the police vacated. They had failed to connect the two most outstanding events of the afternoon— the sky-high bidding for a worthless-looking statuette, and the target practice between the two bidders. The explanation for this error lay in the fact that the auctioneer, who had had the only really good view of proceedings from his podium, fainted shortly after they released him from the vault.

He had the stork statuette in his hand when he came out of the vault. He dropped it when he passed out from shock. Someone picked it up and put it on a table with the other stuff that was to be sold.

Before departing, the police gave a verdict: Two guys who didn't like each other had shot it out.

An ambulance, which had arrived with the swarm of police, carried the swooning auctioneer off to a hospital.

Another auctioneer mounted the stand. "Quiet! Quiet!" he yelled. "Your attention, please!" He beat on the stand with a wooden mallet. "Quiet! The auction sale will be resumed as soon as we get quiet," he bellowed.

Doc Savage, Monk Mayfair and Ham Brooks found seats for themselves.

This auctioneer was large, sandy-haired and serious looking.

Monk Mayfair said, "I hope he's funnier than the other one."

Ham whispered, "I hope the police don't find out that we failed to tell them the shooting started because we started to take a look at that tin bird." He was worried.

"Why didn't we tell them?" Monk wanted to know. "I mean, why didn't *you* tell them? You're so pure and honest."

"Because I didn't want to go to a police station and spend

an hour or two re-telling the story," Ham said. "Why didn't you?"

"I don't wanta tell 'em." Monk looked coy.

"Why not?"

"They woulda run me in their bastille, I was afraid," Monk confided. "On account of our telling them the shooting started because we wanted to look at the tin stork wouldn't have been a very logical story, do you think?"

"I doubt if the police would have believed it," Ham admitted.

"I doubt it, too. So I kept my gapper shut." Monk leaned back comfortably. "The police are very eager to make people out liars."

Ham suggested, "Why don't you try telling them the truth?" He examined his immaculate suit critically. "Things certainly picked up for a few minutes, didn't they." He snapped a bit of lint off his sleeve. "What are we hanging around for?" he asked. "Why don't we go home?"

The new auctioneer had things quiet enough to satisfy him.

He surveyed the crowd with contempt. It was considerably smaller than it had been prior to the shooting.

"Sale is resumed!" The auctioneer hit the stand a bang with the mallet. "You bid, I'll sell!" He scowled at them as if they doubted his word. He yelled, "You make me a price, and you've bought something, brother."

He snatched up the handiest piece of merchandise.

It happened to be the tin stork statuette.

The auctioneer yelled, "What'm I offered for this fine piece of art? And brother, I mean business."

Doc Savage spoke quietly.

"Fifty cents," Doc said.

"Sold!" shouted the auctioneer. "Brother, I mean business, as you can see."

Doc Savage hastily visited the wrapping counter, paid fifty cents in cash and the sales tax for his purchase, and walked out. He was shaking his head slowly in amazement. The auctioneer apparently hadn't known a thing about the fifteen thousand dollars bid on the stork statuette prior to the shooting.

But he got plenty of attention from those who knew what had been bid on it previously. From a beginning of startled gasps, the room went into an uproar of surprised talk.

Not understanding, the auctioneer hammered with his mallet and demanded silence. He didn't get it.

"Hurry up!" Ham urged the package desk clerk. "Don't bother wrapping the thing. I'll just carry it."

A large man with a greasy face was trying to get the auctioneer's attention. He was yelling, "Cancel that sale! I'll pay more." He picked up a chair and hammered the floor with it.

Monk Mayfair went over to the large, greasy man and said, "Buddy, you want to buy that thing?"

"For it I give five dollar," the man said. At the auctioneer, he screamed, "Cancel the sale! She's a mistake! I pay lots more!"

Monk said, "Buddy, would you like to go to the police station and explain why you want that little doo-lolly?"

Round-mouthed, round-eyed, the large man stared at Monk. Monk evidently looked like a cop to him. "I don't want it," the man said. Fear made a bubble of saliva appear at the corner of his mouth. He added nervously, "I just make a buck maybe, thassall."

"Sit down," Monk said.

The man sat down. Doc Savage was near the door with his purchase. Ham was already at the door, waiting. Monk joined them.

They piled into the first taxi which came along. Doc gave the driver an address. The cab got rolling.

"Great beavers!" Monk said. He suddenly doubled up with mirth. "Hah, hah, hah!" he yelled. Amazed enjoyment made his voice squeaky. "Can you beat that? Fifteen thousand dollars bid. And he sold it for fifty cents!"

Ham chuckled. "I wouldn't want to be that auctioneer's blood pressure when he discovers what happened."

Their cab driver was smoking a cigar. He executed a snappy turn into Sixth Avenue, aiming for a pedestrian who was crossing Sixth Avenue at Forty-third Street.

Doc Savage said, "We will return the stork if its value seems greater than the sum I paid."

Monk gulped. "Return it?" He was dumfounded. "Why should we return it?"

"We practically stole it," Doc said.

Ham Brooks snorted. "Listen, I've been hooked by these gyp auction galleries, and they didn't give me my money back. They just laughed at me when I complained. They told me I had no legal redress, and they were right. Now I'd like the pleasure of telling one of *them* to go to hell, that they have no legal redress."

"This place isn't a gyp outfit," Doc said.

Ham grimaced. "You're really going to return it?"

"If I decide we swindled them, yes." Doc was firm on the point.

Monk sighed. "I'm glad I'm not so honest," he said.

III

Doc Savage maintained a headquarters on the eighty-sixth floor of a midtown skyscraper which had been completed just in time to encounter the leasing slump of the early nineteen thirties. Doc's father, now deceased, had sunk some money in the building and in the process had acquired a permanent lease on the eighty-sixth floor. This had been about all Doc had inherited from his father in the way of property, although there had been a large heritage of adventure thrown in.

The elder Savage had been a remarkable man, more than somewhat on the screwball side. Doc had never known him well. His father had always been off prowling the unique corners of the earth. Doc, whose mother had died shortly after his birth, had been placed in the hands of a series of scientists, thinkers, judo experts, wrestlers and what-not, for training. His upbringing had been unorthodox and it was only an act of God that had kept him from growing up into more of a freak than he was.

The purpose of the strange upbringing, as nearly as Doc had been able to learn, was to create for the world a sort of modern Galahad, a righter of wrongs, a punisher of evildoers who were outside the law. Most kids wind up doing exactly the opposite of what their parents expect them to do, but Doc was more or less what the elder Savage had expected him to be. Possibly somewhat less. But the training had made him a man unusual enough to earn, in his own right, a reputation which in some quarters was phenomenal.

The simplest explanation of Doc Savage was that he was a professional adventurer. He was that because he liked it. The unusual, the unique, the exciting, the dangerous, fascinated him. He followed it as a career. Associated with him were five assistants: an engineer, a chemist, a lawyer, an electrical engineer, an archaeologist-geologist.

Monk Mayfair and Ham Brooks were two of Doc's assistants. Monk was the chemist, Ham the lawyer. There was no formal agreement that they were to work for Doc, no contracts or articles of incorporation. They simply worked with him because they liked excitement, too.

Headquarters consisted of a reception room containing an ancient monstrosity of an inlaid desk and a safe big enough to hold a jeep, a library which contained one of the most complete collections of scientific works extant, and a laboratory which occupied over half of the floorspace.

Monk sailed his hat on to the inlaid desk in the reception room.

"Let's see what that thing is," he said.

Doc Savage removed the stork statuette from his pocket and stood it on the desk. It fell over. He stood it up again, and this time it remained erect.

"Won't even stand up," Monk commented. His small eyes were glittering with interest. "Now, what is the thing?"

Ham was positive. "It's a stork," he said.

They studied the statuette from all angles. It was eight and one-sixteenth inches high. Doc measured it with a ruler. It was one and twenty-seven thirty-seconds of an inch wide. It weighed one pound, seven ounces and forty-eight grams. They had it in the laboratory when they found this out.

"It's a stinky looking stork," Monk said. He was growing puzzled. "I could make a better looking stork myself," he added. "The legs on this one are too spindling at the top."

Doc Savage went to a case and got out some chemicals and a piece of apparatus. He was going to run an assay to learn what kind of metal the stork was made of.

"It's not tin," Ham said.

"It's a spindleshanks stork," Monk said. "I hope it's made of platinum."

Ham became excited. "Maybe it's made of some new, rare kind of steel!"

"I would say it was steel," Monk said, excited himself.

Doc Savage made several tests. He did it the hard way, without removing samples of metal from the statuette. He used acids, and did a magnaflux test, X-rays, and some other tests.

He gave his verdict.

"Ordinary high-grade steel," Doc announced.

Even Monk was surprised. "That all?" He frowned at the steel bird. "What do you know about that!"

"It's not even worth fifty cents," Ham exclaimed. "We got hooked!"

Doc handled the bird thoughtfully. He rapped it against the edge of a table. The legs vibrated from the tapping, making a note like a tuning fork.

"Seems to have been formed with an emery wheel." Doc was holding the thing up to the light, turning it so that the marks were more noticeable. "Hand made," was his verdict. "Whoever made it put more than fifty cents' worth of time on it."

"Maybe we can find the owner and get our fifty cents back by selling it to him," Monk suggested.

Doc frowned. He was defeated.

"Maybe this isn't why we went to the sale," Doc said. He sounded confused.

Ham jumped. "Hey!" he said. "Did we go to that sale on purpose? I thought we just happened in there."

"We just happened to go to it on purpose," Doc told him. "You know Billy Copeland?"

"Sure," Ham said. "You don't mean that place was Billy Copeland's Auction Galleries?"

"It was Copeland's place."

Monk knew Billy Copeland, too. Slightly. Copeland was a white-haired old gentleman, hell on wheels with the chorus girls, who conducted a very genteel business of disposing of the odds and ends of estates. His reputation was good with his customers, and while he rarely got hold of a fine piece of art or merchandise, his sales were not junky.

Greatly alarmed Copeland had related over the telephone that morning that his store had been burglarized during the night. Or rather, an attempted burglary had occurred. Four men had broken into the gallery—four men that the watchman saw, although there might have been more—and had attempted to obtain something or other from the collection which was to be sold that day.

"The articles to be sold the following day are always assembled in the rear room the night before," Doc Savage explained. "The four burglars broke into the place, and overpowered the night watchman. They demanded that the watchman tell them where the stuff was which was to be sold today. They were not interested in anything except what was to be sold this afternoon. The watchman refused to tell them, and the burglars were alarmed by a passing policeman and fled before they found what they came after."

Copeland, the auction gallery owner, Doc continued, had become puzzled when he had checked over the articles which were listed in the catalogue for sale this afternoon, and found nothing which in his opinion was worth the time of one man to steal. Much less the time of four men.

Doc glanced at Monk. "Copeland said he thought of us because it seemed unusual to him. I wasn't doing anything, so I told him I would drop around to the auction this afternoon and see what happened."

Monk scratched his head.

"How's Copeland know there'd be an uproar at the auction?" Monk demanded suspiciously.

"He said he didn't. But if the men were after something that was to be sold this afternoon, he reasoned they might bid for it." Doc turned the stork statuette in his hands slowly, looking at it in disgust. "Incidentally, the watchman they overpowered last night was supposed to be hanging around to identify his assailants if he could. I didn't see any sign of him."

"Funny Copeland felt there'd be a mess," Monk said. He was suspicious.

"There's nothing funny about Copeland," Doc Savage said. He hunted and found a piece of tissue paper. "The funny thing is why anyone wants this steel stork." He wrapped the stork in the tissue paper. He dropped it in his coat pocket. "Why don't we go eat?" he said.

"I know a good French place," Ham said.

"I'm as hungry as a curly wolf," Monk said.

Ham examined Monk briefly. "I wouldn't say you were any too curly," Ham said.

The man with the diaper satchel seemed to have been waiting for them on the sidewalk. He came to them in a hurry and said, "Oh, thank God! Thank God, indeed!" He was a long-faced man with sunken cheeks. "I'm so glad I found you, Mr. Savage," he said. He was a sad looking man. "You are Mr. Savage, aren't you?" he added anxiously.

Doc Savage kept most of the astonishment off his face.

"Yes, I am Savage," he admitted.

"I'm so glad," the sad man said. "I knew you were, though. No one else looks quite like you." He clutched Doc's sleeve with one hand and used the other hand to point excitedly. "She's over there," he said.

"Who's over where?" Doc asked. He noticed that the man's satchel was fastened with zippers, but the zippers weren't closed.

"The girl," the man said.

"What girl?" Doc asked.

"Miss Nobel," the man said.

"Miss who?"

"Nobel. Ada Nobel," the sad man said.

Doc turned to Monk, asked, "Friend of yours? You know her?" He was stalling for time. The fact that the man's little bag was not zippered had aroused his suspicions.

Monk's mouth was open. Without seeming to close it, he declared, "Don't know the girl. Maybe she's one of Ham's."

The sad man pointed. "Please!" He was getting frantic. "She wants to talk to you," he urged. "There's not much time."

He was pointing at a sedan. The car was big and black enough further to alarm Doc Savage.

Doc said, "Do you mind?" He reached down and got hold of the handles of the diaper satchel.

The sad man cursed. He tried to jerk the bag free. He struck at Doc, missed when Doc leaned out of the path of the blow.

The sad man cursed again. "Damn you, we want that stork!" he cried hysterically.

The sad man then tried to dash the satchel to the sidewalk. Doc, using both hands and shoving with his shoulder, prevented this. The sad man let go the bag, then endeavored to kick it. Doc blocked the kick.

Now the sad man tried wildly to strike, kick, or hit the bag. He tried with feet, elbows, knees, shoulders. He tried to butt the bag with his head.

Monk had a horrifying thought.

"Nitroglycerine!" Monk screamed. "Run!"

He began running himself. His feet skidded somewhat until he got going, after which he gave a fair imitation of a rocket and vanished around the corner of the building.

Doc held the bag over his head. The sad man jumped,

trying to hit it with his fists. Doc punched him in the middle, and the sad man fell down.

Out of the dark sedan got two men. One wore a blond page boy bob wig, but he was, unmistakably, a man. Both wore blue suits. In their hands were guns. They fired.

Ham was already behind a parked car. Doc joined him. A bullet knocked its way noisily through the body of the car.

Ham said, "I know a place for us!" He was very scared. He added, "Oh Lord, put that bag down!"

Doc placed the diaper satchel carefully under the automobile. He was afraid something would happen when he let go the handles, but nothing did.

Ham sprinted twenty yards, bending low, on the street side of the row of parked cars. The men who had gotten out of the sedan stopped shooting. They were on the sidewalk, and apparently had lost sight of Doc and Ham.

Doc failed to understand why the men weren't pursuing them and shooting at them.

Ham's destination was an iron manhole in the street. Most New York manholes are located in the middle of the street, but this one wasn't. It was about six feet out from the edge of the sidewalk.

Ham wrestled with the manhole lid. "I've had this spotted for over a year," he gasped. He got the lid off the hole. He dropped into the hole.

Doc asked, "What's down there?"

"No bullets, that's a cinch," Ham said. He sounded far underground.

Dropping into the hole, Doc found himself in an orderly tangle of lead-covered cables. Their refuge was a part of the city's underground communications system.

"Close the lid," Ham urged. "Maybe they won't know where we went."

Doc did the opposite, and put his head outside. But cautiously.

From what he could see under the parked cars, he decided the two men had picked up the sad man and were placing him in the sedan. "They've collected their friend," Doc told Ham. "I think they're as scared as we are."

"In case they're not, I think I'll stay here." Ham sounded as if he was shuddering. "What was in that bag? That's what got my goat. That bag!"

Doc said the bag was what had gotten his goat, too. He watched the sedan pull out from the curbing.

"They're leaving," he reported.

Ham mumbled that he was glad to hear it.

The sedan swung out into the middle of the street and turned from sight around the first corner at a modest twenty-five miles an hour.

Doc Savage, continuing to watch, observed an elderly yellow taxicab which pulled out of the side street adjacent to the tall building which housed their headquarters. The taxicab looked familiar. So familiar that Doc blew out his breath in relief.

"Good old Monk!" Doc said heartily. "That's the quickest thinking I've seen in a long time."

"And the quickest get-away, too." Ham was not sharing Doc's pleasure.

Doc observed that the taxicab turned the same corner that had been turned by the sedan carrying the sad man and his two rescuers.

Ham added, "The way Monk ran was something else that helped scare me."

Doc climbed out of the manhole. "You know what Monk is doing? He's trying to grab our fat out of the fire."

"Huh?" There was a falling sound. A splash. "Damn the luck!" Ham wailed. "There's mud in the bottom of this thing!"

Doc said, "Monk ran around the corner to our garage. Monk jumped in that old taxicab we keep in the garage. He got it out in time to follow our friends. I just saw him drive off their trail."

Ham's wail came up from the depths. "My ninety-dollar suit, mud clear up to here," he cried. He was a man who had met a major tragedy.

IV

Spring-of-the-year clouds, peaceful as lambs, filled the evening sky. The late sunlight touched the clouds with gentle salmon tints, made the western heavens warmly palladium red, and, slanting through the eighty-sixth floor windows of the tall building, made a pleasant place of the reception room. The placidity which pervaded the outdoors also filled the reception room, except for the sound of splashing water in the shower in a corner of the laboratory.

The rushing noise of the shower stopped suddenly, breathlessly, as Ham Brooks turned it off. Ham called, "Has Monk phoned in yet?"

Doc said, "No." He was watching the telephone hopefully.

"You think he will?" Ham demanded anxiously.

"Why not?"

"I guess there's nothing else he can do," Ham admitted. "But you never can tell about Monk. When everybody else is walking on their feet, that's the time Monk picks to walk on his hands."

Ham came in, naked, toweling himself. He was astonishingly muscular. He added, "I hope he has sense enough not to get shot."

Doc said, "You can put on one of my suits. Try the second locker."

"Thanks." Ham went back into the laboratory. "Have you opened that diaper satchel?" he called.

"No."

"Maybe there's a bomb in it," Ham said nervously. "A time bomb, maybe."

"There's a bottle in it," Doc said.

"A what?"

"A bottle. A half-gallon bottle."

"How do you know if you haven't opened it?"

"I peeked."

"Why don't you open it and see what's in the bottle?" Ham suggested.

Doc explained, "I'm waiting for you to do that."

"Not me," Ham said hastily. "I don't open any strange bottles, no thanks."

"I think it's just a half-gallon of diphenylchlorasine," Doc explained.

"Come again?" Ham suggested.

"A sensory irritant in the form of a fine powder which mixes with the air and will render a man helpless because of sneezing, coughing, and eye irritation, in a few moments," Doc said.

"Oh. Tear gas?"

"One form of it."

"No wonder the sad-faced guy wanted to break the

bottle!" Ham exclaimed. "By golly, he would have laid us out if he had." Ham seemed to be amazed at the resourcefulness of the sad man. "We had a narrow escape, didn't we?" he added.

Doc said, "Want to hear a guess? I think they planned to gas us if they had to, and search us for the stork statuette. But the scheme didn't quite hatch out."

Alarm seized Ham's voice. "Where's that stork now?" he demanded.

"Still in my pocket."

Ham was silent for a while, thinking. "I'll bet we'll wish they'd got it before this is done," he said.

Silence came into the place again. Doc Savage leaned over and lifted the receiver off the telephone and listened to make sure that it was in working order. It was. He replaced the receiver. After that he sat in morose silence, wondering what had happened to Monk, whether Monk had managed to keep on the trail of the sad man and his two helpers.

In the laboratory, Ham exclaimed, "Goshamighty!" He had looked into a mirror.

"How does my suit fit you?" Doc asked.

"It would fit two of me just fine," Ham said. He entered the reception room, fully dressed.

Doc examined him. "You'll be all right if you don't have to make any quick jumps," Doc decided. "If you do jump out of it, don't run off and leave that suit. It happens to be my Sunday one." Doc indicated the bottle. "You want to open that?"

"Not me," Ham said hastily. "I'll take your word it contains diff—die—whatever you said it was." He backed away from the bottle in alarm.

Doc Savage uncorked the bottle, noticing that this made Ham turn white. "See." Doc passed the bottle neck under his nose. "Diphenylchlorasine," he added. He hastily corked the bottle, sneezing. "One of the tear gases." Tears began to flow from his eyes. He wished he hadn't shown off by opening the bottle. He had been fairly sure it was diphenylchlorasine in the bottle, but he could have been wrong. Good Lord, suppose it had been poison gas in the bottle, he thought.

Ham eyed the steel stork statuette. "I wish there was something we could do while waiting for Monk to call," he said. "I'm getting nervous." The stork was sitting on the inlaid desk.

Doc closed his eyes for a moment. Then he jumped.

"What a dope!" Doc said. He was disgusted with himself. He added, "Ham, look up the telephone number of the Copeland Auction Galleries."

Billy Copeland, proprietor of the auction concern, had a hearty bull-fiddle voice developed by a great deal of bellowing at customers.

Doc Savage listened to the unhappy noises Copeland made over the telephone. "Oh, we'll return it to you if it proves to have real value," Doc said. "We weren't trying to steal it from you. . . . No, I know you didn't say that." He listened to more excited talk from Copeland, said, "Yes, I realize they were bidding thousands of dollars for it, and I can assure that I will consider the statuette to be still your property." He frowned at the telephone. He added, "Providing, of course, you can give me some information. I want to know whom you were selling that statuette for."

Doc listened thoughtfully for at least a minute while Copeland talked.

"When did he die?" Doc asked.

Copeland talked some more.

"Any surviving relatives?" Doc asked. To be certain, he asked again, "None? Are you sure?" Finally he said, "Goodbye, Copeland. No, I want to keep the statuette a while yet. Yes, I know you do. Goodbye."

After Doc hung up, Ham said, "Thinks we're trying to steal the gimmick, does he?"

"He conveyed that impression, but politely," Doc admitted.

Ham snorted. "If he had it, all them strange guys would have been shooting at him instead of us. I wonder how he'd like that. Personally, I would like it fine."

"We'll mention it to him," Doc said, "if he insists on having the statuette back right away."

Ham nodded. "Okay. Whom was he selling the statuette for?"

"The estate of Mason Carl Wentz," Doc said. "Ever hear of him?"

"No."

"Here either," Doc said.

*   *   *

Doc Savage leaned back. "Billy Copeland seemed to think we should have heard of Mason Carl Wentz," he said. He contemplated the ceiling thoughtfully. "This Wentz died about sixty days ago. He died at his home in Arizona." The ceiling needed re-painting. "Wentz had some art objects and antique furniture which went with his estate. The stuff was placed in the hands of Copeland's auction gallery to sell. That's all there is to it. The statuette of the stork was part of Copeland's stuff, of course."

Ham said, "Arizona?" He sounded suspicious. "What would make them bring an estate all the way from Arizona to New York to sell it?" Ham sounded like a lawyer who had caught the defense witness in an important lie.

"Copeland explained that," Doc told him. "New York is a sucker market for antiques and paintings and furniture, so such stuff is shipped here from all over the country to be sold." He shook his head. "Nothing suspicious there."

"Didn't Copeland know anything special about the stork?" Ham asked, disappointed.

"No." Doc went back to watching the telephone hopefully. "He feels that the burglars last night were after the stork, though." He wished Monk would call.

Ham nodded. "It wouldn't take Einstein to figure that out," he remarked. He went over and inspected his reflection in one of the windows. "I wonder if I've got time to go to my club and get a suit that will fit me?" he asked.

"No." Doc stood up suddenly. "I've got a job for you." Doc glanced at his watch, added, "I'm going to leave for a few minutes. While I'm gone, find out what you can about Mason Carl Wentz."

Ham grimaced at his reflection in the window. "Find out about Wentz? Where the heck would I start?"

"Copeland said Wentz was a banker," Doc said. "Start on bankers." Doc put on a hat, a lightweight topcoat. "Use the listed telephone," he added. He pointed at their private instrument, the one with an unlisted number. "Keep that one open for Monk's call."

Doc put the shiny stork statuette in his coat pocket and went to the door.

"You better be careful somebody doesn't waylay you," Ham warned.

Doc said, "I will," and went out.

Doc Savage did not leave the building. Nor did he use

the elevator. He took the stairs, walked down four flights, and walked down the corridor examining the legends on office doors. The door he selected was lettered: J. B. FOWLER, PATENT ATTORNEY, and also said, TOLLIVER JONAS, WORKING MODELS.

Doc went in, asked a middle-aged woman, "Is Jonas here?" The woman said, "Who is calling?" Then she recognized Doc and became excited. "I'll tell him," she exclaimed.

Tolliver Jonas was a young man who walked with a slight jumping movement due to a wooden leg. He was one of the most skilled model makers in the city. His chief business was making working models for inventors.

"Hello, there, Mr. Savage," said Jonas heartily. He had done work for Doc before. "What can I do for you?" he asked.

Doc asked, "You have facilities for casting metal forms, haven't you, Jonas?"

"Small stuff only," Jonas said. "How big would you want?"

Doc drew the steel stork from his pocket. He said, "I want some duplicates made of this."

"That's small enough," Jonas said. He picked up the statuette and examined it. "You want this duplicated? You want it of steel, like this?"

Doc shook his head quickly. "That's what I don't want. Not steel. But use something that might look or feel about the same. Not lead or aluminum, because they would be too soft. Use a reasonable duplicate, but not steel."

"Can do," Tolliver Jonas said.

"Make me about six copies," Doc said.

"Okay. I take it you want them enough like this to fool somebody who didn't know metals?" Jonas was not prying. He was just making sure what Doc wanted.

Doc nodded. "That's the idea. Several people seem to want that thing, and I thought I would keep them happy."

Jonas grinned. "Happiness is wonderful," he said. "How soon do you want the duplicates?"

"Pronto," Doc said. "How soon can I get them? An hour?"

"Oh, hell!" Jonas looked discouraged. "I was just about to knock off for the day." He hesitated, asked, "You want me to stay and do them?"

"I would certainly appreciate that," Doc told him.

"Oh, all right," Jonas agreed. "But don't squawk when you get my bill."

Leaving, Doc paused with his hand on the door knob. "You better keep your door locked while you've got that stork around," he advised.

Jonas was startled. "Sure," he said uneasily. "Sure, I will."

Ham Brooks' hair was mussed. On the desk in front of him was a New York telephone directory, a Los Angeles telephone directory, a New York and a Los Angeles city directory, a copy of Who's Who, and a directory of banking institutions and their credit ratings.

Doc Savage asked anxiously, "Has Monk telephoned in yet?"

"Not yet, damn him," Ham said in a worried voice. "I'm getting scared." There was perspiration on his upper lip.

Doc asked, "What about Mason Carl Wentz, the ex-owner of the stork?"

A telephone rang. "Monk!" Ham gasped. Then he swore, for it was the listed phone. He grabbed up the instrument anyway, said, "Brooks speaking. . . . Oh, I see. When was that? Two years ago. Okay, thanks."

He hung up. "Mason Carl Wentz retired from business two years ago," he reported. "Wentz was a private banker, one of the vanishing Americans. An investment banker. He operated in Los Angeles and New York, head office in Los Angeles. An honest, upstanding and fairly rich man, as far as I can learn."

"What about the Arizona end?" Doc asked.

"Fear's End," Ham said. He sounded as if he wanted to surprise Doc with something.

"Eh?"

"That's the name of the ranch, Fear's End," explained Ham. "Sort of symbolic, don't you think? Here is this old banker, bewildered by the bloody, confused state the world has come to, so he retires and goes off to a ranch in the Grand Canyon country to live the rest of his days unmolested. What better name could he give the place than Fear's End?"

Doc was not impressed by the symbolism. "In the Grand Canyon?" he said. "The Grand Canyon is a national park."

"Not where the ranch is," Ham said. "Or so the banker told me who had been out there. The banker said it was a hell of a place, a million miles from nowhere, and with the kind of scenery around it that would scare the pants off you."

Doc was disgusted.

"Just what," he asked, "did you find out about a steel stork?"

"Nothing," Ham said sourly. "Everyone I asked was perfectly normal about it. They thought I was crazy."

Stillness settled in the room. The ringing of the telephone, and Monk's voice, were the only sounds that could dispel it.

Ham Brooks, crouched anxiously on the edge of a chair, was made ridiculous by the outsize of his clothes. He looked miserable. He looked as if he would like to scream, or shed tears. Ham thought a lot of Monk Mayfair. He never spoke a civil word to Monk if he could help it, but he had a very affectionate regard for Monk. Monk understood this and felt the same way about Ham. He never said anything nice to Ham either. They enjoyed insulting each other and practicing practical jokes on each other. Their comradeship was perfect.

When the telephone rang, Ham automatically picked up the wrong instrument, the listed one. He saw his error. "Monk!" he yelled. He was so excited he couldn't pick up the other phone. Doc got it. "Yes?" Doc said.

Monk's voice said, "I've got myself into a little trouble." Emotion, excitement probably, made Monk sound squeaky.

"Don't keep it a secret," Doc suggested. "Did you follow those fellows?"

Monk said, "You know me—bloodhound Mayfair. I didn't call in before because there didn't seem to be a telephone handy. I'm still on their trail. I'm on Long Island, in a graveyard to be exact. I finally discovered that there was a telephone in the caretaker's shack, and it's the one I'm talking on. The caretaker seems to have gone home for the day."

"What," Doc asked patiently, "are you doing in a cemetery?"

"I followed my game to a house," Monk explained. "The graveyard seems to be the best place to watch the house from. That's very logical, don't you think?"

Doc inquired, "Would you mind telling us where the cemetery is? Or do you know?"

Monk said of course he knew, and he gave the location.

Doc recollected the place faintly. Automatically he began to think of the roads to take to get out there most quickly. This train of thought was wrecked when Monk added, "I got me a prisoner."

"Prisoner!" Doc exclaimed. "You've caught one of them?"

"I caught somebody," Monk said. "I haven't decided just who she is."

Doc swallowed with difficulty. "Who *she* is?" he said.

From the pleased sound of Monk, she was evidently good-looking. He verified this. "She is not too hard on the eyes," Monk advised. "But she has a very sharp way with words."

"Who is she?" demanded Doc Savage.

"I'm trying to get acquainted," Monk explained. "I have told her who I am, thinking that would—ouch!" He gasped in pain, added, "She kicked my shin!"

Doc said, "We'll be right out there." He dropped the receiver on its hook. He told Ham, "Monk has caught a girl."

Relief made Ham gasp. "He's running in form," Ham said. "The old roué," he added.

V

The night had a clammy quality, faintly warm, like a sick man's breath. The sun, vanishing in the west, had taken with it the warmth and pleasantness of the day; the air had become different, lifeless and moist. There was some ground fog through which the car charged bearing Doc Savage and Ham Brooks.

Doc, kicking out the clutch, said, "It's along here some-where." He didn't sound too sure.

"You couldn't prove it by me," Ham confessed.

Doc stopped the car. "We'll walk," he said. The car headlights made two long oyster-colored ghosts in the fog. He added, "No need to ask for trouble." He switched off the lights and the ghosts vanished. "The place has big, brick gate posts."

Their feet made squishy sounds in the grass beside the pavement. It was no better when they walked on the con-crete, because the scuffing was like bones rubbing together. "Nice scary preamble to a graveyard," Ham commented.

"You're not afraid of graveyards?" Doc asked.

"Certainly not," Ham said. "It's the ghosts that inhabit them that scare me." A pair of huge brick pillars loomed. "Isn't that the gate?" Ham asked.

Doc said it must be. He said he had no idea where the caretaker's shack would be, but it would probably be near the gate. "I hope the gates aren't locked," he said. He tried one of the gates, added, "They're not."

The gates, massive, and of rusting iron, made an ungodly moaning sound when Doc opened them. Ham muttered, "If there are any spooks around, that should bring them out."

Doc discovered a building. He approached it warily, said, "Monk?" There was no answer, so he called, "Monk? You there?"

He pushed open the door of the building. The room inside was less than ten feet square, roughly furnished with a stove, a chair, a desk and a telephone.

"This must be where Monk called from," Doc said. He was using a flashlight, holding a palm over the lens to cut down the amount of light. He added, "Monk was here, all right." He had found a note.

The note said, *Gone to watch house—Monk.*

Ham was disgusted. "What house?" he said. "Boy that Monk is a mental giant." His endeavor to sound angry didn't overcome his pleasure at finding Monk had really been here and that nothing drastic had removed him from the premises. "What do we do now, look around?" he asked.

"Might as well," Doc said. He changed the position of the note, wrote, *Hunting you, you dope,* on it, and signed Ham's name. He said, "Let's see if we can find Monk."

Then he observed that the bit of paper the note was written on had a ragged torn edge at the top and also at the bottom. Doc pointed out this peculiarity to Ham.

Ham didn't think two torn edges on the paper was peculiar. "Monk just tore it out of that notebook he uses instead of a memory," Ham said.

"But *two* ragged edges." Doc was not convinced.

"Oh, he'd previously torn a piece off the bottom of the page," Ham said.

They went outdoors. The cemetery was still, black, awesome around them. They had not realized it was quite so dark. The tombstones, the white ones, were faint shapes like frozen wraiths.

They moved forward, wondering when they were going to fall over a marker. "Good God, of all the places he could pick to make us hunt for him," Ham complained. "How big is this city of the dead, anyway?"

"Not large, about forty acres, as I recall," Doc told him.

"Forty acres of tombstones is a lot of tombstones," Ham grumbled.

Doc Savage was wondering if they weren't doing the wrong thing in prowling the cemetery in search of Monk. He was not entirely satisfied about the note. It was not like Monk to fail to say, in the note, where he had gone and be specific about it. Monk was not dumb. Ham didn't think he was, either, although he was continually saying so.

Doc whispered, "Ham." This caused Ham Brooks to start violently. Doc continued, "I'm wondering if Monk couldn't have put more to that note."

"Eh?"

"A map," Doc said. "It would be more like Monk to draw a rough map of where we could find him."

"There wasn't any."

"There might have been," Doc said, "on the bottom of the note."

"Why'd he tear it off, then?" Ham demanded.

"Maybe he didn't," Doc said. "Maybe someone else did."

Ham stopped breathing for a while. Finally he asked, "You trying to scare me?" Uneasiness made his whisper hoarse. He added, "I don't see what on earth makes you think that."

"Well," Doc said, "there's nothing we can do about it now. Let's proceed."

A step at a time, they advanced. Their task was almost hopeless, and they both knew it. As Ham had said, forty acres of cemetery was a lot of cemetery. Especially when it was this dark.

Suddenly Doc heard Ham gasp. "Whoosh!" Ham gasped. Ham sounded some distance away, so they must have become separated. Abruptly Ham said, "Ooo-o-o-o!" He followed this with a gagging sound. He added, "I've found a body!"

"Monk?" Doc demanded.

There was a moment of horrifying silence, while Ham explored in the darkness with his hands. "Not hairy enough,"

Ham said. "I guess it's—ugh! Ouch!" A blow, a grunt, movements, was almost one sound. Ham cried, "Hell, it's alive!"

Doc Savage jumped toward the sound of Ham's voice. He encountered something large and hard. A human-shaped figure. He was about to smash it with his fist when he realized it was a stone or metal statue, probably of an angel, marking a grave.

A gun emitted noise, a sheet of flame.

Ham's voice grated, "Shoot me, will you!" From the way he sounded, it was impossible to tell whether or not he had been shot.

There was a blow, a struggle.

There was a man running off in the darkness, running fast, falling over tombstones and getting up and running again.

The gun sounded three times. The flashes made pale red lightning wink over the graveyard.

Then silence.

Doc Savage, crouching beside the angel, tried to reduce his breathing to soundlessness. The angel seemed to be made of bronze. A dark metal, anyway. Doc began to crawl toward where the gun had exploded.

Finally he distinguished a man's figure. The man was poised. One hand, evidently holding the gun, was upraised.

Doc prepared to spring upon the figure. But the figure called, "Doc?" anxiously.

"Ham!" Doc explained. "In another second, I'd have jumped you!"

Ham said, "Yes, and got yourself shot." He sounded badly shaken. "Boy, that guy was tough. I got his gun by accident, or he would've fixed me good. He felt as hard as nails."

"Could he have been Monk?"

"Not a chance." Ham was positive. "He was lying here hoping we wouldn't notice him, and I stepped on him by accident. He didn't move even then, so I thought he was dead."

Now on the far side of the cemetery, a fight started. It consisted of blows, running, cries of pain, yells, and a bellowing like a bull. The latter belonged to Monk Mayfair.

"That's Monk," Doc said. "Come on!" He ran toward the sound. He demanded, "Any shells left in that gun?"

"Should be two," Ham said.

"Save them." Doc had his hands out in front, feeling for grave markers. "You may need them." He wished they could find a road through the cemetery.

"Listen!" Ham gasped.

There was a new voice. A woman's. It cried, "That man is Monk Mayfair! They have the stork!" She sounded terrified.

Doc wondered why she was yelling that. He found a road. "Here's a lane," he told Monk.

They made more speed now.

The fighting noises had subsided. They had lasted a dozen seconds, probably. It had seemed longer.

But the girl was still crying out. She was saying the same thing: "That's Monk Mayfair. They have the stork!"

The road was black-topped. By running on tiptoes, which they were doing, they made almost no noise. If there had been more fight noises, they would have heard them. There wasn't. There was only the pounding, rather lightly, of a woman's fast-traveling feet.

She was coming toward them. She cried, "It's Monk Mayfair, Doc Savage's aide. They have the stork!"

Doc said, "Pss-s-t! Ham, I'll get her."

They stopped. "You're welcome to her," Ham whispered nervously. "She may have a gun."

The woman was yelling, "Monk Mayfair!" again when Doc caught her. It was no trick catching her. She ran into his arms. He had a hair-raising moment wondering if she had a gun. Apparently she hadn't.

She kicked, clawed, scratched, pulled hair, bit him. He began to wish she had a gun.

With a stroke of brilliance, Ham said loudly, "Doc Savage, whom have you caught?"

The young woman became still. "Are you Doc Savage?" she demanded. She had hold of Doc's hair with both fists.

"Would it make any difference?" Doc asked painfully.

"Yes. The answer is yes."

She released her grip. "They've caught your friend, Monk," she said. "If you expect to help him, you'd better get busy."

Doc thought that the girl didn't sound half as scared as they were. He said, "Ham, stay here with her. And hang on to her. I'll try to help Monk."

*   *   *

Moving with great care, Doc Savage went forward. There was a small hill, then a sharp slope downward, and he encountered a high iron fence which seemed to encircle the cemetery. He reached up, and found the fence could be climbed quite easily. But he did not think that Monk could have been gotten over the fence, conscious or unconscious, so readily.

He heard a car start. It was not far away, about a block distant. He saw the car headlights, saw the light move rapidly, appear and disappear behind houses, and finally vanish down a road.

Listening for two or three minutes, he heard nothing more, saw nothing but some lights come on in some houses, probably lights being turned on by people who had heard the uproar and become alarmed.

Doc went back.

The girl was whispering to Ham Brooks. She was saying, "I kept yelling that way so they would be sure it was Monk Mayfair. I did it to save Monk's life."

"How'd you figure that'd save Monk?" Ham was amazed.

"Because you have that stork. They want it. They'll keep Mr. Mayfair alive and try to trade him to you for the stork." She sounded positive.

"What makes you so sure?" Ham demanded.

"I'm not sure. But it was an idea. I think it was a good one."

Doc called cautiously, "Easy with the gun, Ham." Having identified himself, he joined them. He asked the girl, "Was Monk inside or outside the cemetery when they jumped him?"

"Outside," the girl said.

"On the other side of the fence?"

"Yes."

The men hadn't had to hoist Monk over the fence, then. "How many were there?" Doc asked.

"I don't know. Four at least," the girl said. Fright was beginning to displace the confidence in her voice. "He left me inside the fence. Mr. Mayfair, I mean. He was going to scout the house, he said. He thought it was dark enough for that."

Doc said gloomily, "I think they got away with Monk." He wished he could see what the girl looked like. "What house was it? We'll investigate," he added.

Suddenly the girl began to sob. She said, "I'll sh-show

you." She choked on the words. "I'm skuk-scared," she explained. She resumed sobbing. "I'm skuk-scared of graveyards, too," she added.

"Who isn't," Ham told her. "Here, take my arm. You'll be all right."

They made their way to the fence, and climbed over it. Ham helped the girl over from the inside, and Doc helped her down from the outside. He became somewhat embarrassed.

Doc said, "I don't see how you were so sure they would kidnap Monk, instead of murdering him."

"They're kuk-kidnapers by nature," the girl told him. "They did it to my uncle."

"Your uncle?"

"They kidnaped my uncle, Harrison Nobel," she explained. "They did that in Arizona."

VI

A large gray moth, frightened by what was going on, flew frantically around the living-room, traveling in erratic swoops and darts, twists and turns. Moth-like, it became fascinated by the electric light fixture, made a few scouting turns, then power dived and hit the bulb. A little puff of dust flew off its body, and it flew away drunkenly and landed on the old-fashioned piano. It settled there, looking aged, ill, frightened, dazed.

A little old lady, like the moth, looked aged, frightened, dazed, as she sat in a rocking chair in front of the piano.

She was Mrs. Ivan Merrillee, and this was her house. She was a widow who lived alone.

"H. I. has always been bad," she said. She was discussing her stepson. "Bad, bad, bad," she said miserably. H. I. Merrillee was her husband's son by his first wife, they had learned. She added, "H. I. was in the reform school before he was fifteen."

Doc Savage nodded sympathetically. He was alone, listening to the old lady's story.

Ham Brooks and the girl they had found in the cemetery were outdoors. They were checking on the little old lady's reputation with her neighbors. The name of the girl from the cemetery was Ada Nobel. She was lovely. She was so lovely that Doc was still startled.

"An awful boy," continued little old Mrs. Ivan Merrillee. There was shamed dampness in her eyes. "I know it's awful to talk about my poor, dead husband's son by his first marriage the way I'm talking about H. I. But I can't help it. The boy has shamed me so."

"He was staying here in this house?" Doc asked.

"Only for the last three days, off and on," Mrs. Merrillee answered. "Three days ago was the day he came in from the west, from Arizona, I think."

"What had he been doing in Arizona?"

"I don't know. I hadn't heard of him in five years." Mrs. Merrillee twisted her hands together. "I didn't know but what he might be in jail again." The hands were dry, crinkled, the veins darkly blue-black through the parchment skin. "He had those men with him. I didn't like them either."

"How many men?" Doc asked.

"Four."

Doc asked, "Can you describe them?"

"Oh, yes," said the old lady eagerly.

She proceeded to demonstrate that she couldn't describe them at all. Not so that they could be recognized in a crowd. The way she described them, they were just men. But she was sincerely trying.

Doc asked, "Know what H. I. Merrillee and these four friends of his were up to?"

Mrs. Merrillee shuddered. "Something awful. I think it concerned the sick man."

"What sick man?"

"They had a sixth man along. That is, there was H. I., his four friends, and this sixth man, who was sick." The old lady shook her head sadly. "He was so sick he couldn't get around or talk at all. They told me he was suffering from paralysis, but somehow I'm not so sure about that now."

Doc asked her to describe the sick man. She did.

The sick man was a benevolent, rather mild looking man, about sixty years old. It was evident that the widow had taken an interest in him because he was about her own age. The sick man had white hair, a good complexion, gray eyes, and false teeth. That was all she knew about him, except his first name, which had been Harky. Or at least the men had referred to him as Harky.

H. I. and his friends had taken Harky with them when they fled in great haste a few minutes ago.

Doc described Monk Mayfair, asked Mrs. Merrillee if she had seen him. She hadn't.

Doc asked, "Have you got a photograph of H. I. around anywhere?"

"Yes, I have. A snapshot," said Mrs. Merrillee. She went into her bedroom, came back with a photograph of her stepson. "This is H. I., as he looked several years ago," she said. "He hasn't changed much."

Doc examined the picture. "So this is H. I.!" he said interestedly.

H. I. was the slightly fat man with the cherubic smile, the man who had bid on the steel stork at the auction, then taken a shot at the bell-voiced young man who was the other bidder.

"Thank you very much, Mrs. Merrillee," Doc said. "This is quite a help." Then, because the little old lady looked so frightened, he added, "H. I. may not be in serious trouble."

Mrs. Merrillee shook her head wearily. "He's always been a bad one."

Doc Savage found Ham Brooks and Ada Nobel waiting outside. Doc asked, "What did the neighbors know?"

"The old lady seems to be okay," Ham reported. "She owns the house, has lived there about ten years, and her husband has been dead three years. She belongs to the Methodist church, the Red Cross and a couple of bridge clubs. She has a rascal of a stepson, the son of her husband by his first wife, but he hasn't been seen around for years, until the last day or two."

Doc told Ham who the stepson was. "The fat cupid who bid on the stork," Doc explained.

"Did he grab Monk?"

"Apparently," Doc agreed. "Yes, I think we can charge that up to him."

"Damn him!" Ham was bitter. "He'll probably try to trade Monk to us for the stork."

Doc said, "We might as well go back to the car." He began walking. Ham and the girl walked with him. They passed under a street light and Doc noted that the girl was slender, carried herself well. Not like a showgirl or a trained model. But a nice carriage. Natural.

She hadn't told her story. There hadn't been time. She had said her name was Ada Nobel. She hadn't said how she had met Monk.

Doc spoke to her. "You have a story to tell us?" he asked her.

"Why not?" she said instantly. "I've told you my name. Ada Nobel. I was born——"

"Hold it," Doc said. "Not right now."

He wanted to watch her face while she was telling whatever she had to tell them. It was hard enough for him to tell whether women were lying, even watching their faces.

They crossed over to a sidewalk which followed the edge of the cemetery. It was dark. Sand particles on the concrete walk gritted under their feet.

They came to the cemetery gate. Doc explained, "I think I'll pick up that note Monk wrote. We left it in the caretaker's place."

He went to the shack. It was not far, so Ham and the girl followed him. The night was as dark as a cave, smelled like a cave. It seemed to be getting darker.

Doc started into the shack. His hand, out in front of him, encountered the door, which was closed. He had left it open. He said, "Someone has been here!"

A new voice addressed them. It said, "He's still here." There was a moment of silence. The voice added, "You better stand still, all of you."

A flashlight came on, blazing into their eyes and blinding them. Doc noted that Ham had seized the opportunity to put an arm around the girl. However, Ham's hand, concealed from the man with the flashlight because it was behind the girl, held the revolver he had captured from the assailant in the cemetery.

The man with the flashlight was tall. His face looked dark, greasy. He had a cap pulled down to his ears, and a muffler tied around his throat.

The man demanded, "Who're you?"

Doc Savage frowned at him. "Haven't I seen you somewhere before?"

The man said, "I wouldn't know." In addition to the flashlight, he held a large shiny six-shooter. "I'm the watchman here. I go to get me a cup of coffee, come back and find

238 / A Doc Savage Adventure

all kinds of hell being raised." He scowled at them. "Now what's going on?"

Doc was puzzled. "You seem familiar to me," he said. "Maybe you should know me."

"Hell, I know lots of people." The man sounded somewhat scared. "What's your name?"

"This is Miss Nobel and Ham Brooks. I am Doc Savage," Doc explained.

"Okay. What're you doing here?"

"Looking for a friend," Doc said.

The man sneered. "Visiting hours are nine to five," he said. "Or did you have an appointment with your friend? Maybe he was gonna get out of his grave and meet you, huh?"

Ham Brooks entered the discussion. "Wise guy," Ham said.

"I wanta know what's going on," the man said.

Doc Savage said, "Are you sure I haven't met you somewhere?"

"Wise guy wouldn't know who he's met," Ham said. "Wise guy doesn't like us. Let's get out of here, Doc."

The man with the flashlight and gun said, "I oughta call the cops."

"Call them," Doc told him. "Go ahead."

The man thought this over. He sneered again. "Go on, beat it," he said. "You ain't got no business in here."

Ham said, "Buddy, if you would stay on the job, you wouldn't have trouble around here."

"Beat it," the man said.

Doc turned. "Come on, Ham," he said. He moved over so that Ham could get his revolver back in his pocket without the man seeing the weapon.

They left the cemetery and walked toward their car.

Ada Nobel asked, "What did you want with that note Monk wrote?"

"I wanted to show it to you," Doc explained. "I wanted to ask you about the map on the bottom of it."

"What about the map?" The girl was puzzled. "Wasn't it clear enough? I saw Monk draw it, and it showed the location of the house, and where Monk and I would be watching."

"That's what I wanted to know," Doc told her. "There was no map on the bottom of the note. It had been torn off."

Ham made an astonished noise. "It looks like they were all fixed for us!" he exclaimed. "We walked right into it."

They reached their car. Ham walked around the machine cautiously, then announced that everything seemed to be clear. Doc had the door open. He was standing there holding the door open.

Suddenly Doc jumped back. He said, "I knew I'd seen that fellow somewhere!" He ordered Ham and the girl, "Stay here! Wait for me! I'm going after that phony watchman!"

"Phony?" Ham gasped.

"The watchman was a fake!" Doc was excited, angry with himself. "He changed his voice enough to fool me. He had grease or something on his face, too."

"Who the devil was he?" Ham demanded.

Doc said, "The other bidder on that stork!" He ran back toward the cemetery gate.

Approaching the gate, Doc made as little noise as he could. The gate was still open. He stood outside and listened for some time. There was no sign of his quarry.

Cautiously, mindful that the fake watchman had had a gun, Doc slid through the gate. When he was inside, he heard an automobile start in the distance. It departed into the night.

Doc looked into the watchman's shack. Monk's note was still there. Doc took it.

Ham Brooks and Ada Nobel were waiting in the car.

Doc told them, "That is about as big a fool trick as I have pulled recently." He got into the car, told Ham, "You drive. The way my luck is going, I would probably run through a stop light and get us all arrested."

VII

Ada Nobel was impressed by Doc Savage's headquarters. She kept looking around with an expression of breathless wonder. She said, "This is an amazing place. I've heard of it." She looked out of the windows. "What a wonderful view!" she exclaimed. "You have the whole city spread out before you, haven't you. I've never been to New York before." She sounded excited, really thrilled.

Doc Savage and Ham Brooks were impressed by Ada Nobel. Ham was obviously delighted that he was impressed. Doc Savage wasn't, because he was faced with the job of deciding whether the girl was going to lie to them. The prettier she was, the more trouble he would have, he felt sure. He'd had experience.

Doc explained why they might as well stay here for the time being. "If they intend to trade Monk to us for the stork, they will probably phone us here," he said. "So we had better stay here."

"They will want to trade," Ada Nobel said. "I am sure they will."

Doc maneuvered her to a chair where she would be in bright light. He suggested, "Suppose you tell us why you think so."

"Don't you want my whole story?" she asked wonderingly.

"It wouldn't hurt," Doc admitted.

She nodded. She explained that she had been born in Quincy, Illinois. She had lost her parents when she was eighteen. She was twenty now. Her only father was an uncle, Harrison Nobel. She had been, until a week ago, a stenographer for the Central Packing Company in Chicago, Illinois. The job paid her twenty-eight dollars a week, and her record was good. They could check on this, she explained, by calling a Mr. Givenman, manager of her department at the packing company.

"Now I'll tell you about my Uncle Harky," she said.

Doc Savage nodded. "Please do," he said. He was carefully keeping expression off his face.

"Harky is what everyone calls Uncle Harrison Nobel," she explained.

Harrison Nobel, she continued, had for fifteen years been the private secretary of a banker named Mason Carl Wentz. A fine old man, was Uncle Harky. Mr. Wentz evidently thought so, too, because recently when Mr. Wentz had died of pneumonia, his will had disclosed that his faithful secretary, Harrison Nobel, was a beneficiary.

"Mr. Wentz's will gave Uncle Harky the Arizona ranch," she explained. "There was also a trust fund, the income from which would maintain the ranch and keep Uncle Harky in comfort the rest of his life." She smiled at them gently. "Wasn't that a fine thing for Mr. Wentz to do?"

Doc Savage agreed that it was a fine thing to do.

Ham Brooks was about to split with excitement. Doc caught Ham's eye, shook his head slightly, hoping Ham would understand that he was to keep still. Doc felt they were learning a great deal. How much of it was true, he wasn't sure. He wished he knew.

"Uncle Harky," continued Ada Monk, "wrote me the nicest letter. He said that he was an old man now, and lonesome. He said that he would like one of his own kin around him to keep him company, and that if I would come and live at the ranch, he would pay me fifty dollars a week and my expenses wouldn't cost me anything. It would be like a job, and if I didn't like it, I could quit anytime. Wasn't that nice? I grabbed the offer in a minute."

"You went to Arizona?" Doc asked.

"Yes." The pleasure left her face suddenly. "And the most awful things began happening."

Doc leaned forward. "What were they?"

"Some terrible men were at Fear's End," she said. She shivered. "Isn't that an awful name for a ranch—Fear's End? It's such a scary place, too. Right in the canyon, such incredible walls all around. You feel so small. Like something was sure to fall on you any minute. I tell you, I never dreamed of such a place."

"What about the terrible men?" Doc urged.

"They were holding Uncle Harky a prisoner in his own ranch," Ada Nobel said. She sounded angry. "There was an awful fat man named Merrillee. H. I. Merrillee. He had four friends as bad."

She was busy remembering for a moment. She shivered. "At first, they tried to make me think nothing was wrong," she continued. "But I saw something was. I didn't know what to do. I wanted to call the sheriff, but there was no telephone."

She clenched her hands. Her nails were neat, and the polish on them was the color of a robin's breast.

"They left with Uncle Harky before I could do anything," she added. "I followed them. I followed them all the way to New York. I knew they were coming to New York after something they called a stork, and that they had taken Uncle Harky along so he wouldn't make trouble for them. They drugged him. They first drugged him at the ranch, something in his coffee. I think they tried to drug me, too, but my coffee tasted bitter and I didn't drink it."

Doc asked, "How did you know a stork was involved?"

"From what I overheard at the ranch. I did a lot of snooping at the ranch, you can bet."

"What happened after you got to New York?" Doc asked.

"Why, I just kept following them. I wanted to locate Uncle Harky. Then I was going to call the police in and save him."

"Why were you in the graveyard tonight?"

"I was watching that house. I knew H. I. Merrillee was staying there. I'd trailed him there."

Doc asked, "Didn't you know your Uncle Harky was in the house?"

Ada Nobel's hands flew to her face. "No, no!" she gasped. She lost color. "Was he?" she cried. "And I didn't know!"

Doc told her that the widow, Mrs. Merrillee, had described a drugged man who answer Harrison Nobel's description as to name, Harky. He gave her the description of Harky's appearance which he had received from the widow.

"That's Uncle Harky!" the girl cried. "I couldn't have saved him!" She burst into tears.

Her sobbing, violent, grief-stricken, made Doc Savage uncomfortable. He glanced at Ham. Ham was uncomfortable, too.

The telephone rang. Ham, eager and apprehensive, clutched at the phone. "Yes?" he said. "You have? All right. . . . Yes, that's enough." He hung up, looking disappointed. He told Doc, "That was one of the men I was checking on Wentz with. A lawyer. He says that Wentz's will gave Fear's End to his secretary, Harrison Nobel, together with a trust fund to maintain the place."

Doc Savage went into the laboratory and began mixing a mild sedative which would quiet Ada Nobel.

Ham came in, closed the door, and whispered, "What do you think?"

"I don't know," Doc said. "Her story checks with what we know." He shook his head, added, "But a good job of lying would check, too."

"What the hell do you suppose they want the stork for?" Ham asked.

Doc finished mixing the sedative. He said, "I think I'll go get the stork, show it to her, and see what happens." He handed the glass to Ham. "Get her to drink this if you can. It'll quiet her."

Tolliver Jonas, the model maker, opened the door of his office for Doc Savage. "I thought you were going to be back in an hour," Jonas complained.

"Something came up," Doc said. "Have you got the imitation storks made?"

"See what you think." Jonas led the way into his workroom. He indicated a table, said, "There they are." There were seven shiny storks sitting in a row on the table. "Which one would you say was the original?" Jonas asked.

Doc eyed the storks in amazement. "The middle one?" he ventured.

"Hah!" Jonas was pleased. "The one on the end," he said.

Doc began putting storks in his pockets. "You did a fine job," he said. He tapped a few of the storks against the table edge. "The original one makes a deeper ringing sound than the fakes," he said.

"Dammit, you didn't say you wanted them tuned up," Jonas said.

Doc assured him, "These will be fine." He added, "Send me the bill. And don't throw the hook in too deep."

Jonas grinned. "I'll hook you plenty," he said.

Ada Nobel was quieter. The sedative was having some effect. Color was back in her cheeks, she had dried her eyes, and she had made herself a new face.

She examined the stork, fascinated. "How on earth did you get it?" she asked.

Doc Savage told her about the auction. Then he asked, "Is that the stork all the shooting is about?"

"I don't know," Ada Nobel said. "I never saw it before. But of course it is. What has happened proves it is."

Doc asked, "What is it?"

"I don't know." She looked at them in surprise. "Don't you know?"

"We haven't the shade of an idea," Doc assured her.

She put down the stork suddenly, as if it might come to life.

"Isn't this all the strangest thing?" she remarked wonderingly.

"Do you feel better?" Doc asked.

She nodded. "Yes, thank you," she said gratefully. She added, "Except that I feel a little dizzy. Maybe it's just the excitement, and the fact that I have been losing sleep."

Ham Brooks became solicitous. "There is a couch in the library," he said. "Why don't you stretch out in there and get some rest? Or would you rather go to a hotel?"

"No, no, I don't want to go to a hotel," Ada Nobel said hastily. "I want to stay close to you." She blushed a little. "I mean, in case you should find Uncle Harky," she explained.

Ham helped her into the library. The moonstruck way in which he did it made Doc want to kick him. Ham was always complaining about Monk being a pushover for anything in skirts, but in Doc's opinion Ham was a more ready victim.

"Your tongue is hanging out a foot," Doc said when Ham came back into the room. Doc was disgusted.

"She's lovely," Ham said ecstatically. "She gave us lots of very good information, too, didn't she?"

Doc gave him a sour look. "Of which you believed every word, no doubt."

"Certainly." Ham examined Doc pityingly. "You haven't the slightest ability to tell when a woman is lying and when she isn't, have you?"

"Have *you*?" Doc demanded.

"Certainly."

Doc was irritated. His ideas about women were being lambasted, and by Ham Brooks, who was notoriously gullible game for the fair sex. Ham, Doc reflected, should be taught a lesson.

On impulse, Doc said, "Ham, you go downstairs to the lobby. Keep an eye on the elevator indicators, and when you see an elevator leaving this floor, get ready to follow Miss Ada Nobel, who will be skipping out."

Ham stared. "You're nuts," he said.

"You get down in the lobby," Doc said. He was indignant, because he suspected he was making a fool out of himself. "When the girl appears, shadow her. Don't let her see you. I want to know where she goes and what she does."

Ham became suspicious. "Do you know something about her I don't know?"

"Only what my judgment of women tells me," Doc said briefly.

Ham snorted. "If you think Ada Nobel will doublecross us, your judgment of women isn't worth a dime," he said.

He left with another snort.

* * *

Doc Savage contemplated the stork statuette on the desk. He suspected he might have made a fool out of himself. It would not be the first time, so it did not particularly worry him about being ridiculous. What did bother him was the possible psychological reason for his behavior. He wondered if, subconsciously, he wasn't trying to show off around a girl.

Another thing that bothered him was why he had told Ham that Nobel Ada would flee. He didn't know exactly why he had told Ham that. A hunch. The accusation had just seemed to come from his lips. He wondered if that was the way mediums, if there was such a thing as a genuine medium, got their predictions.

He went into the library. "Feeling quieter?" he asked.

Ada Nobel smiled at him. "Much better," she said. She yawned prettily.

"I'm going to be in the laboratory for a while," he said. "I've locked the outside door. Ham won't be back for a while. The stork is on the desk, in case you shouldn't feel sleepy and want to look it over."

"Thank you, but I'm quite sleepy." She closed her eyes.

Doc went into the laboratory. The telephone had an extension bell there, so if they got a call about Monk Mayfair, he would hear it.

The storks made his pockets heavy. He took them out, and hid them in various places around the laboratory. He would carry one, he decided. He wished he had thought to give Ham one to carry around. There were now plenty of storks, so he thought it would be nice if everyone who wanted a stork should have one. It might make things more peaceful, and maybe Monk would get turned loose.

Doc hid all the storks except one. He put that one in his coat pocket. He didn't know what more to do to kill time, so he went to the door and opened it and looked into the library.

Ada Nobel wasn't on the couch in the library.

She wasn't in the reception room, either.

The stork wasn't any longer on the desk.

Doc Savage was deeply shocked. He thought: My God! I have finally learned to read the female character!

VIII

Doc Savage felt so good that he took a shower and put on his second best suit. A glance from the window appraised him of lightning winking in the sky, and remembering how intensely dark the night had been, he surmised there would be rain. It never rained for only an hour or so at this season in New York, usually it wasn't satisfied with less than a week. He laid out a raincoat and an umbrella. There was nothing better than an umbrella to hide your face on a damp day on the street.

Then Ham Brooks called on the telephone. "What're you pulling on me?" Ham demanded.

"Did you follow Miss Nobel?" Doc asked smugly.

"How the hell did you know she was going to skip out?" Ham sounded like a man whose entire code of evaluations had been torpedoed. He demanded suspiciously, "Or did she skip? You didn't send her out on an errand, did you?"

"Leaving was her own idea," Doc said. He added, "She took the stork statuette off the desk."

Ham was stunned.

"Dammit, why didn't you say so!" he cried. "I'll grab her right now and take it away from her."

Doc said hastily, "No, no, don't do that. Just follow her and see where she goes and what she does."

"But if I lose her and the steel stork—"

"Never mind the stork," Doc said. "We've got them to give away now."

"Huh?" Ham demanded, confused. "Say, you haven't gone off the beam, have you? Where'd we get more storks?"

"I had them made," Doc said. "We've got half a dozen." He listened to Ham's snort of surprise, then added, "If we need more, we can get them. We can order them by the gross, I imagine."

"You sound too damned pleased," Ham said.

"I was right about the girl," Doc reminded him.

"Sure, for the first time in your life you were right," Ham retorted. Ham was discomfited. "Where's the genuine stork?"

"In the laboratory, hidden in a bottle marked 'poisonous lizard preserved in alcohol,'" Doc explained.

"You want me to keep track of the girl?"

"On second thought," Doc said. "I'll help you. Where is she now?"

"Having a good attack of jitters, and a sandwich in the Penn Station restaurant," Ham explained. "The one on the north side, downstairs. I'm in the telephone booths out in the hall, east."

"Be there in a minute," Doc said.

"What about if they call in to trade Monk?" asked Ham uneasily.

"I think this is probably hotter," Doc said.

The eighty-sixth floor of the building was exclusively Doc Savage's premises, but this did not mean he had all the space in the building at that level. The normal layout of the building had not been disturbed to accommodate him. The hall, for instance, was like the halls on the other floors, except that only one door had a name on it.

There was quite a battery of elevator shafts. The eighty-sixth floor was called the top floor, but actually it was only figuratively the top. Above it was located a roof restaurant and night club, an observation tower, and a shop which sold gimcracks to sightseers. There was also the machinery, enough to fill a young factory, of the elevators, and a water tank and the other stuff found on top of buildings.

At any rate the eighty-sixth floor was not isolated. Anyone who wished could reach it, either by the elevators or the stairs.

Leaving his door, Doc observed a man standing by the elevators, facing the other direction. Doc kept an eye on him. He was not alarmed, but he was cautious. Drunks sometimes strayed down to this floor from the night club, particularly at this hour of the morning.

Doc approached the elevator and the man. The man was long. Suddenly realizing there was something familiar about him, Doc dropped a hand in his coat pocket, grasped the stork, and held it so it would look like a gun in the pocket.

The man turned around. He said, "I think I've made some mistake."

"Somebody has," Doc agreed.

The man was the fake watchman at the graveyard. The bell-voiced bidder on the stork at the auction.

"I came up here to talk to you," the man said. He spoke in his normal high, bell-like voice. "I got cold feet and changed my mind. I was about to leave," he added.

Doc watched the man closely. He said, "You had better change your mind again."

"I think I will," the man said.

Doc said, "Put up your hands."

Obeying, the bell-voiced man said, "My gun is in a holster under my right armpit."

Doc felt for the gun. "Left-handed, eh?" he remarked. He got the gun, a large single-action six-shooter of the Buffalo Bill variety. "Have a license for this?" Doc asked.

"A license good in California," the man said. "Look in my billfold. If they reciprocate on those licenses, it's good here. If they don't, it's not."

The man's billfold was a limp affair of sweat-stained brown leather. It contained about eleven hundred and twenty or thirty dollars, or at any rate eleven one-hundred-dollar bills. There was a driver's license, an old 1A-H draft card, credit cards for the Hotel Ambassador in Los Angeles, the Muehlbach in Kansas City, the New Yorker and the Waldorf in New York City, and a private detective's license entitling the bearer to practice in California. The description of bearer on these documents, where there was a description, fitted the tall bell-voiced man, gave his age as 42 (he looked much younger than 42), and his name as Theodore La France.

"Theodore La France, private detective," Doc remarked.

The other nodded. "And sucker, you might add," he said.

Doc Savage rang for an elevator. "Any objections to talking while we move?" he asked.

"None at all," La France said. "Do I get my gun back?"

Doc shook his head. "Not right now." He noted that the man had wiped the dark grease off his face, and no longer wore the cap and muffler. Doc added, "You did quite a job of fooling us at the cemetery."

"You mad about that?" La France asked.

"Should I be?"

La France shrugged. "Some people don't like to be fooled, is all."

An elevator was stopping. "No one does," Doc said. He

put the six-shooter under his belt, where his coat would hide it. It was too large to go in his pocket. "Let's not talk now," Doc added.

The elevator contained four men and four women, all a little high. Doc and La France got aboard. One of the women, a brunette, squealed, "It's Doc Savage! How are you, honey?" She tried to kiss Doc. He had never seen her before. She cried, "I wanna kiss!" She smelled of bourbon and gardenias. Her escort, a small fat man, said, "Stop acting a fool, Rose." Rose, belligerent, said, "Who's a fool?" The fat man said, "By God, I get you home, I'll show you." Doc Savage's face was getting a darkly cooked lobster color. He was very glad when the elevator got to the lobby.

Doc and La France hurried away across the lobby. "Your public?" La France asked.

"There's a night club on the roof," Doc told him uncomfortably.

Darkness filled the streets. The streetlights looked hotly white, dispelled the blackness at the corners, in the middle of the blocks. There was not a pedestrian in sight, and only two taxicabs. Rather than have an argument with a cab driver over such a short haul, Doc decided to walk to Penn Station. It wasn't far.

Doc was careful not to get ahead of La France as they walked. The man looked lithe, tough. He could probably hit a nasty blow from behind.

Lightning crawled across the sky, jaggedly, redly. There was no thunder.

"Let's have some words," Doc said.

Quickly, eagerly, Theodore La France said, "You know my name. Ted La France. Private detective. Los Angeles. My identification proves that. Here's something else you can check on: I was employed by Mason Carl Wentz's investment and banking firm for several years, before he dissolved his banking business and retired to his ranch in Arizona."

Doc said nothing.

La France added, "You can check on that by calling Wentz's former banking associates in Los Angeles."

Thunder went rumbling boisterously across the heavens, although there had been no visible lightning. "You bet I'll check on it," Doc said. The lightning bolt that had made the thunder must have been above the thick clouds. "Go ahead with more words," Doc added.

Rapidly, La France said, "Here's something I can't prove: Mason Carl Wentz paid me five thousand dollars a year ago, in return for which I was to investigate his death, no matter when and how he died."

Pennsylvania Station looked enormous ahead of them. It looked like a cathedral. Doc remarked, "So you are investigating the banker's death?"

La France nodded. "A little more than that," he added. "You might say I'm doing something for my country, I hope. You saw my draft card. Over age. As a matter of fact, I didn't try to enlist, either, and since then I've become a little ashamed of that."

"What does patriotism have to do with a banker's natural death?"

"You'll see."

"Was his death natural?"

"Sure. Pneumonia. Type three, and a serum would have saved him, or sulfa. He couldn't get it. You couldn't get a buzz-bomb into that ranch in the wintertime, if the Lord wasn't kind with his weather."

Doc Savage decided to be cautious and not use the main entrance to Penn Station. He said, "All right, you were hired by Wentz before he died to investigate his death if he did die. Then what?" He pushed open a swinging door.

"I investigated," La France said. He went ahead of Doc into the station.

Stale air, smelling of rain and railway station, hit them. "Keep talking," Doc suggested.

La France nodded. "Well, his death was natural. I found that out. But I turned up something else, something I had long suspected." La France kept abreast or a little ahead of Doc with long, rangy steps. He added, "Wentz had too many alien friends."

"Alien friends?" Doc pretended to be puzzled.

"Enemy aliens. Japs. Germans. Austrians." La France sounded dramatic. "People who were citizens of countries we were fighting."

They were walking in a low-ceilinged corridor. "What does the fact that Wentz had alien friends mean?" Doc asked. They passed a door that smelled strongly of washroom antiseptic.

"It means they tried to kill me when they knew I had found it out," La France said.

"Who?"

"Who what?"

"Who tried to kill you?"

"Oh. A fat guy named H. I. Merrillee and some friends of his."

Doc pretended surprise. "Let's not talk for a minute," he said. They were coming near the restaurant. Doc's eyes searched for Ham Brooks.

There was a drunk sprawled on a shoe shiner's chair in a little alcove. The drunk seemed to be asleep, head twisted around, hat over his eyes, hands drooping. The pretending drunk was Ham Brooks. Evidently he saw Doc Savage, because one of his drooping hands made some gestures, which Doc decided meant Ada Nobel was still in the restaurant.

Looking about, Doc Savage decided the best place from which to watch Ham Brooks and the lunchroom door was the interior of an all-night newsstand-bookstore-fountain opening off the passage. Doc said, "Let's go in here. Can you drink a malt?"

La France jerked his head at the restaurant. "They probably make better malts in there."

"I like the malts in here," Doc assured him. They entered the place. "Two malts," Doc told the attendant. By sitting on the stools, they could see Ham. Ham made an airman's okay signal, a circle with thumb and forefinger, to tell Doc he was okay where he was.

Doc said to La France, "Let's hear more."

La France scowled at the clerk. He lowered his voice, resumed his story, saying, "Here is where I got confused. H. I. Merrillee and some friends were at the ranch, which was inherited by Harrison Nobel, old Wentz's secretary. Some of H. I. Merrillee's men must have been watching me and found out I was nosing around the alien friends angle, because one of them took a shot at me, and ruined the hell out of my five-dollar hat."

Doc remarked, "I don't see anything confusing about that."

La France grimaced.

"The stork statuette," he said. "That's what confused me. H. I. Merrillee was after it. He was scaring the hell out of old Harrison Nobel trying to make Nobel tell him where it was. Nobel didn't seem to know."

Doc interrupted. "How did you learn this?" he asked.

"By gumshoeing around the ranch after dark," explained Theodore La France. "I wore my ears out flattening them against keyholes."

"I see."

"I don't. I don't see for nothing," said the detective. "Here's the rest of the story. H. I. Merrillee suddenly discovered the stork statuette had been shipped off to New York to be sold in an auction gallery with Wentz's other pictures and books and furniture and stuff. So H. I. Merrillee and his men grabbed old Nobel, and came hell-bent for New York, with me right on their tails. There's a girl in the picture, too. I don't know who the hell she is. She followed them to New York, too."

Doc asked, "Did H. I. Merrillee know you were doing all this following?"

"Not until I bid against him at that auction, I don't figure he did," said the detective.

"Why did you bid at the auction?"

"I wanted to see what would happen."

"You bid fifteen thousand dollars."

La France grinned. "I would have bid a million. I didn't have that, either."

The clerk put their malteds in front of them. "Then what happened?" Doc asked.

"After the whirlygig in the auction room, I got back on H. I. Merrillee's trail," the detective explained. "He was staying at his stepmother's on Long Island, so I went back there to watch him. That graveyard was a good place to watch from, so I was watching from there when you showed up."

Doc tasted his malt. "And then you played caretaker," he said. The malt was terrible.

Ted La France nodded. "I was in a dither to know what the hell was happening," he explained. He sipped his own malt. "I didn't know it was you when I stopped you. Finding out who you were gave me a jolt, I can tell you." He glared at the malt. "Cripes, is this what you call good?"

"Their malts are very economical here," Doc said. He asked, "Why did you come to see me?"

"Because I don't know my eye from a hole in the ground about this mess," said Theodore La France. "I think there's something damned big and mysterious afoot. I think some foreign, alien angle is involved, and I think it's our duty as patriotic Americans to find out what the hell it's about."

"You want me to help you?" Doc inquired.

"No, the other way around. I want to help you," said La France. He attacked his malt again, took two swallows and gave up. "Economical, you say! They're twenty-five cents! Cripes!"

Doc said, "It seems to me we could work together." He added, "One swallow of these malts, and you don't want any more malts for a month. That's where the economical comes in."

At this point, Ham's hand made an alert gesture. Doc moved hastily until he could peep at the restaurant door.

Theodore La France became alarmed. "What's going on?" he wanted to know.

"Detective business," Doc said.

"Huh?"

"We're following the mysterious girl, Ada Nobel," Doc said.

"Why?"

"She's got a statuette of a stork," Doc explained.

"Godamighty!" exclaimed the detective.

Ada Nobel came out of the restaurant. She carried a small newspaper bundle, evidently the stork. She walked away without seeming to notice Ham Brooks.

Doc told La France, "The race is on. Let's go."

IX

Hot, zig-zagging, awe-inspiring lightning raked the sky above the mouse-gray stone front of the hotel in the Forties between Fifth Avenue and Sixth Avenue. Thunder belched out of the stormy sky the moment the lightning bolt collapsed, and with a whoop and a rumble dived into the canyon-like street, rebounding in violent echoes, pouring into the hotel lobby in a cascade of violent noise, further frightening the already alarmed hotel clerk.

Ham Brooks emphatically repeated the lie he had just told the clerk.

"We're police detectives," Ham said. He used the belligerent manner police detectives use. "I want to sit in on your telephone switchboard, and I don't want any argument about it. I haven't got time to argue." He glared at the terrified clerk. "Or would you rather have Clancy here"—Ham jerked his head at Theodore La France—"take your pants to jail?"

"Go ahead and listen," the clerk said. He stood by and wrung his hands.

"Get a natural look on your face," Ham told him. "Nothing is going to happen to you or the hotel."

Doc Savage came down from upstairs. He told Ham Brooks, "I listened at the keyhole. Apparently she is alone in her room. I could not hear any voices. She seemed to be walking the floor."

"Maybe she was packing," said Ham. "She would do a lot of walking back and forth if she was doing that."

Doc dismissed this. "She did not pause as if she was picking up things. She kept going."

Ham nodded. He frowned at La France. He didn't know who La France was. "Where do you come into this?" Ham demanded.

Doc asked the hotel clerk, "What's your name?"

"Mr. Davis," said the clerk nervously.

Doc suggested, "Mr. Davis, will you go over to that chair yonder and sit there, so you can't overhear our conversation."

The clerk hastily complied with the suggestion. Doc asked Ham, "What did you do to the clerk to scare him like that?"

"Nothing," Ham said innocently. "He must have a nervous nature." Ham indicated La France, asked, "What about this fellow?"

Doc told Ham the story Theodore La France had told him, Ham listening with rapt expression. Doc had nearly ended the story when the PBX switchboard began buzzing. "You had better get on the job, telephone girl," Doc said.

"Holy cats!" Ham was staring at the telephone board. "It's her! It's her calling!" he gasped. He grabbed at the keyboard.

"Disguise your voice!" Doc exclaimed. "Don't forget that."

In a very prissy voice, Ham said, "Number please?" He listened, then turned his head to demand wildly, "How the hell do you work one of these switchboards?" He grabbed a fistful of plugs. "What do I stick where?" he demanded.

Doc showed him what to do, and they listened to Miss Ada Nobel's call.

Miss Ada Nobel called a number, Circle double naught five three. The instrument rang for some time, then a voice answered. "Yeah?" the voice said. "Whatcha want?"

"Get hold of H. I. Merrillee," Ada Nobel ordered. "And give him a message."

"Huh?" The voice sounded frightened. "Whatcha say? Whoosis?"

"Ada Nobel," she said.

"Don't know no Ada Nobel," the voice complained. "Whatcha wakin' people up this timea night?" He didn't sound in the least sleepy.

Ada Nobel became angry. "Listen, you!" she snapped. "You get hold of your pal Merrillee and tell him that Ada Nobel has the stork, and she's willing to do business."

The man pretended to be bewildered.

"Don't know whatcha talkin' about," the man said.

Ada Nobel said, "Brother, you pass the word along if you know what's good for you."

The man hesitated. "Where you at?" he asked.

Ada Nobel gave the telephone number of the hotel. "Call me there," she said. "Tell Merrillee that."

The man said defiantly, "Don't know no Merrillee." He hung up.

Ham Brooks was amazed. "By jove, she's doublecrossing us. You *can* read the female mind, Doc."

Pleased, Doc said, "Ham, grab a taxi and get over to the nearest newspaper office, which will have a cross-numbered telephone directory. Find out the address of Circle double naught five three. Then go up there and get on the trail of this person she called, if you can."

Ham reached for his hat. "What'll I do when I find him?" he asked.

Doc snorted and said, "What'll he do, he asks. Dress him up in a Santa Claus suit and take him to the North Pole. I'll bring the Christmas tree." Doc grimaced. "What'll you do with him!"

Ham departed, grinning.

Doc Savage summoned the hotel clerk. He explained that he wanted to be called immediately, in order to listen in on any telephone calls from Miss Ada Nobel's room. Would the clerk summon him? The clerk would.

Doc Savage beckoned Detective Theodore La France, and retired with him to a small dining room adjoining the lobby. Through the glass doors of the dining room, they could watch the hotel clerk.

Detective La France chuckled. "This reminds me of old home week," he said.

"What did you expect?" Doc asked.

"Miracles," La France admitted. "I've heard about you. You've got more reputation, in certain quarters, than the emperor of hell. The way I heard it, you just snapped your fingers and all evildoers were consumed by a flash of fire." He laughed softly. "Here you are acting like any other detective. Imagine!"

"Stick around," Doc told him. "Maybe we can produce a fiery flash for you."

The hotel clerk was confused. He lowered the hand with which he had beckoned, said, "I—uh—incoming calls to Miss Nobel. I didn't know—do you—"

"Let's have it," Doc said. He completed the connection. He listened to H. I. Merrillee's fat-man voice address Miss Nobel. "Okay, toots," said Merrillee. "What you got on your mind?"

Miss Ada Nobel spoke with much dislike in her voice. She said, "What I've got isn't on my mind, it's in my hand. The stork statuette."

H. I. Merrillee hesitated. "Sounds very dreamlike to me, toots."

"I snitched it from Doc Savage."

"Nice work if you got it," said H. I. Merrillee.

Ada Nobel said, "You've got my uncle, Harrison Nobel, and Monk Mayfair."

H. I. Merrillee spoke hastily. "Now you're in the woods, sister. About those parties you mention, I know nothing. A flat nothing." He hesitated, then ventured, "What was that about a trade?"

"I'll swap you," said the girl. "The stork for Harrison Nobel and Monk Mayfair."

Merrillee, surprised, asked, "What's Monk Mayfair to you?" He added, with considerable feeling, "I wouldn't give ten cents for that guy. He's made us more trouble than a barrel of alligators."

Miss Nobel explained her stand. "I stole that stork from Doc Savage, who intended to trade it to you for Monk Mayfair if he could. I'm just adding Uncle Harky to the jackpot. But I feel I owe it to Mr. Savage to get Monk Mayfair free. Mr. Savage isn't going to be too pleased with me as it is."

Merrillee was silent a while. "Some very beautiful sentiments," he said. After being silent some more, he said, "Listen, toots. It's a deal. A quickie, see. You give us the stork. We give you Harky and Mayfair."

"Good," Miss Nobel said. "But there is a catch: I don't trust you."

"Sure, sure, you're a cautious chick. That's okay." H. I. Merrillee lowered his voice confidentially. "Here's the act: give us half an hour. Be at that coffee doughnut place on Broadway. Sit at the window. Put the stork on the table, so one of us, walking past outside, can see that you got it. Then we'll walk Harrison Nobel and Mayfair past to show you we got them. Then we'll make a quick deal. How's it sound?"

"It sounds good," said Ada Nobel.

"It is good, toots," said H. I. Merrillee.

This ended the negotiations.

Ham Brooks had some perspiration on his forehead. He wiped the sweat off while saying, "There was nobody home at Circle double naught five three. The bird had flown the coop. I guess he had gone to tell H. I. Merrillee the news." Ham put his handkerchief away. "Has Merrillee called yet?"

Doc gave the gist of the deal he had heard consumated over the telephone.

Ham expressed suspicions. "That quick, eh?" he remarked dubiously. "No preparations at all, you might say. And at that place on Broadway." He shook his head. "Broadway is crowded, even at this time of night. How does Merrillee know that the sidewalk won't be jammed with cops?"

"He doesn't," Doc said. "Which means, if you ask me, that the thing will never get that far."

"How far will it get, do you think?"

"Probably as far as the first dark alley, where Miss Nobel will be rapped over the head, then the statuette taken from her," Doc surmised.

Ham thought so, too. He asked, "What do we do about it?"

It was decided that Doc and Detective La France would take up a position in the street in a taxicab. Ham would wait farther down the street, in a darkened doorway. Fearing Miss Nobel would leave any moment, they took up their positions at once.

Detective La France lit a cigarette, after Doc had declined one. La France asked, "What do you suppose this cockeyed thing is all about?"

Doc countered by asking, "What do you know about this H. I. Merrillee?"

The driver of their cab cocked an ear toward their voices. Doc leaned forward and slid shut the glass partition with a bang. The driver snorted.

La France said, "Merrillee? I checked that baby's record. He's no good. His nose never has been clean."

"Did you ever obtain information concerning his recent activities?" Doc asked. He believed the driver could hear what they were saying even with the glass partition closed.

La France evidently was aware of the driver, too. Lowering his voice, he said, "The feds tried to glue an espionage rap on him about a year after the war began. It didn't stick. But the sandpapering they gave him scared him out to Flagstaff, Arizona, where he bought a beer joint." Suddenly opening the glass slide, La France said to the driver, "Buddy, ain't you afraid you'll split an eardrum?" The driver scowled at him, said, "If you don't like it, get the hell out." La France said, "I'll get the hell right down your throat, that's what I'll do!" The driver said, "Any time you're ready, snooks."

Doc Savage was saying, "Here, here, stop it!" when La France reached through the opening and got the driver's neck. La France called the driver a dirty name. "You tend to your damned business," he said. "Or you'll rot it out in a federal jail."

The driver was frightened. "Hell, why didn't you say you were feds," he complained.

After that, they had peace. Detective La France did not resume talking. Doc did not ask him any more questions. Doc wondered if he had started the row with the driver in order to stop conversation about the case.

* * *

Half an hour passed.

Forty-five minutes passed.

They were alarmed.

Doc Savage took his eyes off his watch, said, "The girl was to meet them in half an hour. She hasn't come out of the hotel."

Theodore La France said, not too flatteringly, "You guys are hot detectives, aren't you?" He opened the cab door. "Me, I'm going to see if that hotel has a back door."

Doc was startled. He was flabbergasted. "She might have been afraid they would waylay her, and used the back door," he said. He jumped out of the cab. "We'd better see."

"We've been outslicked," said La France positively.

The cab driver now didn't think much of them.

"Wise guys," he said. "Feds!" He snorted.

Ham met them at the hotel entrance, and they went in together. Detective La France became excited, pointing. "Look at that!" he cried.

The hotel clerk was sitting at the switchboard. He was bent over, his face resting among and mashing over the plugs and cords. His nose was in a pool of blood. His hair was nearly parted on the back of his head, where split and bruised scalp showed.

"Look for a back door," Doc told Ham. Doc felt the clerk's wrist, located a pulse. "He's not dead," Doc said.

Ham was back. "There's a back way out. It leads into an all-night restaurant on the next street."

"See if our party went through the restaurant," Doc ordered. He added sharply, "Why didn't you do that before you came back?" He picked the clerk up and carried him to a divan.

Detective La France said, "I'll go up and see if the girl is in her room."

"How do you know what her room number is?" Doc demanded.

La France scowled. "I don't," he said. He added, "You trust me about as far as you could throw a bull by the tail, don't you?"

"Just about that far," Doc admitted. He decided the clerk couldn't be revived immediately. "We'll both see about the girl." He made for the stairs, keeping a wary eye on La France.

Ham appeared. "The girl didn't go through the restaurant," he reported. "But three men did." He shrugged, added, "One of them could have been H. I. Merrillee."

"Upstairs for us," Doc said. He told Ham, "I didn't mean anything barking at you a minute ago."

A strip of adhesive tape, two inches wide, the color of a scraped bone, ran exactly across Ada Nobel's eyes. Another one like it crossed her mouth. She was tied like a package with two sheets, two blankets, tightly knotted.

Doc told her, "This may hurt," and picked the adhesive tape off her mouth. She said, "They got the stork!" He said, "Yell if this hurts," and loosened a corner of the other adhesive tape, pulled. The loosening tape made a sandy tearing sound. When it reached the girl's eye lashes, she screamed.

"We'll have to soak it off," Doc said. He didn't pull any more at the tape. "Who were they?" he asked.

"Merrillee and two others," she replied. "They outsmarted me."

"You weren't the only one," Doc told her. He wasn't pleased with himself.

A red light was glowing at intervals on the switchboard. When it glowed, a buzzer whirred simultaneously. This had been going on for some time, and now it stopped, and the board was still for perhaps a minute. The board was still, but the roaring of the rain falling in the street filled the hotel lobby. A guest came dashing in, holding a newspaper over his head, and stopped in astonishment when he saw the bloody-faced clerk lying on the divan. The guest hesitated, frightened, uncertain, then finally he tiptoed across the lobby and went up the stairs, intent on having nothing to do with whatever had happened. Now the switchboard light began to glow red and buzz again.

Thunder ran rumbling through the sky, rain roared freshly down. Doc Savage came down the stairs. Ham Brooks, Ada Nobel and Theodore La France were with Doc. The tape was still over the girl's eyes, and Ham was helping her.

The whirring board caught Doc's notice. He hesitated, undecided whether to pass it up, then went over and plugged in and pushed a jack handle.

Doc said, "Number, please."

H. I. Merrillee's voice laughed in his ear.

"You smart so-and-so," said H. I. Merrillee. "I spit in your ear, see." He made a spitting noise. "I spit in your ear, bub. How do you like it?"

"I don't like it," Doc admitted. "And you won't either, when the marbles are all counted."

"I saw you guys go into the hotel a while ago," H. I. Merrillee said. "You know, you scared the hell out of me. I didn't dream you had a trap set for me. We just went in the back way of the hotel to give the girl a little crossing up." He laughed the shaky laugh of a man who had just heard ice crack under him. "When I saw you and Ham Brooks and that stinker, La France, go into the hotel, you could have wiped my eyes off with a stick."

Doc said coldly. "Keep talking. We want to trace this call." He knew Merrillee was telephoning from one of the railway stations or from a subway station somewhere. He could hear the station noises in the background. He could hear a loudspeaker, faint, shrilly female.

The threat scared Merrillee into business.

"I got a little promise to make you," Merrillee said. "You leave me alone if you want to see that bull ape of yours again."

He hung up.

Doc took off the phone headset. His movements were slow, worried. Ham was staring questioningly. Doc told Ham, "That was H. I. Merrillee. He threatens bodily damage to Monk if we continue our activities."

Detective Theodore La France shoved out his lower lip sarcastically. "Scared you out, eh?" he said.

Doc Savage shook his head slowly. He closed his eyes. He was thinking, examining his memory closely.

His thinking was about the background of sounds which had come over the telephone while H. I. Merrillee was talking. He remembered the tinny voice in the background, shrilly female.

He said thoughtfully, "Railroads are masculine, aren't they?"

"Huh?" Ham Brooks stared at him. "What say?" Ham was startled.

"They announce trains in depots and they announce planes at airports," Doc said. He became excited. "This was a woman announcer. I don't think they have lady announcers in the railway stations yet. But they have them at the airport."

He wheeled on Ham Brooks. "Ham, get out to La Guardia Field as fast as you can. I have a strange feeling that our friends have lit out for Arizona by plane."

X

At Tulsa they were telling the customers that westbound flights would probably be cancelled. At Amarillo, they were getting ready for a stackup of westbound ships. At Tucumcari, CAA airways radio station, one of the operators was on vacation, and they were snowed under. It was a madhouse. At Albuquerque, private fliers were running around like scared ostriches trying to find hangarage for their planes, and those who discovered they were going to have to take their ships out and take what was coming, screamed like eagles.

Old man weather was about to pop. At Salt Lake, Tulsa, Denver, Fort Worth, Albuquerque, the meteorology boys were bending over their maps and connecting points of like barometric pressure with isobar lines. They looked alarmed at what they saw.

West of Kingman on Airway Green 4, it was clear as a crystal. From Kingman east to Winslow, it was instrument. But at three o'clock in the afternoon, Winslow CAA teletype tacked an X on its sequence. X meant take-offs and landing suspended. Closed. The old man was there.

"Oh, boy!" Ham Brooks said.

Doc Savage contemplated the instrument panel of his plane with no enthusiasm at all. The instrument panel had a full blind flight group, and the instruments were as good as they come. But he was not happy. No pilot who has ever flown into a stinker wants to fly into another one. Doc had been in a couple.

He had been riding the Winslow beam, in the N quadrant, but close enough to get the twilight A. The Winslow call was dot dash dash then three dashes. WO. The range N went off, and the Winslow operator gave the weather. It made Doc much less happy.

"Oh, boy!" Ham Brooks repeated. "If we set down at Winslow, they'll never let us off again."

"The remedy for that is simple," Doc explained. "We will not set down at Winslow."

Detective Theodore La France jeered at them. "Scared, ain't you?" he said. "What the hell are you scared of?"

"I hope you'll never find out," Ham said sincerely. "Indeed, I do."

"Hah. I'm not afraid," said Mr. La France.

Ham nodded pityingly. "You have never met our approaching friend which we scientific boys refer to as cAw."

"As which?"

Ham waved generally westward. "A continental arctic air mass, or cAw as he's called," he explained. "Nobody knows why he came down here at this time of year. Nobody invited him. God knows, nobody wants him. He's a wild harum-scarum from the Arctic, and he's out to whoop and roar among the gentle warm air masses."

"What is this, a kiddie story?" asked Detective La France.

Ham looked through the skylight. There was high cirrus, like strips of shed snake hide. Cirrus like that was composed of frozen ice particles.

In the west, gleaming silver and ebony castles stood in the sky. These were what the weather man called cumulo nimbus clouds. Inside them, you could find winds so violent no man had ever measured them. There were reliable reports of five-hundred-mile-an-hour winds in such clouds.

Ham shivered.

Ada Nobel moved to Ham's side. She demonstrated how much she knew about meteorological signs of the devil.

"Aren't the clouds pretty," she said.

The police report came over the other radio, the multi-band. It was from Kansas City. Ham was manning that set, and he copied the message with a pencil.

He said, "I guess they pulled out of Kansas City, all right." He handed Doc what he had copied.

The message read:

No individuals your description used airlines. But hospital plane chartered by two men claiming be doctors taking two patients answering your description Monk Mayfair and Harrison Nobel destination given Los Angeles. Hospital plane is Beechcraft NC 23875 painted white. Full instruments. Left Kansas City contact flight rules hour 22:10. Shall we check itinerant private plans for more men your description of H. I. Merrillee and others.

MORGAN, Kansas City Police.

"What's that?" Detective La France wanted to know. Ham let him read it. La France said, "Dammit, they didn't take an airliner." He scowled. "What does that mean, hour twenty-two-ten?" he added.

"Hour twenty-two-ten would be ten minutes after ten last night," Ham said.

"Why do you flying guys change everything all around?" La France demanded. "Hell, they're way ahead of us, aren't they? Beechcraft, is that a fast ship?"

"It's a pretty hot job for a private ship," Ham told him. "Yes, they're a long way ahead of us."

"Why the hell didn't it occur to you they might charter private planes?" demanded the detective. "Some detectives, I must say."

Ham scowled at him. "It did occur to us, Sherlock," Ham said. He didn't like La France. "But what they did was rent the plane ahead of time. More than one plane, no doubt. That hospital ship wouldn't carry all of them."

"Couldn't you guys have had them stopped at some airport?"

Ham became enraged. "You've got more back sight than a horse has flies. Why don't you spout those bright ideas early enough to do some good?" He poked the detective's chest with a finger. "If you want my opinion, we could take the good you've been to us and put it in a gnat's eye, with some room left!" he added.

"Quit punching me in the chest!" La France said.

Ham examined the sleuth's ample nose. He was tempted to see if it would flatten. But Doc Savage said, "Sit down, Ham." The bronze man was impatient. "See if you can find an airport that has seen that hospital plane."

Forty minutes later, Ham released the microphone button and yelled.

"Montrose! Montrose, Colorado!" he yelled. "Nine o'clock this morning, they loaded fuel there!"

"Sure it was this hospital plane?" Doc asked.

"Positive. The lineman at the field got the NC number on the gas ticket. Same ship." Ham was elated. "You know what that means," he said.

Doc Savage nodded. "They're heading for the ranch, Fear's End," he said. "They're coming in from the north, probably across the Uncompahgre plateau."

Doc clipped a Grand Canyon sectional aeronautical chart on the mapboard.

"We'll try to make the ranch," he said.

The plane gave a jump like a spanked mule. One wing went up, and there was the stomach pulling sensation of a furious sideslip. Disturbed air pounded fuselage and wing surfaces.

"There's what I mean," said Ada Nobel.

The detective, Theodore La France, looked out dubiously at the troubled world. "What if a guy gets airsick?" he asked.

Ham dismissed this airily. "You don't. You just tell yourself you won't, and you don't."

"Why don't you?"

"Airsickness is all imagination," said Ham, emphatically.

The plane hit a downcurrent. For ten seconds the bottom was out. It was worse than out. They lifted up as if ghosts had hold of them, only the safety belts holding them in their seats. Ada Nobel shrieked, "What's that?" Ham said, "Only a downcurrent." La France said, "Jeepers!"

The ceiling was about fifteen hundred. The trouble was that the fifteen hundred feet was measured above the floors of the canyons around them.

Ahead there was a front. Doc had concluded it wasn't too bad just now, had decided to go through. There was a sort of hole. Flying into a hole in a cold front wasn't the wisest thing to do, but it was that or go back to Albuquerque or some place like that and sit it out. Possibly for days.

Slinking, coiling, uncoiling, black and gray like Siamese cats, the cumulo-nimbus clouds were all about them. There was lightning. They could see it spurt and flash, hear it wanging the heavens, its thunder like sixty-gun salvos. Each lightning flash illuminated the red fuel tank caps on the wings, one labeled two hundred fifty gallons, the other three hundred gallons. Hundred-octane gas, about as explosive as dynamite, if one wanted to think about that.

Wind, invisible, terrific, suddenly got them. It sucked them upward. Doc tilted the plane on its nose, and his jaw muscles made walnuts in front of his ears. A cumulo-nimbus cloud was sucking them up into its internal workings. Doc watched the airspeed, giving the plane all the dive he thought the wings would take, or a little more.

Ham went white, then green. They went up into the cloud. The wind was certainly more than four hundred miles an hour. Into the cloud. It was as black as the inside of a goat. And several times as unpleasant.

They spun out of the cloud a few moments later. Ham knew they were spinning. He could tell it by the way forces were tearing at him, wrenching him against the belt. But, when he saw the naked rocky earth gyrating in front of him, he had the absurd feeling that he was going to have to reach up and put his hair back on his head.

Doc got the plane levelled out.

Ham grabbed for a paper sack. He was violently airsick.

Detective La France leered at him. "Imagination, huh?" La France said.

Sunlight, peace, quiet, placidity, enveloped them the moment they were out ahead of the front. Ham went back to the lavatory with his paper sack, sheepishly. He returned shortly without the sack.

"It's beautiful!" exclaimed Ada Nobel, meaning the weather.

"Lovely," Ham agreed, wondering why the hell he had to be the only one who got airsick. He looked down, added, "The Grand Canyon from the air." He didn't think it was so lovely. He thought it was something to scare the roar out of a lion.

Doc had climbed the ship. It was about four thousand feet up and the air, while not smooth, was crystal clear. The sun, piling its glory against the clouds behind them, made an awe-inspiring backdrop for the greatest spectacle of nature that the world offers. The Grand Canyon.

Westward and southward was Grand Canyon the town, with its fancy tourist lodges, and Bright Angel trail snaking down to the bottom of the canyon. Two days' trip by donkey. To the right was Cameron, the painted desert beyond, a waste as bald as a skull.

Ada Nobel stared at the canyon country. "You don't get the feeling of frightening smallness that you get on the ground," she said.

"Wait until we get down in it," Ham said. He saw Doc beckoning. "Doc wants you."

Doc Savage wanted to re-check about the ranch landing strip. How long was it? What direction did it lie?

"It's nearly half a mile," Ada Nobel explained. "It's smooth. I walked over it one day. It runs roughly north and south. It's on the top of a kind of shelf on which Fear's End is situated." She examined the chart. "Here," she said. "Right here."

Doc nodded. He switched on the radio transmitter, his idea being to get a CAA radio station, either Winslow or El Morro or Milford, and tell where he was landing, then ask that planes with armed men to sent in after him if he didn't report himself safe tomorrow. But there was too much static. He couldn't raise anything. He switched to code, tried that. No better luck. Static, blasting and continuous. He put the microphone back in its clip.

He told Ham, "We're on our own. But don't advertise it."

Ada Nobel looked back at the storm front. "I'm glad we're out of that," she said.

"We're not," Doc told her. "We're just ahead of it. It's coming this way. And from the way the weather reports read, it's going to center over the canyon area."

She looked worried. "There is no hangar at Fear's End."

Fear's End was astonishingly near the bottom of the canyon. They had flown only a few minutes, but they had covered terrain that no man had ever traversed afoot, and probably never would.

Ages ago, the river had cut its way down to hard, level, rock strata, and for a while, a few centuries probably, it had squirmed across the rock, cutting a fairly wide and flat valley. Then it had found a soft place, and eaten its way downward another thousand feet to the place where it now raced, a swollen, muddy, frightening snake of water.

The result was a shelf of fairly level ground not quite a mile long, and nowhere more than three hundred yards wide. Soil had settled here, enough to support a growth of coarse desert grass and scraggly pinon trees.

Doc Savage looked it over, thought: It sounds large, when you speak of the dimensions.

But the shelf was small against the titanic immensity of the canyon walls. Two minutes ago, he hadn't been able to pick it out at all.

He told Ham, "We'll drag the area, but good. Stand by for landing procedure check-off."

Ham nodded. "Looks like enough room from here."

The landing strip had been cleared among the gnarled pinon trees. It was not wide, not more than a hundred and fifty feet. But it seemed smooth. And it was with the prevailing wind.

Doc said, "There's no white plane there." His face was tight with disappointment.

"I don't see where they could hide it, either," Ham agreed.

The ranch buildings were prominent. They were of native stone, but the rooftops were gay, brilliant. The place looked peaceful.

Doc dragged the landing strip. The third time he went over, he did so in a hair-raising sideslip, so that he got a good view.

Ada Nobel said excitedly, "I see someone at the ranch house! More than one man!"

Doc nodded. He let down the gear, adjusted the throttles, hit a glide, set the flaps, did the two dozen other things that had to be done simultaneously. There was an interval when he was aware of nothing except the runway, the feel of the plane.

Detective La France said, "Hot dog!" He was relieved. "We made it, didn't we?" he added. He started for the door.

"Stay in your seat," Doc told him. "We'll taxi back to the other end of the runway."

"Why?"

"In case we have to get off again in a hurry," Doc said.

Doc locked a wheel brake, fed the opposite motor throttle, got around, and taxied downwind, guiding the heavy ship with the brakes. At the far end of the runway, he came into the wind, locked the brakes. He sat for a while, letting the motors run cooler, watching the surroundings. Everything seemed all right. He cut the switches.

"All right," he said. "But let's not be in a hurry."

His jacket had been hanging over the back of his seat. He gathered it up, somewhat clumsily, and an object fell out of the jacket pocket, skipped along the cabin aisle.

"Hell's bells!" Detective La France ogled the object

which had dropped. "For the love of Heaven!" he added. The object was a metal stork statuette.

Ham pretended astonishment. "Where'd that come from?" he demanded.

Doc picked up the stork. "It fell out of my pocket," he said. He put it back in his jacket pocket. "Let's look around."

La France blurted, "But I thought they had the stork!"

"Oh, they have one, too," Doc told him. "Would you like one, too?" Doc opened a handbag. He took out three more storks. "You might as well have one," he said, and handed a stork to La France, a stork to the girl, a stork to Ham. "Everyone might as well have one," he added.

No one seemed to be able to think of anything to say.

Doc got out of the plane. He walked out on the runway, studying the ground. From the tire prints he found, he decided that one plane had landed recently and taken off. From the distance between the tire tracks, he thought the plane could have been the Beech, the hospital ship.

Ham grew excited about the tire tracks. "The Beech," he said. "I'll bet it was the Beech!"

Doc nodded. "In that case, you'd better keep your eye peeled," he warned.

Ham said, "I got a better idea." He climbed back into the plane and got a machine pistol, and his coat. He put his coat over his arm, covering his hand which held the small rapid-firer. "They better not start anything," he said bloodthirstily.

XI

The man had gentle, sheep-like eyes. He was not a large man, and his shoulders were stooped from years of work at a desk and over a stenographer's notebook. Recent suffering had not been able to erase the gentleness from his face.

He opened his arms when Ada Nobel cried, "Uncle Harky! Oh, Uncle Harky!" He received the girl into his arms, saying, "Ada, my little niece." He patted her shoulder tenderly. "I'm so glad to see you," he told her.

In front of the ranch house stood three other men, all of whom Doc Savage had met previously. There was the small sad man who had carried the diaper satchel in New York, when Ham and Doc had been so scared in front of their headquarters' building. The other two men had also been present on that occasion, one being the fellow with the blond wig, Doc was sure. The other man had been in the car with him at the time.

These three gentlemen were smiling, but it was obvious they had been told to smile. Otherwise they showed signs of uneasiness.

Doc decided he had nothing to say. He was astonished.

Detective La France, amazed, demanded, "What the hell is this? What *is* this, anyway?" He seemed frightened, too.

Ham Brooks had the three onlookers covered with the submachine gun under his coat. "Where's Merrillee?" Ham demanded. "Where's old cupid-face, eh?"

Harrison Nobel patted his niece's shoulder again. "You poor darling," he said. Ada began crying.

Ham stalked over to the sad man. He demanded, "You got any more diaper satchels around?"

The man grinned thinly over fear.

"Come on, you so-and-so!" Ham told the sad man violently. "Speak a piece for me. Let's see what you've got to say. Where's Monk Mayfair?"

The sad man began to tremble. "I ain't got nothin'," he said.

Ham suddenly hit the man in the stomach with his left fist. "You've got something now," Ham told him. The sad man fell down.

Harrison Nobel cried, "Wait! Oh, please wait!" He fluttered toward them. "Please, gentlemen, please." He sounded as if he was about to sob. "There's been a terrible mixup. Please let me explain," he pleaded.

The sad man lay on his back and made gagging sounds. "I've got a notion to kick a kidney out of you," Ham told him. "Where's Monk Mayfair?"

Detective La France looked at Ham in amazement. He was impressed by Ham's ferocity.

"Let me talk to you," Harrison Nobel urged. "Come inside, please, and let me talk."

Doc Savage said, "Take it easy, Ham. Let's hear their story."

His two friends helped the sad man to his feet. They didn't have a natural color, and they were sweating.

In the southwest, clouds were like a herd of grazing dark sheep in the sky. They looked deceitfully peaceful, harmless. One cloud was standing up higher than the others. It looked like a herder taking care of the nice peaceful sheep.

The living room of the ranch house was beamed in stained wood. The walls, which were about three feet thick, were unfinished naked native stone, the floor was a mosaic of flagstones. The fireplace was enormous, pleasant, and there was a magnificent elk head above the mantel. The elk horns had sixteen points and a button.

Harrison Nobel twisted his hands together and said, "I'm so glad you will listen. I know how—"

"Hold it a while," Doc said. "Wait until Ham gets back." Ham was prowling the ranch, searching for Monk Mayfair.

Detective Theodore La France was staring at one of the three men. Not the sad man, but the one whom Doc suspected of wearing the blond wig in New York. Suddenly the detective said, "I think you're the blankety-blank who took a shot at me!"

The man recoiled. "You're crazy!"

The detective bristled. "You ruined a five-dollar hat for me, you rat!"

The man's jaw fell. "Oh, cripes!" he exclaimed. "Was it about a week ago?"

"By God, I thought you were the one!" La France shouted. He started toward the man.

"No, no, wait," the man cried, retreating. "I thought it was one of them Navajo Indians prowling around the place. They come down here and steal stuff. We have to scare 'em off, and that's why I took a shot at the prowler."

"What a lie!" the detective said.

Discouraged, Ham came into the room. He said, "I didn't find Monk." He suddenly removed his coat from his arm and hand, exposing the submachine gun. "But I'm going to, you bet!" he added angrily.

Doc ordered, "Hold it!" He nodded to Harrison Nobel, said, "What've you got to say?"

Eagerly, wildly, Harrison Nobel said, "A banker named Wentz built this ranch, and I was his secretary." He poured out words as if there wasn't much time. "I inherited the place when—"

"We know how you inherited it," Doc said.

Thrown off stride, Nobel faltered, mumbled, "I—that

is—I guess Ada, here, has told you I sent for her? She was working in Chicago, and I offered her a job."

"Why?" Doc asked.

A breath, relieved, rushed between Nobel's teeth. "That's what I want to tell you!" he exclaimed. "A companion. You see, I need a companion very much because—because—" He floundered like a ham actor portraying a confession scene. "I'm mentally unstable!" he blurted. "I—my nerves—a nervous breakdown. I'm afraid that—well not insanity exactly, but delusions. Awful delusions."

Doc examined him curiously.

"What kind of delusions?" Doc asked.

"The last one was about a little statuette of a stork," said Harrison Nobel.

A wind, a small vagrant wind, whirled under the eaves of the ranch house, sighing softly. It was as full of promise as a tiger's breath.

"This," said Doc Savage politely, "is very interesting. Continue."

Harrison Nobel twisted his hands together.

He said, "I had a crazy spell recently. For some reason, or rather no reason at all except a desire that existed in my demented mind, I had to get my hands on the stork statuette." He nodded at the three men. "These are my friends, who were visiting me." He started in surprise, added, "Oh, I haven't introduced you gentlemen, have I?"

He introduce the trio. Sad man was named Jonas McBride, of Los Angeles. The other two were Mr. Horn and Mr. Giesing.

Doc Savage was watching Nobel. He did not think he was watching a crazy man, or one who had ever had a crazy spell, with or without delusions. Doc did feel sure he was watching a thoroughly scared, greedy and desperate man.

"My friends," explained Harrison Nobel, "didn't know what to do to humor me. They decided I would be all right if I could get the stork. So we went to New York after it." He paused uncomfortably. "I'm afraid my friends were overzealous in their efforts to get it."

Nobel lifted his head, gazed at them levelly.

"You see, that explains all that happened in New York," he said.

Silence came into the room and took hold of everyone for a while.

"Nuts!" Detective La France said skeptically.

Doc Savage voted a silent agreement.

Ham Brooks slapped his submachine gun. The sound caused everyone to jump.

"Where's Monk Mayfair?" Ham demanded.

Nobel dropped his eyes. "I'm awfully sorry we put you to so much trouble, and worried you so about your friend," he said. "Mr. Mayfair is in New York, I suppose. He was having a good drunk, the last we saw of him."

Ham's face got wooden. "Monk doesn't drink."

"I'm sorry." Nobel was not looking up from the floor. "He said, after we told him the whole story, that he was disgusted that so much hell could arise over something so inconsequential, and what he needed was a good toot. We had some liquor, which we gave him. He was rather inebriated when we last saw him."

Ham said, "Monk doesn't drink." He moved the machine gun a little, as if he was going to use it on them.

Nobel watched the rapid-firer. Terror made him pale, ill-looking.

Doc asked, "What became of Merrillee?"

"Oh, my friend Merrillee? Oh, him." Nobel shrugged. "He didn't come back to the ranch with us. He has his business to take care of, and his vacation was over." Nobel lifted his head, looked at them. "I'm so sorry this thing has created such an uproar. So very sorry. I wish I could recompense you in some measure. Will you, perhaps, stay here at the ranch and rest?"

He didn't sound as if he wanted them to stay at the ranch.

"We certainly will," Doc Savage said. "That's very fine of you," Doc added. "We may pay you quite a visit."

They were put, Doc and Ham and La France, in a guest cottage off by itself. It was a fine pleasant cottage which had been built by the banker to make his millionaire clients feel at home. There were big Navajo rugs on the floors, and the furniture was made of such native materials as cactus wood, pinon wood, cowhide, deerskin.

Ham was indignant. "Why the hell," he demanded, "did he tell us a string of lies like that?"

La France looked doubtful. "You think he was lying?"

"Don't you?"

"I don't know." La France scratched his head. "It did sound fishy."

"Sure he was lying." Ham slapped his submachine gun. "If I was half a man, I would go back to the house, give them a chance to tell the truth, and shoot their heads off if they didn't."

Doc looked at Ham uneasily. Ham sounded as if he might do what he was threatening to do.

Far away, faintly, there was a rumbling. It began softly and gathered volume, but did not become particularly loud. It was just a strange, frightening sound, a popping and crackling and rumbling. It was thunder.

Doc said, "That storm is going to pile in here before we know it." He turned to Ham, suggested, "You and La France had better find ropes and sledge hammers and stakes and stake down the plane, so it won't be blown off the shelf into the canyon."

Ham agreed. He said, "All right, but I'd rather shoot some sense into somebody around here." He cradled the gun over his arm, and he and La France went out.

Doc Savage made a quick search of the guest house. They had gone over it before, but they made sure there wasn't an ambush. Now he hunted for something else, anything. He didn't know what he would find. His nervous excitement merely urged him to hunt, and he hunted. There was nothing.

Discouraged, he went outside. He walked to a spot from which he could see Ham and the detective. They were cutting and driving stakes. Their sledge and axe blows rang out, echoes making each sound come back twenty-fold from the canyon walls.

Ham and La France stopped pounding. They were fascinated by the echoes. They could not resist a shout or two, to see what would come back.

"Liar!" Ham shouted. And cascading back from the echo chambers came, "Liar-liar-liar." About twenty of them.

In the southwest, the cloud banks were taller, darker, more nodular. Now and then a tongue of lightning would lick out of one.

Ham and the detective came back. They were excited. Ham's mouth was down at the corners, his jaw out.

"Doc," Ham said. "Doc, somebody got to the fuel line. Our gasoline is all out on the ground."

"You mean the plane tanks are empty?" Doc demanded.

Ham nodded. "Somebody who knew how to use a crowbar used it."

"They don't want us to get away," La France said. The detective was hoarse. His fingers were twitching.

Doc said, "Harrison Nobel and his three friends didn't do it." His eyes swept the surroundings nervously. "They couldn't have done it. They haven't been out of our sight long enough."

"We're isolated here!" La France wailed. "Can't we use the radio and get help, or something?"

Ham scowled. "That's right. Harrison and his three friends couldn't have opened that gas line. So someone else did."

"Merrillee, perhaps," Doc said. He sounded grimly satisfied with the situation.

XII

Harrison Nobel put the palm of his right hand against his cheek. "Your gasoline—gone! Gone?" he said. He was like a startled girl. "You must have sprung a leak when you landed." He lifted his binoculars, turned around, tilted his head back and scanned the heights of canyon wall above the ranch.

"Must have," Doc said without emotion.

The storm was fighting a war in the distance, southward toward Bright Angel. It sounded exactly like a war, too. A little more of it, perhaps. The thunder, cascading through the canyon in volleys of echoes, was the cannon fire.

"Storms here always terrify me," Nobel said. He twisted the focusing screw of the binoculars nervously. "The concussion of thunder sometimes dislodges great boulders which roll down." He shuddered, added, "Big as houses! Bigger!"

Detective Theodore La France ran around the corner of the ranch house. "The horses!" he cried breathlessly. "Where are the horses?"

"Horses?" Nobel didn't lower his glasses. "We don't use horses here. We use donkeys."

"Well, donkeys!" the detective yelled. "Where the hell are the donkeys?" Terror made his voice ugly.

"They broke out of the corral last night and wandered off," Nobel said.

"My God!" the detective cried. "How do we got out of here then?"

Nobel shrugged. "Walk, I imagine." He lowered the binoculars. "It takes about a week to climb to on foot. Too bad, isn't it?"

Lightning struck a forked red tongue out of the storm. The tongue must have been five miles long. And the storm gave a terrific gobble of thunder.

The sad man, who had been introduced as Jonas McBride of Los Angeles, came to the ranch house door. "Dinner is served," he said.

"Dinner?" Detective La France was startled.

"I thought we might as well eat," said Nobel.

The sad man repeated, "Dinner is served." He was looking at Ham Brooks. It was a hateful look. The look said that he hated Ham because he remembered how Ham had hit him in the belly. I've put arsenic in your soup, the look said.

Doc Savage went inside. He found Ada Nobel. She jumped up eagerly, glad to see him. He knew, by the tight way she held his arm, that she was frightened.

He whispered, "What do you think?"

"There's something horrible going on here," she whispered back. "Uncle Harky isn't himself. He isn't himself at all. He's—different—like—as if—"

"As if he were acting?" Doc suggested.

She began to tremble. "I'm afraid Uncle Harky has joined up with them," she said.

Doc looked at her intently. "How do you feel?"

"Feel?" She was puzzled.

He nodded. "Feel, yes."

She thought about that for a moment. "As if—as if I had hold of a sack, and there was a wildcat in the sack." She shuddered. "Not a wildcat, because they're little. A tiger. A man-eating tiger," she added.

Surprise made Doc release a rush of breath. That was exactly how he felt, too. He released another deep breath. He decided he had enough of it.

"Let's open the sack," Doc said.

"Can we?" Her eyes were wide with wonder.

"I think so."

She clutched his arm eagerly. "Let's do. Oh, let's!" she said. "I'm tired of this stalking around, nothing happening, nothing that seems to make sense."

"All right," Doc said. "Hold your hat."

The dinner table was long. The linen was expensive, if not exactly spotless. The silver was costly. Ham scowled at it, said, "The setting is a little elaborate for a can of beans."

The sad man said coldly, "Beans is what we've got."

Doc Savage prepared to start the fireworks. He drew out a chair and sat down.

"McBride," he said.

The sad man's name was evidently really McBride, from the way he looked around. He said, "Huh?"

Doc became very friendly.

"Mack, old boy," Doc said, "don't you think we might as well stop fooling them?"

McBride batted both eyes. He said, "Huh?" again.

"I mean, old boy, what's the object of going on with it?" Doc asked. He was even more friendly. "After all, we might as well wind it up now."

McBride began to look sick. "I don't know whatcha talkin' about," he said.

"Sure you do. Storks." Doc laughed with resounding comradeship. "I know this isn't the way you figured it, Mack. But why don't we cut it short?"

Stiffly, mouth working, McBride got to his feet. "Damn you, I don't know what you're talking about!" he said.

Doc laughed again. He reached in his coat pocket, brought out a stork, planted the stork on the table. He said, "Here's the stork. We sucked them in with the phony we gave them, didn't we, Mack?" Doc laughed some more. "Really took them in, didn't we?"

McBride looked at his two friends. They were watching him with animal-like intentness. "Oh hell, guys!" McBride appealed to them. "You don't think I'd—here, here, now! Dammit, this is a rib!" He sneered at Doc Savage. "You liar," he said.

McBride's two friends looked at the stork Doc had put on the table. The animal air about them grew. One said, "A phony stork!" He thought for a moment, added, "By God, no wonder we got it so easy."

Harrison Nobel was now looking quite ill. "Gentlemen," he ventured weakly. "Gentlemen." He didn't seem to know what more to say.

One of McBride's two friends stood up. "We got a phony stork," he said, unbelievingly. "A fake stork."

He backed away from the table. He told his friend, "This splits it, Goose."

The other, Mr. Giesing, was confused. He had been holding a fork, which he now put down. He reached inside his coat.

Alarmed, Ham yelled, "Keeperhandoffthatgun!" At the same time, he grabbed the handiest missile, the pot of beans, and hurled it in Mr. Giesing's face, pot and all.

On the floor in a shower of beans, Mr. Giesing used his head. He scooted under the table. He made quite a noise.

His friend used the confusion to produce a flat, dark pistol. With it, he shot the sad man, McBride, in the head.

Harrison Nobel shrieked and ran out through the door.

Ham Brooks grabbed frantically for his submachine gun, which he had placed on the floor beside his chair. In his haste to get it, he fell from his chair to the floor.

Ada Nobel stood up. Then she threw up her arms, waved them, tottered, screamed, fell to the floor, disappeared under the table as if she had been swallowed.

Doc Savage had a feeling the man with the gun, whose name was Mr. Horn, was going to shoot at him next. Doc seized the table edge, lifted it, heaved it up on its side. This put the table between himself and Horn.

Upping the table to its edge disclosed that Mr. Giesing had seized Ada Nobel, was going to use her for a shield.

Detective Theodore La France had been sitting in a chair at the end of the table. He still sat in it, although now there was no table in front of him. He was holding his napkin.

Mr. Horn aimed at two or three points on the table top, indecisively. He couldn't see Doc or Ham. Then he didn't shoot. "Ah!" he said. He'd spied the stork. Jumping to the stork, stooping, picking it up, occupied him for a broken second.

Mr. Giesing now gained his feet. He was holding Ada

Nobel to his chest with his left arm. She struggled. He said, "Be still!" Hit her over the head with his fist.

Mr. Horn was withdrawing with the statuette of the stork. "Scram, Goose!" he said. "We'll shoot ta hell outa them from outside."

A bolt of thunder crashed outside, loosening an unbelievable amount of sound outside the door. Loud as the gunshot had been, this was louder.

Doc put a shoulder against the bottom of the table, shoved and skidded the table toward Mr. Horn. This caused Mr. Horn to retreat hastily, as Doc had known it would. While Mr. Horn was withdrawing, Doc made a rush for Mr. Giesing.

Giesing didn't have his gun out yet. He saw Doc was going to try to hit him with a fist. He dodged behind the girl, ducking his head from side to side like a rooster in a fight. Doc Savage feinted with his left hand, which caused the man's head to bob into view on the other side of the girl's head. Doc hit the head as hard as he thought he could without smashing his hand.

Mr. Giesing loosened his hold on Ada Nobel and backed away. His nose would never be the same again. He retreated as far as the wall, where he fell down. He blew a large, scarlet bubble.

Doc Savage had hold of Ada Nobel, and he ran her to the floor behind the table.

Mr. Horn fired at the table. The bullet came through the table easily. It made a small hole around which splinters stood on their ends.

Ham Brooks, sitting on the floor, had his submachine ready. He glared at the table bottom, which hid the enemy from him, and demanded, "Shall I kill them?"

Doc Savage got hold of a chair. He said, "No, just bark them like you would a squirrel." He threw the chair over the top of the table as hard as he could. "For Heaven's sake, shoot that thing," he urged Ham.

The chair Doc had thrown hit a wall, bounced back, rolled noisily over and over.

Ham aimed at the table bottom, braced himself, pulled the trigger. He got a snapping noise. He could have made a louder noise with his fingers. He looked silly, got a cartridge in the barrel, and tried again. This time the results were satisfactory. Ham fired about twenty shots, stopped. Everybody's ears rang like small bells.

There was a dragging noise. The sound was made by Mr. Horn dragging the dazed Mr. Giesing out through the door, but Ham did not know this.

"Want some more?" Ham demanded.

The dragging sounds ceased.

Ham said confidently, "Got them." He started to stand up. Doc lunged, jerked Ham down flat. Two bullets came through the table top, narrowly missing them.

Horn's voice said, "This ain't over with!"

The door slammed.

Detective La France still sat in his chair. But now his eyes were closed.

Doc Savage ran to the wall near the door, reached out swiftly and tried to yank the door open. It was locked. A shot roared on the other side. A cloud of splinters flew. But Doc had jerked his hand back.

Ham Brooks put a five-shot burst through the door. He took two jumps to the right, sent another five shots into the panels. He listened.

Mr. Horn told them, from the other side of the door, what he thought of them. He was joined, not as strongly, by Mr. Giesing. Both of them finished by inviting Doc or Ham, or both, to come through the door.

"Better save your ammunition," Doc told Ham, who was aiming at the door again.

Ham dampened his lips with his tongue. "We better get out of here."

Doc shook his head. "Too much open space around the house. They could pick us off."

A slight sound brought them around wildly. But it was only Ada Nobel getting to her feet. Her confusion was understandable.

"Where is Uncle Harky?" she asked.

"He showed more judgment than any of us, and ran," Ham explained.

The girl looked dazed. "What happened?" she asked. Then she put a palm on each side of her head and pressed.

Suddenly Doc Savage jumped at her, grasped her, brought her to the floor. She had been standing in front of a window, an easy target for anyone outside. He pointed this out to her. "I'm sorry," he apologized. "But you must be careful."

She thanked him. She said, "Thank you." This caused Doc to look at her sharply, and wonder how soon he was going to have a hysteria case on his hands. It wasn't the time for polite thank yous. Or was it? If you had enough grip on yourself to be drawing-room polite when—

"'S matter?" Ham was pointing at La France. "What's the matter with him?"

Doc looked at the detective narrowly. "La France!" he called. The man on the chair was motionless, unresponsive, eyes tightly shut.

Turning Ada Nobel around so that she wouldn't see, Doc made a series of gestures—aiming one hand like a pistol at La France, making hammer-falling motions with the thumb of the hand, then raising his eyebrows quizzically—by which Ham understood he was to see whether Detective La France had been shot.

Having investigated, Ham said, "No holes in him." He nudged La France. "Hey, you, wake up!" Ham said. Then, hit by another thought, he gasped, "Heart trouble!" But after holding the detective's wrist, he reported, "Pulse like a fire hose."

Ada Nobel demanded, "What's happened to Mr. La France?"

"He threw a la-de-dah on us," Ham explained. He gave La France a shove, then had to catch the detective to keep him from falling out of the chair. "Fainted," Ham explained.

The girl giggled. "I was going to faint," she said. "I don't think I will, now. It—it would be sort of an anticlimax, don't you think?"

"That's the attitude," Doc told her. "That's exactly the attitude."

Doc Savage was not watching her. He was gazing intently at Detective Theodore La France. Certain ideas which he had held about Mr. La France began to crystallize into rock-solid certainty. The most solid idea was that La France had not fainted. He was faking.

The major part of Doc's early training had been in medicine and surgery. He still practiced, of late years having specialized in brain operative procedure. He was not egotistic in considering himself an authority on fainting.

Fainting, which a layman usually thought was a snap to imitate, was almost impossible to feign. Shutting the eyes and becoming limp wouldn't fool many doctors.

The detective was faking.

XIII

Somber, sooty, alive, the gloom of the storm came into the room. Noisy, too. Thunder and lightning played continually, the echoes making it a deafening conglomeration of sound.

Ham Brooks made a cautious survey from the window, blinking his eyes when the lightning flashed. Impressed, he muttered, "Kind of noisy. We couldn't hear them if they did shoot at us, probably." He looked about uneasily, and his eye lit on the enormous fireplace. "I wonder what a man could see from up there," he said. He went over and put his head in the fireplace.

Doc Savage went over to Theodore La France. He held the detective's wrist, finding, as Ham had said, that the pulse was as strong as the pulse of a pump in a fire hose.

"A very impressive faint," Doc remarked.

"Isn't he silly?" Ada Nobel said. "After all his big talk."

Ham, his head in the fireplace, said, "There's a kind of a roof over the top of the chimney." He sounded as if he was in a hole. "Say, I bet we could see something from the top without being seen." He touched the side of the fireplace and got his fingers very sooty. He withdrew and suggested, "Doc, why don't you climb up and have a look?"

"Why don't you?" Doc asked.

"I don't think I could make it." Ham put his sooty fingers behind him.

"You're afraid of getting a little dirty," Doc said.

Then Doc got up and made an elaborate business of looking around the room. "Where's the stork?" he demanded. "They got it, didn't they?"

Ham suddenly forgot about the fireplace. "My God, was it the real stork?" he demanded.

"No, they got another fake," Doc said. He made sure his voice was loud enough for Detective La France to hear. "Here's another stork in my other coat pocket," he added. He produced the stork.

Amazed, Ham demanded, "How many of those things are you carrying on you?"

"This is the last one."

"Is it the real one?"

"Yes."

"All they've got to do now is take it away from you," Ham said.

Doc agreed with this. He added, "They might do it, at that." He pretended to think about this, added, "I shouldn't be carrying it on my person."

"Hide it," Ham said.

"That's a good idea," Doc agreed. He went over to La France. "Everybody will think La France is carrying a fake, too. If it was the real one, it would probably fool them."

"I don't think so much of that idea," Ham said hastily.

Doc bent over La France. He got La France's stork out of the man's clothing, went through some motions, and put a stork back in La France's pocket. It was the same stork. The stork Doc put in his own pocket was the same one he had been carrying, the genuine one.

Ham got the mistaken impression that La France was now possessor of the genuine stork.

"I don't think that's so hot, letting him carry the stork," he complained.

"Are you going to climb the chimney?" Doc asked.

"No." Ham was displeased. "Climb it yourself."

Doc Savage decided he would go up the chimney, which was constructed of rough stone, and easily mounted. He told Ham Brooks, "Watch that door. I don't want to be caught up in there." He suggested to Ada Nobel, "You better watch the windows."

Theodore La France now opened his eyes, showed signs of life. He asked, "Where am I?" He grabbed his forehead, added, "I feel awful!"

Doc said, "You fainted."

"Oh." La France groaned. "I guess I'm a lily." He stood up, essayed a step or two. "Will walking around hurt me?" he wanted to know.

"Walking should be good for you," Doc said. "Do not overdo it, is all."

Doc entered the fireplace. The chimney was amply wide and deep for climbing, but the layer of soot was extraordinarily thick. Doc climbed a few feet.

"La France," Doc called.

The detective put his head in the fireplace. Doc immediately slipped, lost his grip, and fell. He did not injure himself, but he brought down a cloud of soot and ashes.

Soot and ashes splattered over the hearth.

Doc dusted himself off. "What I wanted to ask—does that chimney top give a good view of the neighborhood?" he said.

"A fine view," La France admitted.

Doc nodded. "I'll tackle it again, then." He entered the fireplace once more. "Give me a lift up," he said.

La France, standing in the soot and ashes, gave Doc a lift up, groaning impressively as he did so. Doc climbed.

The chimney top did give a fine view of the surroundings. The only trouble was that there was enough brush to hide an army, and the howling violence of the storm, sweeping down on Fear's End, would soon wrap everything in blinding curtains of rain.

Doc climbed down again.

He looked about in surprise.

"Where," he demanded, "did La France go?"

Ham Brooks had one eye to the bullet holes in the door, trying to see whether there was an ambush outside. Ada Nobel was watching through the window. They both whirled, stared, showed unbelieving amazement.

The detective assuredly wasn't in the room.

"Didn't he go up the chimney?" Ham demanded.

"No."

Ham exclaimed, "Ada, why did you let him leave through the window?"

"I didn't," the girl cried. "I didn't! I never—where *did* he go?"

The mystery of what had become of La France held them speechless. There seemed to be no other way out of the room except the door, the chimney, the window.

Suddenly the storm pounced upon Fear's End. The lightning laid down a dozen ear-splitting bolts outside the door, rain followed this barrage, rain and hail together, so that the outer world became white and sobbing and terrible. In different parts of the house, the rain began breaking windowlights.

Doc Savage said, "I hope I didn't get La France to step into that soot for nothing." Doc began inspecting the floor.

The deposit of soot and ashes which Detective La France had gotten on his shoes when he stepped into the huge fireplace opening to aid Doc Savage made his footprints easily discernible.

Ham said admiringly, "So that's why you got him into the fireplace!" He shook his head in wonder. "How the blazes did you know he was going to skip?"

Doc looked wise. He hadn't known.

La France's tracks progressed to the east side of the room, where they stopped. Ended. Disappeared.

"What the devil!" Ham exploded.

Ada Nobel was also confused. "Where did he go?" she wanted to know. "Through the wall?"

Ham snorted. "What do you think he is, supernatural?"

Doc was scrutinizing the wall. "La France had soot on his hands, too," Doc pointed out. He hunted and finally found an oval black smear on an entirely normal looking section of the log wall.

There was nothing whatever to indicate that the thumb had been pressed there for any good reason. But Doc put his own thumb in the same spot. Nothing happened. He pushed. Then he understood. The log, from the other side, must be shaved to a thin shell; pressing on it closed some sort of closely adjusted contact on the other side.

With a flourish, without noise, a secret door opened.

"Good God!" Ham was amazed. "A secret door!" He began to think it was funny. "Sort of like Aladdin and the lamp. Maybe there's a genie, too."

Doc said, "Keep your eyes open." He wasn't feeling funny.

The opening was quite ample in width, although they had to stoop to enter. Inside it was dark. It was as dark as it had been in that cloud which had sucked them into its innards for a few moments. There were also steps, stone steps.

Doc made sure he could get the door open again, then closed it, increasing the darkness. He whispered, "Take off your shoes, so we'll make less noise." The shoe-removing occupied a while. "All right, stick together," Doc whispered.

He went down the steps, very slowly, feeling his way. The stone steps were rough. They hurt his feet.

Ham Brooks seemed to think the secret door and dark passage were funnier and funnier, because he giggled. Doc, aggravated, rammed an elbow into his ribs. "Ouch!" Ham gasped. Ada Nobel whispered, "Sh-h-h." Then she added, "There's a fork in the passageway. Right here, I think."

Doc investigated. There was indeed a fork. He whispered, "Wait here." He followed the branch about forty feet, around two turns, reached a door, opened it cautiously, discovered he was looking into the living-room of one of the guest cottages.

The thunder was making a great deal of noise outdoors. Rain was coming down in oyster-colored ropes.

Doc went back to Ham and the girl. Ham whispered, "I can hear voices. Listen!"

The door, big, heavy, was of steel. It was about a foot thick, and was a regulation vault door. It was, in fact, the door to a vault.

The vault itself was as large as a room, apparently excavated in the solid stone, and lined with steel. The ceiling did not seem to be more than seven feet, the width about twelve, the length eighteen or so. Entirely around the walls, except for the space where the door opened, there were steel filing cases, shelves, cabinets. There was no dampness.

Monk Mayfair, tied hand and foot, considerably battered, lay on the floor. His mouth was taped shut.

H. I. Merrillee was there with a gun. He was saying, "It's time we wound this thing up, and I'm going to do it." The cupid smile on his face was gently evil.

With Merrillee—and being menaced by his gun—was Harrison Nobel and Detective Theodore La France.

There was no one else.

Harrison Nobel said, "Finish and be damned. You are not living up to your part, so I'm not going to deliver on mine." He sounded weary, scared beyond any capacity to scare more.

Merrillee said, "The boys just lost their heads."

"Maybe," Nobel agreed. "Yes, I guess they did."

"Then what are you kicking about?"

"Look," Nobel said. He was stubborn. "You said that if I was to help you, nothing would be done to my niece. That's the only reason I gave in."

"Well, hell, we—"

"Hell, nothing!" Nobel interrupted Merrillee. "You said for me to tell that goofy story about me being crazy, and maybe Doc Savage, Ada and Ham Brooks would go away hunting Monk Mayfair. So I told the story. So what did you do while I was telling it? You opened the gas line on Savage's plane so they *couldn't* leave."

"They didn't believe the story," Merrillee said hastily. "They wouldn't have gone."

"You never gave them a chance." Harrison Nobel looked intently at Merrillee. He called Merrillee six or seven nasty names. "The hell with you!" Nobel finished. "The deal is off."

Merrillee's cherubic smile slipped somewhat. "I'll put it on again," he said.

Detective Theodore La France cleared his throat nervously. "Don't forget to count me in on any deals," he said.

They whirled on him. Merrillee said, "Damn you, you had to stick your nose in!"

Detective La France snorted. "Nobel knows the spot. I've got the stork." He sneered at Merrillee. "What have you got, except two bits' worth of talk?" He scowled at Merrillee, added, "Maybe we'll make a deal with *you*, not you make one with us."

The detective was selling a bill of goods. "Who d'you think you are?" he demanded. "Who d'you think you are, huh?"

He pushed out his jaw and answered his own question. "You're a lug who did some business with some aliens, and found out old Mason Carl Wentz was holding a lot of property for aliens, property they knew damned well the United States government would confiscate, if the United States government found out about it." He paused, sneered at Merrillee. "You're a chiseling traitor against your own country," he added.

Merrillee wasn't impressed. "Go ahead, you thin-witted Sherlock. Get your say." Merrillee's tone implied that later he would have plenty to say.

Detective La France sneered at Merrillee some more, demanded, "Brother, you're not the only one who knew Wentz was keeping a lot of property for aliens. Did you think so? Well, you weren't." The sleuth tapped his own chest. "Me. I knew it. And I was out to find it. And I would have found it, too. I did get the stork."

Merrillee was interested.

"You sure," he asked, "it's the real stork?"

"Certainly I'm sure."

"You better prove it."

"I'll prove it, all right," said La France indignantly. "Just get old Nobel, here, to show you the place. I'll prove it's the stork."

Merrillee swung on Harrison Nobel. "All right, where's the spot?"

The old man retreated. He shook his head. "I won't tell you. Not until Doc Savage and my niece are away from here."

Merrillee cursed. "Damn it, we're trying to get them away from here! Trying to drive them off."

"You're trying to kill them," said Nobel. His voice was heavy.

Suddenly, in the passage behind Doc Savage, there was noise. Footsteps. Hurried ones.

Detective La France heard them, yelled, "What's that?"

"Horn, that you?" Merrillee shouted loudly.

Mr. Giesing's voice answered him. "It's me," Mr. Giesing said. "Hey, you better help. Savage, Brooks and the girl are outa the house. They musta got away in the storm—"

He came down the passage slopping rainwater off his clothes. Behind him came another man. Their breathing was quick, rushing.

"Hell!" Mr. Giesing had bumped into Doc Savage.

Doc surmised Giesing would have a gun in his hand. He was correct in this. Doc got hold of the weapon. But he lost it immediately, because the weapon was slick with mud. Giesing must have fallen down in the storm and landed in the mud.

Throwing his weight against Giesing, Doc drove the man's head into contact with the tunnel wall. Stunned, Giesing lost his gun.

Ham had hold of the other man.

Merrillee, yelling, "What's going on here?" lifted his own gun and started for the vault door.

Ada Nobel screamed, "Uncle Harky!"

Electrified by her voice, Harrison Nobel sprang upon Merrillee. He tried to grab Merrillee's gun, didn't get it, got the wrist instead. They wrested one another about. Merrillee's gun spoke once, blam-m-m! deafeningly. About a yard of fire seemed to come out of its muzzle.

Detective La France yelped and fell to the floor. He had been hit in the body by the bullet.

Merrillee and Nobel, struggling, making spitting sounds, so great was their effort, fell to the floor, writhed.

Monk Mayfair, his small eyes protruding with excitement, rolled over, doubled his legs, and kicked H. I. Merrillee in the head. Merrillee, stunned, released Nobel, but still fought for possession of the gun.

Nobel, not realizing Monk Mayfair had managed to get into the fight although tied and gagged, did what he thought was necessary for his life. He turned the gun against Merrillee. He shot Merrillee in the stomach and chest until the gun was empty.

By now, Doc had finished battering the senses out of Giesing.

It was suddenly still.

"Ham?" Doc asked.

"O. K.," Ham said. "Is this all of them!"

"Miss Nobel?"

"I'm all right," she said.

Doc went into the vault. He pulled the tape off Monk's lips, ignoring Monk's squalls of pain. Doc asked, "How many more are there?"

Monk yelled, "Ouch! My face!" His little eyes snapped with indignation. "You mighta left some hide on my face!" he shouted.

"Is this all—"

"How many'd you get in the tunnel?" Monk demanded.

"Two."

"That's all," Monk said. "There were just Merrillee, McBride, Horn, Giesing, and that accounts for them."

"They had more men than that in New York," Doc said.

"They just used some local talent temporarily," Monk explained. "What about turning me loose, huh?"

Ham came into the vault. He stumbled over Detective Theodore La France. Looking down at La France, Ham remarked, "Fainted again."

But Detective La France was dead.

XIV

Vibrating below A above middle C, the tuning fork sounded unpleasant. It was unpleasant because listening to it was becoming monotonous.

The tuning fork—which was actually the genuine stork—made a fairly loud note. Loud enough that it could compete with the storm sounds, now that the storm was about over. The storm, the violent cold front of it, had gone whooping and flashing and thundering up the canyon.

Monk gave the fork another rap against the vault wall. "I wish you knew the right spot," he told Harrison Nobel.

"I do, too," Harrison Nobel agreed. "But it's just that wall, around where you are somewhere."

"Didn't you see Wentz open the secret part of the vault with it, ever?"

Harrison Nobel shook his head. "Only once. And just a glimpse. He was using the stork right where you are, just about."

"Okay." Monk rapped the stork legs against the steel vault wall, held them a fraction of an inch from the vault, and moved them around.

Ham Brooks demanded, "How is that going to work?"

"Vibration," Monk told him. "You take two tuning forks of the same frequency, start one vibrating, hold it close to the other, and that one will start vibrating, too. It's something you call synchronism, or something."

Doc Savage addressed old Harrison Nobel. Doc asked, "If you knew about this secret vault opened by the tuning fork, why didn't you open it before all this trouble started?"

"Oh, I didn't know about it," Nobel explained. "The first I knew was when Merrillee and his gang showed up and began trying to get the stork. I'd forgotten all about the stork, and had put it in with the other stuff that was shipped to New York to be sold at auction."

Monk turned his head, asked suspiciously, "How about the time you saw Wentz using it in here?" Didn't you remember that?"

Nobel shook his head.

He explained, "I just thought, that time, that Mr. Wentz was playing with the stork, just listening to it vibrate."

"But Merrillee told you different?"

"Oh, yes." Nobel looked uncomfortable. "He explained there was a secret vault, full of property of aliens which Mr. Wentz was holding, in an effort to persuade me to join up with him."

Doc Savage asked, "Was Theodore La France actually what he said he was, a detective, who had an agreement to investigate Wentz's death regardless of whether the death was natural or not?"

"Yes." Nobel nodded. "Mr. Wentz, because of his connections with so many aliens, probably feared his death might not be a natural one."

Monk Mayfair said, "I bet there isn't any secret vault."

There came a loud, very loud report. With it, a blinding flash. A whistling sound. A great quantity of blinding vapor suddenly poured out of vents in the walls. It hit their eyes and lungs like fire."

"Gas!" Monk dropped the tuning-fork-stork. "My God, gas!" He dived for the door. "Run, everybody! We're in a death trap!" he yelled.

The door of the secret vault had opened.

The secret vault—it was only about six feet square— contained a good deal of currency. About twenty suitcases full, although not all of the greenbacks were of large denomination. Ham Brooks fingered some of the greenbacks admiringly. "The kind you can spend, tens and twenties," he remarked.

Doc Savage was looking through metal drawers. He was impressed by what he was finding. Jewelry, unset jewels, some bonds and stocks, several bars of platinum, about a double handful of sparkling diamonds.

"No gold?" Monk Mayfair asked. He seemed discouraged by not finding gold.

"Did you ever try to buy any gold the last few years, lame-brain?" Ham Brooks asked him. "An American citizen can hardly get his hands on any, much less an alien."

Doc Savage noted that each lot of the valuables had a name attached. He indicated one of the names. "Fritz Gaephart," Doc said. "I remember that fellow. They tried him on an espionage charge about six months ago."

Ham said, "I've recognized some more of the names, too."

Harrison Nobel nodded. He said, "All of these people are either aliens who were going to be put in isolation camps and knew it, or spies and saboteurs who were afraid they might get caught."

Doc Savage asked, "Wentz, the banker. How did he get into this business?"

"I imagine it was profitable," said Nobel. "I imagine he charged them plenty. And also, Mr. Wentz was a German by birth."

"That might explain it," Doc admitted.

Monk Mayfair went over and examined the mechanism which had caused all the rumpus when the door opened.

"Tear gas," he remarked. "Darned lucky for us it was tear gas." He investigated further. "Hey, we should have shut off the light in the vault. Then the tear gas wouldn't have been fired. There's an arrangement of magnets that make it go off."

"I wish," said Ham Brooks, "that you had such an arrangement of magnets." Ham had been contemplating Ada Nobel. Evidently he felt Monk was going to be some competition. "To make you go off, I mean," he told Monk additionally.

Monk winked at him. "Miss Nobel and I are going off on a mule-back ride around the canyon this afternoon," Monk told him.

Astonished, angry, Ham demanded, "How the hell'd you manage to make a date?"

Monk admired a package of fifty-dollar bills. "I must have magnets," he said.

DANGER LIES EAST

I

At three o'clock he was dead.

But five hours earlier, when he was quite alive and alert, he sauntered from the doorway of the Blair House. The Blair House was a rather good hotel on Park Avenue in New York City, and he had been waiting—loitering, if one was frank about it—in the lobby of the place. He did not live there. Outdoors it was chilly and the sidewalks were wet and the air felt damp, although there were no visible raindrops.

He took a cab to the airport. He took a plane to Washington.

Airline passengers are expected to give their names, and he gave one. He gave a name. It was Alexander Trussman. It was not his name. As a matter of fact, no one ever did learn his name. The name of Alexander Trussman fitted him in a way, and in another way it did not. If the name of Alexander Trussman sounds foreign to you, it fitted him. He was young, tall, dark-haired, dark-eyed, dark-skinned.

When a dumb-looking lout of a newsboy tried to force a newspaper on him outside the Blair House, he refused the super-salesmanship rather angrily, snapping, *"Imshi!"* This word *imshi*, meaning to be gone, or scram, was of a language spoken pretty generally in the Near East. The term Near East being applied broadly to that part of the world between the Mediterranean and the Indian Ocean, the Caspian Sea and the Gulf of Aden. Mr. Alexander Trussman, to give him the name he had given himself, looked sorry that he had used the word.

At noon, three hours before he was dead, he ate the lunch the airline served its passengers.

In Washington, he took a taxi to the Houghton Hotel, but did not register. He loafed in the lobby. He did not have luggage of any sort. A few minutes past two, he left the Houghton, and was walking on Pennsylvania Avenue when he began showing signs of distress.

First, he perspired freely. It was cold in Washington, a city which seems always to be too hot or too cold, too dry or too wet. He burst out into a sweat, then a chill, and displayed all the symptoms of a man suffering from an attack of violent illness. He also showed signs of being a man who wanted desperately to go ahead with what he was doing. Being ill mustn't interfere. It mustn't. He fought his nausea and weakness, but it did no good. Finally he knew he could not go on.

He had been following a man. He gave that up suddenly. He wheeled from the sidewalk, entered a drug store, got two ten-dollar bills changed into quarters and dimes—this took a long time and his skin was lead-gray before it was done—and he carried the money toward a telephone booth. But he collapsed before he reached the booth.

Presently there was a group of curious spectators around the sprawled man. One of the spectators, who had conveniently entered the drug store a moment before, pushed forward and took charge.

He was not a doctor, but he said, loudly, "I'm a doctor. Let's see what goes on here."

This man, who was thick and wide and homely and hairy, did some pulse-feeling, tongue-examining and eyeball-inspecting. Mostly it was mumbo-jumbo.

"Mild heart attack," he announced. "I'll take him to a hospital."

The manager, who was a little nervous about such things happening in his drug store, asked the name of the man who had collapsed.

"How the hell do I know?" asked the "doctor."

The manager wanted to know the doctor's name.

"Doctor Doesmith," said the "doctor."

"Shall I," asked the anxious manager, "make a report of this to the police?"

"I'll make all the reports that are necessary," said the phony medico. "Chances are there won't be any. This guy has a chronic ticker difficulty, and the probability is that he will live to be a hundred. Now and then he will cave in like this, is all."

The manager was completely fooled, and he let the hairy ape carry Mr. Alexander Trussman outside and put him in a sedan which was rather too conveniently waiting.

The "doctor" took his victim to a hotel. It was a good hotel, one that didn't have to worry about its reputation, consequently a man with moxie could get away with stuff that would have gotten him thrown out of a lower-grade place. By dint of pouring some whiskey from a bottle on Mr. Alexander

Trussman, the apish man got him upstairs to a room, leaving everyone with the conviction that he was just bringing his drunken pal home.

It was then two-forty.

The hairy ape put his burden on the bed. He punched Mr. Trussman in the belly a few times and said, "Wake up, you so-and-so." But this did not get results.

The hairy ape's name was Mayfair. Lieutenant Colonel Andrew Blodgett Mayfair, to give him his full title. He was one of the world's outstanding industrial chemists, and had so been recognized for a number of years. It was generally agreed that he was too contrary and lazy to work at his profession except when he was broke or when he had strained his credit with his friends to its utmost. His friends were wise to him, so his credit didn't stretch far. The thing he preferred to do, and which he did most of the time, was pursue excitement.

It was inevitable that Mr. Mayfair should be called Monk. And he was. He did not mind.

Monk did some more belly-punching of his victim and said, "Come on, wake up, chump!" Still there were no results.

Going to the telephone, Monk gave a number and asked, "Ham?... Well, what are you waiting on?... Sure I got him. Like a sitting duck. He's here in the hotel room now. Notify Doc, and then come on up.... No, he hasn't talked yet. He thinks he's pretty sick. Okay. Fifteen minutes."

Monk concluded the conversation, turned, and discovered he had been careless. His victim, Alexander Trussman, had slid silently off the bed and was slipping out through the door into the hall.

"Here!" Monk yelled. He dived for the door. He had started too late. Mr. Trussman, forcing activity over his sickness, slid through the door and, taking the key along, got it closed and locked on the outside.

Monk did some roaring. He roared very well, sounding like he looked, a bull ape. The door was too stout for mere twisting and wrenching, and he drew back with some idea of caving in a panel with his shoulder. At that point, he remembered there was another room, a connecting door, and the second room had a door into the hall.

"Dumb cluck!" said Monk with feeling. He meant himself. He bolted into the adjoining room, knocking over furniture without noticing or caring what he was knocking over, and plunged out into the hall.

"Oh, oh!" he said, greatly pleased.

Mr. Trussman had collapsed in the hall. He had made about twenty feet, which had taken him almost to the door with the little light above it that said EXIT in red, and which would have admitted him to the stairway. "Crockett!" gasped Trussman. "Tell Crockett—"

Monk ran to Mr. Trussman, stood over him and blew vigorously on his fist. He was tempted to see whether Mr. Trussman would appreciate the feel of the fist. What stayed him was the conclusion which he drew—a wrong one, but he didn't know it—that Mr. Trussman had fainted.

Monk carried the man back in the room and dumped him on the bed. After that Monk didn't turn his back and do any telephoning. It was an unnecessary precaution, though, because the man was now dead. It was three o'clock.

Ham was Brigadier General Theodore Marley Brooks, and he preferred that no one call him Ham, including his friends. Everyone called him Ham whenever possible. . . . Ham was a lean, dapper man, an authority on clothes, and an example always of what to wear for the occasion. He was an eminent lawyer, often mentioned as one of Harvard's most brilliant alumni, but his attitude toward the practice of law was much the same as Monk's toward the practice of chemical engineering. Ham preferred excitement. He had better judgment than Monk with money, however, and was usually broke no more than once a year. He was also Monk's friend, in an evil-eyed sort of way.

Ham Brooks came into the hotel room dawdling a cane and told Monk, "God, you look awful."

"I look like I always do," Monk said, surprised.

"That's what I mean," said Ham.

"Cut it out," said Monk. "There's our friend." He pointed at the motionless figure on the bed and added, "Resting quietly."

Ham examined the man. "He's not very active, is he? . . . Is there any doubt but that he was following Doc?"

"Not," said Monk, "a bit. He trailed Doc to his hotel, the Blair House, in New York, and then followed him on the plane to Washington, and was following him around Washington when fate caught up with him."

"What fate?" Ham asked.

"Me."

"Go ahead, be funny. Make like a clown, with a dead man lying on your bed."

"He isn't dead," said Monk smugly.

"What's wrong with him then?"

"He ate lunch on the plane," Monk said. "And I put some stuff in his soup and he ate it. I was afraid there for a while that he wouldn't like soup, but he did. He ate every drop."

"What did you put in it?"

"A small diabolical concoction of my own which won't hurt him a bit," said Monk. "It made him as sick as a dog. The effects should be wearing off by now, though."

Ham frowned. "What was the idea of giving him this mickey of yours?"

"To scare the hell out of him and soften him up for questions."

"Have you asked him any questions yet?"

"He didn't answer them."

"Oh, then you've got nothing out of him," Ham said, using a tone that cast doubt on Monk's ability.

"Crockett."

"What?"

"Crockett . . . Tell Crockett—" said Monk. "That's all that's come out of him."

"What made him say that?"

Monk decided not to tell Ham that, due to a momentary lapse into stupidity on his part, Trussman had nearly escaped, but had collapsed in the hall, and at that time had mumbled the words: Crockett. . . . Tell Crockett—

"Danged if I know why he said it," Monk remarked.

Ham eyed Monk intently. "What's the reason for all this?"

Monk shook his head. "Search me."

"You don't know?"

"Nope."

Ham said suspiciously, "You're lying."

"A lawyer! Accusing somebody of lying!" Monk sneered. "What do you know about that! The pot calls the kettle black."

* * *

Ham Brooks, puzzled, but not entirely disbelieving, although he knew Monk would rather tell him an untruth than a fact, said, "Naturally I know you would tell me exactly why we are here and what we are doing and what Doc Savage is doing that caused this fellow here to follow him. I'm sure you would tell me—if it was choked out of you. But for your information, I don't know why I am in Washington. How did you get here?"

Monk said, "Doc calls me in New York. He describes this guy. He says he thinks this guy is following him. He says for me to make sure, then grab the guy. Doc says that if the guy is following him, let the following proceed to Washington before I grab him, and then take him to the Rimes Hotel, which is this hotel, where a room will be reserved in my name, or two rooms in fact. I am to bring my captive here, and telephone you at a number Doc gave me, and you will know where to find Doc. That is the prescription I get. I follow it. Here I am. Now is that frank and honest, or isn't it?"

Ham thought it was the truth, so he said, "I think you're lying. . . . However, my experience was something similar, except that Doc telephoned me to grab the first plane to Washington, rent these two rooms for you, rent one at another hotel for myself, wait there, and if you call me, and say that everything has gone well, I am to telephone Doc at one of two places. . . ." Ham glanced at Alexander Trussman. "I wonder if he can hear us?"

"Him?" Monk grinned at Trussman. "Maybe we'd better ask."

Ham went over and punched Trussman. He didn't like the reaction, and looked, somewhat horrified, at his finger. With great revulsion and difficulty, Ham Brooks forced himself to make one of the most positive tests for learning whether life is extinct. He touched one of the man's eyeballs. There was no sensitivity.

Hoarsely, Ham said, "Was it your idea, giving him the drug?"

"Sure," Monk said. "Why?"

"It'll probably get you electrocuted, or whatever they do to you for murder in the District of Columbia," Ham said.

"Huh?"

"Your friend," Ham explained, "is slightly dead."

II

Clark Savage had always considered it a great misfortune that he was a big bronzed man who was as conspicuous in a crowd as—Monk had once put it this way—the fig leaf on a fan dancer. His noticeable physical size and muscularity had on more than one occasion nearly been the end of him. In another profession, it would perhaps have been an asset, but he could well do without it, and he made a practice of dressing as quietly as possible, in plain suits, and using a low voice and an unobtrusive sort of politeness. Too often, this was mistaken for spectacular modesty, and did no good at all.

Doc was also hampered by a reputation. He did not like publicity, and discouraged it whenever possible, with the unfortunate result that he was considered somewhat of a man of mystery. Consequently he was pointed at, whispered about, discussed at cocktail parties. And there was another end result of being thought of as a genius—when he was handed a job to do, it was usually something that everyone else had gagged on. He did not mind this. Trouble was his business. Trouble and excitement.

He was not a detective, although frequently his work was something that a high-grade detective would have done. He was a trouble-shooter and, regardless of whether it sounded corny or not, his usual object was to right wrongs and punish evildoers who were outside the law. This was a rather Galahadian motivation for what he did, and he usually denied such high ideals if they were mentioned to him, and certainly never expressed it that way himself. He had been trained for the work by his father, who had possibly been a little cracked on the subject of crooks, particularly of the international sort. Doc as a child had been handed over to a succession of specialists and scientists for training, and his youth had not been at all normal. But the results were remarkable, in that they had produced Doc Savage, who was supposed to be able to do anything.

Walking into Monk Mayfair's room in the Rimes Hotel in Washington, Doc felt anything but a superman. His general impression was that someone was making an ape out of him.

301

"Hello, Monk—Ham," he said. Then he saw their facial expressions. "What is wrong?"

"We got a little complication," Monk said uneasily.

"Yes?"

"It's there on the bed," said Monk.

Ham Brooks explained, "I think what Monk means is that the man is dead."

"What!" Shocked, Doc Savage went to the bed.

Monk blurted, "For God's sake, Doc, *is* he dead? Tell us?"

Doc made an examination and stood back.

"Dead," he said.

Monk retreated behind a chair as if to take refuge from this fact. "But he can't be, Doc. He just can't be."

"What did you do to him?" Doc Savage asked.

"I didn't kill him."

Ham said, "All he did was give him poison in some soup on the airliner."

Monk was upset. He said, "Cut it out, Ham. Rib me some other time. I tell you, he couldn't have died from that stuff I gave him. It would only have made him sick."

Doc Savage frowned. "Let's have a full story of what happened," he said.

Monk did not leave out anything. He related the most trivial incidents. One got a strong impression that Monk felt that, while he was a noted chemist, it wouldn't do him much good in case he went on trial for murder. Monk covered everything that had happened, and threw in the part that he had not intended to tell Ham, the bit of action when, as Monk was telephoning, Alexander Trussman, to use the name the man had given the airline people, had slipped out of the room and locked the door. But, Monk explained, he had found the man collapsed in the hall, so it had turned out all right after all.

"How long," asked Doc Savage, "would you say the man was out of your sight?"

"You mean after he got through the door and locked it?" Monk said.

"Yes, between then and the time you first saw him lying in the hall."

"Only a jiffy," Monk said.

"Can you be more specific than that?"

Monk scratched his fingers uncomfortably in his bristling reddish hair. "Well, to tell the truth, it didn't seem like more than four or five seconds," he said. "But it might have been longer, because I was plenty in an uproar. Time kind of fools you when you're excited."

"How long, at the longest?"

"Sixty seconds," Monk decided. "A minute."

"And did you hear any sound from the corridor during that time? Any sound through the door?"

Monk tried to remember. "I guess maybe anything I heard I would have thought was the guy beating it. . . . No, I didn't get any noises."

"Any voices?"

"The guy wouldn't be talking to himself, would he?"

"No voices?" Doc asked patiently.

"No." Monk was puzzled.

"And when you went around through the other room into the hall," Doc said, "did you see anyone when you came into the corridor?"

"This guy here."

"Anyone else?"

"No."

"Was the man on the floor?"

"Yes," Monk said. "I ran to him, and it was then that he said, 'Crockett. . . . Tell Crockett—' That was all he said."

"Was it spoken distinctly?"

"Yes. . . . Slow, though. Like he was forcing it out, and concentrating on it while he did so."

"Did you," Doc asked, "get the feeling that he was telling you, or trying to tell you, something about someone or something named Crockett?"

Monk considered this point. "No. I think he didn't know what he was doing. I think this was just in his mind—telling Crockett, whoever, Crockett is—and he concentrated on it and said the words without knowing what it was all about. . . . Say, when he went into the drug store before I caught him, maybe he was going to telephone his Crockett."

Doc asked, "How much change did you say he got?"

"Change?"

"Didn't you say he got two ten-dollar bills changed into quarters and dimes in the drug store?"

"Say, that was a hell of a lot of change, wasn't it?" Monk said. "I wonder where he was going to telephone to? The moon? Let's see . . . twenty bucks! Why, you could telephone practically anywhere for that."

Doc got back to the line his questioning had been following.

He said, "You're positive you didn't see anyone else in the hall?"

"Just this guy here."

"Where was the stairway door?"

"About ten feet from where he was lying."

"Was the door open?"

"Closed."

"And you didn't hear anyone on the stairs going up or down?"

"Nope. I take it you think somebody else was out there in the hall?"

Doc spoke grimly. He said, "That would help explain how this penknife blade got into his spinal cord."

The blade from the knife—it had been broken off—was not very long. It did not need to be. Not more than an inch and a half, which was ample, for Alexander Trussman was a thin and bony young man without much padding of flesh over his spinal column.

Monk was relieved. He was so relieved he was shaking. "To kill a man like that, and quick," he said, "you'd have to know how to do it, wouldn't you? I mean that it isn't an ordinary way to use a knife."

Ham Brooks said, "I don't see what you've got to be happy about. He's still dead. And the police are still going to feel it was odd he died on your hands."

Monk said he wasn't scared of the police. Well, maybe moderately scared. In a week or two he might be able to sleep nights. "But the point is," he added, "that I know now that stuff I fed him in the soup didn't kill him. Somebody was waiting in the hall, and did it to him when he tore out of here."

Doc Savage said, "We had better make some inquiries."

Their inquiring was complicated by the fact that Doc Savage said they wouldn't notify the police about the murder yet. The total result of the questioning of a few bellhops, two cleaning women and some maids was nothing. No one had seen anyone who could be immediately identified as the murderer.

"Why not notify the police?" Ham Brooks asked Doc Savage.

"You think it will get us in trouble?"

"I know blamed well it will, and so do you," Ham said. "As an attorney giving you advice, which you didn't ask for, I can assure you they can and probably will lock us all up."

Monk was also perturbed. "Doc, just what's the idea of taking this chance?"

Doc Savage explained when they were back in the hall upstairs, but not in the room with the body, where, he said, it was just possible a microphone might have been planted for eavesdropping.

"Microphone!" Ham gasped. "For crying out loud! What are we mixed up in, anyway?"

He did not know, Doc said. He explained that he had received a telephone call from a Mr. Lawrence Morand, of the State Department. Did they know Mr. Morand?

"I've heard of Morand in the State Department," Ham Brooks admitted, "in about the same way that you hear of Paul Revere in connection with the Revolutionary War. He's sort of an expert giver-of-alarms, isn't he?"

"That," Doc said, "is about as good a description of Morand's position in the State Department as I have ever heard."

"What did Morand want with you?"

Doc shook his head. "I do not know. Morand was very secretive, over the telephone. He asked me to come to Washington, using the utmost care to avoid being conspicuous, and said he had a job for me that he thought was along my line. I wasn't too hot about the secrecy, and I had some experiments under way in the laboratory in New York, but when I tried to talk my way out of this job, Morand got pretty emphatic. So I gather it is something big."

Ham scratched his head and said, "If Morand is in it, it's something to do with foreign relations, isn't it?"

"Probably. Morand's department is foreign relations."

Ham indicated the body on the bed. "He's a foreigner of some sort, judging from his appearance. Do you suppose he was connected with this call from Morand?"

"What other guess is there?" Doc asked.

"Then you're not going to notify the police about the body until you talk to Morand?" Monk asked.

Doc said he thought Morand would appreciate doing it that way.

"Morand sounded," Doc said, "as if the world had started to fall over and he was holding it up with one hand and fighting bumblebees with the other."

III

The Honorable Lawrence Morand was an erect, white-haired man of much dignity and about sixty years, nearly forty of them spent in the devious jungles of international diplomacy. Many men look disconcertingly unlike the parts they occupy in affairs, a fact that is sometimes a little jarring to confidence. But Morand was reassuringly the picture of a career diplomat. One knew he could lift a teacup, flatter a politico's mistress, bribe a government functionary, and possibly order a genteel throat-cutting, all with equal aplomb and ability.

Coming forward behind outstretched hand, Morand said, "How are you, Doc? I haven't seen you since London in '45. You're looking fine. How are the rest of your organization? Monk and Ham still conducting that interminable quarrel?"

Doc said things had been fine up until that telephone call from Morand, but since then . . .

Morand held up a manicured hand. "Do a favor for me, eh? You know the statue of the three monkeys. Say nothing, hear nothing, see nothing? If you don't mind, I am going to occupy the position of the three monkeys with regard to you."

Doc said, "It is evil, isn't it, that the monkeys do not see, hear nor speak?"

"Could be. Anyway, I have not seen you, I have not heard from you and I shall not speak of you. Is that confusing?"

"A little," Doc said.

Morand indicated a chair. "Sit down. I'm a little embarrassed about this. You see, I need your help. More properly, we needed your help some weeks ago, and didn't have sense enough to realize it."

Doc said, "This isn't beginning to sound good."

"I'm afraid it isn't."

"No?"

Morand grimaced. "I don't think you're going to be happy, but I don't think you will be surprised either."

"What are you getting at?"

"I guess I'm apologizing," Morand said. "And trying to say that I imagine you are accustomed to being called on when things are in such a mess that nobody else can handle it. In other words, when the potato gets too hot, they hand it to you."

Doc Savage said that he began to get the idea, and he had been afraid it would be something like this. "The question in your mind," he said, "is, will I take the potato? Right?"

"Will you?"

"Let's see the potato first."

Morand nodded and said, "I don't except any blanket promises out of you. . . . Have you been following the political situation in the Near East? Oh hell, I know you have. The newspapers have been full of it for that matter. . . . What is your general impression of it?"

Doc said, "Everyone mad at everyone else. The Arabs are mad at the English, the Americans, the Palestine Jews, and they distrust the Russians. The Egyptians are irritated with the English, they think the Americans have no business monkeying around, and ditto for the Russians. In India, one religious sect is ready to fly at the throat of the other, and both of them are drooling for an English throat. . . . You know I've been out of touch with the situation over there. What are you asking me for?"

Morand grinned with no humor. "Your picture isn't so far from the truth. Let me give you some inside stuff." Morand talked, and Doc listened, and much of what he heard he had already known, as far as the general picture in the eastern Mediterranean area was concerned. He had known, without being exactly sure of the facts, that most of the dissension had fairly well settled down to a question of whether or not there would be an armed uprising.

"The dissatisfied factions," Morand explained, "have rather generally coagulated, undergone a clotting process which has placed them, not exactly under one leadership, but ready to follow that leader if he gives the word. In other words, it has gotten to the point where one man, their religious symbol, can make it war or a peaceful settlement, as he wishes. And if it turns out to be fighting, it'll be war, and I mean a real war. I'm afraid—and don't think I'm being a wild-eyed old maid when I say this—as bad as the one we finished a few months ago."

Doc Savage made no comment. An international crisis was usually dry stuff to discuss, unless one knew the problems posed and the personalities and intricacies involved. It only stopped being dry when the army of one little country marched into another little country, and some bigger nation or group of large nations that had some time or other signed a treaty guaranteeing its sovereignty jumped into it, and another combine jumped on them. Like Poland and the Reich. It wasn't dry then. It was wet and red with the blood of millions of men.

Doc stirred uncomfortably. When you talked of nations, it was never as if you talked of men; the personalities were not there. As an example, the man lying dead back in the hotel was very real. Here a Mr. Morand of the State Department had given him a picture that could mean the death of a thousand men, and it was not the same at all. A thousand men? That was ridiculous, of course. The number would be hundreds of thousands and quite possibly millions. But talking it and thinking of it was not as biting as having seen with his own eyes one man dead.

"These generalities bother you?" Morand asked.

"Only that it's hard to break out in a cold sweat over generalities," Doc said. "Although I'm beginning to."

"Uh-huh," said Morand. "Here in the State Department we're not supposed to call a spade a spade—if the spades are too big. But anyone who is not a fool knows the world is split pretty much into two factions, and some people assume that, by God, if we've got to have a war in twenty years, let's fight it now and get it over with for good. With that kind of defeatist feeling around, all that is needed is for someone to get his toes stamped on, and he's going to start swinging. It's a damned sad travesty on the human race, but there it is."

Doc made no comment. He was shocked. The general tone of this sounded as if he were going to be handed the job of stopping a war before it got started. When it was stated bluntly that way, it was a little wild for belief.

Morand leaned forward. "Nesur," he said.

"Nesur?" Doc echoed.

"Yes. The name—does it mean anything to you?"

Doc hesitated, then nodded. "Yes. Nesur. The leader of a minor religious sect. Sort of a holy man, with a few thousand followers."

Morand grinned unhappily. "Not minor, Doc. A couple of years ago, this fellow Nesur was reported to have Nazi leanings, and so he was sort of eased into exile. Quite an effort was made to disgrace him and blacken his name. To tell the truth, I had a hand in that myself, although since I've wondered just how smart I was. The fact is, I never had any real proof the fellow did have Nazi sympathies. I think maybe we made a mistake."

"Nesur is back?" Doc asked.

"That's right." Morand nodded. "He's back, and he must be quite a guy, because we've suddenly come to realize that he is the key to the whole mess. I don't know how he did it, but if he says start fighting, they'll start fighting."

"Will he?"

"Will he what?"

"Say start fighting."

"Unless you can talk him out of it," Morand said, "we're afraid so."

Doc jumped. "Now wait a minute! What's this? What are you trying to hand me?"

"Your job," Morand said, "is to get hold of Nesur and talk him out of violence."

"Where is he?"

"We don't know." Morand shrugged wearily. "We've looked for him for months, and if we could have gotten hold of him a few months ago, he could have been quietly spirited out of the picture, one way or another. But that's out of the question now. If anything violent happens to him, and the blame can possibly be pointed at us, the fat will be in the fire."

"Why does Nesur want to start trouble?"

"We can't figure that out either."

"I take it," Doc said, "that you don't know much about him."

"We don't. Oh, we've got pictures of him and his early history."

"This," said Doc gloomily, "is the potato?"

"This is it."

Doc took the job. There was not much else he could do. He thumbed through a folder on Nesur which Morand gave him. It contained Nesur's photograph. A tall dark, rather grim young man with the usual aquiline nose and piercing eyes. Not a distinguished face. But one that Doc realized he would remember.

Reading, Doc found the man had been born in a desert village, and had led, in general, the sort of life that most religious leaders lead, except that there had been no education abroad, either in England or America. It was possible to understand why the man would dislike the English and Americans, because he had been pushed around by them a few times—but not until he had started the pushing himself.

"But I hardly see why he has a motive to start the kind of fracas this one would be," Doc said.

"We don't get that either," Morand admitted. "But he hates Americans. He hates them like poison."

"This a recent hate?"

"That's another funny angle. His dislike for Americans—and it amounts to an attack of hydrophobia—began only a few months ago. We don't know why."

"Where can he be found?"

"Somewhere east of Gibraltar," Morand said. "And I'm not being funny." Morand then stood up and added, "Do you know Sherman McCorland?"

"McCorland? No."

"One of our men in the Near East. He's here in Washington now. Going back by plane this evening. I'll introduce you, and you can call on him for anything he is able to furnish you in the way of assistance."

Sherman McCorland turned out to be a lean whip of a man with startling red hair, a reddish leathery skin, and in spite of these fundamental qualities for a rough-looker, a smooth man who had almost too much polish.

"Delighted!" said McCorland. "I've heard of you, Mr. Savage. Most impressively, I must say, too."

The flattery was obvious enough to be a little overdone. Doc did not react very favorably. He said, "I understand you are returning to the Mediterranean today."

McCorland was adept enough to sense that he had made an unfavorable impression, and to realize why. He became more casual, admitted he was leaving today, said that he could be contacted—or there would be someone who would know where he could be found—in Cairo, Jerusalem and Tehran. He gave Doc the addresses.

Morand explained, "McCorland has been our main man on Nesur."

"I'm not proud of my results, either," McCorland said.

"You have no idea where I can find Nesur?"

McCorland shook his head. "You can pick up as much as I know in listening to bazaar gossip anywhere in the Near East. In Libya, Tripoli, Saudi Arabia—Nesur is everywhere. And nowhere. Frankly I haven't the least idea where his hangout is. But if I get a line that is worth anything, I'll let you know."

"Do that," Doc said.

Before McCorland left, he made a statement. His mouth was quite grim when he made it. He said, "I take it you know, or have been told, that it's probably a third world war we're fooling with."

Doc was left with the impression that McCorland was not a fool, and that the man had been worried, and had had something on his mind that he hadn't mentioned. Doc suggested this to Morand. Morand laughed. "We brought him into Washington and ate him off up to here. He's just had the damnedest bawling out any man ever had. Of course he's got something on his mind."

"That might explain it."

Morand suddenly snapped his fingers. "Damn!"

"What's the matter?"

"I guess I'm a little embarrassed because we gave McCorland so much hell," the State Department executive explained. "Because I forgot to have McCorland tell you about a source of information you might be able to use. Oh, well, I can give it to you."

Doc said that the way it looked to him, information was one thing he was going to need. "Go ahead," he said.

"It's a woman," Morand explained. "Rather remarkable character, I hear. I've never met her. Headquarters in Cairo. Sort of a dabbler in international intrigue, and pretty good at it, too."

Doc asked, "How would a woman dabble in international intrigue?"

"I don't intend to sound like a spy thriller," Morand said. "But this baby is, I understand, something out of the pages of a book. Kind of a lady queen of the thieves, or something like that."

"She might know where this Nesur is?"

"Yes. Crockett would know if anyone did."

Doc Savage raised possibly a half inch off the floor without any visible force being applied to him.

"Who?" he asked.

"Crockett. The lady fearful we're talking about," Morand said. "Yes, she would have contacts that would know where Nesur is. She seems to get her finger in everything." Morand peered at Doc Savage. "What's the matter with you? Ache somewhere?"

Doc said, "Have you got a portfolio on this Crockett?"

"Oh, sure. We've got those on almost everybody we might use, or who might try to use us. I'll have it sent in for you."

Presently the folder on Crockett, Miss Eunice Lee, was in Doc's hands, and he turned at once to her photograph to see what this sinister wrench looked like. She looked like a school teacher, probably around the third grade. Pretty, wide-eyed, innocent. You could imagine her as the quietest one in a crowd. He shuddered and said, "One of those, eh?"

Morand grinned and said, "I wouldn't mind meeting that babe. Sometimes I feel the same about an atom bomb, though."

Doc read the stuff in the folder on Crockett, Miss Eunice Lee. The startling thing was that until about five years ago she had led the life of a perfectly normal American girl, but then she had gone to Cairo where she had inherited the estate of an uncle named Ira Crockett. It didn't say what the estate was. But there was plenty after that, for there were evidences that Miss Crockett had done about everything from smuggling Jewish refugees into Palestine—five thousand at one lick—to causing the unexplained disappearance of various Iranian, Italian, Turkish and Italian important persons, including a boatload of Nazi big shots together with quite a lot of loot they were supposed to have with them.

"How does she get away with this?" Doc asked.

"That's simple. She's smarter than the guys who try to catch her."

Doc finished the documentation on Crockett.

"A couple of questions," he said. "First, who knows that I am taking this job, or was going to have it offered to me?"

"Me. McCorland," Morand said. "That's all."

"No one else?"

"No."

"Crockett wouldn't know about it?"

Morand laughed. "She's not that good," he said.

Doc Savage decided to hold off and give Morand a shock about the man who had died in the hotel mentioning Crockett's name. Doc felt that Morand had given him very little information, probably as a matter of deliberate forethought, feeling that the detail the State Department had couldn't be worth much or it would have gotten them farther than it had.

"To go back to Nesur," Doc said. "Why is he hiding out?"

Morand grinned sheepishly. "Oh, he's got reason enough."

"What reason?"

"Well, if we could have gotten him located a few months ago, he would probably have gotten chased back into exile by some little group that opposed him or was jealous of him. Officially we wouldn't have known anything about that, of course."

"No wonder he dislikes you."

"Oh, I wouldn't say that. There's a lot of that stuff goes on in Nesur's circles."

Doc said thoughtfully, "You fellows have to pull a lot of close-to-the-line stuff, don't you?"

"Us?" said Morand innocently. "Not on your life. We're the open-faced friends of the whole earth, we are."

"You mean you don't get caught?"

"Well," said Morand, "what do you think?"

"Then your department is pretty good at arranging little matters and not getting caught?"

"I wouldn't say we're perfect," Morand said smugly.

"Could you do a little favor for me?"

"Sure."

"All right. There's a strange body in our hotel room. A murder victim. Quietly take it off our hands, will you?"

"Oh, my God!" Morand yelled. "A body!"

IV

In the lobby of the Rimes Hotel, Ham Brooks was waiting. Ham looked alarmed, and when he saw Doc Savage enter, he hurried forward.

"Doc, we've got another complication upstairs," Ham said.

"Another body?" Doc asked.

"I wish it was," Ham said. "It's a man named Homer Wickett, who says he's the hotel manager. He walked in on us and saw the body."

"Walked in on you?" Doc exclaimed. "Why would he dare—"

"The managers of these flea-bag hotels will dare anything," Ham said. "This Homer Wickett unlocked the door and came in without warning. He had a master key. Of course he saw the corpse and began raising cain. He said he wasn't surprised. He said we looked like a pack of murderers to him. He said there had been a report of strange goings-on in the hall—probably the rumpus when the fellow got killed—and he had come up to investigate."

"How did he recognize that it was a body so quickly?"

Ham squirmed uncomfortably. "Well, Monk happened to be putting the body in a trunk when he came in."

"Trunk?"

Ham nodded. "We had to do something with the body, didn't we? Well, Monk went out and bought a trunk, and he was going to put the body in it."

"And then what?"

"Well, Monk knows a fellow here in Washington he doesn't like. A fellow he had some trouble with over a chorus girl. Monk was all for sending the trunk to this fellow."

Doc Savage said bitterly that it was a very poor time for gags, that the gag would be in bad taste at any time, and particularly now, when they were involved in a matter which might very well develop into a world conflict. He was fully serious about what he thought, and he told Ham so. He made Ham extremely uncomfortable.

"And on top of handing us a job they can't handle, that fellow Morand in the State Department refused to have anything to do with taking the body off our hands," Doc added.

"You can't blame him much," Ham said uneasily. "If that got out, half the Senators would fall out of their seats. . . . But to get back to this trunk notion, that was all Monk's idea—"

"Listen, I've seen you two cook up a screwball notion before," Doc said. "What about this fellow you were going to send the trunk to? Did he cut you out with the chorus girl, too?"

"How did you know—" Ham swallowed, and changed to: "How do you think we had better handle this?"

"We'll have to get the hotel man out of the picture for a while," Doc said.

"I'll enjoy knocking him cold, if that will do."

"And we'll send the body to Morand, as long as you've got a trunk for it," Doc said.

Mr. Homer Wickett was a short, wide man with amazingly blue eyes and corn-colored hair. He was not an albino, although his coloring was close to that of one. He had an Oklahoma whang in his voice, and knew a remarkable procession of cusswords, which he was using on Monk. But he fell uneasily silent when Doc Savage and Ham entered the room. Monk was relieved to see them.

"This guy," Monk said, "has cussed ten minutes solid without repeating himself." He indicated the body and added, "It's a wonder he didn't wake up Mr. Trussman, here."

Doc said bitterly there was nothing humorous in the situation.

"I don't feel humorous," Monk said gloomily. "I think I'm a little hysterical."

"Murderers!" said Homer Wickett, not too firmly. "Murderers! And in my hotel! You'll not get away with it."

Doc asked grandly, "Do you know who we are?"

Homer Wickett indicated that he didn't, except that he held the conviction this probably wasn't the first crime they had perpetrated. That set him on the subject of what he thought of them, and he resorted to obscenity again.

Ham moved around behind the man while he was swearing, and swung a fist suddenly. The fist collided satisfactorily with Homer Wickett's jaw, and the man fell.

"Hitting him wasn't necessary," Doc said.

"He sort of worked me up to it with that cussing," Ham explained.

Monk had his fill of Homer Wickett also. "I wish we had another trunk, and we'd leave two bodies on doorsteps," Monk said.

"Get your fingerprints wiped off anything you may have touched in the room," Doc ordered.

Ham explained they had already done this. They had wiped the whole room, practically.

"All right, we'll get the trunk and the body out of here before that fellow wakes up," Doc advised.

Ham blew on his knuckles. "We'll have plenty of time before he wakes up."

Monk picked up a blackjack which had skidded partially under the bed. It was quite a serviceable piece of skull-cracking equipment, made of excellent leather.

"Homer Wickett's," Monk said. "I think I'll take it along. Do a service to such future guests of this hostelry as Mr. Wickett may not like."

They edged the trunk out and into a freight elevator. The elevator operator kept an eye on them to see that they paid their bill downstairs before carting the trunk away. They paid the bill. They were careful not to inquire about the health of Mr. Homer Wickett.

Homer Wickett revived in time. Not soon. But in the course of events he came to the conclusion that the great beast that was growling and biting at his head was really non-existent, the growling being his own. At least the growling stopped when he stopped.

Homer Wickett did not waste any time once he was hooked up with consciousness again. He rolled over, staggered to his feet and got out of there, noting only that the body and trunk were gone.

The operator of the elevator which took Homer Wickett downstairs did not treat Wickett as if the man were a hotel official. The operator merely glanced at Wickett, then away, apparently concluding the man was another drunk. That was all right with Wickett.

No one in the lobby gave any indication of knowing Wickett, or of having seen him before. Nobody spoke to him. Mr. Ginsbruck, who was actually the manager, gave Homer Wickett a passing frown of disapproval. The assistant manager, a Mr. Freel, did the same after he saw Mr. Ginsbruck do so.

Wickett was very glad to get out of the hotel. He hurried two blocks north and one block east and walked in a more leisurely fashion, and presently an automobile swung over to the curb and he got in. The pick-up was neatly arranged. Had anyone been following Wickett, he would undoubtedly have been given the slip.

The man driving the car was young and agreeable-looking, but gave the impression of having no special characteristics at all. He was about as conspicuous as a single grain in a double handful of corn. His ability to seem a part of the human race probably accounted for his not having been hanged long ago. His name, to those who wanted to address him, was Clyde.

"I guess they had a car rented," Clyde said. "Anyway, they loaded a trunk in a car and were on their way."

"You didn't try to follow them?" Homer Wickett asked in an alarmed voice.

"I'm not that simple-minded about following orders," Clyde said.

"Good. I'm glad you let them go."

Clyde glanced at Homer Wickett, who was obviously his chief, and remarked, "They push you around?"

Wickett nodded. "I half-way expected the apish one to do it. He's got a reputation for solving his problems with his fists. But it was the lawyer, Ham Brooks, who walloped me." Wickett compressed his lips bitterly, separated them and said, "Which he'll wish he hadn't."

"Think they took the job of finding Nesur?" Clyde asked.

"I think so."

"They say so?" ·

"I don't know. I was unconscious for—say, how long was I in there, anyway?"

"Half an hour, I'd say."

"Half an—" Homer Wickett was amazed. "That fancy-dressing lawyer packs more of a punch than you would think."

"They impress you much?"

"Eh?"

"You think they're the hot rocks they're reported to be?"

Wickett looked at the driver bitterly. "Let's not kid ourselves."

Clyde expressed some emotion or other by shooting his eyebrows up and bringing them down again, and said, "I think this is one of the few times in my life I've seen you impressed."

"That could be," said the other man sourly.

They drove in silence for a time. Clyde had a destination

in mind, but in reaching it he was using all the means he could think of for shaking pursuit. He had not seen anyone following them, however.

Later Clyde asked, "The blackjack?"

"The blackjack? They took it," Homer Wickett said with satisfaction. "I knew they would. It was a fine item, and I guarantee you that any man would carry it off after he took it away from a possible assailant."

"You think maybe they suspect you?" Clyde inquired.

"Oh, Christ! Of course not. You think they would have gone off and left me there on the floor if they had had an inkling of the truth?"

Clyde said he didn't think this would have been the case. He added, "Since they've got the blackjack, you're in a position to kill them any time you want to."

"Just about," admitted Homer Wickett proudly. "Granting of course they carry the blackjack with them, which I imagine they will."

V

A TWA Constellation, only forty-three minutes off schedule on the New York-London-Cairo flight, deposited Doc Savage, Monk Mayfair and Ham Brooks in Cairo. As a matter of general precaution, they waited until the rest of the passengers had debarked down the very tall portable stairs, then watched to see whether newspapermen or other suspicious individuals were lying in wait for them. The matter of their fares, $428.70 each, had been disturbing Monk, and he demanded, "Do you think the State Department will pay that if we turn in an expense account?"

Doc Savage had his face to a porthole. "When Morand receives the body in the trunk, I doubt if he will okay any expenses, unless it would be the cost of a rope to hang us with."

"I told you we should have presented the body to this guy who did me and Ham a dirty trick," Monk said.

The coast seemed to be clear. They left the plane and were cleared by customs without flurry, and without getting any comment on their names. Their passports carried only their initials, and no titles, and listed their occupations as business-men, importers, which shaded the truth a little.

In a taxi headed for a hotel, Ham said, "I have the most futile feeling about this. Where do we start? What do we do? Just begin asking people where Nesur is?"

Monk said sarcastically, "That's a great idea."

"Have you any shining notions?" Ham demanded.

Monk had one. "See this Crockett, Miss Eunice Lee. We know she must be mixed up in it, because of what that poor cuss said in Washington before he died."

Doc Savage admitted he thought this was as sensible an idea as any.

Monk, who had seen her picture, said, "I wish she were a little more sexy-looking."

Their driver, on instructions, took a scenic route into town. All three of them had been in Cairo before, so the idea of the sightseeing was not the scenery, but whether anyone was trailing them. They had not cabled ahead for hotel reservations for the same reason.

Their car moved in the streets that netted the rocky slopes of the Mokattam hills, and passed the citadel, actually the south-east angle of the city. Doc glanced at the structure, recalling the spectacular view from its ramparts, the complex wonderland of mosques, lofty towers, gardens and squares, and, beyond, the wide river with its freckling of small islands.

Ham said, "What about the native quarter for a hotel? Say somewhere on Muski Street or Rue Neuve?"

"A good idea," Doc said. He leaned forward and, addressing the driver in English, said, "Can you take us to a pretty good hotel? One in a part of town where we can have some fun."

The driver turned around to see how Doc meant this. Doc leered meaningly. The driver grinned.

"*Aiway!*" the driver said. "Yes, very much, *la yasidi.*"

"What the hell!" gulped the startled Monk.

The last thing anyone with half his wits did in Cairo was take the recommendation of one of the cut-throat cab drivers on a hotel.

The hotel was a dump. It opened off a narrow street full of characters who, if they were half as sinister as they looked, were pretty tough.

Doc drew Ham Brooks aside. "You speak a pretty good English dialect, don't you?"

Ham nodded. "I can only stumble along in Arabic, but I can sound like any kind of an Englishman you want."

"Do it with a touch of Cockney," Doc said. "Not too much Cockney. Or do you think Monk could get away with it better?"

"He ain't got nothin'," Ham said. He said it in Cockney, so that it sounded more like, "Uhee yin't gawt nah'th'n."

Doc frowned. "Don't overdo it that much."

"Okay."

"Go talk to our cab driver," Doc said. "Ask him if he knows of a man named Ole Hansel."

"Who," demanded Ham, "is Ole Hansel?"

"A name I just thought up," Doc said.

"Oh. . . . What does Ole look like? That robber of a cab driver might ask that."

"A Swede who had an Arab mother," Doc said. "He will be about six feet two, weigh over two hundred and have a pronounced scar on his left cheek. An old knife scar about three inches long. He speaks Arabic fairly fluently."

"For crying out loud. Who is the guy?"

"Ask the driver and see if he knows," Doc said.

"Well . . . all right."

"Then have a fuss with the driver over the fare he's charging."

"That," said Ham, "I can see some sense to. That robber is trying to hang it on us."

Doc Savage and Monk were preparing to go to their room when they heard a rumpus in the street. Doc listened with interest. Ham, using his Cockney dialect, which he had toned down so that it sounded quite genuine, was telling the driver off.

"Whoee!" Monk breathed. "Where did Ham learn to cuss like that?"

"I don't believe the hack driver knows Ole," Doc said dryly.

The row ended with the driver in flight, and Ham came stamping inside. The proprietor of their hotel began to look worried, probably wondering if his new guests were the suckers he had presumed they were.

They entered their room, and Monk scowled at the hotel owner. "What's the market on the rats you've been raising in here?" he demanded.

Before Monk could go further into his ideas about their

room, he caught Doc's eye. Doc shook his head. The hotel owner left them alone. He seemed discouraged.

Doc said, "After this, Monk, see if you can't sound like an Englishman. You can fake the dialect, can't you?"

"What kind of an Englishman?"

"The kind of a fellow who would be possibly a gold prospector in the back country hills. The laborer type preferably."

"A dumb one, eh?"

"That shouldn't be any trouble for you," Ham suggested.

Monk scratched his head. "I don't get it."

Doc Savage went to the door to see whether the proprietor had loitered outside to eavesdrop. Apparently he hadn't.

"There isn't much doubt," Doc said, "but what this woman, Eunice Lee Crockett, is a sharp operator. We are not going to walk in on her and get anything out of her. From what I gathered out of reading the dossier the State Department had on her in Washington, she has pulled just about everything in the book and gotten away with it. That means she is as wary as a cat in a dog kennel. A forthright approach would get us nothing."

Monk and Ham were interested. "But I don't get this English accent stuff," Ham said.

"You two," Doc explained, "are a couple of discharged English soldiers. You were in the desert and around Cairo during the war, and you heard about the possibility of gold deposits in the hills over toward Jeb Garib. That's not too far away, and will do as well as any for a spot. After you were mustered out of the English army, you took up prospecting. You had a large half-breed Arab-Swede for a partner. When you found gold, it was this Arab-Swede who found it. His name is Ole Hansel. A large man with a knife scar on his face. Ole found the gold, and he scrammed out and deserted you. But you two learned Ole had found the lode, and you're hunting him to make him divide up, or tell you where it is, so you can stake claims."

Monk said, "Hadn't you better describe this Arab-Swede better than that?"

"You'll see him in a minute," Doc said.

"We will! The hell!"

"In about an hour," Doc added, "you're going to find

him. . . . No, better take longer than that. You had better make some inquiries."

"Where do we inquire?"

Doc Savage named three places, and gave the addresses. Monk had heard of one of them and he whistled. "That's the toughest night spot in town, as I recall," he said.

"You can be as tough with this inquiring as you want to," Doc explained. "The idea is to attract some attention to yourselves."

"I see."

"You're brighter than I am if you get this," Ham told Monk. "And I freely doubt that you are."

"What you are going to do," Doc explained patiently, "is build up this fellow Ole Hansel as a swindler."

"Yeah, but who is Hansel?"

Doc said, "Let's fix him up now."

Doc Savage's skin already had a metallic bronze tan that would pass for that of a half-caste. His hair and eyes, however, were totally out of character. A dye treatment—when Monk and Ham saw that Doc had brought along the dye, it dawned on them this was no spur-of-the-moment idea—took care of the hair. Doc's eyes were an unusual light brown, a sort of flake-gold effect, with the gold seemingly always in motion. He used contact lenses, tinted somewhat, to get more of a change in the character of his eyes than Monk or Ham had expected. The scar was easier, put on with a collodion which contained a chemical irritant that would redden the skin in the neighborhood of the scar.

Finally Doc changed to older and more shabby clothes.

"I won't be wearing these when you find me," he said. "I'll pick up local stuff."

"Where will we find you?"

"It will help out the effect if I sent a messenger to you with the information. Right now, I'm not sure where I will locate."

"This is still a little ahead of me," Ham said. "What do we do when we find you?"

"We'll stage a fight. I'm a fellow who has swindled and double-crossed you. So act accordingly."

"How good do you want to make that?"

"Impressive. But let me escape."

"And then?"

"Use this place for headquarters. I'll contact you here."

"What if we're thrown in jail?" Monk asked, looking alarmed. "I've heard these Cairo jails are a little discouraging."

Doc shrugged. "In that case, lodge a complaint against me."

"You mean tell the swindler story?"

"Yes."

Monk nodded unhappily. He ventured the opinion that if their real identities came out, and they were connected with that fellow Alexander Trussman who had been murdered back in Washington, the circumstantial evidence—their hiding in disguise in Cairo—would probably fix them up nicely with a couple of chairs, wired for electricity.

"You had better sound like a genuine Englishman then," Doc said.

Doc Savage left the hotel by climbing to the roof, jumping an easy gap to another roof, and dropping almost fifteen feet to a balcony, then another twelve feet or so to a grimy street filled, at the moment, only with smells and heat.

He walked rapidly. Cabs were scarce here, because the inhabitants of the section were either not affluent, or took pains not to seem so. However, the shops of the Muski section were within walking distance.

Doc picked a first-class shop, one catering to men, and purchased a wardrobe, using the sort of taste he imagined an Arab-Swedish gentleman would have. He could see that he was not making a good impression. The one-hundred piastre notes with which he paid for his somewhat loud suit were carefully scrutinized by the shop cashier.

Next, Doc found lodgings. The place where he located was not a hotel in the conventional sense, although it did open off the usual winding narrow street. But this thorough-fare was spotted at intervals with elaborate *sebil*, public fountains, and the pedestrians had more class. The house had been, rather recently, an Arab home. It was built around the court—this court form of construction was almost universal—and it had a great deal of stained glass and elaborate woodwork.

The central alcove of the suite was an enormous room with a fountain and a startlingly fancy lantern arrangement above it; there were inlaid cabinets around the walls, and the small niches called *divans* with cushioned seats that had given the name divan to most reclining couches in America.

He did not use his own name. He registered as a Mr. Ahmed Himar, the first name that came to his mind.

He had spoken Arabic, using the Egyptian handling of the language, since leaving Monk and Ham, and he continued to use it.

The *lukandah* where he had checked in was on Arnab Street, and according to the information Morand of the State Department had given him in Washington, Miss Eunice Lee Crockett lived on Hamanah Street, which was in the neighborhood. No more than, unless his memory of Cairo was frayed, the equivalent of about four American blocks from where he was.

He was wrong. It was three blocks. . . . The house of Crockett, Miss Eunice Lee, was not impressive from the outside. But then few private homes in the old quarter of Cairo were.

The entrance was a naked, bleak arch of stone large enough to pass a good-sized truck. A burnoosed native who had all the earmarks of a beggar sat crosslegged under the arch, and thrust out a hand when Doc passed.

"*A tini, a tini,*" the man mumbled. "*A tini piastre.*"

Doc paused. The native repeated this plea for a piastre. Doc asked in Arabic, "Is this the home of the woman named Crockett?"

"*A tini, a tini—*"

Doc, picking up the part he intended to play, asked the beggar how he would like three of his ribs kicked in, or better still, how would he like to be fed to a dog? "Answer my question, you breath of a camel," Doc added.

The beggar said there was undoubtedly something dead and rotting in the neighborhood, else why should a jackal visit the place? He said this conversationally. It was quite an insult, the way he did it.

Doc dusted his hands elaborately and remarked, "A dung heap." He went on to a second archway, much more elaborate, inlaid with pearl and gilt, and made a commotion against a huge door.

The door did not open at once.

He heard the beggar say something. It was Arabic, sounded like, "*Hu jada shatir,*" which translated roughly to the statement that Doc was a clever fellow. The tone gave it the effect of, "A wise guy, eh?"

Doc wondered if the beggar had a pushbutton signal of

some sort accessible. He hadn't seen one. More likely the fellow was there to flank attack anyone at the door if necessary. Obviously the beggar was one of the household.

Doc knocked on the door again, and kicked it a few times for good measure.

The door was opened by a very fat, very blonde, very pleasant looking woman of better than forty years of age who addressed Doc in good American. "Son," said the woman, "shirts are made to be kept on."

Doc was very nearly startled into replying in English. He caught himself, and spoke Arabic. "I have business with the woman called Crockett," he said.

"All right, keep your shirt on, this is the place," the fat woman said. She looked Doc up and down, added, "Son, they had something large in mind when they made you, didn't they?"

"*Shu hadha?*" Doc said bluntly. He wondered if this was still the equivalent of, "What goes on here?" His Arabic wasn't as fluent as he had hoped. That, or he was getting nervous.

"Oh, for God's sake, don't you speak any English?" the woman asked.

"I want to see the woman called Crockett," Doc said, sticking to his Arabic. "You, as anyone can see, are not her."

"No English, eh?" The woman sighed. "That's two strikes on you, son."

"What?"

"Big and dumb, aren't you?"

"I did not come here to listen to guinea cackle," Doc announced.

He started to push past the woman. He felt that sort of behavior would fit the part he was acting.

Astonishingly, there was a gun in the fat blonde woman's hand. It was a small flat gun with inlay and pearl handles and a hole larger than a pencil for the bullets to come out. He was a little confused about where she had had it.

"Do you," she asked, "want to become a nasty mess on our doorstep?"

She said this in Arabic.

Doc pretended considerably less awe of the gun than he felt, and said, "I am here to see Eunice Lee Crockett. Will you take me to her?"

"I've heard you say that a couple of times already," said the woman. "But you left something out."

"What?"

"The nature of your business."

"It's private business."

"Just how many times a day," she asked, "do you suppose I hear that?"

Doc shrugged. "I'm not interested. Do I see Miss Crockett, or not?"

"Not."

Doc registered thwarted disgust. It was not difficult. He had no idea who the woman might be, but he suspected she was a capable character. She was an American. At one time she had been quite beautiful, he imagined, and flashy. Relieved of about a hundred pounds now, she would still be striking.

Doc scowled at the gun and said, "I think I'll come in."

"You do," she advised him, "and you'll leave rolled up in a rug. . . . Son, I don't know what you've heard of Crockett, but it must have been awfully undependable information, or you wouldn't be standing there acting tough. That could get you what we used to call back home a pine overcoat."

Doc was dubious. She didn't look that tough. But could her looks be depended upon?

"How much," Doc asked finally, "would I have to tell you about my business?"

The fat woman shrugged. "Enough for me to decide whether it's monkey business."

That gave him an opening for a question that had been puzzling him, and he asked, "What is your connection with Miss Crockett?"

"That," said the fat woman, "would be a long story. Call it secretary, advisor, companion, whipping-boy and a red flag in front of idiots like yourself."

"Miss Crockett is here?"

"Sure. But a fat chance you have of seeing her if you don't pass inspection with me."

Doc shrugged.

"This business of mine," he said grudgingly, "is about a gold mine."

"Whose gold mine?"

"Mine."

"I'll bet," said the big woman skeptically. "I'll just bet."

"You think I'm a thief?" Doc yelled. He looked angry.

"Why not? Why else would you be here?" She began laughing, and added, "And why else would you be so indignant about being called a thief? . . . What do you want here, anyway?"

"Some help," Doc said, dropping his anger quickly enough to show her it was feigned.

"What king of help?"

"A sort you might find some profit in giving," Doc said.

"You don't talk your head off, do you, when it comes to facts," said the fat woman. "Oh, well, come in. . . . We'll have a little reception for you, and see what develops."

Doc Savage walked in, not getting the point about a reception, but rather pleased with himself. He supposed it merely meant he was to meet Miss Eunice Lee Crockett, lady adventurer or *femme* sinister or whatever she was.

It did not mean this.

He did not find it out, though, until he had handed the large lady his hat when she held out a hand for it, and then he had stood there, as confident as a goat looking at the picture on a tomato can label, and listened to the woman say, "That's nice. It would be a shame to ruin a good hat." Promptly he was hit over the head from behind with something or other.

VI

Doc Savage did not fall after he was struck, but he came unhooked from reality. He stood there and his arms hung down. He couldn't think of anything particular to do. . . . Unexpected head blows had always held more terror for him than almost anything. There was a kind of black, abysmal, meaningless shock about a head blow that upset him. The moment of unexplainable surprise afterward was a thing of terror, like being pushed into a chasm. If you were knocked out, it was not as bad, although still bad enough, because unconsciousness would come quickly. But it was worse when you were dazed, and trying to get organized, figure out what had happened and why, and defend yourself.

The fat lady had not hit him. That was sure. Neither had the beggar. Who, then?

He turned to see. He turned holding his legs stiff, for the knees felt as if they would bend either way on slight provocation. He got partly around, and saw there was not just one. There were three of them, all big men, men nearly as large as he was, with clean shiny skins and the kind of faces that men have the world over when they only know how to make a point with their muscles. One was smoking a cigarette lazily.

The fat woman said, "Your arm must be getting weak, Abraham." And the man with the sap, a tube of goatskin with some loose shot in the end, looked pained and swung again. Doc bent his head a little and the weapon skated over the top of his head, not hurting him much worse than if he had been hit with a hammer.

Doc still did not go down. Moreover he could think after a fashion. He wondered if he should cut loose and do as well as he could, which might be better than they expected, providing they didn't know who he was. Or did they know? If they did, there was no percentage in letting himself be sapped down. If he did, there was always the chance some fisherman on the Nile in a few days would paddle over to see what the seagulls were fighting over, and find whatever was left of him by then.

He solved it by walking in close to Abraham. He hit Abraham in the middle with his right fist while he was putting his left arm around Abraham's waist. It was about as far around the waist as around a barrel. He did not have enough arm for it. He pumped his right into Abraham again, and the barrel convulsed and Abraham became a weight pulling him down toward the shiny floor. The floor was mother-of-pearl. He hadn't noticed that before. A floor like that would cost money.

By pushing against Abraham as he fell, he got the great bulk to topple. Abraham, troubled by what the two punches had done to his stomach, made a series of hacking and whooping noises and was again disinterested in using his sap any more. In falling, he brought up against the other man, with the result that they both landed on the floor.

Doc was off balance. In stumbling around trying to remain on his feet, he stepped on Abraham and his companion as often as possible. And presently he managed to hit the third assailant somewhere, and that one was on the floor too, his cigarette making a shower of fire.

"Whoeee!" said the fat woman. She sounded as if she was calling hogs. "Whoeee!" Then she added, "A real rough boy." She did not sound much disturbed.

I've probably overdone this, Doc thought.

The beggar came and stood in the door. When he appeared, he was bold and decisive. But then he saw what was going on, and was undecided.

Doc scowled at the cigarette on the floor, then the fat woman.

"You," he said, "can jump in the lake." The actual words which he used in Arabic were a little at variance, having to do with a sea trip by camel, but the inference was the same.

He walked out.

The beggar looked at him, did not do or say anything. This beggar was clean. Genuine Cairo beggars were never clean.

Doc kept walking. Not very straight, but he kept walking. When he got his legs tracking better, he tried a little running.

Sherman McCorland's red hair looked redder in Cairo. Otherwise he was much the same lean whip of a man that he had been when Morand had called him into the State Department office in Washington and introduced him to Doc Savage as the man in Cairo to call on for small favors.

"Good God!" said McCorland. "Are you injured?"

Doc was not injured, but he had bandaged his face rather completely in order to cover the phony scar, which was quite a bit of trouble to remove and replace. Doc had taken the contact lenses off his eyes, so he looked pretty much like himself now.

"Not seriously," Doc said. "I want you to do me a favor."

"How in Heaven's name did you get to Cairo so soon?" McCorland demanded. "You must have taken the plane immediately after nine."

Doc said that might have been. "I want some gold," he explained.

"Gold?"

"Not much. A couple of ounces. But it should be placer

gold—not stuff that has been milled out of ore—and it should
be from some part of Egypt if possible."

"What do you want it for?"

"Can you get it—without anyone knowing anything much
about it?"

"Why do you want it?" McCorland repeated.

"A private matter."

"Has it something to do with your finding Nesur?" asked
McCorland.

Doc shrugged and said, "Do we have to go into this?
Morand gave me the impression you knew what discretion was."

McCorland stiffened. He didn't like that. He said, "You
pick a sweet way of asking a favor."

Angry now, Doc said, "Skip it, then." He went toward
the door and had his hand on the knob when McCorland
said, "How soon will you need this gold?"

Doc stopped. "Right away. Half an hour."

McCorland punched a button. A native came in, and
McCorland asked for his hat and stick. The native left. "If you
want to wait here," McCorland told Doc, "I'll see what can
be done."

"Placer gold," Doc said. "Dust. Very small nuggets.
From Egypt, or at least from Africa."

"I heard you," McCorland said. "I'm sorry if I seem
abrupt, discourteous or unduly inquisitive—or a trifle irked
over what might seem to me a trifling request for an absurdity
in the face of such an urgent situation."

Doc Savage examined the other man's face. "What do
you mean, urgent?"

McCorland frowned. "Haven't you heard?" He shook his
head and added, "But you probably haven't, because you can
have been in Cairo only a few hours. I cabled this information
to Morand only a few moments ago."

"What information?"

"A report—how true it is, I can not say, but I am terrified
of its authenticity—that Nesur has definitely decided on
hostilities, and that the word will go out quite soon. Not
longer than twenty-four hours. Sooner if there is evidence of
British and American knowledge of the decision."

"That means," Doc asked grimly, "that our time is
shaved down to twenty-four hours?"

"Yes, obviously."

"Get the gold dust," Doc said.

* * *

When Monk Mayfair and Ham Brooks came to call on Doc Savage, Doc was rubbing the placer gold between two chunks of rough sandstone. The nuggets were too large for his purpose, and he was reducing them in size.

Monk and Ham came in without knocking, and Monk said, "Hello there, Ole Hansel. Right nice diggings you got for yourself here."

Ham closed the door.

"Where's the English accent?" Doc asked Monk briefly.

"Righto, gov'nor. You want the bloody trouble started right off?"

Doc shook his head. "Sit down. I didn't expect you this soon. That messenger must have broken a record getting to you."

Neither Monk nor Ham took chairs. They were nervous. Ham said, "We asked half a dozen places for Ole Hansel."

Doc nodded. "That's good."

He spread the particles of gold he had just reduced in size out on a paper on the table. Arrayed there also were two packages of cigarettes, new ones, which he had opened.

Doc proceeded, with infinite care, to insert particles of gold into the cigarettes, not less than half a dozen tiny pieces to each cigarette. For this he was using a needle-thin rod sliding inside a tiny tube; he would place a few flakes of gold in the thin tube, insert it in the end of the cigarette, and with the rod ram it out so that it lay in the tobacco.

He had thus prepared one package of cigarettes, and three fourths of the other package. He proceeded to finish the job, examining the end of each cigarette with a small magnifying glass when he finished to make sure his trickery was not obvious.

Ham leaned over to look at the cigarettes. "How'd you know what brand to use?"

Doc told them about his attempt to see Miss Crockett. "The fellows who crawled me were evidently her goon squad," he finished. "One of them was smoking this brand of cigarette."

He re-sealed both cigarette packages, wrapped them carefully, and put them in his clothing.

He said, "Before we start our fracas, here is some bad

news McCorland gave me: He says that this holy man, Nesur, has decided on violence, and the word will go out in about twenty-four hours."

Monk rubbed his jaw gloomily. "That's going to push us." He shook his head, added, "In Washington, the idea of some holy man on the other side of the world causing a war didn't seem much more than so much talk. Walking around through the native quarter here in Cairo, the way we've been doing the last few hours, you get a different idea."

"Heard anything?" Doc demanded.

"Nothing to help us find Nesur," Monk said. "But we did run across Nesur agitators at work. They're not underground about it at all. These guys we heard were doing it from soap boxes. You'd think they were on Union Square."

"If they're out in the open with it, they must be pretty sure of themselves," Doc commented.

He finished his preparations.

"Okay for the fuss," he said. "I'm Ole Hansel and I know where there is a gold mine you should rightfully share. Act accordingly."

Their previous conversation had been in low voices. What followed was louder. Presently they had worked up a noisy quarrel.

Monk produced the showy blackjack he had taken from Homer Crockett, the man Monk still presumed was the manager of the hotel in Washington. "This thing should be good window-dressing," Monk said, and made a pass at Doc with the blackjack.

They struck a few blows, broke up some furniture, fell on a bed and smashed that down. Presently, when the thing looked good enough, Doc took to his heels. Monk and Ham pursued him. They made all the commotion they could going through the building.

The owner of the place and half a dozen servants had gathered. Doc dived through them, upsetting one, and gained the street. Once outside, he settled down to running, doubling around corners, heading for the section of sidewalk shops. Presently he had lost Monk and Ham off his trail.

He thought the whole thing had looked genuine enough.

Doc decided to delay his return to his hotel. It was likely that the management would summon the police, and Doc wished to avoid complications there. So, for the next hour and a half, he browsed through the more crowded part of the old city, the Muski, and the Copt and Jewish quarters to the north. He visited several of the bazaars and markets in the huge buildings called *khans,* listening to the talk of the polyglot peoples—Cairenes, Nubians, Bedouin Arabs, Levantines, Syrians, Armenians, Greeks, Italians, French, English.

He was interested in the thing Monk had mentioned. That there was open agitation by Nesur's organization under way.

There was. He got a sample of it in a side street not far from the mosque of El Azhar, which for a long time had been the chief theological seminary of Islam.... As Monk had remarked, it was a little like Union Square, where a man could climb on a soap box and vent his opinions.

The organizer doing the talking here was probably small fry. But he was adept, knew his subjects, and the points he wanted put across.

One folk, one leader, one nation. That was his cry. It was basic and ancient. It had come down through the centuries, from the mouths of men who were welding people together for a purpose, good or bad. In union there is freedom, in union there is power. United we stand, divided we fall. The same cries had rung out over blood in American history; they were great words there, and heroes had said them. But men with dark souls had said them in other nations too, and Doc remembered the mottoes that had been plastered over Nazi Germany before the war: *Ein volk, ein Ehrer, ein Reich.* One people, one leader, one nation. Prelude to holocaust. How many had died then? Fifty million? Did anyone know?

This was grim stuff. That fellow there, that street spieler, wasn't just raving dream-stuff at the crowd. There was a confidence about him. Doc could feel it. And he knew the crowd could feel it.

There was no appeal to violence, and the Palestine problem, boilhead of the whole thing, was mentioned only by implication. . . .

Doc returned to his hotel slowly. He was worried. Morand, in Washington, had not exaggerated. This was only Cairo, and Cairo was on the outskirts of the problem. How much hotter it must be in Baghdad, Tel Aviv, Damascus, and for that matter in Karachi, Delhi and Calcutta.

The hand of Nesur was already well raised. If the hand held a match to light the fuse, there was no man to say where it might end.

It was stuff that, put in words, did not have awful urgency. He imagined how some Americans would regard it in their newspapers. *Jaffa, Basra, Beirut? What are they? Towns?*

Nesur? Who's that? The hell with it, let 'em fight it out. How did the Dodgers do today? . . . And maybe one thing would follow another and again ten million of them would be packing guns, or perhaps twenty this time.

He scouted his hotel. It was quiet. There seemed to be no police about. He entered, and the manager came to him at once and said, "We shall have to ask you to leave."

"Those two fellows started the trouble," Doc argued.

"You will leave anyway, please."

Doc shrugged and said, "If that's the way you feel," and went on to his elaborate suite.

The fat woman who had been at Eunice Lee Crockett's house arose from a chair.

"Maybe you did have something to offer," she said. "Crockett wants to talk to you about it."

Doc concealed pleasure carefully. It was working.

VII

Mr. Homer Wickett, erstwhile phony manager of the Rimes Hotel in Washington, D. C., was the first passenger off the four-o'clock plane from points west—Paris, London, New York, Washington. He was trailed closely by the man called Clyde and was, as anyone could see, in a hell of a hurry, and about the same state of temper.

"Where's Nate with the car?" he demanded.

Nate was a dark-skinned, thick-browed Italian. The car was a French custom body on an American chassis, and had cost approximately fifteen thousand dollars. There was already another man in the car, a roundish bald-headed man with a hard-skinned pale face that always looked as if it had just had a coat of oil and a polish. He wore spectacles with flashy shell rims in which several small gems, imitation ones, were set. Wickett addressed him as Galsbrucke.

"You get my cable, Galsbrucke?" Homer Wickett demanded.

"I got four of them," said the bald, spectacled man.

"Four is all I sent.... All right, where is this fellow Savage?"

The bald man looked uncomfortable. "He was in the American embassy offices about noon, seeing McCorland. He evidently wanted two ounces of African gold dust, because McCorland went out and got some."

"Gold dust?"

"Yes."

"Why?"

"I am sorry, I do not know," said Galsbrucke.

Homer Wickett cursed at some length, indicating there had been, as he put it, too much fumbling around with this thing, with nobody knowing enough about anything.

Clyde rode in front with Nate, the driver. Clyde was bleak-eyed and expressionless, carefully masking the fact that he was quite ill. He did not like airplane travel, and he liked it least of all over oceans for the very simple reason that once as a small boy while swimming in the surf off Atlantic City, N.J., he had been attacked by a hammerhead shark and had, he had always felt, barely escaped with his life. He was now in no state to care in the least what happened.

Homer Wickett finished his swearing and asked, "All right, where is Savage?"

"From McCorland's office, Savage walked through the bazaars and shops—"

"Where is he?"

Galsbrucke winced. "My man lost his trail."

Wickett's face took a slight bluish cast. "Who lost him?"

"Sabi. Hassam Sabi."

Wickett said, "Clyde."

Clyde did not stir and gave no sign of hearing.

"Clyde!"

The tone would have cracked a rock. Clyde lifted sick eyes. "Huh?"

"You know Hassam Sabi?" Wickett demanded.

"Yeah. Guy we picked up in Tehran. Why?" said Clyde weakly.

"I want you to put a knife in him," Wickett said.

"Oh, for God's sake!" gasped Galsbrucke. "The poor devil did his best—"

Wickett spat. "His best wasn't good enough, then," he said. "Listen, Galsbrucke, you'd better get it through your shiny skull that the situation is desperate. I'm going to get some action if I have to see throats cut right and left, yours included." He leaned forward and bellowed at the driver, "What are you waiting on? Get me to my office, and quick."

The office was not outwardly elaborate, but the interior was probably as fine as any in Cairo. It was located in a penthouse structure on top of one of the buildings in the newer section of the city near the river. If there was a more luxurious office in town, it would go hard on the architect who had designed this one if Homer Wickett found it out. He frequently made this statement, for he was a man who liked to take his emotions out of his mouth in balls of fire. This was always impressive, because he was not a four-flusher.

"I want Savage found," he told Galsbrucke. "You get that? I want him found."

"We are trying. We had no idea he was in Cairo until he appeared at the embassy to see McCorland."

Wickett got a little purple. "Weren't you watching the airport?"

"We—I—"

"Were you?"

"Well . . . no."

"Galsbrucke," said Wickett thoughtfully, "I think your stupidity is going to cause you to have an unfortunate experience —*if you don't find Savage in the next couple of hours!*" The last was said in a tone that caused all the pigeons to leave the roof outside the windows.

The man was pacified somewhat, however, by a couple of drinks and a light dinner that featured the form of skewered lamb called shish kebab. He told Galsbrucke sourly that he hadn't had much luck stopping Doc Savage in Washington. "He was in town and out before we got our breath," he explained. "However, I did plant one of those blackjacks on two of Savage's assistants, or on one of them, anyway. And that should enable us to take care of one or more of them."

Galsbrucke, anxious to change the subject to a more pleasant one, asked, "Would you care to look over some of the reports that have come in?"

"Might as well," Wickett said.

The reports were from the branch offices and field managers of the various petroleum interests owned or controlled by Wickett and the men associated with him.

An oil scout in Iran reported that the Central-Oklahoma-

United Oil Company No. 7 well had come in for two thousand barrels at thirty-seven hundred feet. This was doubtless quite secret information, and important, because it meant that a new field had proved out. It was a matter that involved many millions of dollars, but not in Mr. Homer Wickett's pocket. He had no oil holdings in Iran.

He did have holdings in Oklahoma, Illinois, California, Mexico and China. He had a refinery in Oklahoma, one in Indiana, one in Mexico. These were his personal holdings. They were not held jointly by the combine. They were Mr. Wickett's. But there were other oil leases, producing wells, drilling operations, areas under lease and being doodlebugged for oil in various parts of the world, refineries, pipelines, tanker concerns, and even a not inconsiderable chain of service stations, all controlled by the combine of which Wickett was spark plug.

There were reports from most of these holdings. The regular routine. Wickett looked them over, and they were pretty good. But not good enough to satisfy him. He was a man who quite probably would never be satisfied.

Wickett had a few things that were good in him, but much more that was bad. His intensity and his drive, his skill and his business sense, could have made him a genuinely great man. But he had in him the thing that in another sense Hitler had: he did not know when to stop. An excess, if it was a means to an end, meant nothing to Wickett. Bribery, murder, robbery, meant nothing if he could gain by them. He was a man in whose hands power was a grisly thing.

And he had power.

It was not yet dark when Galsbrucke came hurrying into Wickett's office. Galsbrucke looked relieved.

"We've spotted Monk Mayfair and Ham Brooks," he reported. "There was a fight at a hotel in the native quarter, and the participants, or two of them, were a couple of phony Englishmen, one big and apish, the other slender. One of my men, Cagle, had sense enough to realize the coincidence, so he investigated and found Monk Mayfair and Ham Brooks."

"Where are they?" demanded Wickett.

Galsbrucke handed him a slip of paper bearing an address. Wickett read this, then tore it up, growling, "Listen, don't let anything get in writing about this affair. Nothing! You understand."

"Yes, sir."

"Is Doc Savage with them?"

"No."

"Where is he?"

Galsbrucke lost some of his elation and confessed, "I don't know yet."

But Wickett was not as enraged by this as Galsbrucke had expected. Wickett swung back in his chair. He contemplated the ceiling for a while, then remarked, "The chances are that one of them has that blackjack. The question is, who."

Galsbrucke jumped. "The blackjack? Why, the one named Mayfair has it."

"How'd you find that out?"

"My man, Cagle, saw it in his hand. It seems Mayfair has a habit of fondling it."

Wickett laughed. Then he scowled. "You crazy fool, you didn't tell this Cagle that blackjack had any particular significance, did you?"

"Oh, no—"

"Did you tell anybody?"

"No. No indeed."

"Then how in the hell," yelled Wickett, "did Cagle happen to notice it." He didn't sound as if he believed Galsbrucke.

Galsbrucke explained nervously. "Cagle mentioned the man Mayfair taking a blackjack out of his pocket occasionally. The subject came up when Cagle was telling me that Mayfair seems to be a very tough customer."

"You bet he's tough," Wickett said. He was satisfied. He rubbed his jaw thoughtfully. "The point is, do we get rid of Brooks and Mayfair immediately, before the fool mislays that blackjack or somebody takes it away from him? Or do we wait for Savage?"

"You're going to—to—" Galsbrucke swallowed.

"The word, Mr. Galsbrucke, is kill," said Wickett. "When you are talking about something as direct as murder, never use an evasive word."

VIII

Miss Eunice Lee Crockett said, "Who is it?"

The fat blonde woman said, "Tiny. . . . Bearing an offering."

"Come in, Tiny."

The fat woman said to Doc Savage, "Would you mind holding your hands up a minute?" He did, and she slapped her hands on the obvious places where he might be carrying a weapon, and some places that were not obvious. Then she pushed the door open and said, "Walk into the web, fellow."

Doc Savage went in.

He had not known what to expect of Eunice Lee Crockett. He had seen her picture, of course. And her record in the State Department dossier. Her picture was that of a sweet little thing, but her record was as a combination of Cleopatra and Anne Bonny, the lady pirate.

Well, she looked like her picture, anyway.

"Won't you sit down," said Miss Crockett.

The room was an office, quite formal and quite New Yorkish, but not specially elaborate. He took the visitor's chair at the corner of the desk.

She had not offered to shake hands. But he had not expected her to.

In a pleasant voice, she explained, "It is too bad your first visit was unfortunate, but you see we have odd visitors here sometimes. We took the trouble to check on you, and a certain fight that happened at your hotel indicated your story might have something."

All this was said in Arabic, which she spoke fluently but with an American accent.... He was so busy weighing and measuring her that he didn't realize he was supposed to say something. Finally she said, "Well? What have you to sell?"

"Oh, that," Doc said. He began lying. He told her the story he had outlined to Monk and Ham; he was Ole Hansel, with two partners, and he had found a gold mine. He had found the mine—Doc made a point of that, indicating that he and his partners had quarreled, and separated, and so they had no right to the gold mine, although they seemed to think differently.

"I want them taken off my neck if necessary," he said. "I don't think they're going to bother me much, because they haven't any legal rights to back them up."

"Were any papers signed?" asked Miss Crockett, as calmly as if she was a school ma'am asking a sixth-grader if he knew what a divisor was.

"No."

"What else do you want?"

"Money from you to develop the mine," Doc said. "For that I will give you a generous share, say ten per cent."

Miss Crockett smiled. "Ten per cent?"

"Yes."

"For you, you mean?" she said.

He had not supposed she was dumb. Now he concluded she wasn't, and that she was a Shylock besides. Although, considering that he was holding himself forth as nothing less than a double-crosser and a crook, there was some justice to her side. . . . He found himself arguing with her as if there was really a gold mine, and she was really going to crimp him out of the lion's share of it.

In the end they compromised on an even split.

"Now," she said, "it's up to you to prove you have a gold mine."

He said that was easy. He would take her out and she could watch her men pan gold out of the pay sand.

As promptly, she said they would do that. "How far is it from Cairo?"

"Not more than two hundred miles."

She was startled. "That close? . . . Can an airplane land near the spot?"

He nodded.

"Then we will go there early in the morning," she said. "You will sleep here tonight."

Staying here was something he hadn't bargained for. He had intended to consult with Monk and Ham about future plans. But Miss Crockett was already pushing a button.

A servant appeared—one of the big fellows with whom he'd had the fight on his first visit—and took him to a room. The servant seemed to carry no malice.

The room was large, pleasant, and, like most of the house interior, more like an American mansion than a Cairo manse. An indication, he imagined, that the proprietress often got homesick for the U. S.

The servant left the room, closing the door. . . . There was a clicking sound. Doc whirled, hurried to the door, and tested it.

He was locked in.

He slept soundly though. And the next morning, on the way out to a private airport, he got his cigarettes planted. He merely borrowed a cigarette from one of the big men, whose name was Ali, and took the package out of Ali's hand in order to extract the cigarette, and made a switch. Later, while they were waiting for the plane to be pushed out of a hangar, he pulled much the same switch on the other big man. The latter's name was Wazzah. It was probably a nickname, because the word was Arabian for goose.

The plane was a little five-place cabin job made in Michigan. In the party were Miss Crockett, the fat woman, the two big men Ali and Wazzah, and himself. That was all the plane would hold, and he wondered who was going to fly. Miss Crockett would, it developed.

He was handed a chart when they were in the air. He pretended to be upset by the unfamiliarity of an aerial chart. He was upset all right, but not by the chart. He was upset because he had to find a likely gold mine in a country he had never seen, and find it from the air.

An hour and fifty minutes later, he selected what seemed to be a likely place, and pointed it out. "There," he said.

The plane landed.

"Bring the gold pans," said Miss Crockett.

This was desert country, so normally there wouldn't have been a discernible drop of water within miles. But the rainy season was with them, and so there was, if anything, an over-abundance of water in the sinkholes and pools.

He led the way.

"There," he said, pointing.

Miss Crockett said she didn't see any tracks. Shouldn't there be tracks if he had been prospecting around the place.

He looked wise and asked, "Would I leave tracks and let them know where I had been prospecting?"

He had a bad minute when he thought Ali and Wazzah were going to begin panning without smoking. But he got that fixed up by bumming another cigarette off them. The power of suggestion was enough. Both big men lit up cigarettes, dipped up gravel in the gold pans which Miss Crockett had brought along, and went to work.

There was disgust when the first panning showed no gold. But the next one showed flecks of pay, and spirits revived. The third panning was quite rich, and after that, every panning except one, taken at various points up and down the stream, showed gold.

*   *   *

Miss Crockett was pleased, and also surprised. "That sand," she said, "is running near a hundred piastres to the panning. With modern mining methods, the return would be fabulous."

Doc said smugly that it would. Then he put the bee on Miss Crockett. He had, Doc explained, a wailing need for money for expenses, and now, seeing that there was a fine gold claim being shared between them, how about Miss Crockett advancing a trifling amount in cash. Say about twenty thousand piastres.

Miss Crockett said nothing doing. Doc complained loudly. He explained, with gestures, the horrible things his creditors might do to him unless he got some cash. "Would you buy ten per cent of my share for cash?" he asked. Miss Crockett was more interested in that, but said she would have to think it over.

The two big men, Ali and Wazzah, had lifted their ears.

During the flight back to Cairo, Doc managed to sell Wazzah a tenth interest in his half of the mine for twenty thousand piastres.

The fat woman did not become aware of this. She was riding ahead of them, and was bulky and silent in Arab garb, including veil.

But Ali overheard. He was disappointed. To placate Ali, Doc unloaded another tenth on him for the same price Wazzah had paid, twenty thousand piastres.

Neither Ali nor Wazzah had the purchase price handy, but insisted they could get it, and quick.

"You are getting a great bargain," Doc assured them. "You have robbed me of my eyes, practically."

At the airport, Miss Crockett left them for a while, accompanied by the fat woman. But both returned shortly, and Crockett said they would now go to her house and prepare the papers of agreement, and the necessary moves to get control of the gold claim from the government.

Doc agreed. He was not very enthusiastic, since he wanted privacy so he could contact Monk and Ham. It had now been almost twenty hours since he had seen them.

But they went to Miss Crockett's house, and Doc saw no prospect of getting away immediately. The bickering about details went on and on. The deals with Ali and Wazzah came to Miss Crockett's notice.

"You're a fool to sell so cheaply," she told Doc. "But it's your funeral. Ali and Wazzah are faithful servants of mine, and if someone has to skin you, I'm glad they're doing it."

"When can I leave?" Doc demanded.

"Not for an hour or so at least."

The scheme seemed to be going all right. . . . Whether it would end as he had expected it to, Doc wasn't sure. He was beginning to have some doubts.

This elaborate piece of connivance was based on human nature—Miss Crockett's human nature. His first idea of what she was like had been taken from the State Department dossier on her. Now he was not as certain. She was different. Either that, or she was the smoothest article of deceit he had ever seen.

The delay was tough to take, too. Some of his impatience might be coming from that. If this holy man, Nesur, was going to put out the word for violence within twenty-four hours, the time was getting very short. The twenty-four-hour report might have been a rumor. It might not. McCorland had seemed frightened about it.

He studied Miss Crockett as they discussed, argued. Smooth, all right. According to the information he had on her, she had led the ordinary day-to-day life of an Ohio girl until five years ago. Grade school, high school, teacher's college, then a job teaching in a small Ohio town; the usual friends, he imagined; the usual hobbies and the usual social life. And then she had come to Cairo where she had inherited the estate of an Uncle Ira Crockett. . . . That she should then become a fabulous figure of intrigue, accredited with feats that were equalled by few men, was startling. It would have been startling in any case. But for an Ohio school ma'am. . . .

Three men came in. Arabs. They were big men, as big as Ali and Wazzah.

Doc understood instantly that Miss Crockett had been waiting for them. He knew it certainly when one of the trio nodded at him, and asked Miss Crockett in English, "Does he speak English?"

"I've been wondering," Miss Crockett said. "But report in English anyway."

"There was no gold," the big man said.

"What?"

"No gold. We panned up and down that creek bed for some distance, as well as panning where you had panned. There was not a single flake of gold."

Miss Crockett smiled without humor. She looked at Doc Savage.

"Salted," she said.

She spoke English. Doc pretended not to understand. Miss Crockett, he realized, could handle herself in an emergency. She was no more excited than she had probably been in Ohio when one of her students added six and six and got ten.

Doc inquired what was up. "*Shu hadha?*" he asked.

Miss Crockett explained. "You were trying to sell me a phony gold mine," she said. "You were very slick. I don't see how you managed it yet—the salting, I mean. But you did."

"*Ma yumkin!*" Doc said. Impossible.

"It's lucky I was cautious enough to send a second crew to investigate," Miss Crockett said. "Bulad, here, is a mining engineer, and he says there is no gold, so there is obviously no gold. What about it, Mr. Ole Hansel?"

Doc pretended indignation. He said again it was impossible.

"Is your name Ole Hansel?" Miss Crockett asked.

Doc shrugged. "I guess not. . . . Do you want to listen to an explanation?"

"Not," said Miss Crockett, "until I pick up your two friends who helped you pull this." She stood up and gave orders. She was going after Monk and Ham. "And you'll come along," she told Doc.

The ride wasn't particularly pleasant. They went in two cars, and Ali kept a gun in his hand. Around a corner from the second-rate place where Monk and Ham were staying, Miss Crockett ordered the car parked. The other car parked behind them, and the three big men approached.

"Bring the two men," ordered Miss Crockett. "Bring their baggage, too. Pay their bill, bring their baggage, and them. You understand?"

Bulad, the mining man, nodded. "They may not want to come peacefully."

"Then persuade them."

The trio departed.

Doc stirred. Ali gouged him with the gun snout warningly.

"Look here," Doc said. "I don't want those two hurt."

"So they're friends of yours?" Miss Crockett said.

"Yes."

"They won't be hurt—much."

Doc leaned forward. "There is no reason why you should not listen to an explanation." He spoke Arabic. "The story is simple. We want jobs. We had heard about you, Miss Crockett, and we surmised you did not employ fools. So we simply did something to prove we were not fools."

"Jobs?" She seemed surprised. "You want to work for me?"

"Yes."

"Why?"

He could not very well tell her it was because she knew where Nesur was, and he hoped to get that information. He shrugged and said, "It would be a privilege."

She frowned a while over that. Suddenly she asked, "How did you fake the gold?"

"The cigarettes."

"What cigarettes—oh! Oh, I remember. Ali and Wazzah were smoking." She glanced at Ali and his companion. They looked bitterly disgusted with themselves. "Where did you get those cigarettes?"

"From our pockets," Ali muttered.

Doc explained about the switch. He demonstrated the sleight-of-hand by which he had done it.

Miss Crockett began laughing. "That was a smooth piece of work," she said.

She was still laughing when the explosion came slamming into the street, around the corner, throwing itself on them with unbelievable abruptness, thrusting their clothing against their bodies, then, a second later plucking the garments away from their skin, and sucking windows out of buildings, sucking up dust in the street.

Time, for a few seconds, became a kind of cavity. The blast had come, gone. Like a big whip that had popped. Surprise seemed the only thing in their brains. Incredulous wonder. That, and the blank shock on their faces, the dust crawling up in the street, and the greater dust coming rolling now in a great cloud around the corner toward Monk and Ham's hotel. . . .

Doc said thickly, "Monk..."

He was really out of the car and running into the dust before he planned any movement at all. He kept going. He

346 / A Doc Savage Adventure

ran headlong. In the dust he could smell the fumes of cordite, the mellow-sweet stink that spreads after the explosion of an artillery shell. Other feet ran behind him.

The fat woman had remained at home. It was odd this popped into his mind now. But it did. It seemed to have no bearing on anything, but it was what he thought of.

Just before he reached the corner, an Arab boy appeared. The boy was about eighteen, and he was walking backward, both hands pressed to his face and blood leaking through his fingers.

Doc gripped the boy's arm. He said, "What happened?" English. He changed to Arabic. *"Shu hadha?"*

Very clearly through the hands still to his face the boy said, "Some men came from the hotel. They carried baggage. There was a pushcart by the curb. It blew up as they came near."

The explanation was utterly lucid. "Sit down," Doc said to the boy. "Wait for a doctor."

The boy said, "Thank you, sir," and then fell forward loosely on his face.

Doc Savage went on. The dust was thick in the street and in the dust nothing lived. Some things were burning, not blazing but smouldering and smoking. Some wood, possibly parts of the pushcart, and cloth on a body or two.

The blast had been amazing. It had cleaned out a hole, where the pushcart had been, that a man could stand in knee-deep. Paving stones and sidewalk stones had been pushed with great force against the buildings, and one building wall had come down, making a pile of stone and brick on which was spread, like frosting on a cake, white bedclothing from some room above.

Doc went to the first body. It was the mining engineer, Bulad. To make sure of identification was not easy, particularly if one was squeamish about exposed anatomy. But he decided it was Bulad.

The woman called Crockett came up beside him. She said, "It's Bulad."

She sounded as she should sound. Strained, with illness pushing against restraint. Horror crowding against determination.

She said, "Your friends killed him."

She sounded all right with that, too. Her voice had all

the revulsion and condemnation it should have. It was what she logically should think.

Doc went forward to another body. He did not walk easily nor did he easily look down at the body. Evidence that a body was there, really. For here was where the wall had come down, covered the body, all but an outflung arm from fingertips to midway between elbow and shoulder. If there had been any clothing on the arm, the explosion had stripped it away completely, and the arm was blackened and did not have its former shape.

Doc leaned down. He all but fainted. He could see that a great block of stone had hit so that its edge had severed the arm from the body that was deeper in the rubble.

By the arm's fingers lay the flashy pigskin blackjack that Monk Mayfair had taken off Mr. Homer Wickett, who had said he was a hotel manager in Washington.

Doc picked up the blackjack and dropped it in his pocket. There was no indication on his face that he knew what he was doing nor why.

IX

Homer Wickett had once read somewhere that many of history's great men, or notorious ones, had been victims of spasmophilia; which was a five-dollar psychiatrists' word meaning a tendency toward convulsions. It had relieved him not a little to read this. He himself had been addicted to tantrums when he was opposed, and it had worried him. He feared it might indicate insanity. But this thing he had read had tagged it with greatness, so he was no longer bothered. He had heard that Hitler had frequently fallen to the floor in a tantrum and chewed the carpet, and he understood exactly how the fellow felt. It was, Wickett supposed, an affliction of empire builders, something that went with a certain type of genius. He himself had constructed a petroleum empire, and he certainly had occasions when he went completely berserk.

Wickett was treating himself to one of his better fits now. He had finished striking and cursing the man who had brought him the bad news. Now, alarmed not so much by fear that he had killed a man as by fear that he might have needlessly killed a rather valuable henchman, Wickett had recoiled into a chair and was sitting there in muscle-knotted rigidity.

The man he had struck down had fallen in front of the large desk, and Wickett, in kicking him repeatedly in the head, stomach and ribs, had propelled the body partly into the knee-hole area of the desk. The man lay there now. He was breathing.

He was a tall gray-haired man of about thirty-five who spoke several languages fluently, and could as a usual thing be depended upon to accomplish almost any devilment that was assigned him. He had worked for Wickett for years. Once before Wickett had struck him, about seven years ago in a New York hotel when he had unfortunately been the one to tell Wickett that the U. S. government was shutting off Wickett's petroleum sales to the Nazi government.

Homer Wickett began slowly to rock back and forth. His face was pale, his lips compressed.

Clyde came in. Clyde was wearing the same suit he had worn when he served as chauffeur for Homer Wickett in Washington. Behind Clyde was the roundish bald-headed Galsbrucke. They were excited.

"We got them!" Galsbrucke said excitedly. "They passed the pushcart! You should have heard the explosion here. Did you?"

Wickett looked at the men in a wooden pale-faced way and did not speak.

Clyde said, "We were a couple of blocks away and didn't actually see it, but that explosion was something to take your hat off."

"There isn't the slightest doubt!" said Galsbrucke.

Wickett said nothing.

Clyde frowned. "Something wrong, chief?"

Wickett jerked a little. His mouth opened slowly and a guttural trickle of sound came out; in a moment they realized he was cursing them, the world, and all things.

Startled, Clyde moved around the desk. He saw the unconscious man lying partly under the desk.

"For God's sake!" Clyde gasped. "It's Lansdowne! What did he—what's going on?"

Galsbrucke ran around the desk, observed the man also and said something stunned and appropriate. Then he ducked wildly as Wickett made a sudden swing at him with his fist.

The one blow was the only one Wickett released. He began to shake, not loosely, but tightly like a taut cord, and he yelled, "Where is Nesur?"

It was Galsbrucke's time to look stunned. He said, "Lansdowne is staying with Nesur..." Blankly, like an idiot, he stopped.... Lansdowne was there on the floor! He said, "What—" and did not finish.

Wickett, stabbing a hand at Lansdowne, screamed, "The fool! The idiot! The imbecile sat there in Gaza for a week watching an empty hole. Nesur had gone. Gone! And the consummate boob didn't know it!"

He kicked the body under the desk, and it moved slightly and groaned.

"Where is Nesur?" Galsbrucke blurted.

"Lansdowne doesn't know!"

"But that—oh, that's awful," Galsbrucke said, sounding as if he wanted to wring his hands. "The fat's in the fire. Everything depended on keeping Nesur under our thumbs."

Wickett screamed that he didn't need to be told this.

Clyde put in a question. "Why did this Nesur scram that way?"

Wickett cursed Clyde and asked if he was too dumb to guess. "Nesur was probably getting suspicious of us," he said.

Clyde rubbed his jaw.

"Has anybody thought of that babe, Crockett, in connection with this?" he asked.

Quite a prolonged silence followed this. Clyde used it to pull Lansdowne out from under the desk and tow him into the bathroom—there were living quarters as well as offices in the suite—and splash him with some water, give him a stiff drink of whiskey, and help him wash his face.

Lansdowne improved. They spent some time agreeing on the sort of fatherless so and so Mr. Wickett was.

"How the hell," said Clyde, "could Nesur be missing a week and you not know it?"

Lansdowne's shrug was bitter. "Nesur had been sticking close to the hideout."

"Afraid of us?"

"I thought he was afraid of the Americans and the English," Lansdowne said. "God knows, he should have been, the amount of spadework we've done on him to make him think the Americans and English were his poison."

Clyde said, "I was afraid we were going to overdo that."

"I told Wickett that. I told him that very thing," Lansdowne said. "But would he listen? Hah!"

"The chief pushes too hard," Clyde admitted. "You figure maybe Nesur had started to think we weren't his great friends and maybe the Americans and English weren't the stinkers we had them painted?"

"It could be."

"That would be a hell of a note," said Clyde.

"It would indeed," admitted Lansdowne sourly. "We have spent two years building this up.... Persuading Nesur to come out of exile, building himself up again as a holy man, getting an organization together. All that was a lot of work."

Clyde nodded and said he had been thinking about that. "Nesur," Clyde said, "is at the point now where he can step out and lead an uprising against the English. He can call it a holy war or call it a war of independence, or call it anything he wants to for that matter. And he's pretty sure to be able to get the backing of every disgruntled man in the Near East."

"That's a fact," Lansdowne said.

"Isn't it also a fact that, regardless of whether Nesur's campaign to throw the foreigners out succeeds entirely, the foreign-held oil companies are going to get thrown out on their ears?" Clyde said.

"Yes."

"Okay. Wickett figured he was going to be the man to get the oil business that was taken away from the companies that now have it."

"Of course."

"That's big stakes," Clyde remarked.

"About as big as you can count them," Lansdowne agreed.

Clyde was sagely thoughtful. "Like I said a minute ago, it would be a nice set-up for someone to step in and take over."

"What do you mean?"

"That dame," Clyde said.

"Crockett?"

"Uh-huh. She's been known to grab the walnuts after somebody else shook the tree.... You remember that boat-load of Nazi bigwigs who sailed from Greece with their loot when it got too hot at home? Talk is she got the walnuts there."

Lansdowne swore thoughtfully.

"We'd better tell Mr. Wickett," he said.

*　　*　　*

It was not a very easy job to tell Mr. Wickett that Eunice Lee Crockett might have, by a cunning move, put herself in a position to harvest the crop Mr. Wickett had spent two years planting and cultivating.

Reluctantly—he seemed quite sure Wickett would have another fit when he heard this—Lansdowne confessed that for the past three weeks or so, and up until a week previously when it was now presumed Nesur had disappeared from his hideaway in the city of Gaza, there had been a man known as Wazzah around Gaza. And this Wazzah, it was rumored, was a henchman of Miss Eunice Lee Crockett.

Homer Wickett didn't have his fit. He merely said he was tempted to kill everybody in the room.

"We've got to get that woman," Wickett said.

"You think she would know where Nesur is?"

Wickett bitterly requested Lansdowne not to be stupid. "Of course she would know. That babe knows everything she's not supposed to know. As a matter of fact, the old reprobate of an uncle she inherited her organization from used to finance Nesur. Nesur was sort of the old goat's protegé. After the English chased Nesur into hiding a few years ago to keep the Mediterranean section quiet, it was Crockett's uncle who provided a retiring-place for Nesur. . . . Hell, Nesur would consider this dame his friend."

Clyde said proudly, "That was my idea, too. Crockett will go ahead and provoke trouble, and get those oil concessions for herself."

Homer Wickett rather astonished them by doubting this.

"I don't know about that," he said. "But we're going to grab this Crockett woman."

"If we're wrong, that's going to make Nesur mad," Clyde said. "They're friendly."

"We'll make him think we were protecting him. We can fix up some sort of hokum he'll believe."

"How about saying she was plotting with this Doc Savage?"

"That might do it," Homer Wickett admitted.

The discussion got down to practical plans about Miss Crockett. Should they seize her? How? That might be easier talked than done. Galsbrucke's suggestion that they simply eliminate her, possibly using the method that had just been employed on Doc Savage's aides, was voted down by Wickett, who pointed out that the primary object was Nesur. Catch Miss Crockett, and grind out of her the whereabouts of Nesur, if she knew. That was the program.

The telephone rang, and Clyde answered. He said, "What? What? Oh, yes," and passed the instrument to Homer Wickett, adding, "For you."

Wickett had trouble understanding what was being said over the phone. He could not get it straight and said, "Come on up here. Something must be wrong with the connection."

Clyde frowned after the other ceased speaking and replaced the instrument on its cradle. "Didn't sound to me as if it was a bad connection," he said.

Homer Wickett nodded. "Scared."

"Nate, wasn't it?"

"Yes."

"Nate doesn't scare easy," Clyde said. "I wonder what the hell is wrong?"

Nate did not leave them in doubt when he got there. He arrived in a wild-eyed run.

"Pushcart—dynamite—didn't get Savage's men," Nate said by jerks. "Guys killed—Crockett's men—had gone to get this Monk and Ham and came out of the hotel carrying the blackjack."

X

Doc Savage, when he found Monk and Ham were safe in the hotel—this did not happen for some time—was knocked speechless by relief. He could do nothing but stare at the pair, then abuse them joyfully, after which he demanded what had happened.

"Three guys showed up out of a clear sky," Monk explained. "They caught us by surprise. They said they were going to take us to this Crockett woman. We said we weren't sure we liked the idea. They said it made damned little difference."

"They were from Crockett, all right," Doc said.

Monk nodded. "So we gathered finally. Anyway, to continue the story, they said they were going to move us out of here lock, stock and barrel. We objected to that, too, and refused to carry our baggage, which they had to pack, too.

They put all our stuff in the bags. They searched us and put
what we had in our pockets in the bags, too—except that
blackjack of mine. One of them decided to take that for
himself. . . . Well, two of them left, and pretty soon we heard
an explosion."

"Two left carrying your bags?" Doc asked.

"Yes."

"Then what became of the one who stayed here?"

"Him? He tore out of here when he heard the explosion."

Doc gave them an outline of what had happened since
he had seen them, explaining that Miss Crockett had bitten
on the gold mine trick, then discovered she had been on the
point of being hoaxed. "Of course the whole idea was to
convince her we were slick shysters ourselves and good men
to have in her organization," Doc finished. "But I am not
sure how that is going to work out. . . . I think maybe we've
been misled—the girl may not be the rooting-tooting crook
we were led to think she was."

"Where is she?" Ham demanded.

"She was down on the street," Doc said. "I missed her
there. . . . I don't know whether we had better hunt her up,
either."

"Why not?"

"It's just possible," Doc said, "that this scheming isn't
going to turn out the way we thought it would. Our plans
were based on her being pretty unscrupulous." Doc rubbed
his jaw, considering the point. "I'll tell you what," he said.
"We had better clear out of here, and I'll talk to the State
Department man again, McCorland. See what has developed."

"Want us to go along?" Ham asked.

"Better, yes," Doc said. "I have a hunch that explosion
was aimed at you two fellows. If it was, this neighborhood
isn't healthy."

McCorland was in his office, and seemed quite surprised
to see them. He had not met Monk and Ham. Doc introduced them, and they shook hands.

"Have you found Nesur?" McCorland demanded.

"Not yet," Doc said.

McCorland shook his head uneasily. "Time is getting
awfully short, I'm afraid. All reports indicate that the time
limit Nesur had set to reach a decision has elapsed, the
decision has been made and awaits only its execution."

Doc nodded. "There doesn't seem to be much uneasiness here in Cairo."

"Well . . . No, no actual fighting yet," McCorland admitted. "However, something happened about half an hour ago that gave us a bad shake. There was an explosion over in the native quarter, and at least two men were killed. There may have been more. One of the dead men has been identified as a fellow in the hire of that woman, Crockett. The killing may have been the beginning of general violence."

"I don't think so," Doc said.

"Why not?"

"The blast may have been an attempt to kill Monk and Ham."

"What! Great God, you mean someone tried to murder them?"

It looked that way, but there was no way of being sure, Doc explained. He did not go into details.

An embassy clerk entered, leaned over, and whispered into McCorland's ear. Doc did not get what was said, but McCorland jumped. Then McCorland looked at them. Doc Savage got the impression McCorland was irked by something that had just happened.

"There is a friend of yours here," McCorland told Doc.

Friend? Doc wondered who. Was that sarcasm? Was it Miss Crockett?

It was Morand. Morand from Washington. Morand neatly barbered and in whites, as dapper as if just stepping into the Mayflower Hotel in Washington for a cocktail at the end of the day.

"Listen, why didn't you let me know they were here?" Morand snapped at McCorland. "I told you to."

"I was going to send word," McCorland said hastily.

McCorland, Doc realized, was irked by the presence of Morand, his superior officer, in Cairo.

Morand came toward Doc, smiling bitterly. "I don't know whether to shake hands with you or not," he said wryly.

"Something happen to our beautiful friendship?" Doc asked.

Morand nodded. "Somebody," he said, "made me a present in Washington."

"Is that so?" said Doc innocently.

"A body in a trunk. . . . You wouldn't know anything about it, I suppose? If you do, you'd better not admit it."

"A body!" Doc said. "Imagine!"

"Uh-huh. Funny thing, too. . . . Fingerprints of the fellow were on file with my department. Seems he works for a certain lady I recall mentioning to you, a Miss Crockett."

Doc suggested that this was quite a coincidence.

"It sure was. It scared the hell out of me. So I took a plane to Cairo in a hurry. Came over to see if you needed protection," Morand said.

Doc Savage said that, in view of the kind of lousy progress he had been making, what Morand should have brought along was a couple of first-grade miracles.

"You mean you aren't getting anywhere?" Morand demanded.

"Not anywhere."

"I'll bet," said Morand suspiciously. "What you mean is that you're not going to tell me what you're doing, isn't that it? Okay. All I can say is that if that shenanigin you pulled in Washington is a sample, nobody had better find out what you are doing."

Doc shook his head gloomily. "No, seriously—the results so far are awful."

Morand grinned dubiously. "That so? I seem to recall that you've produced results a few times in the past. . . . Anyway, can I be of any service?"

Doc nodded.

"There was an explosion," he said, "in the native quarter not quite an hour ago. It killed, I think, at least two men. They were also employees of our Miss Crockett."

"That's a hell of a coincidence, too!" Morand exclaimed. "Listen, what are you doing? Knocking off her mob by ones and twos?"

"No. . . . I have a hunch that explosion was intended to get Monk and Ham. No proof. Just a hunch."

"The devil!"

Doc said, "The way I'm working this, I can't very well confer with the Cairo police about it. But you can. So I wish you'd do that, and egg them on all you can."

"Oh, you want the explosion-makers caught?"

"Certainly."

"Any idea who it is?"

"No. . . . The same outfit who killed that fellow in Washington, probably."

356 / A Doc Savage Adventure

Morand frowned thoughtfully. "About this explosion," he said. "Did something blow up? Some object with wheels on it, I mean? Or with legs? A camel or a car or something?"

"A pushcart," Doc said curiously. "Why?"

Morand swung on McCorland. "Mack, how many cases like that have there been in the last couple of years?"

McCorland shrugged. "There have been so many bombings that I don't keep track—"

"You kept track of these," Morand said sharply. "I asked you to."

"Oh, you mean specific instances where a victim came near an object and it blew up.... There have been at least half a dozen," McCorland said.

Suddenly interested, Doc Savage took over the questioning. He demanded, "Were all of these explosion murders in Cairo?"

McCorland shook his head. "No. Two were in Jerusalem, one in Tel Aviv, one in Cairo, one in Athens, and I don't recall where the other one was."

"Haifa," said Morand.

"Yes, Haifa," McCorland agreed. "I remember now."

Doc demanded, "In each case, the victim or victims came near a movable object, and it exploded?"

"Well, as nearly as could be ascertained, yes."

"Who were the victims?"

"Just natives," McCorland said.

Morand frowned and said, "Come on, McCorland, don't be secretive with Savage. He's here to help us out on something we can't crack."

McCorland's neck darkened. "Yes, sir." He turned to Doc and explained, "The victims were, we have reasons to presume, men interested in, or involved in, the political picture in the Mediterranean area, the eastern end."

"Men who opposed Nesur?" Doc demanded.

"Well..."

Morand interrupted sharply. "There's kind of a funny thing about that. Some of them opposed Nesur. Some of them were in his organization. One of them in particular was a man named Mohammed Nimjah, who was the sheik of a bunch of Iranian inland tribesmen, and supposed to be very close to Nesur."

"Then the purpose of the murders isn't clear?" Doc asked.

"I wouldn't say that. . . . McCorland, tell him the rumor that went around about that."

McCorland hesitated. "It was just unproved talk."

"Tell him."

Reluctantly, McCorland said, "Well, I think it was totally unfounded rumor, but there was a whisper that a man, or group of men, who wanted to be close to Nesur and guide his destiny, were killing off men who were trying to do the same thing, or were about to turn Nesur against them."

"By guiding Nesur's destiny," said Morand, "Mr. McCorland means making a hell of a profit out of it."

"Profit on what?" Doc asked.

"Oil, for one thing."

"That's ridiculous," said McCorland sharply. "The oil concessions are tied up now by American, British and Russian interests."

"Uh-huh. There could be changes made," Morand said.

Doc Savage suddenly dropped the question-and-answer session. He swung to McCorland and asked, "Can you get me a camera? A small pocket Kodak will do. One with film in it, though."

McCorland hesitated. "Well, I don't know—"

"Get him the camera and film, dammit," Morand said sharply. "No wonder we haven't made any progress, if this is the kind of cooperation you have been giving Savage."

"He hasn't asked me for cooperation!" McCorland snapped. He left the room.

Doc told Morand, "It's a wonder some of your associates don't slit your throat sometime, the way you talk to them."

Morand snorted. "Or send me bodies in trunks, eh?"

Monk Mayfair and Ham Brooks had been listening without taking a part in the discussion, but now Monk said, "We never left any trunk with a body in your hall."

Morand eyed Monk bitterly. "Hall? How did you know it was in my hall? All I've said is that it was on my doorstep?"

Doc said hastily, "Why didn't you tell us about plotters close to Nesur? And oil possibly being behind it? It seems to me there was a remarkable lot you didn't tell us."

"Didn't want to burden you with details," said Morand. "Hell, what we knew wasn't doing us any good. If all the details, meaningless and otherwise, that we have on this thing were put in print, it would make a book longer than *Gone with the Wind*. I didn't want to give you a headache with all that stuff."

Ham Brooks said, "When we work for the State Department, it's always like this. They want miracles from nothing."

Morand grinned. "We've gotten them a time or two, haven't we?"

McCorland came back with a camera, a small folding Kodak, and asked, "This do?"

"Fine," Doc said. "Is there film in it?"

"Yes."

Doc put the camera in his coat pocket with the blackjack which he had picked up on the explosion scene. He said, "All right, now I want to see a fellow who develops film."

"Right now?" Morand blurted.

"Immediately."

"But you haven't take any pictures yet."

"Nevertheless," Doc said, "I want the film in this camera developed."

About two blocks from the American diplomatic building, there was a photographer's shop patronized by tourists. The photographer spoke English, and it developed that he did his own film processing in the back. Yes, he could put the film through immediately, if it was a matter of importance. Doc assured him it was.

The man went in the back room, put the film in a tank in darkness, and ran it through developer, hypo and wash. Doc said, "Let it wash just enough to clear."

The man did that, then held the film to the light.

"What do you know!" he said. "Nothing on it."

"Why should there be?" said Morand.

"Wait a minute," Doc Savage said. "You mean there is no image on the film, but why?"

"It looks as if it was light-struck or something," the photographer explained.

"How could light get to that film?" Morand demanded. He wheeled on McCorland. "Did somebody doctor that film by exposing it to light so Mr. Savage couldn't take pictures on it?"

"No, no, the film was fine." Doc dropped the film on the darkroom work-bench. "The film served its purpose."

"What purpose?" asked Morand.

"The purpose of convincing me," Doc said, "that I had better get some sheet lead and wrap that blackjack in it."

"What?" Morand was confused. "What the hell is this?"

Doc was examining the work-bench in the darkroom. It was a common practice to cover darkroom work benches with sheet lead as a protection against the chemicals used in photography, and this bench was so covered.

"How much," Doc asked the photographer, "for a sheet of this lead about a foot square?"

They made a deal.

Morand did not understand it. He was still puzzled when Doc Savage, Monk and Ham left him.

XI

The beggar was sitting cross-legged in his usual place outside the door of Eunice Lee Crockett's house. He contemplated Doc Savage gloomily and said, "Back again, eh?" in excellent English.

Doc, pretending not to understand the English, told the man not to trouble himself about moving. *"La tukallif khatrak,"* Doc said.

"Who do you think you're fooling, Mr. Savage?" the beggar asked.

Doc concluded from the man's tone that this was not a tricky fishing for betrayal. The man was sure of Doc's identity.

"So the fat is in the fire," Doc said.

"And blazing merrily," agreed the beggar.

"Miss Crockett know who I am?"

"I imagine so. She told me."

"Oh."

"She said she must be getting very stupid, or she would have realized it earlier."

"What are our chances of seeing her?" Doc asked.

"Pretty good. Walk on in."

Doc frowned. "Will we be able to walk out again?"

"I wouldn't be surprised," said the beggar. "At anything, I mean."

Doc walked on to the door, which was opened at once by the fat woman. The latter, veiled, grim-eyed, said nothing.

"Are we going in here?" Monk demanded, alarmed.

"I think it will be safe enough," Doc said.

"Your confidence," said the fat woman gloomily, "is an astounding thing."

Monk confessed that it astonished him, all right, and they went into the house, first into the vaulted hall, then into rooms that were like the rooms in a nice house owned by somebody with plenty of money in Cleveland, Ohio.

Miss Crockett joined them. She came in slowly and grimly, pretty much as if she were stepping into the corral with the horse that had just kicked the end out of the stable. She was a little pale, but it did not offset her determination.

Monk evidently considered her much more lovely than her photograph, because he made a round mouth of surprise, and thoughtfully moved over enough to block Ham Brooks' view.

Miss Crockett spoke two words to Doc Savage. She made them sound as if she had dropped something nasty on the floor.

"You lied," she said.

Doc nodded amiably. He was puzzled at their reception, but keeping his amazement under wraps. He was surprised that there should be a reception at all.

He said, "I didn't do much else but lie to you, as a matter of fact. . . . What do you say we declare a holiday and stick to the truth?"

She stared at him glassily and said, "How did Armi get killed?"

"Who?"

"Armi?"

Doc shook his head. "I don't believe I knew anyone by that name. . . . Wait. Do you mean a fellow who was using the name of Alexander Trussman in Washington?"

She said, "Armi went to Washington."

"Let's see if his description matches," Doc said, and was no more than fifteen words into a description of Alexander Trussman, the man Monk had seized in Washington, and who had been murdered, when Miss Crockett began nodding her head.

She said, "I have heard his body was found in Washington."

Doc nodded. "Would it get me anywhere if I told you how that happened?"

"What do you mean?"

"You look and sound as if it would take somewhat less than an earthquake to shake your faith in us."

Bitterly, she said, "I want to know about Armi. He was very devoted to my Uncle, and always faithful to me.... Further than that, he was Nesur's closest friend."

Doc said, "Nesur's friend—" blankly. That, he thought, was very bad. It would not be good for Nesur's opinion of Americans, which he understood already was nothing to pin hopes on.

The fat woman had taken up a position at the door. In a thicker, hoarser voice, she suddenly said, "Is Armi dead?"

"I'll tell you about that," Doc said, and did so. He gave the whole story chronologically. Morand of the State Department had called him to Washington and Armi—or Alexander Trussman—had turned up on Doc's trail. Monk, at Doc's instructions, had seized Trussman, or Armi, and the man had made a break for liberty and gotten as far as the hall, locking the door so that Monk could not pursue immediately. When Monk got into the hall, Armi was on the floor. Doc explained about the method of murder, a pen knife blade in the spine. He said, "We have no clue except that whoever used that knife knew spinal anatomy.... Now, that's the truth. I don't know whether you believe it, but it happened that way."

The fat woman had become quite pale and Miss Crockett was also two or three shades off color.

Doc said, "You have figured out my assignment by now. I am supposed to find Nesur and persuade him to take a look at the truth."

"And the truth is?" Miss Crockett asked.

"A moratorium on shooting," Doc said. "Violence isn't going to show anyone a profit, either in human rights or money."

"I wouldn't," said Miss Crockett stiffly, "be so sure about the money."

"Eh?"

"I am going to describe a man to you," Miss Crockett said. "If you know him, or have seen him, tell me."

She began describing a short wide man who was almost an albino, with amazingly blue eyes and corn-colored hair, a man with an Oklahoma twang, a man who, if they had heard him talk, would use a lot of profanity....

"Homer Wickett!" Monk yelled.

"Who?" demanded Miss Crockett.

Monk told her about the hotel manager who had come into the Washington hotel room and seen Alexander Trussman's, or Armi's, body.

"You were made fools of," said Miss Crockett bitterly. "That man—his name is really Homer Wickett, and he had a lot of gall to use it there in Washington—is head of an utterly unscrupulous oil syndicate."

Doc Savage dragged a chair over and sat on it. His knees felt a little too flexible. This was not the first time in his life he had felt a fool, but it was certainly one of the occasions. He was completely discomfited, and for a moment debated trying to cover up, pretending to be more wise than he had been. He decided against it.

"I guess we were taken in," he admitted. "But in that case, this Wickett probably killed Armi, or Alexander Trussman as we knew him. . . . Would Wickett do that?"

"Wickett would kill his own mother," the girl said grimly.

Doc used the silence that followed to decide to see how many cards he could get laid on the table.

"Let's go back to Nesur a moment," he said. "There is a good chance that he misunderstands our State Department, and they in turn misunderstand him. . . . I'll give you an example of the kind of thinking that fellow Morand and his whipping-boy, McCorland, indulge in. Take you, Miss Crockett. I was assured that you were a combination of Mata Hari, Cleopatra, Blackbeard the Pirate with skirts, and I don't know what else. I took their words for that. Probably I knew better, but I didn't have any other information."

She frowned. "You thought I was a crook?"

"Sure. Why do you think I went to all that trouble to stick you with a phony gold mine—but you caught on to what I was doing? Incidentally, the thing *was* figured for you to catch on—I banked on you checking up on Monk and Ham before we did business, which would mean you would have them trailed back to their hotel, make inquiries, and learn that I had first checked in there with them. When you found that out, you would be suspicious. You were, weren't you?"

She was a little taken aback. "Yes."

He finished. "I had been led to think you were a crook, so you would admire slick ways and be apt to hire us. And once in your employment, I was going to try to find out where Nesur was. That, in general, is the whole picture. But the point is that the State Department boys were mistaken about you, so Nesur could be mistaken about them."

"What makes you think they are mistaken?" she asked.

"I know a little about character." He flushed. "I don't claim to read women. But somehow I've had a feeling of being on solid ground with you. I don't think you are any tea party hostess, and I do believe you're an adventuress. But I do figure you as being in it for excitement, rather than greed."

She seemed pleased by that. She said, "That's really as truthful an appraisal of myself as I've heard. . . . Would you like to know how I came to get into this thing I'm in?"

He would have preferred the story some other time. But he was too satisfied with the progress he seemed to be making with her to chance making her angry. . . . Nesur? What about this report that Nesur had put out the word for violence to begin? Was it true? Could the harm be undone? . . . He was inching slowly toward the answers, he supposed.

Eunice Lee Crockett was talking, and some of the things she was saying he had heard from Morand or read in the State Department dossier on her. She had been a schoolteacher in Ohio, and lived a completely ordinary and dull life. She had known she had an Uncle Ira Crockett in the Mediterranean area somewhere, but she had not seen Uncle Ira in years, and recalled him only as a crisp little old man, full of chuckles and cunning little sayings, who had bounced her on his knee when she was twelve years old, and, she had thought, a little too big for knee-bouncing.

Uncle Ira's death had been a surprise, and the fact that he had willed her an estate a bigger surprise. But she had come to Cairo to see about the inheritance. She found that Uncle Ira Crockett had rather hoped that she would carry on his business, if it could be called a business. She said, "Uncle Ira was a kind of adventurer and sharpshooter, I found," she explained. "And his organization was still intact. I didn't know what to do. I was awfully shocked at first, for I thought Uncle Ira had been a crook and nothing else. But I did have the sense to investigate, and I found that he hadn't done anything really crooked, and in the end I decided to carry on for a while. To my surprise, I found I had a knack for scheming and planning, the kind of a knack Uncle Ira had had. Of course, the organization pretty much ran itself at first. Armi, the man you know as Alexander Trussman, was a great help during that period. . . . Anyway, in a few months, I found we were carrying on as usual."

Doc decided now was as good a time as any to take a chance on a direct question.

"Mind giving us the picture in this Nesur thing?" he asked.

"I'm coming to that."

"Good."

Miss Crockett glanced at the beggar, the fat woman. The latter was inscrutable behind the veil. The beggar said, "I had better go back on watch duty, hadn't I?"

"Be a good idea," said Miss Crockett.

The beggar went out.

The fat woman stirred, decided to take a chair. Monk and Ham had also seated themselves. It was still in the room, except that somewhere the conditioner that was making the air cool whirred softly.

Nesur, Miss Crockett said abruptly, had been in some respects a protegee of her Uncle Eli Crockett. . . . Doc nodded to that. He had surmised as much. . . . "Nesur and I became friends, naturally," Miss Crockett continued. "During the war, Nesur was forced into exile by British diplomatic pressure. I do not think that was a wise move by the British, nor do I think they would have done it had they not been misled into thinking Nesur had Nazi sympathies. This was never true. Nesur's enemies got the story going, and the British believed it. . . . But the point I'm making is that Uncle Eli furnished Nesur with a refuge to which he fled in exile."

"That didn't exactly antagonize Nesur," Doc suggested.

"Naturally not. . . . When Nesur decided to make a comeback as a leader, he first discussed it with me and with Armi—Alexander Trussman. Frankly, Nesur needed money for his campaign, and wished me to finance it. I won't bore you with my philosophy, but what I finally did do was this: I loaned Nesur money for his organization and campaign expenses. But I did not take an active part in Nesur's comeback, except as a friend—until quite recently."

Doc showed interest with tilted head, upraised eyebrows. She added, "A series of murders got me interested."

"Murders?"

Miss Crockett nodded. "First, some of Nesur's political enemies were killed. It looked as if Nesur was getting some unwelcome help."

"Unwelcome?"

"Of course! Nesur is no murderer!"

"But who—"

"That's what we wondered," said Miss Crockett. "Then a couple of men in Nesur's organization were murdered, and we began to see the light. Someone close to Nesur was scheming, and he had killed two men who had found out about the scheming."

Doc frowned. "These murders—were they done with explosions?"

"Yes."

"The victims were killed by an object, usually a wheeled vehicle, blowing up when they came near?" Doc demanded.

"Once it was a burdened camel."

Doc leaned back. "Morand, of the State Department, is puzzled about those murders, too."

Miss Crockett nodded. "The rest is very simple. . . . We suspected Homer Wickett. We began watching him. Homer Wickett went to Washington, and Armi followed him. That is how Armi, or Alexander Trussman, happened to be in the United States."

"I wonder why Armi was following me?" Doc pondered.

"I can show you a cable that will answer that," Miss Crockett said. "It says that Armi had learned Homer Wickett was plotting against your life, and so Armi was going to trail you and protect you. . . . Wait, I'll get the cable and show you—"

She had half risen. Now she remained that way, neither in the chair nor quite on her feet, for a moment. She had been arrested by a sound outside, a sound that Doc had presumed came from the street and was merely someone passing. Miss Crockett must have decided the sound was meaningless also, because she moved from the room.

Ham Brooks, who was seated nearer the outer door, said, "Doc, that noise she heard, I think it might be—"

The door burst open and the beggar came in. The beggar came in stiffly, with short mincing stiff-legged steps, like an old-time Chinese girl with bound feet. His head was bowed and his hands were clasped to his throat and through his fingers a red flood was coming to spread over his robes. He did not say anything to them. He merely took his hands from his throat and sank to the floor, dead.

Monk Mayfair said, "For God's sake! What—"

A man jumped through the door and took Monk by the neck.

The man used one hand, his left, for the neck-taking, while the other prepared to wield a bloody knife on some part of Monk, undoubtedly the first part that came handy. Doc Savage discouraged this by throwing a chair.

The thrown chair hit the man and knocked him unconscious and knocked him away from Monk. The man fell partly through the door, which was still open. Hands came into view from the outside and took hold of the man and began dragging him away. Another hand containing a gun came through the door. Out of the gun came lead and noise. In a moment another gun joined the first one.

The room became active. Everyone in it seemed to have somewhere to go in a hurry, or something urgent to do. Ham Brooks helped the situation, or muddled it, by lifting a chair, taking a swipe at the chandelier and knocking all the lights out, plunging the room into darkness.

Doc Savage threw a vase at one of the guns, and scored a bullseye on the gun hand. The owner of the hand must have been hurt badly, because he stepped into plain view, as if going out to see what had pained his hand so badly. Behind Doc, a pistol cracked. The man in the door fell down. The fat woman had scored exactly between his eyes.

It now became evident that the ruckus here was a diversionary action. Because, from another part of the house, began coming shouts, screams, fast movement.

"Miss Crockett!" shrieked the fat woman in a remarkably hoarse voice. "Oh, my God! Miss Crockett—they're after her!"

Doc Savage thought so, too. He was moving. He said, "Monk, Ham, be careful!" And he went toward what he supposed was the best route to the back of the house. At least the fat woman was heading for the same door.

He beat the fat woman through, and they went down a hall, through a room, through another room, and through a lot of rooms and out into a narrow street and back again and through more rooms and finally into another street. But by now the house was quiet, the streets were quiet, and the only noise was a man in the house dying noisily. He was the man the fat woman had shot. He was giving the lie to the accepted face that a bullet between the eyes is supposed to kill instantly.

Ham Brooks put the facts in words. He said, "They got Miss Crockett! They got her, and got clean away."

After half an hour of chasing through the streets asking questions, this was a proven truth.

Doc asked the fat woman, "Do you think Homer Wickett got her?"

"Yes. He didn't do it personally, but those were his men."

"Where would they take Miss Crockett?"

"I don't know. I have no idea." It was a wail.

"Why did they take her?"

"Because she knows were Nesur is." That also was a wail, more distraught.

XII

Morand, of the State Department, assisted his hair to stand on end by running his fingers through it in a wild way.

"If people keep getting killed around you," he said, "I don't know how long you are going to continue getting away with it, Doc Savage or no Doc Savage."

Doc said impatiently, "Get the Cairo police to pick up Homer Wickett. Or is your influence that strong?"

"I think it is," Morand said. "But brother, you had better know what you are doing."

McCorland, who had been a shocked listener, chimed in, "I'll say you had better know."

"What do you mean?"

"Homer Wickett," said McCorland, "is an influential man. He will raise hell by the bucketful if we have him arrested."

"Let him," Doc said. "But I doubt if the police will lay their hands on him."

"Why not?"

"He's probably hiding out. . . . Incidentally, have either of you any idea where he would be hiding?"

"Of course not," McCorland said. "I hardly know the fellow. Doubt if I would know him if I saw him."

"You have," Doc demanded, "no idea where they might have taken Miss Crockett?"

"I don't see," said McCorland bitterly, "why you are so upset over what may or may not have happened to a tramp of a woman."

Morand looked vaguely alarmed. He seemed to feel that Doc might have fallen for Miss Crockett, and that McCorland was irritating Doc.

"McCorland," said Morand. "You get hold of the Cairo police and have this fellow Homer Wickett picked up."

"I don't think that's a good idea," said McCorland.

"I don't give a damn what you think!" Morand yelled. "Get on the phone and have the Cairo cops pick him up. Don't give me a lot of argument. The way you've balled this whole thing up, I'd think you'd be ashamed to show your face."

McCorland went out, and Morand jammed his hands in his pockets and said he was going to give up his job and take up something easy on the nerves, like lion-taming.

Doc Savage said, "There's one thing I've been intending to ask you. . . . You've got a pretty good check on this Eunice Lee Crockett's organization, haven't you?"

"It's not perfect," Morand said. "But it rather pleases me."

"What about a fat woman called Tiny?"

"Well, now," said Morand, "there you make a liar out of me right away. Not much on her. Not even a name. Been seen with Crockett off and on for a couple of years, and been in the Crockett household steady for the last few days."

"Then you don't know anything about her?" Doc demanded.

"If you pin me down," said Morand, "not a thing." He scratched his head. "Say, now, somebody has been tipping off this Homer Wickett about the girl's movements, and it could be this fat woman doing the ratting. You may have something there."

Doc said time would tell what they had.

He then waited for McCorland to come back and report that the Cairo police were on the lookout for Homer Wickett.

Doc arose and put on his hat.

"I think we've got a line on where Wickett is," Doc said.

"But I'm not going to tell you about it and have you balling up my plans."

He walked out.

Monk Mayfair, Ham Brooks, the fat woman and the man named Ali were waiting in a touring car near the U. S. State Department offices. They had the general appearance of having something definite on their minds. Doc did not waste time discussing international relations.

He said. "You all know McCorland by sight?"

They did.

"Ham," Doc said, "you have the embassy telephone wires located?"

"Yes."

"Cut them," Doc said. "And the rest of you get on the job watching for McCorland to leave the embassy."

They separated rapidly, after arranging a system of signals for re-assembling. Doc Savage walked with Monk Mayfair, and they took up a position in a side street where they could watch a likely looking door.

Monk did some jaw-rubbing and asked, "You figure it's a safe bet McCorland is selling out?"

"We're not betting too much on it," Doc said. "I think we're justified."

"Just what gave McCorland a dark complexion for you?"

Doc shrugged. "Information doesn't leak out of the State Department like water through a sieve without reason. McCorland seems a logical reason. The moves we've made apparently have gone right to Homer Wickett."

"It could be a clerk or some menial."

"Maybe—here in Cairo. But what about Washington?"

"Huh?"

"No one but Morand and McCorland in Washington were supposed to know we were being called in on the Nesur matter," Doc said. "Morand told me that. Regardless or not whether Morand's head seems good only for a hat rack, the man is honest. Honest the way the State Department is honest, anyhow, which sometimes leaves room to wonder. . . . McCorland is the logical leak."

"Or Morand."

"That isn't impossible," Doc admitted. "If McCorland doesn't mine out, we'll try—"

McCorland came out of the side door they were watching.

"Nice enough," Monk said, and went to signal the others.

McCorland sauntered like a man with no cares along Junub Street to an intersection with an avenue with a very English-sounding name—Whitechapel Road—and turned right. He looked more as if he were pretending to be unconcerned than unconcerned, like a man walking a dog. He bought a flower for his lapel.

Suddenly McCorland got into a car in a parking area, evidently his own car, and after that nothing went slowly. They could barely keep track of him, although there were two carloads of them, Doc and Monk in one machine, Ham and the others in the second.

The pursuit—they were hoping it wasn't exactly that, hoping McCorland hadn't seen them on his trail—ended when McCorland's car pulled into a pretentious estate well on the outskirts of Cairo.

"It's lucky he went straight here like a shot," Monk said. "Or we wouldn't have been able to follow him."

Their car was nearly a quarter of a mile behind McCorland's. Doc pulled off at once, and parked. The other car drew up alongside them, and Ham leaned out and asked, "How do you fellows know McCorland didn't just go home? Maybe he lives there."

"If he does," Doc said, "the State Department had better look into how he can afford such fancy diggings."

They conferred about their next step, and decided it would be to get closer and look over the house and grounds.

The house was more California-film-star than Egyptian in architecture, and so were the grounds. The building was rambling and tile-roofed with yellow shutters, red door trim, and many flowers. The grounds, while not a jungle, were thick with shrubs.

Monk was saying it should be a lead-pipe cinch to crawl through the shrubbery and close in on the house when a man got off a bus at an intersection and came walking toward them. He wore a burnoose and was hurrying.

Ham whispered, "I think I've seen that guy somewhere before."

Doc had the same feeling. He said, "Monk, drop off and get behind him." Monk turned left and stopped behind some kind of large bush. Doc and the others walked slowly. The man behind them apparently had not recognized them.

Suddenly he did recognize them. He wheeled without delaying about it, and started back the way he had come. But he had passed Monk. A moment later he and Monk were face to face.

Action flared briefly. The man tried to get something from under his burnoose, and Monk hit him. The man fell. Monk said, as they came up, "If these guys have to wear sheets like a spook, they should have a better system for carrying their guns." He stood up with what the man had been reaching for. It was a .45 automatic.

The fat woman said, *"Aiwah!"* explosively. It was the first time Doc had heard her speak Arabic. Arabic was plainly her native tongue.

"Know him?" Doc asked.

She nodded, the veil fluttering. "I have seen him around. He is one of Homer Wickett's men, I believe."

"Or an employee of the U. S. State Department," Ham suggested.

Doc settled that by searching the man and bringing up a small package which he opened. There was a phial inside. He uncorked the phial, then gave his opinion of what it contained. "Scopolamine," Doc said. "Administered hypodermically, it's what they call truth serum. . . . Would a State Department man be carrying that around?"

"Radi kathir!" gasped the fat woman. Again she used Arabic. The phrase meant generally that things weren't good.

"I doubt," said Doc, "that Miss Crockett will appreciate any more delay on our party. . . . They obviously kidnaped her, and that suggested they wanted to question her. The truth serum suggests the same thing."

Monk leaned over and hit the unconscious man again. He then dragged the fellow into the bushes, and used the burnoose to tie him hand and foot and gag him. "That should hold him for the time being," Monk said.

Ali had hardly said a word. Now he said something unintelligible in Arabic. His face had changed until now it looked like a fist. He wheeled suddenly, walked toward the house.

"What's the matter with him?" Monk blurted.

"He is going into the house," the fat woman said. "He is

very angry." She looked at them woodenly and added, "So am I. . . . And I, too, am going into the house."

"Take it easy," Doc said, "and we'll all do that together."

Ali had looked, acted and sounded crazed and desperate, but it developed that his caution had not been overcome. He did not just walk into the house. He went in through a window. He made no more noise than a mouse on a cheese. Doc was not over fifty feet behind him.

"This isn't giving us much chance to look over the ground," Doc said, "But it may be all right. It's fairly sure to be noisy. . . . Ham, you and Monk take the other side."

Monk moistened stiff lips. "Any special instructions?"

"No. Just go in and do what needs to be done."

Monk and Ham moved away silently. The bushes they had disturbed ever so slightly were still trembling when there was a shot in the house.

One shot. Then Ali's voice came loudly, bitterly, attributing to someone the characteristics of a leprous camel. He sounded sincere. This called forth two shots, then a scream that began low and thick and rose and climbed higher and higher until it seemed to go away into the zenith like a rocket, taking with it the life of the one who screamed.

Doc chose a window. The fat woman chose the same one. She was remarkably silent, like a big cat. Once through the window, they were in a room furnished with the sort of modernistic furniture one sees in apartments on Central Park West or Riverside Drive. They did not tarry there.

They were nearly across the room to another door when a woman dived through the door. She was a woman they had never seen before, a half-caste, but beautiful the way a Pekingese lap dog is beautiful. Something to be kept, petted, and utterly impractical for anything else.

She saw them. She made a kind of mewing sound. She was down on the floor. Like that. She had fainted.

Doc stepped over her and met a man coming headlong toward him. The man had his face twisted, looking back, and he did not see Doc until they were together. They hit hard. Both were about equally surprised, but Doc's reflexes were miles ahead of the other, and he had hit the man two blows before the fellow got organized at all.

The fat woman, pointing wildly at the man Doc held, explained, "Wickett!"

That was hardly necessary. Doc already knew he was Wickett. He had met Homer Wickett in the Washington hotel.

Doc had, for a moment, a feeling that the fight was all over. Everything finished. Wickett in hand. Miss Crockett probably somewhere to be rescued. It was temporary state of mind, however, because someone stepped up from behind and struck him over the head.

He had been taken unaware. It was fortunate that the one who hit him used only a fist. But the blow was well-aimed and well-swung and did not hurt much more than having a piano drop on his head.

Vaguely he had the impression that he was down on his knees. Homer Wickett was out of his arms. He had just faded away. Impossible, of course, but that was the effect. The blow had him in a fog and the fog was filling with men. They came into the hall; he could not tell you how many, but three or four.

He did what he could. The floor felt soft under him, soft and spongy. He heard someone saying not to shoot, that a bullet might hit Mr. Wickett. This was said over and over, in Arabic and in English, and it must have been effective because there was no shooting.

The fat woman was in it, too. She did very well, swing, kick, and kick and swing, and was not like a woman at all. Presently her burnoose was torn off; one rip, and she was stripped naked to the waist. Only then she was no longer a she, but a short, thick, coffee-skinned man, well-muscled, who was fighting in a way that showed he had been in a fight before. A ridiculous figure, because the veil was still over his, or her, face, and it flapped about wildly.

Suddenly there was no one left to fight in the hall. There had been only two, instead of what had seemed like several, Doc realized. He must have been more dazed than he had supposed.

The soft floor—the floor wasn't really soft. He had been kneeling on Homer Wickett, or standing on Homer Wickett, during the fight. He leaned down and slugged the man. It probably wasn't necessary.

He stood erect.

"Miss Crockett!" he called.

There was absolutely no sound. But he found her. He

found her not three seconds later, sitting in a chair in a large room done in soft creams and tans, with a towel stuffed in her mouth and another towel tied around her neck. Her face was purple. But, when he got the towel loose from her neck, and the other towel out of her mouth, she began breathing deep and hard, as if she would never again get enough of breathing.

Presently Monk and Ham entered the house. They came in via the front door, sheepishly, and Monk said, "The windows in the back have all got bars on them. We couldn't get in. We—"

Monk stopped and stared at the fat woman—man.

"A guy," he said.

Doc said, "Search the house. And be careful. We may not have all of them."

Monk pointed at the fat woman, or man, and said, "What, who—"

"Search the house."

Ham Brooks said, "Come on, stupid," to Monk. He picked up a gun someone had dropped on the floor. He pointed it at the floor and pulled the trigger to see if it was loaded. It was. He and Monk went out of the room.

There was a scraping and scratching sound in the adjoining room, coming toward the door, and it proved to be Ali, pulling himself along painfully, dragging his legs.

"Ali!" Eunice Lee Crockett screamed.

"I'm all right," Ali said. "Bullet broke both legs, is all. I'm all right."

The man who had been a fat woman said in precise English, "I think we have reached a satisfactory settlement, and it is perhaps best that I be going."

He took tentative steps toward the door, turned to ask Doc Savage:

"You have no objections to my leaving?"

"If you think it would be better, okay," Doc said.

"Frankly, I believe it best," the man said. "All this killing would hardly contribute anything desirable to my reputation."

"Probably not," Doc said.

Still the man hesitated. "Could I—ah—it may be difficult, I know, but could you neglect to mention my presence to the police?"

"I could," Doc said.

"I should be most grateful."

"You had better get going," Doc said, "and show your gratitude later."

The man gathered a burnoose off one of the unconscious men on the floor. He wrapped it about himself. He adjusted the veil. He seemed sheepish about doing this, becoming a woman again. He left without saying anything.

Presently Monk and Ham returned, and Monk said, "There's nobody else—hey! What the hell! The fat dame—guy! Where—"

"There was no fat woman, or man," Doc said.

"What?"

"Let's not get complicated. Keep it simple," Doc said patiently. "There was no fat person with us at any time."

XIII

When the night came, it was still and black, except for a flickering of heat lightning far out in the desert to the west. A policeman padded about, turning on lights.

Another policeman, this one a Lieutenant, came in and asked, "The swimming pool is empty—will it be all right to put that thing in there?"

Doc Savage said, "That should do. Yes, put it in the pool."

Morand was talking over the telephone. He was saying, "Yes, charge McCorland with murder. . . . I don't give a damn if he is—the State Department doesn't back up murder. Charge him with that. He was in it with them. He was selling them information." He hung up.

Doc asked, "The police find anything in Homer Wickett's office?"

"I don't know how the hell I'm going to explain this to Washington," Morand complained. "I'm supposed to be able to pick honest associates. . . . Wickett? Oh, his office—sure, they found a lot of stuff showing he is head of an oil syndicate."

"No evidence he had had murders done?"

"No."

"Then this exhibition in the swimming pool should be interesting," Doc said.

The object the police had placed in the pool—there was

no water in the pool—was not large. About six by seven by eighteen inches. A box.

Doc said, "Stand back. The farther back the better. That is one of the bombs Homer Wickett used. One like it killed those men in Cairo today."

There was a general retirement to cover.

Doc took out the blackjack. He unwrapped the lead sheeting from around it.

"Know what a Geiger counter is?" he asked Morand.

"Sure," said Morand. "The newspapers were full of them when the atom bomb tests were made. They're a gadget that reacts to the presence of radioactive material in the neighborhood."

Doc nodded. He hefted the blackjack. "Say that the loading material in this blackjack was radioactive—had been exposed to radium emanations for a time. Say that it had been, and it was brought near a Geiger counter, which is not necessarily a large piece of apparatus, there would be a reaction. The reaction might be caused to close a relay, which would set off an explosive."

Morand said, "Throw it, and let's see."

Doc slung the blackjack into the empty pool where the bomb had been placed, at the same time throwing himself flat on the ground, or attempting to do so—he did not quite get down before the explosion came.

After the universe had come apart and gone together again, Morand said hollowly, "My God! So that's the way they were killed! Something radioactive was planted on them, and then the bombs were placed where they would eventually pass near."

"Think that will hang Homer Wickett?" Doc asked.

"Want to bet it won't?" Morand asked, in a pleased voice.

Doc Savage had lost his hat somewhere in the house during the goings-on earlier in the afternoon. The loss had escaped his mind, but he thought of it now, and began hunting, and presently learned that a policeman had picked up the hat and tagged it as an exhibit in evidence. The officer retrieved it and gave it to Doc.

"You leaving?" Morand demanded.

"Might as well," Doc said. "By the way, doesn't your department have a way of getting priority on plane reservations? Could you get us three back to New York at an early date?"

"Yes, sure, I—wait! Hold on!" Morand's face blanched. "My God, you're not letting me down!"

"What do you mean, letting you down?"

"This thing isn't finished!"

"Sure it is."

"Like hell!" Morand yelled. "You haven't found Nesur! Holy cripes, you haven't accomplished anything you came over here for!"

"Oh, that. You mean finding Nesur and convincing him we weren't bad eggs?"

"Of course. We'd better talk that over and lay some plans—"

"All taken care of." Doc put on his hat. "You can stop worrying about it." He moved toward the door.

"Wait a minute! What do you mean, taken care of? And stop worrying? Listen, that Nesur situation is so damned serious that I sweat snowflakes when I think about it. And if you're kidding me—say, *are* you ribbing me? Or did you fix it up somehow?"

"You can hang up your worries, Morand."

"Listen, tell me how—"

"You'll figure it out." Doc opened the door. "You lads are very wise. . . . Incidentally, I hope you're wise enough to leave Nesur alone from now on. I think he would appreciate that."

Doc went out, closing the door.

Miss Crockett fell into step with Doc Savage. She had been patched and renewed where necessary. She looked bright, relieved, and there was considerable emotion in the way she took Doc Savage's arm.

"Is Morand—did you have to tell him?" she asked excitedly.

He shook his head. "Morand, and the police too, know that Homer Wickett brought you here to force you to tell where Nesur was. That is all they need to know."

"Then you didn't tell them about the fat woman?" she demanded.

"No."

"And they don't know the fat woman was Nesur?"

"No. At least I think not. A fat woman is the last thing they would expect Nesur to be masquerading as, I imagine."

She laughed. She trilled her relief. "That's good," she said. "I think Nesur, more than anything else, wouldn't want it known he had pretended to be a woman. Nesur is really quite a guy."

"I saw that. He did all right in the fight," Doc said.

"Nesur liked you," she said. "He'll appreciate your keeping his identity secret."

"I hope so."

"Oh, he will!" she said earnestly. "He was really in hiding from Homer Wickett's men, you know. He came to me, and said he was sure there was something going on, because some of his close associates had been murdered. He asked me to help, and I did."

Doc nodded. He gestured lightly and said, "Do we have to go on and on about politics and death. After all, don't we get a breathing spell?"

She looked up at him.

"Why, yes, we should, shouldn't we?" she said.

They walked along. He didn't say anything more. It was dark out here. The heat lightning ran warmly back and forth in the west, and to the right were the lights of Cairo, all scattered over a great area and looking like the lights of any other city, which was a deceptive way for them to look.

As deceptive, he thought, as a breathing spell could turn out to be. Whatever that meant—or whatever it would prove to mean in the uncertain years ahead of the world, so long as men misused power.

THE MAN OF BRONZE

FIVE FABULOUS DOC ADVENTURES

☐ **DOC SAVAGE OMNIBUS #5**
26996-8 $3.95
NO LIGHT TO DIE BY
THE MONKEY SUIT
LET'S KILL AMES
ONCE OVER LIGHTLY
I DIED YESTERDAY

Look for them at your bookstore or use this page to order: